JUST BEYOND™

THE SCARE SCHOOL

Published by

JUST BEYOND™

THE SCARE SCHOOL

Written by
R.L. Stine

Illustrated by
Kelly & Nichole Matthews

Lettered by
Mike Fiorentino

Cover by
Julian Totino Tedesco

Barnes & Noble Exclusive Cover by
Tim Jacobus

Just Beyond created by
R.L. Stine

Designer
Scott Newman

Assistant Editor
Michael Moccio

Editors
Whitney Leopard
Bryce Carlson

JUST BEYOND: THE SCARE SCHOOL, September 2019. Published by KaBOOM!, a division of Boom Entertainment, Inc. Just Beyond is ™ & © 2019 R.L. Stine. All rights reserved. KaBOOM!™ and the KaBOOM! logo are trademarks of Boom Entertainment, Inc., registered in various countries and categories. All characters, events, and institutions depicted herein are fictional. Any similarity between any of the names, characters, persons, events, and/or institutions in this publication to actual names, characters, and persons, whether living or dead, events, and/or institutions is unintended and purely coincidental. KaBOOM! does not read or accept unsolicited submissions of ideas, stories, or artwork.

For information regarding the CPSIA on this printed material, call: (203) 595-3636 and provide reference #RICH – 845270.

BOOM! Studios, 5670 Wilshire Boulevard, Suite 400, Los Angeles, CA 90036-5679. Printed in USA. First Printing.

ISBN: 978-1-68415-416-6, eISBN: 978-1-64144-533-7

Barnes & Noble Exclusive Edition
978-1-68415-511-8

PART ONE

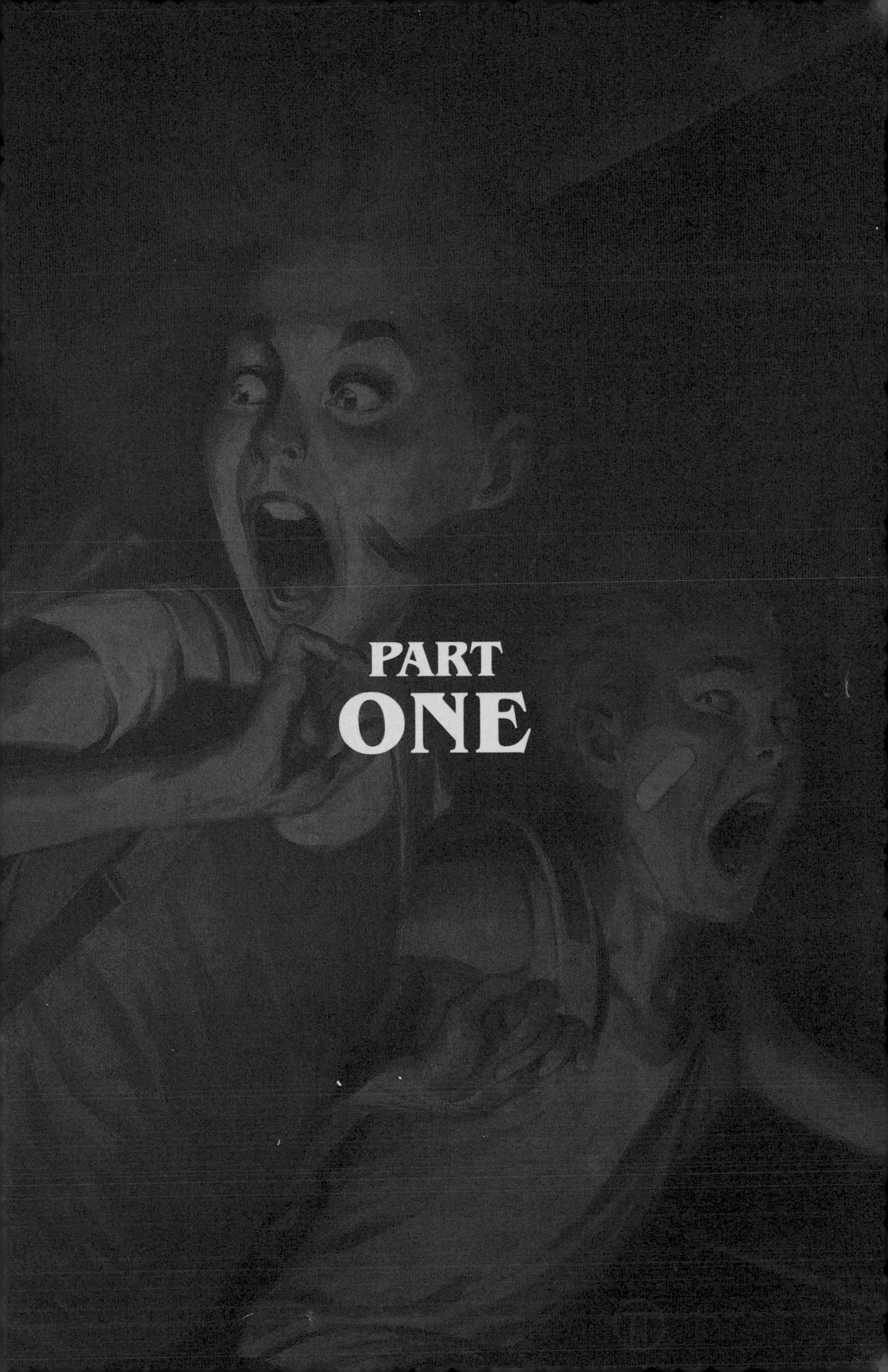

CHAPTER ONE
THEY SENT A DROGG

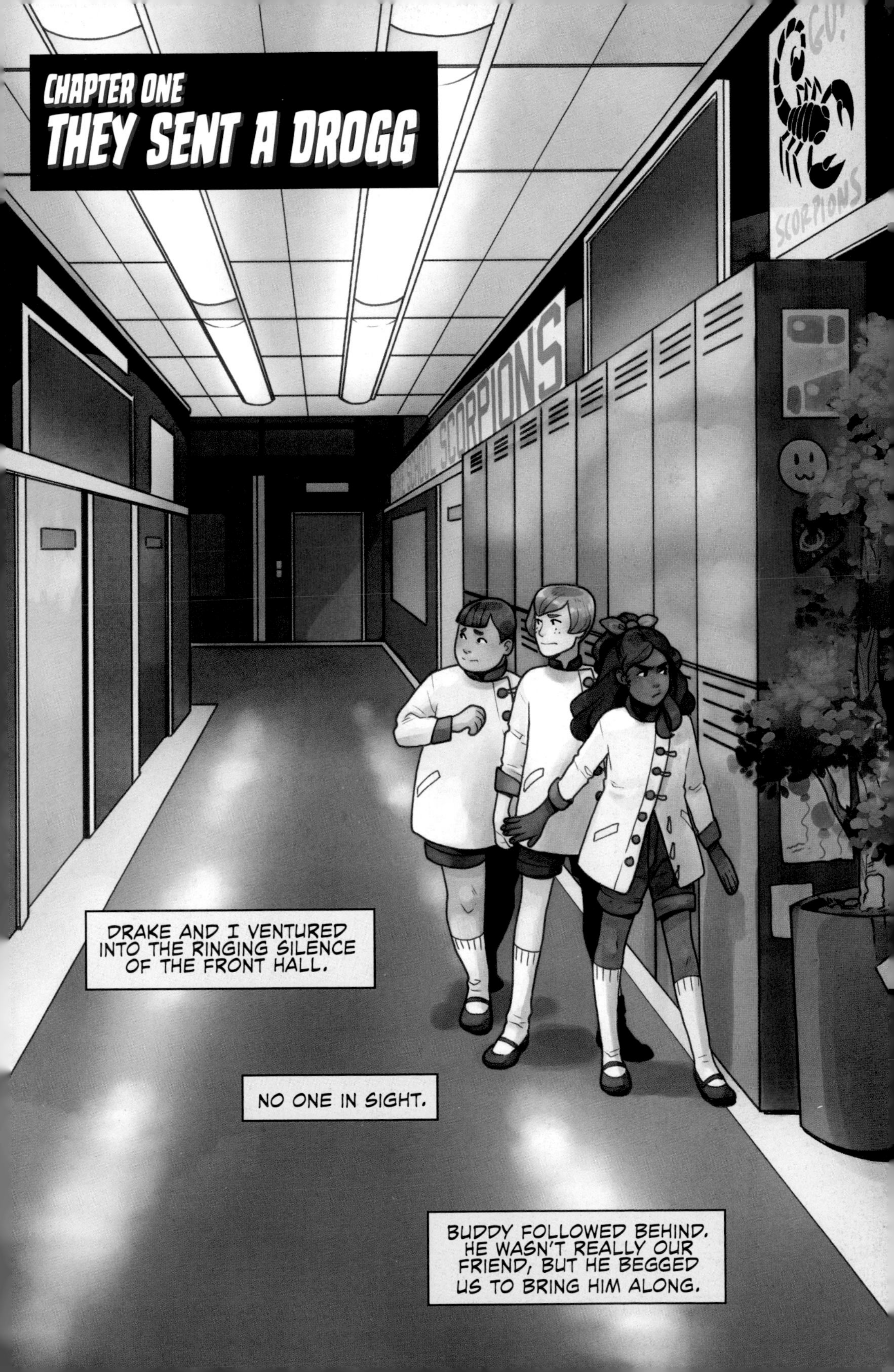
SCORPIONS
SCHOOL SCORPIONS
SCORPIONS
DRAKE AND I VENTURED INTO THE RINGING SILENCE OF THE FRONT HALL.
NO ONE IN SIGHT.
BUDDY FOLLOWED BEHIND. HE WASN'T REALLY OUR FRIEND, BUT HE BEGGED US TO BRING HIM ALONG.

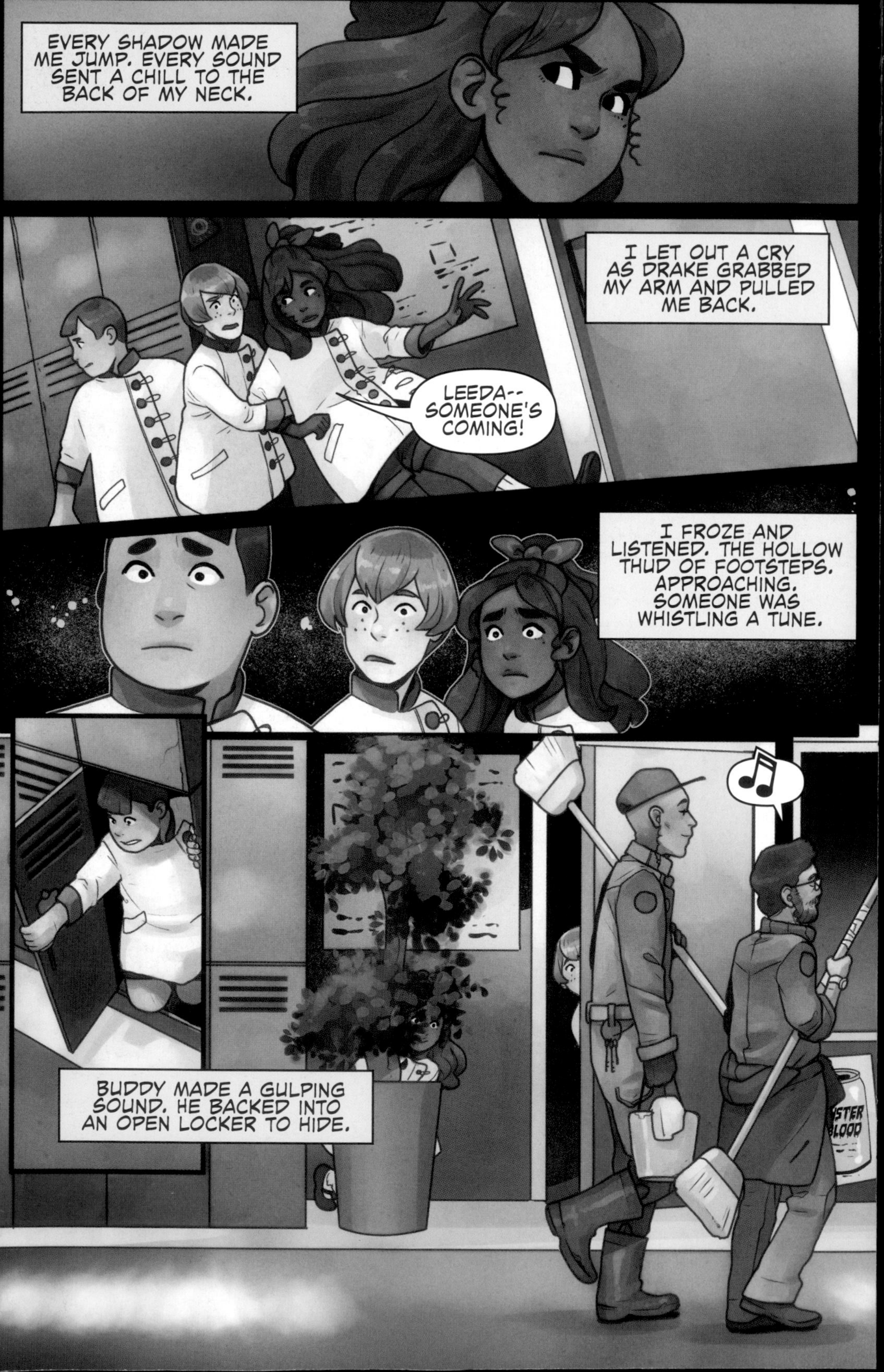

EVERY SHADOW MADE ME JUMP. EVERY SOUND SENT A CHILL TO THE BACK OF MY NECK.
I LET OUT A CRY AS DRAKE GRABBED MY ARM AND PULLED ME BACK.
LEEDA-- SOMEONE'S COMING!
I FROZE AND LISTENED. THE HOLLOW THUD OF FOOTSTEPS. APPROACHING. SOMEONE WAS WHISTLING A TUNE.
BUDDY MADE A GULPING SOUND. HE BACKED INTO AN OPEN LOCKER TO HIDE.

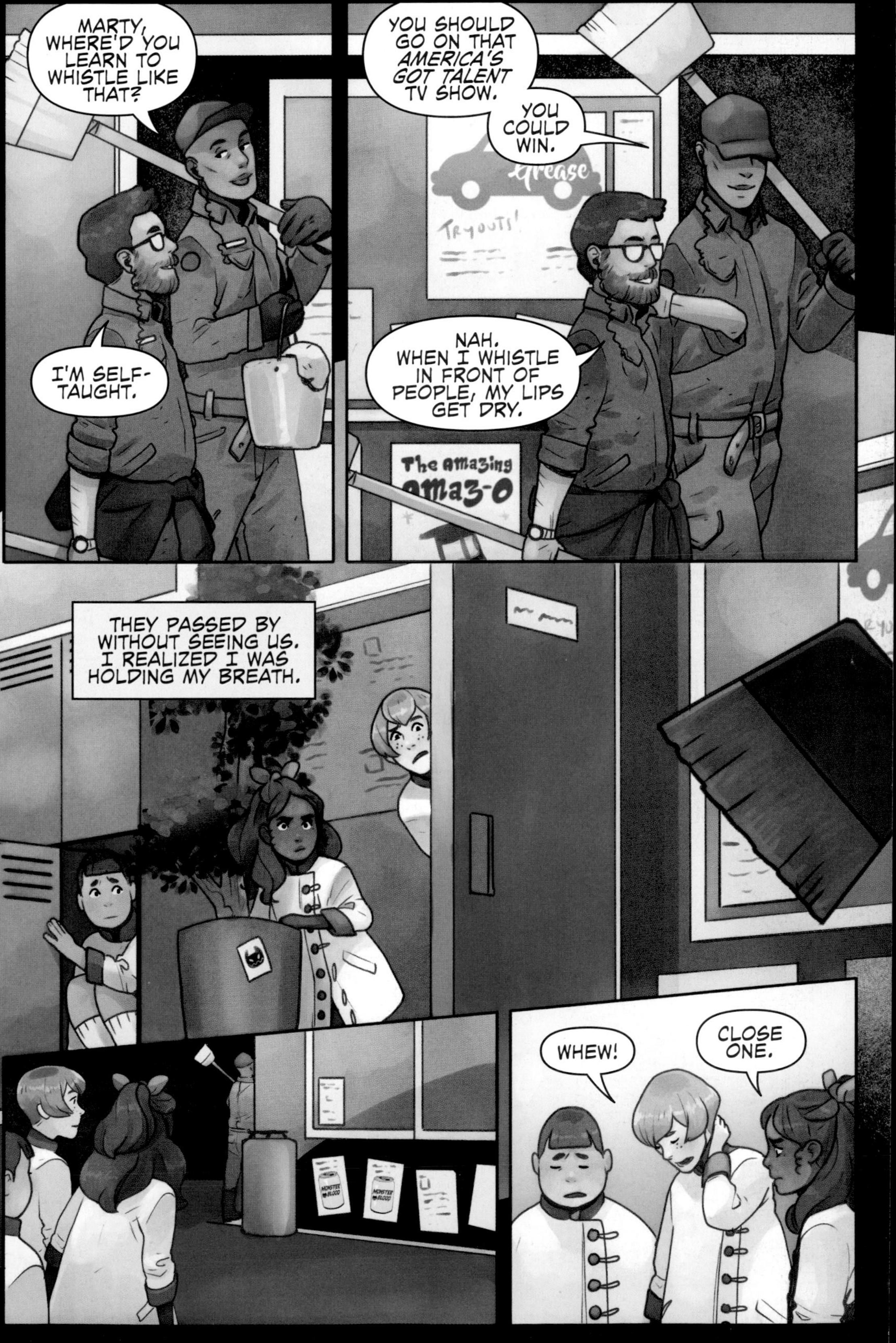
MARTY, WHERE'D YOU LEARN TO WHISTLE LIKE THAT?
I'M SELF-TAUGHT.
YOU SHOULD GO ON THAT *AMERICA'S GOT TALENT* TV SHOW.
YOU COULD WIN.
Grease
TRYOUTS!
NAH. WHEN I WHISTLE IN FRONT OF PEOPLE, MY LIPS GET DRY.
The amazing amaz-o
THEY PASSED BY WITHOUT SEEING US. I REALIZED I WAS HOLDING MY BREATH.
MONSTER BLOOD
MONSTER BLOOD
WHEW!
CLOSE ONE.

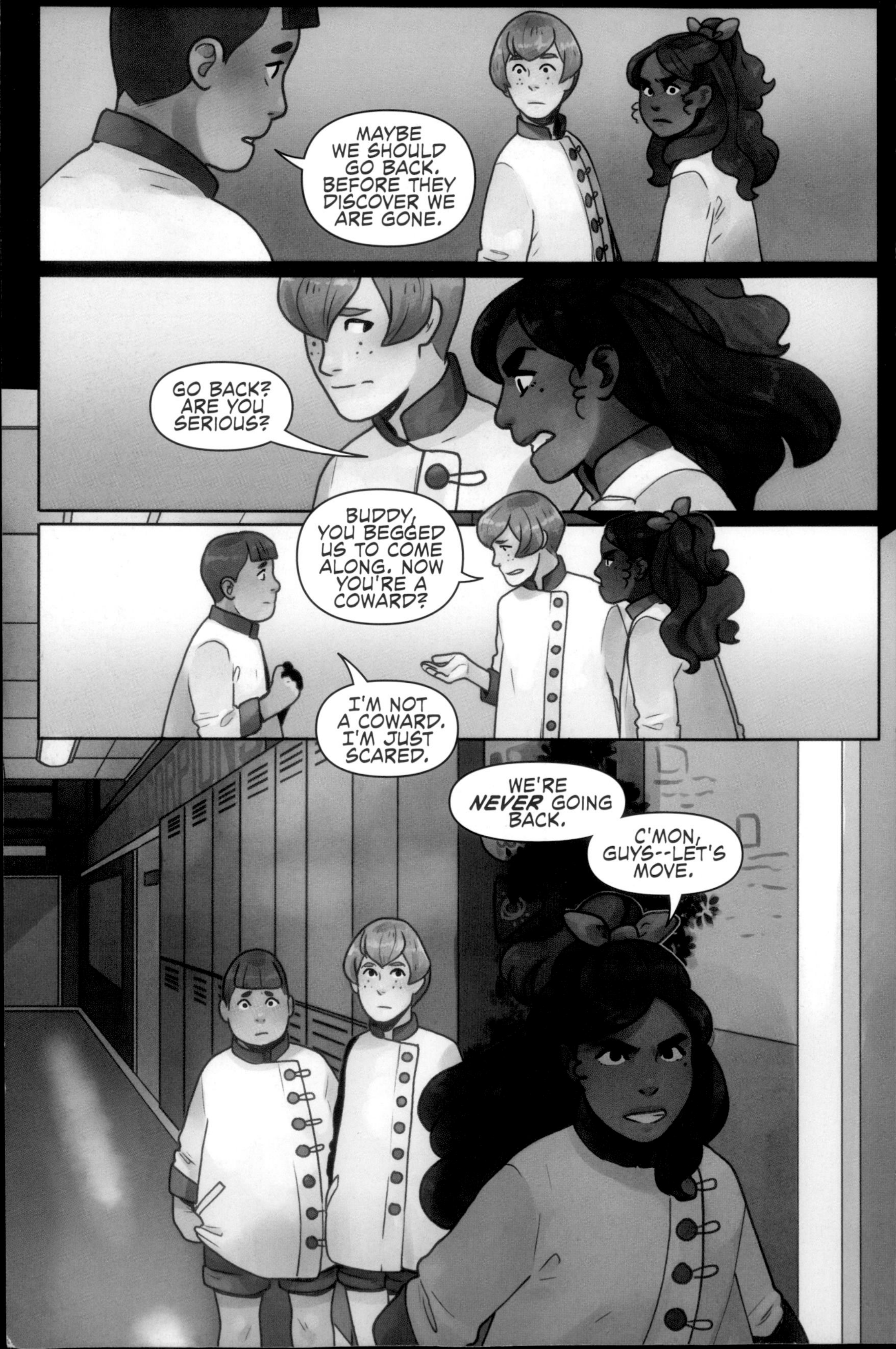
MAYBE WE SHOULD GO BACK. BEFORE THEY DISCOVER WE ARE GONE.
GO BACK? ARE YOU SERIOUS?
BUDDY, YOU BEGGED US TO COME ALONG. NOW YOU'RE A COWARD?
I'M NOT A COWARD. I'M JUST SCARED.
WE'RE *NEVER* GOING BACK.
C'MON, GUYS--LET'S MOVE.

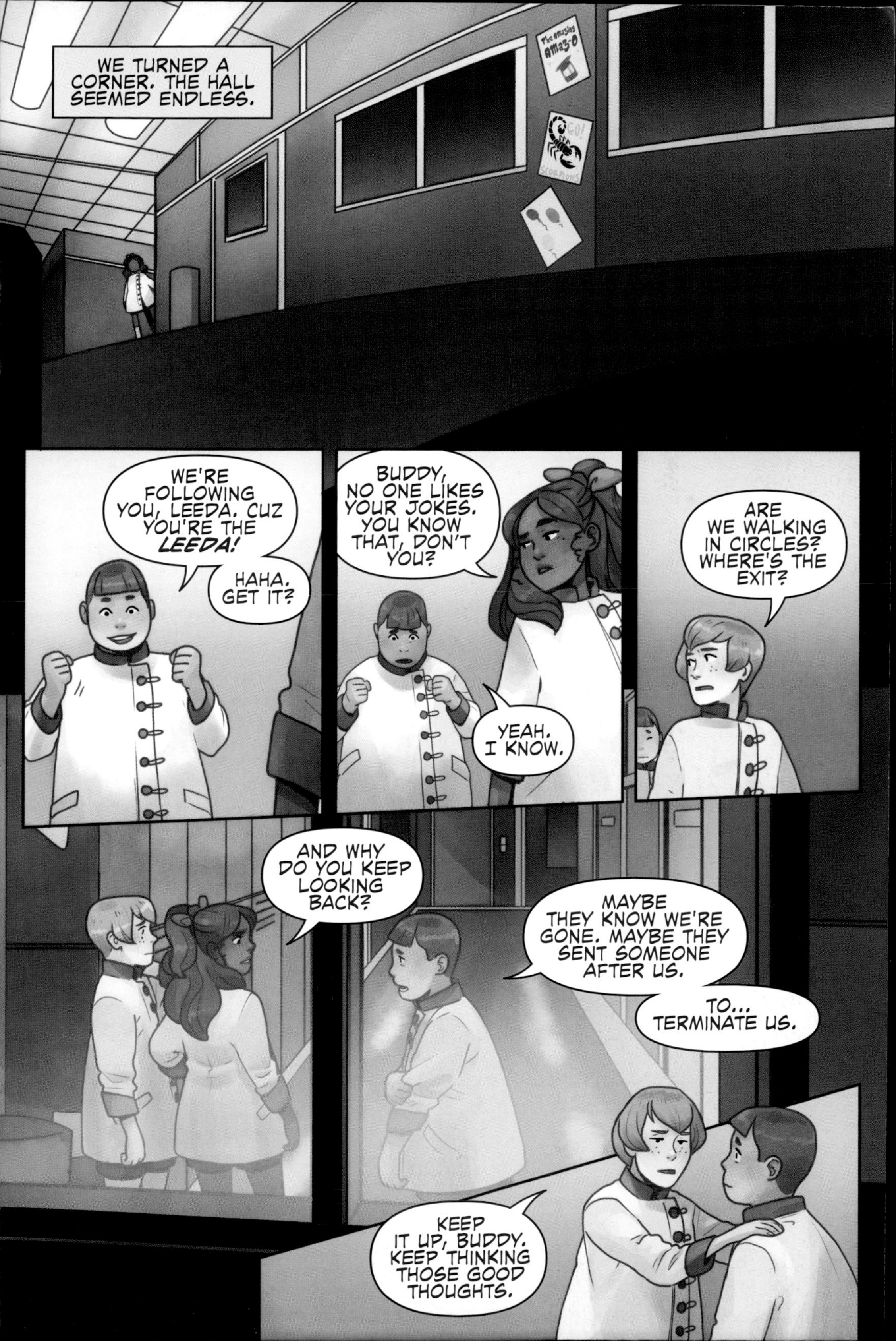
WE TURNED A CORNER. THE HALL SEEMED ENDLESS.
WE'RE FOLLOWING YOU, LEEDA. CUZ YOU'RE THE *LEEDA!*
HAHA. GET IT?
BUDDY, NO ONE LIKES YOUR JOKES. YOU KNOW THAT, DON'T YOU?
YEAH. I KNOW.
ARE WE WALKING IN CIRCLES? WHERE'S THE EXIT?
AND WHY DO YOU KEEP LOOKING BACK?
MAYBE THEY KNOW WE'RE GONE. MAYBE THEY SENT SOMEONE AFTER US.
TO... TERMINATE US.
KEEP IT UP, BUDDY. KEEP THINKING THOSE GOOD THOUGHTS.

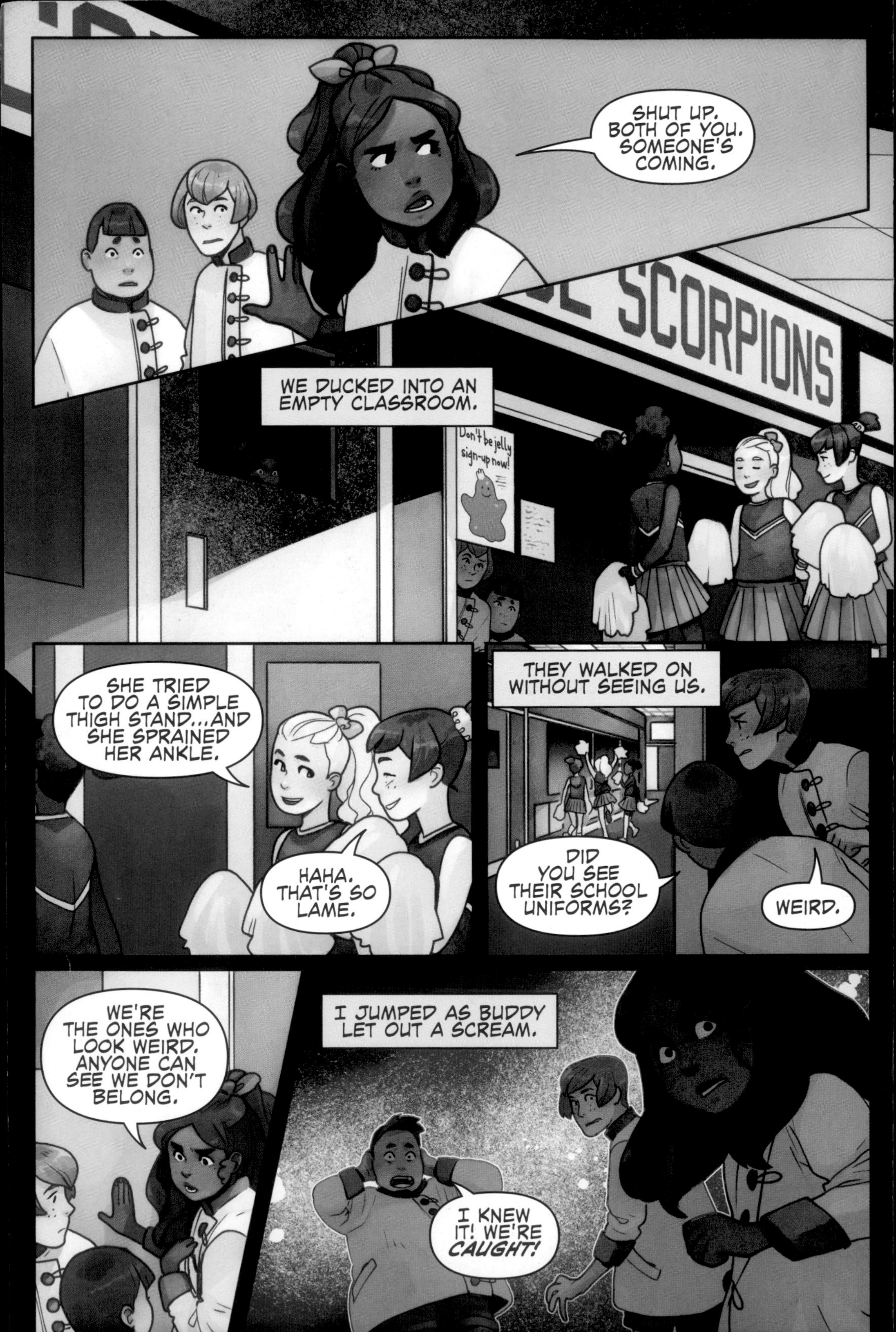
SHUT UP. BOTH OF YOU. SOMEONE'S COMING.
SCORPIONS
WE DUCKED INTO AN EMPTY CLASSROOM.
Don't be jelly sign-up now!
SHE TRIED TO DO A SIMPLE THIGH STAND...AND SHE SPRAINED HER ANKLE.
HAHA. THAT'S SO LAME.
THEY WALKED ON WITHOUT SEEING US.
DID YOU SEE THEIR SCHOOL UNIFORMS?
WEIRD.
WE'RE THE ONES WHO LOOK WEIRD. ANYONE CAN SEE WE DON'T BELONG.
I JUMPED AS BUDDY LET OUT A SCREAM.
I KNEW IT! WE'RE *CAUGHT!*

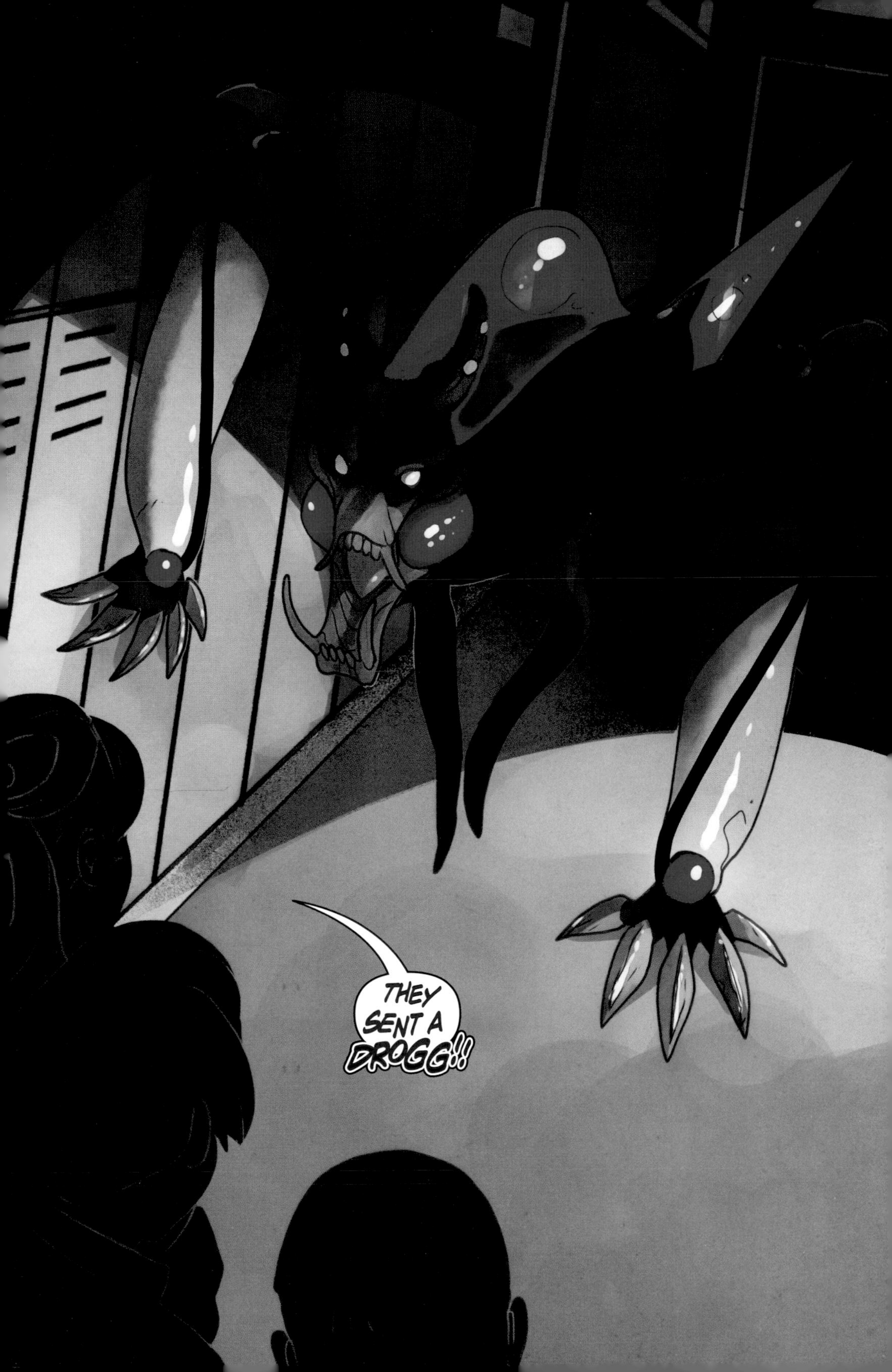
THEY SENT A DROGG!!

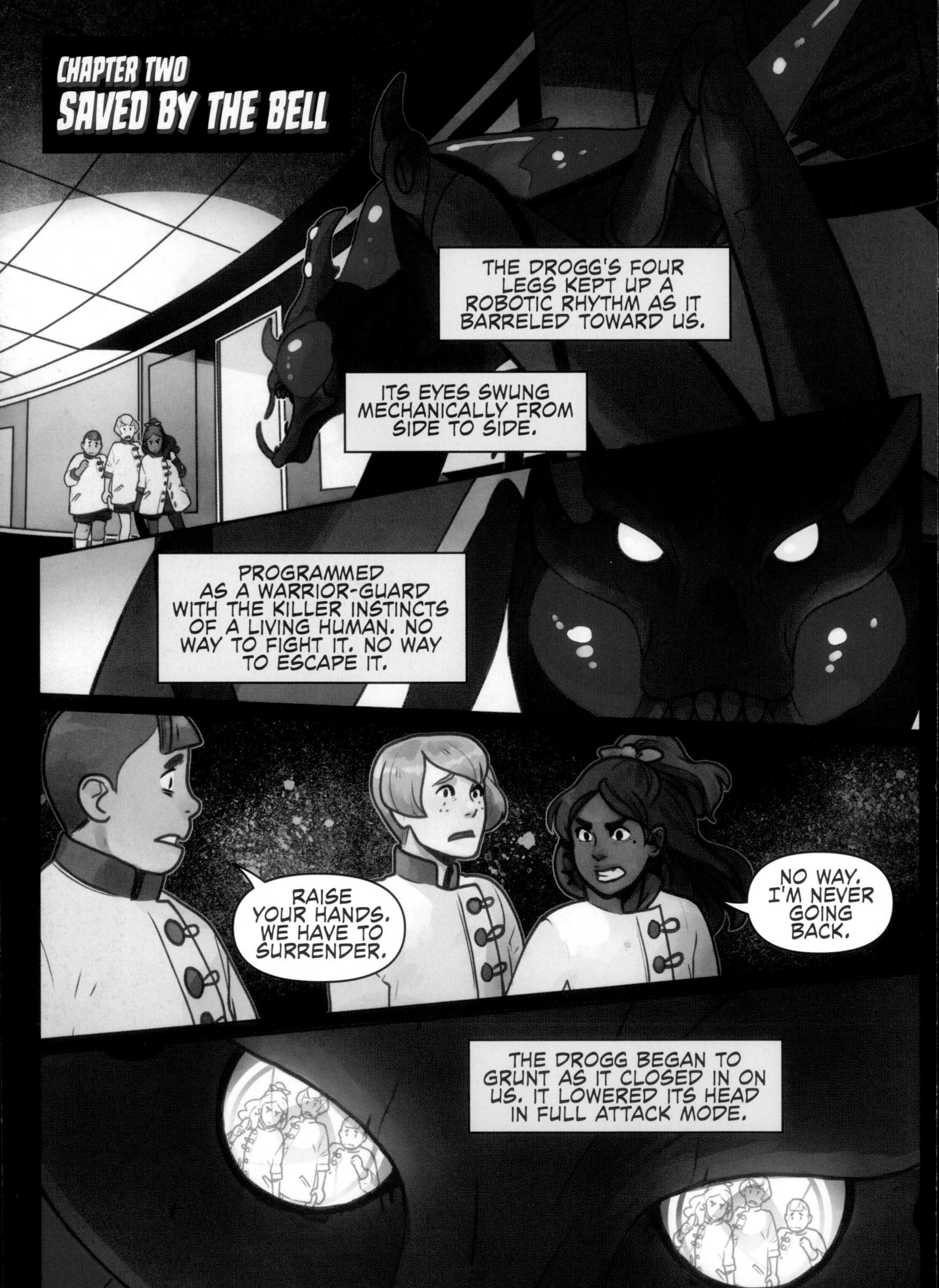
CHAPTER TWO
SAVED BY THE BELL
THE DROGG'S FOUR LEGS KEPT UP A ROBOTIC RHYTHM AS IT BARRELED TOWARD US.
ITS EYES SWUNG MECHANICALLY FROM SIDE TO SIDE.
PROGRAMMED AS A WARRIOR-GUARD WITH THE KILLER INSTINCTS OF A LIVING HUMAN. NO WAY TO FIGHT IT. NO WAY TO ESCAPE IT.
RAISE YOUR HANDS. WE HAVE TO SURRENDER.
NO WAY. I'M NEVER GOING BACK.
THE DROGG BEGAN TO GRUNT AS IT CLOSED IN ON US. IT LOWERED ITS HEAD IN FULL ATTACK MODE.

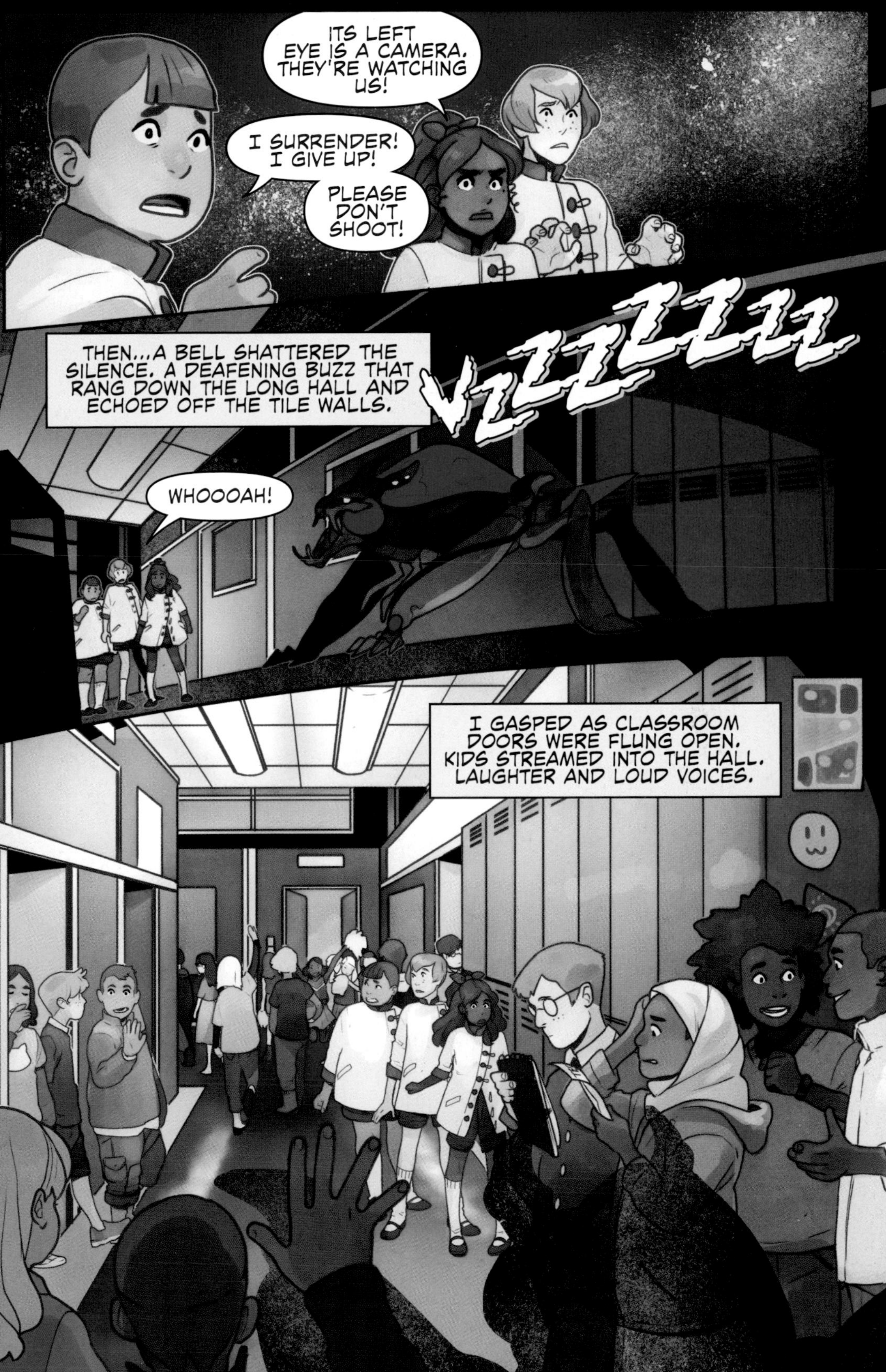
ITS LEFT EYE IS A CAMERA. THEY'RE WATCHING US!
I SURRENDER! I GIVE UP!
PLEASE DON'T SHOOT!
THEN...A BELL SHATTERED THE SILENCE. A DEAFENING BUZZ THAT RANG DOWN THE LONG HALL AND ECHOED OFF THE TILE WALLS.
VZZZZZZZZ
WHOOOAH!
I GASPED AS CLASSROOM DOORS WERE FLUNG OPEN. KIDS STREAMED INTO THE HALL. LAUGHTER AND LOUD VOICES.

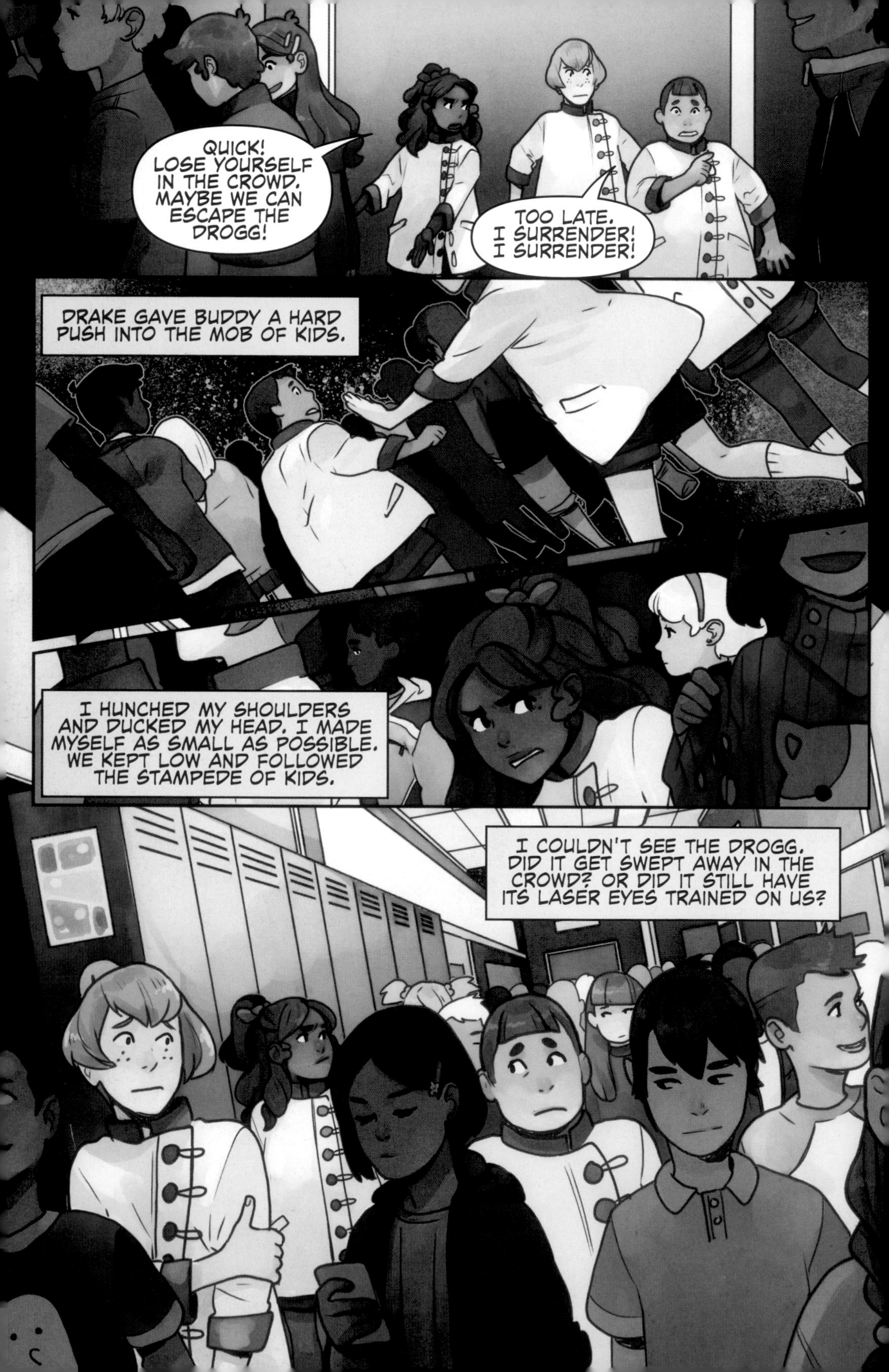
QUICK! LOSE YOURSELF IN THE CROWD. MAYBE WE CAN ESCAPE THE DROGG!
TOO LATE. I SURRENDER! I SURRENDER!
DRAKE GAVE BUDDY A HARD PUSH INTO THE MOB OF KIDS.
I HUNCHED MY SHOULDERS AND DUCKED MY HEAD. I MADE MYSELF AS SMALL AS POSSIBLE. WE KEPT LOW AND FOLLOWED THE STAMPEDE OF KIDS.
I COULDN'T SEE THE DROGG. DID IT GET SWEPT AWAY IN THE CROWD? OR DID IT STILL HAVE ITS LASER EYES TRAINED ON US?

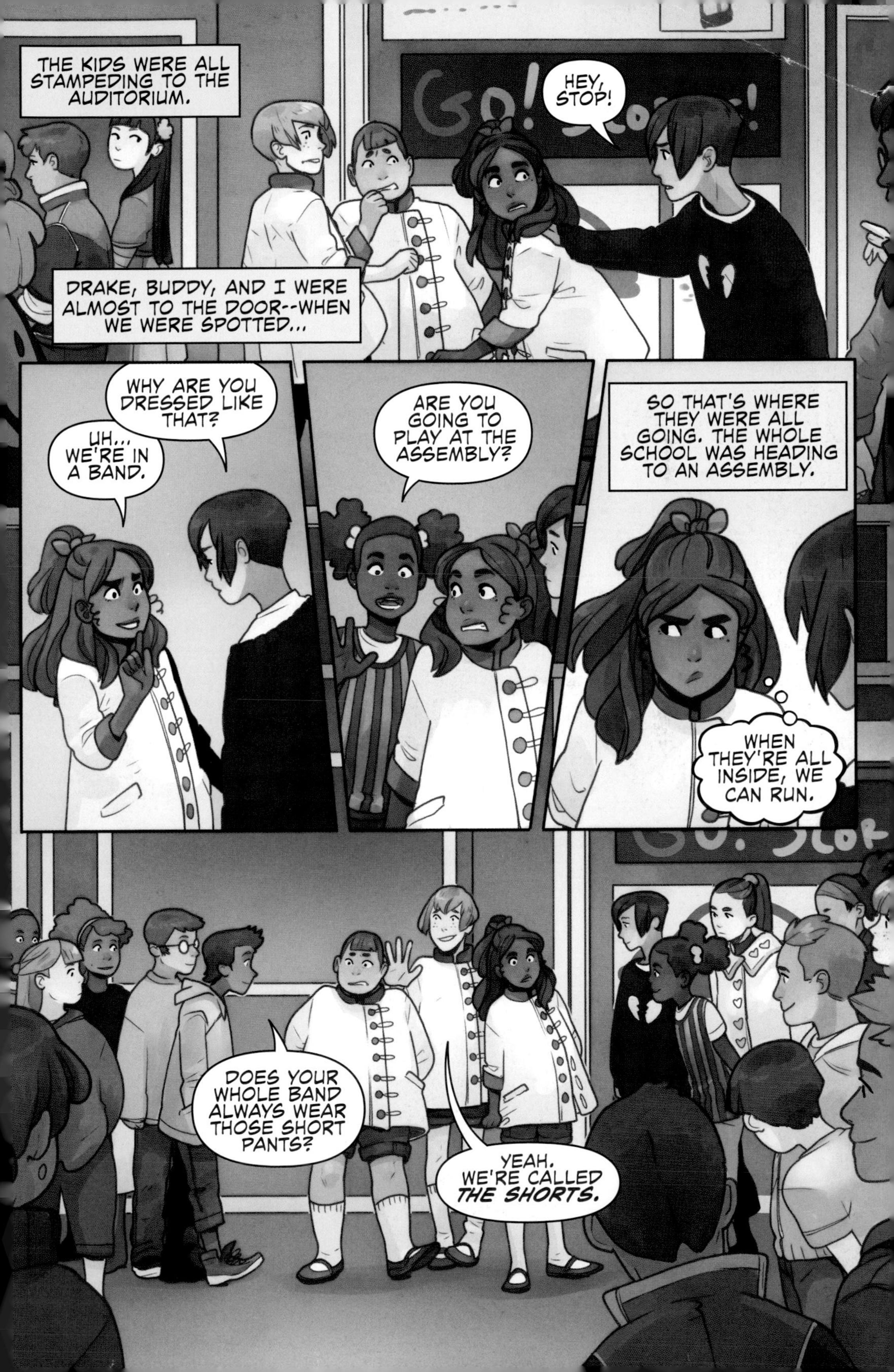

THE KIDS WERE ALL STAMPEDING TO THE AUDITORIUM.
HEY, STOP!
DRAKE, BUDDY, AND I WERE ALMOST TO THE DOOR--WHEN WE WERE SPOTTED...
WHY ARE YOU DRESSED LIKE THAT?
UH... WE'RE IN A BAND.
ARE YOU GOING TO PLAY AT THE ASSEMBLY?
SO THAT'S WHERE THEY WERE ALL GOING. THE WHOLE SCHOOL WAS HEADING TO AN ASSEMBLY.
WHEN THEY'RE ALL INSIDE, WE CAN RUN.
DOES YOUR WHOLE BAND ALWAYS WEAR THOSE SHORT PANTS?
YEAH. WE'RE CALLED *THE SHORTS.*

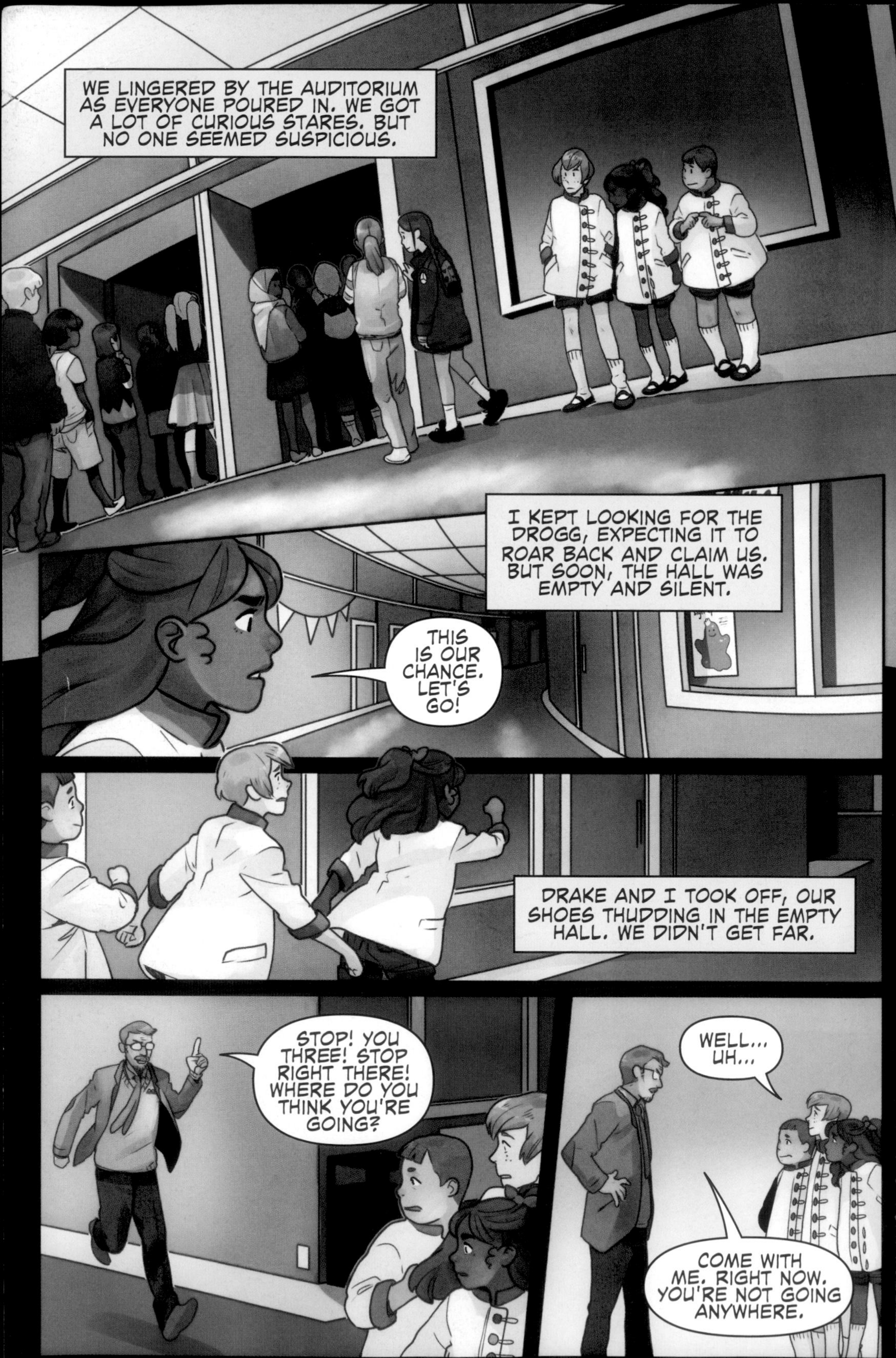
WE LINGERED BY THE AUDITORIUM AS EVERYONE POURED IN. WE GOT A LOT OF CURIOUS STARES. BUT NO ONE SEEMED SUSPICIOUS.
I KEPT LOOKING FOR THE DROGG, EXPECTING IT TO ROAR BACK AND CLAIM US. BUT SOON, THE HALL WAS EMPTY AND SILENT.
THIS IS OUR CHANCE. LET'S GO!
DRAKE AND I TOOK OFF, OUR SHOES THUDDING IN THE EMPTY HALL. WE DIDN'T GET FAR.
STOP! YOU THREE! STOP RIGHT THERE! WHERE DO YOU THINK YOU'RE GOING?
WELL... UH...
COME WITH ME. RIGHT NOW. YOU'RE NOT GOING ANYWHERE.

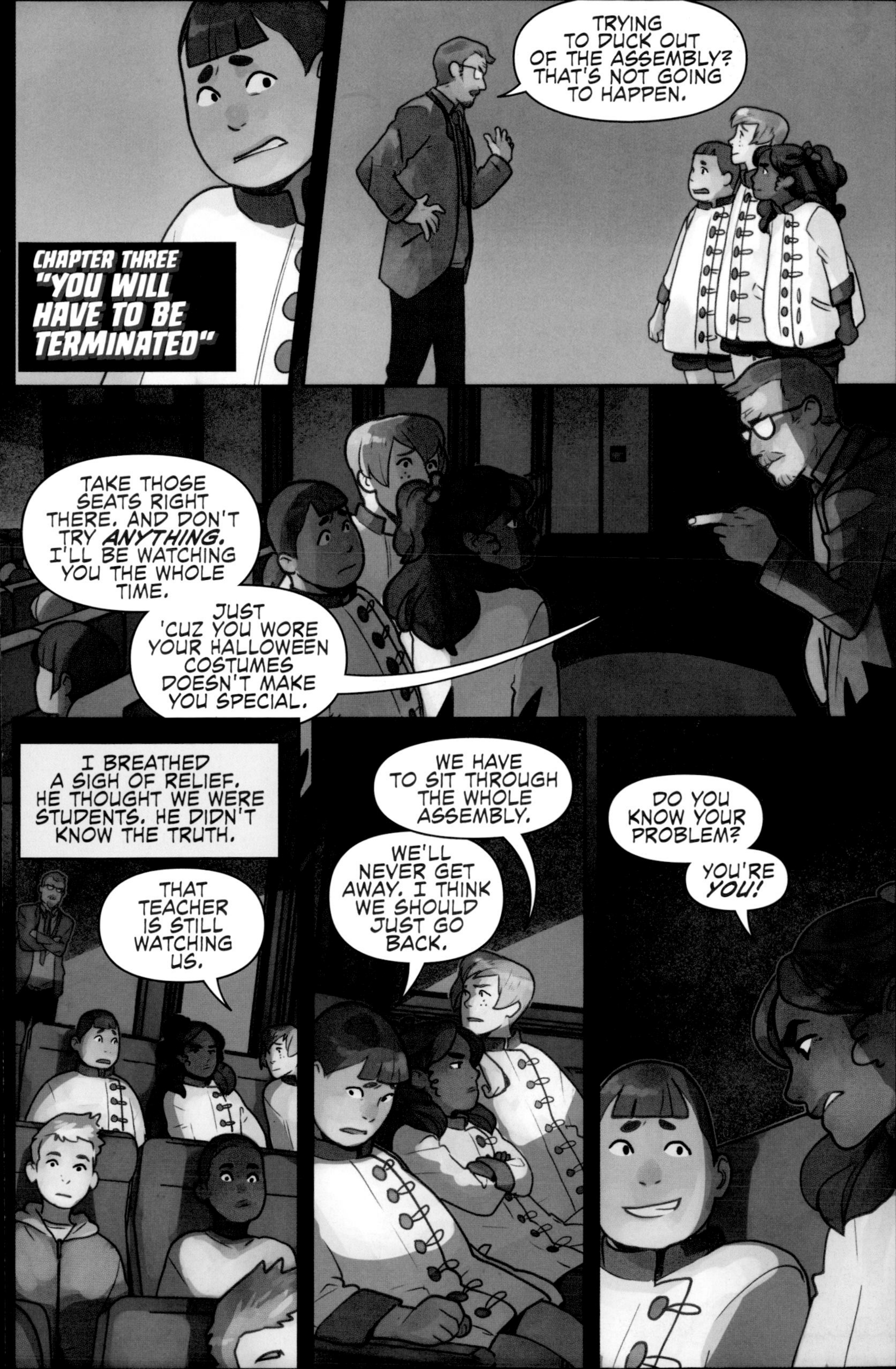
CHAPTER THREE
"YOU WILL HAVE TO BE TERMINATED"
TRYING TO DUCK OUT OF THE ASSEMBLY? THAT'S NOT GOING TO HAPPEN.
TAKE THOSE SEATS RIGHT THERE. AND DON'T TRY ANYTHING. I'LL BE WATCHING YOU THE WHOLE TIME.
JUST 'CUZ YOU WORE YOUR HALLOWEEN COSTUMES DOESN'T MAKE YOU SPECIAL.
I BREATHED A SIGH OF RELIEF. HE THOUGHT WE WERE STUDENTS. HE DIDN'T KNOW THE TRUTH.
THAT TEACHER IS STILL WATCHING US.
WE HAVE TO SIT THROUGH THE WHOLE ASSEMBLY.
WE'LL NEVER GET AWAY. I THINK WE SHOULD JUST GO BACK.
DO YOU KNOW YOUR PROBLEM?
YOU'RE YOU!

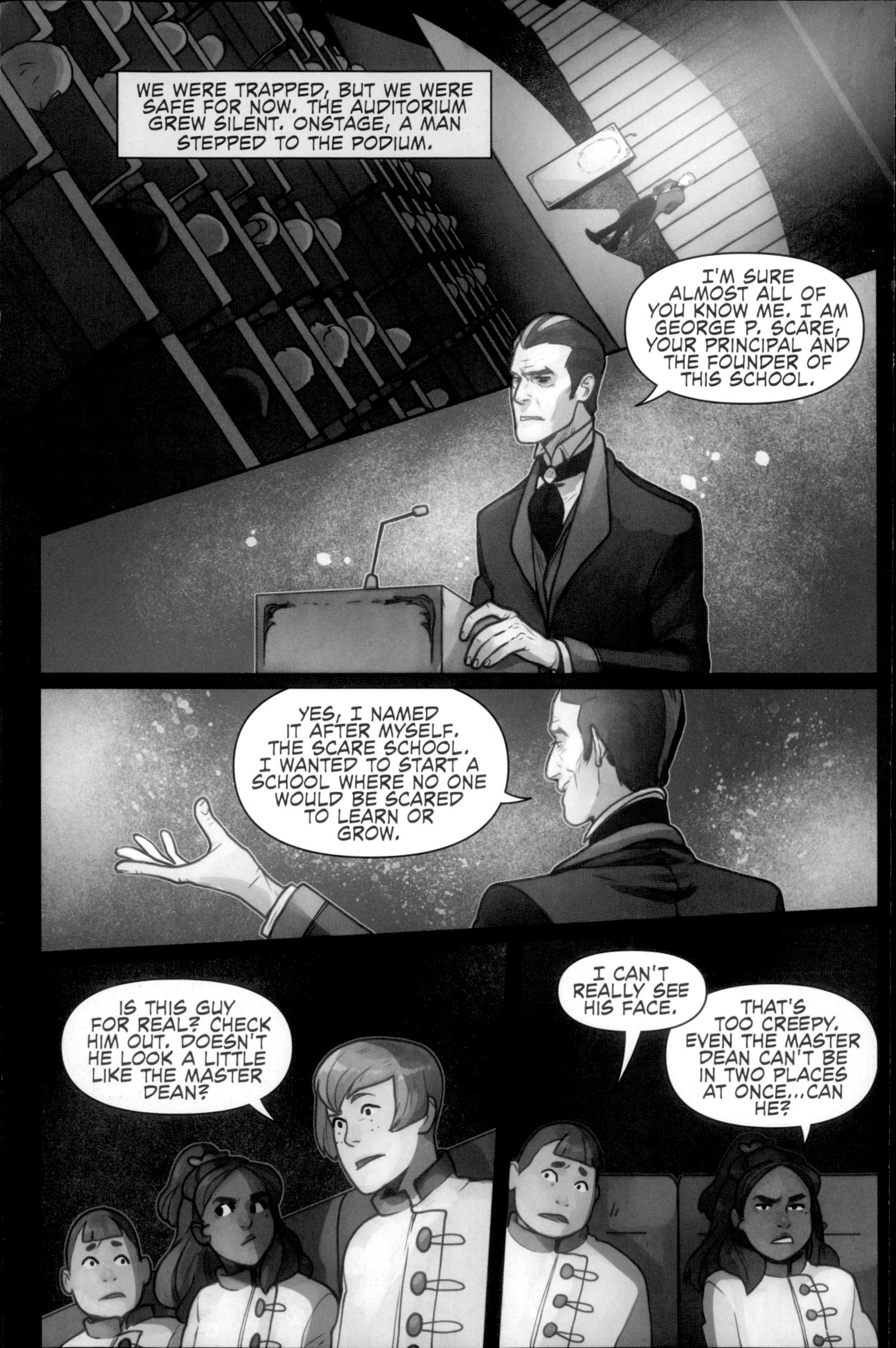
WE WERE TRAPPED, BUT WE WERE SAFE FOR NOW. THE AUDITORIUM GREW SILENT. ONSTAGE, A MAN STEPPED TO THE PODIUM.
I'M SURE ALMOST ALL OF YOU KNOW ME. I AM GEORGE P. SCARE, YOUR PRINCIPAL AND THE FOUNDER OF THIS SCHOOL.
YES, I NAMED IT AFTER MYSELF. THE SCARE SCHOOL. I WANTED TO START A SCHOOL WHERE NO ONE WOULD BE SCARED TO LEARN OR GROW.
IS THIS GUY FOR REAL? CHECK HIM OUT. DOESN'T HE LOOK A LITTLE LIKE THE MASTER DEAN?
I CAN'T REALLY SEE HIS FACE.
THAT'S TOO CREEPY. EVEN THE MASTER DEAN CAN'T BE IN TWO PLACES AT ONCE...CAN HE?

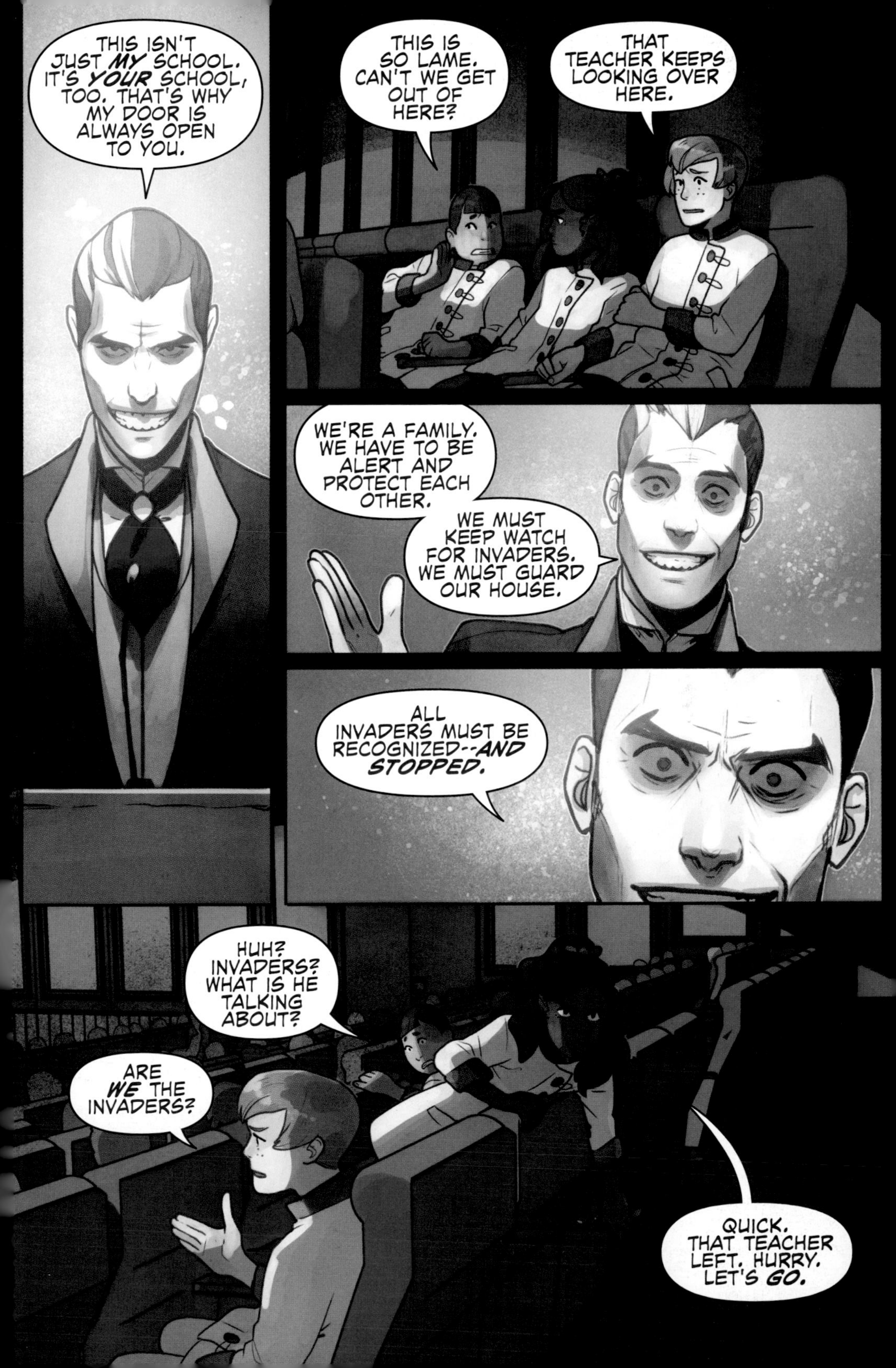
THIS ISN'T JUST MY SCHOOL. IT'S YOUR SCHOOL, TOO. THAT'S WHY MY DOOR IS ALWAYS OPEN TO YOU.
THIS IS SO LAME. CAN'T WE GET OUT OF HERE?
THAT TEACHER KEEPS LOOKING OVER HERE.
WE'RE A FAMILY. WE HAVE TO BE ALERT AND PROTECT EACH OTHER.
WE MUST KEEP WATCH FOR INVADERS. WE MUST GUARD OUR HOUSE.
ALL INVADERS MUST BE RECOGNIZED--AND STOPPED.
HUH? INVADERS? WHAT IS HE TALKING ABOUT?
ARE WE THE INVADERS?
QUICK. THAT TEACHER LEFT. HURRY. LET'S GO.

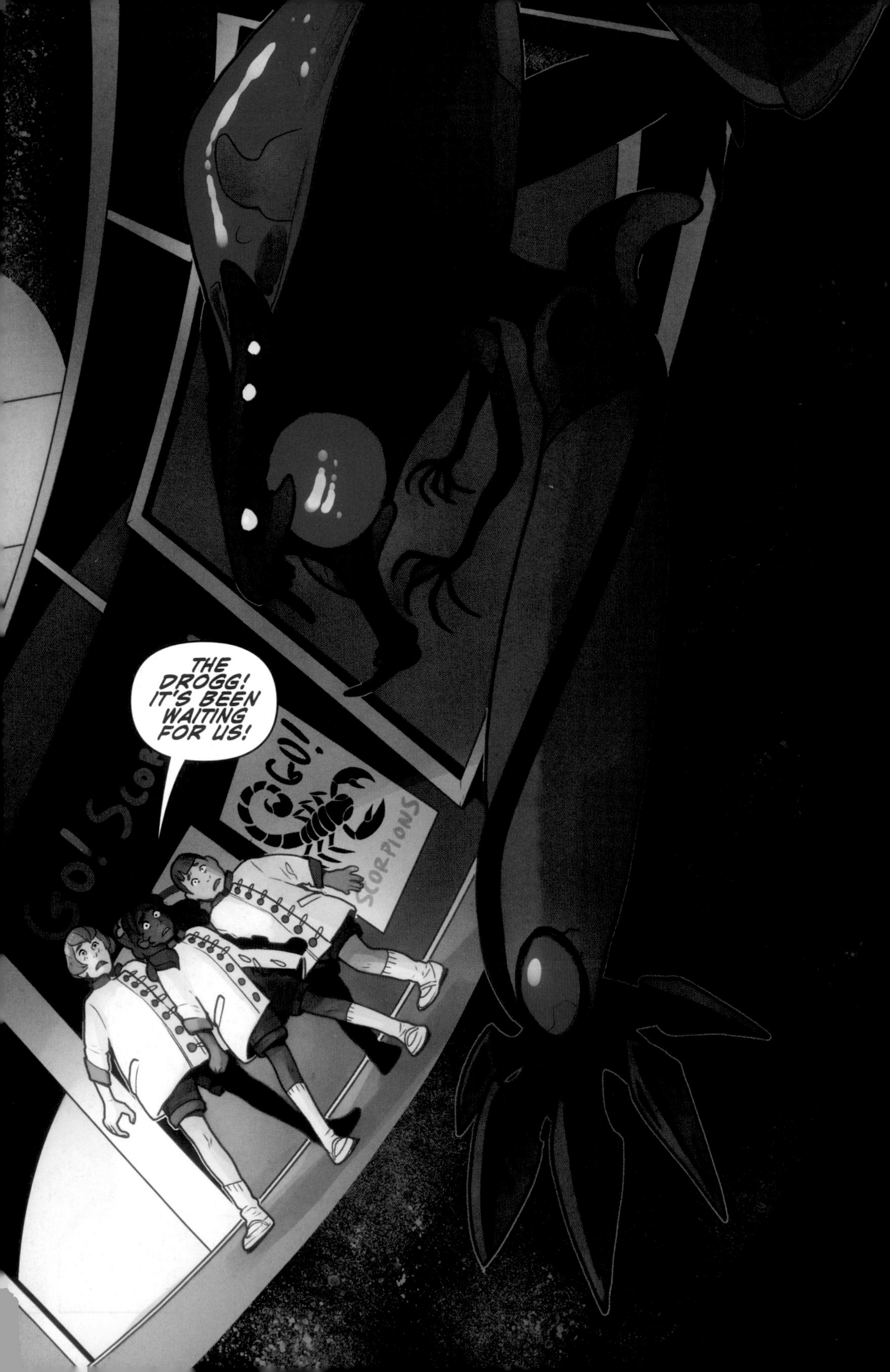
THE DROGG! IT'S BEEN WAITING FOR US!
GO!
SCORPIONS

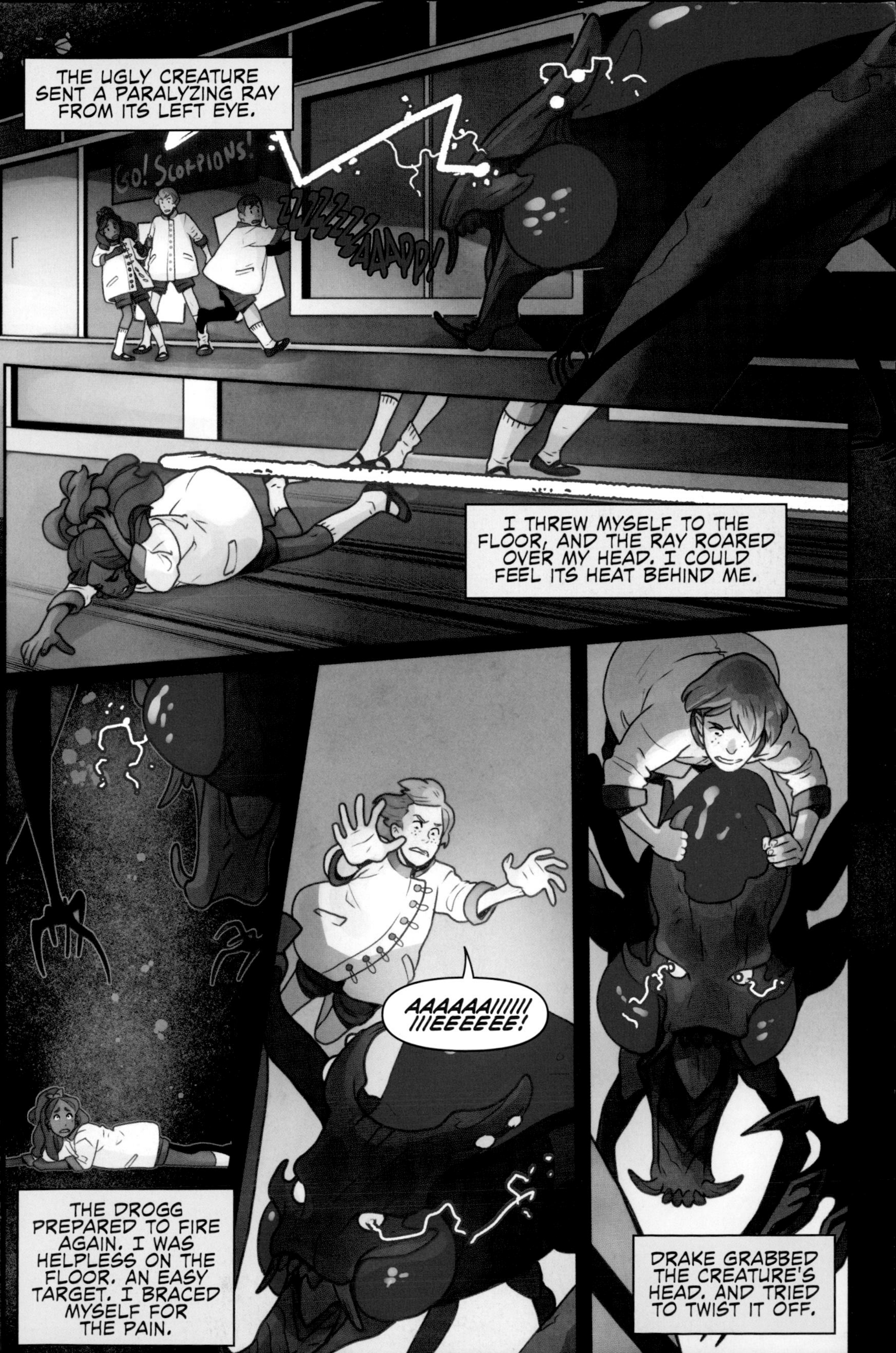
THE UGLY CREATURE SENT A PARALYZING RAY FROM ITS LEFT EYE.
GO! SCORPIONS!
ZZZZZZZZAAAPP!
I THREW MYSELF TO THE FLOOR, AND THE RAY ROARED OVER MY HEAD. I COULD FEEL ITS HEAT BEHIND ME.
THE DROGG PREPARED TO FIRE AGAIN. I WAS HELPLESS ON THE FLOOR. AN EASY TARGET. I BRACED MYSELF FOR THE PAIN.
AAAAAAIIIIIIIIIEEEEEEE!
DRAKE GRABBED THE CREATURE'S HEAD, AND TRIED TO TWIST IT OFF.

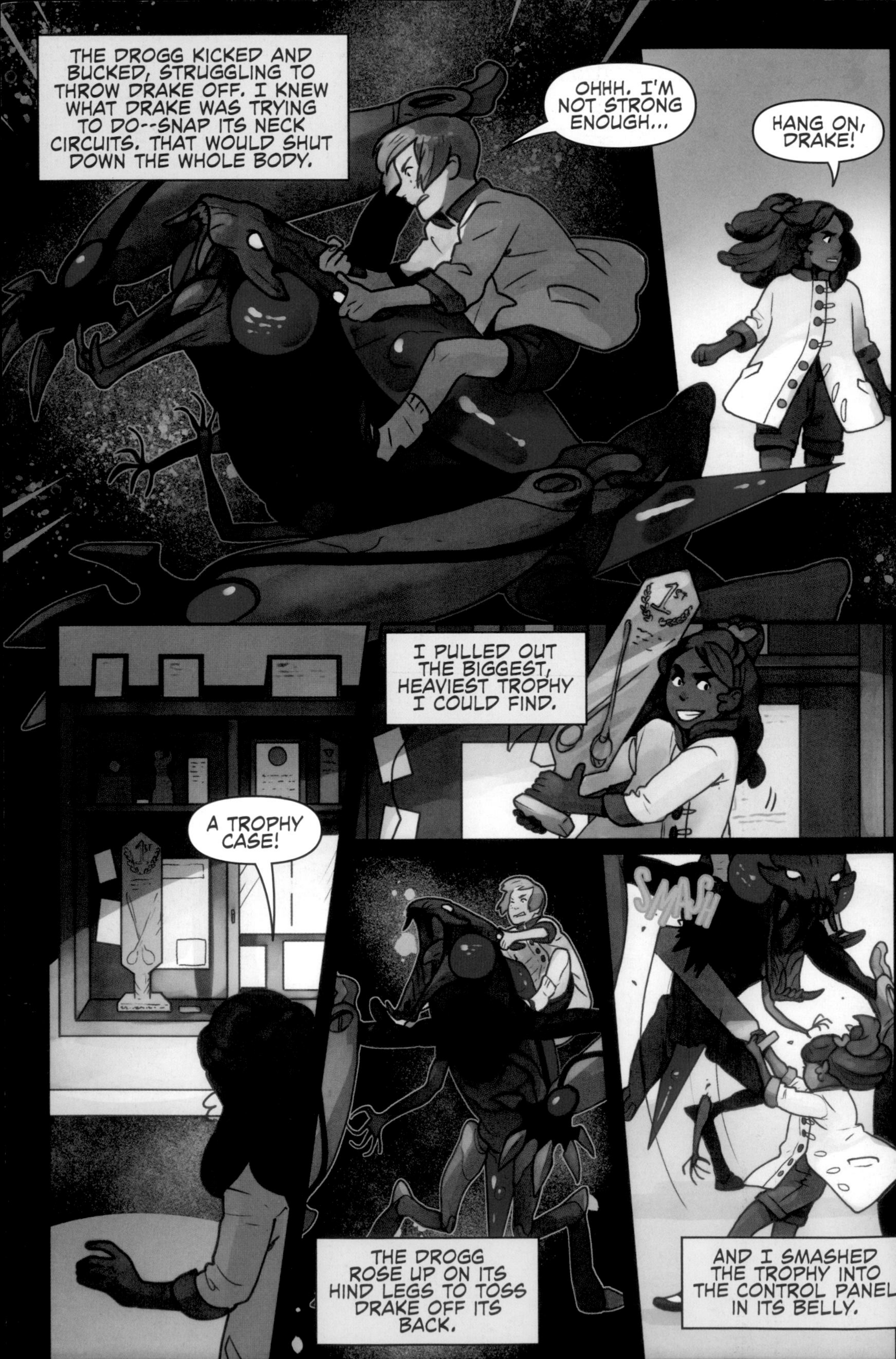
THE DROGG KICKED AND BUCKED, STRUGGLING TO THROW DRAKE OFF. I KNEW WHAT DRAKE WAS TRYING TO DO--SNAP ITS NECK CIRCUITS. THAT WOULD SHUT DOWN THE WHOLE BODY.
OHHH. I'M NOT STRONG ENOUGH...
HANG ON, DRAKE!
A TROPHY CASE!
I PULLED OUT THE BIGGEST, HEAVIEST TROPHY I COULD FIND.
THE DROGG ROSE UP ON ITS HIND LEGS TO TOSS DRAKE OFF ITS BACK.
SMASH
AND I SMASHED THE TROPHY INTO THE CONTROL PANEL IN ITS BELLY.

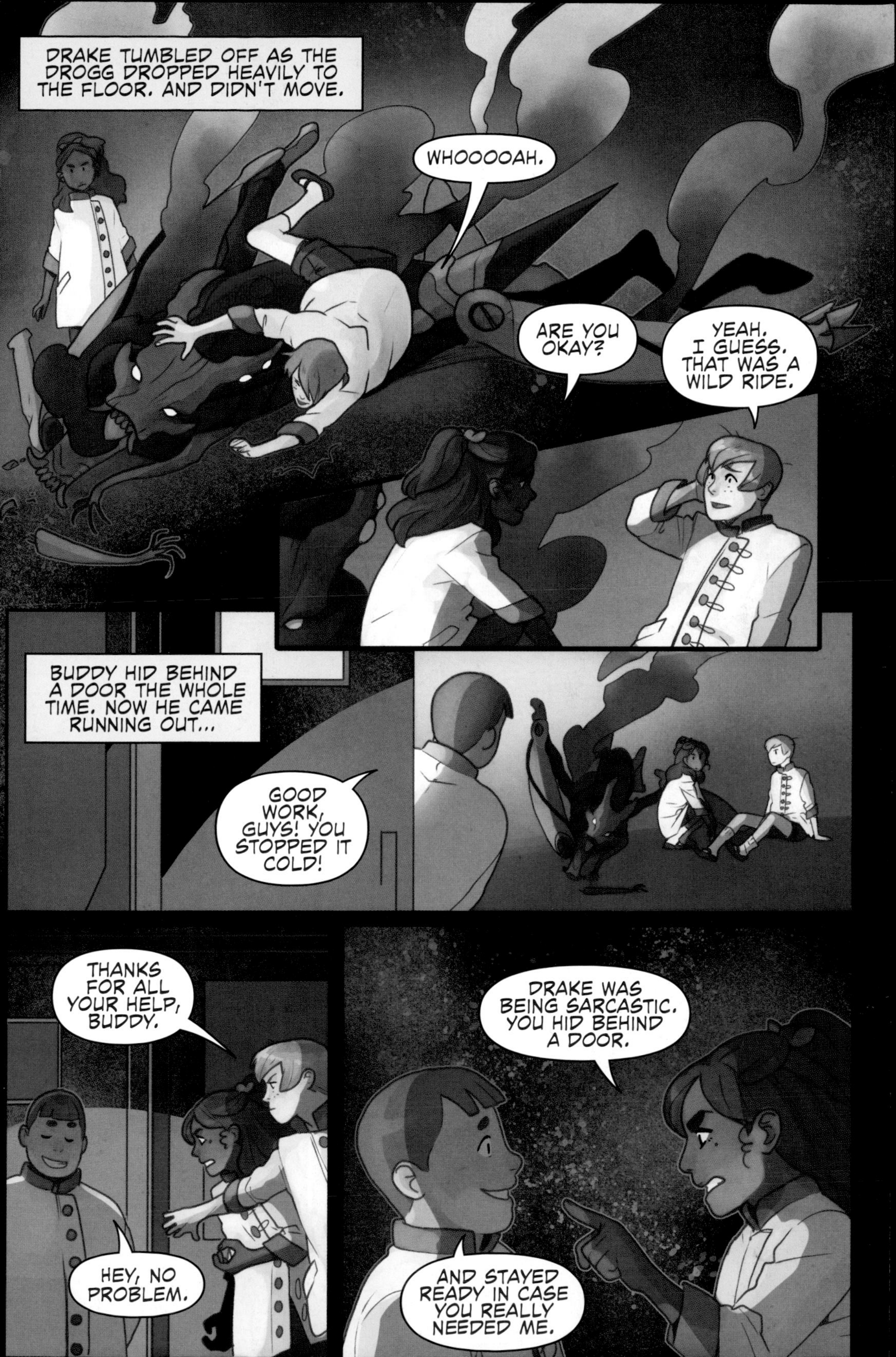

DRAKE TUMBLED OFF AS THE DROGG DROPPED HEAVILY TO THE FLOOR. AND DIDN'T MOVE.
WHOOOOAH.
ARE YOU OKAY?
YEAH. I GUESS. THAT WAS A WILD RIDE.
BUDDY HID BEHIND A DOOR THE WHOLE TIME. NOW HE CAME RUNNING OUT...
GOOD WORK, GUYS! YOU STOPPED IT COLD!
THANKS FOR ALL YOUR HELP, BUDDY.
HEY, NO PROBLEM.
DRAKE WAS BEING SARCASTIC. YOU HID BEHIND A DOOR.
AND STAYED READY IN CASE YOU REALLY NEEDED ME.

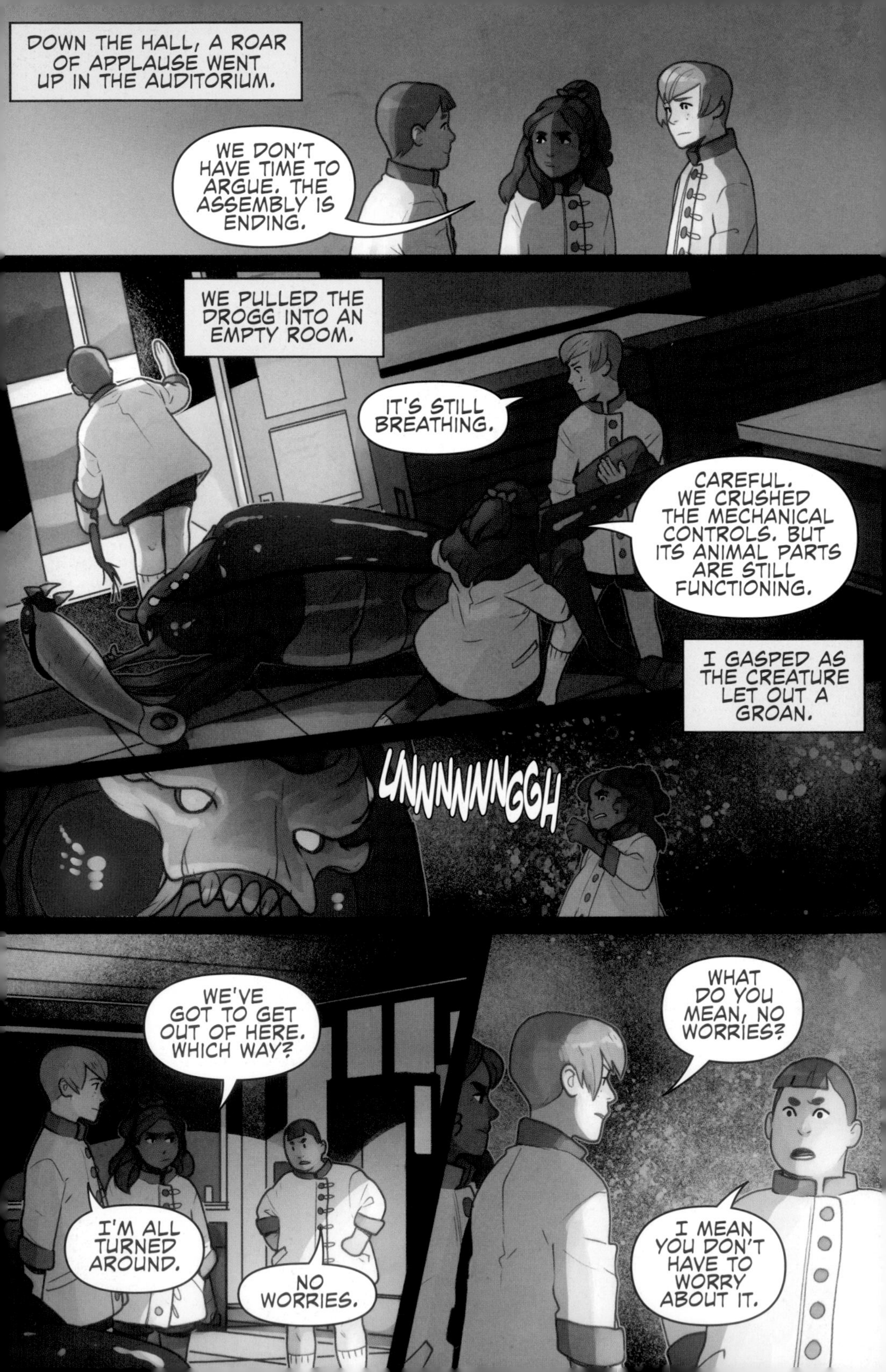
DOWN THE HALL, A ROAR OF APPLAUSE WENT UP IN THE AUDITORIUM.
WE DON'T HAVE TIME TO ARGUE. THE ASSEMBLY IS ENDING.
WE PULLED THE DROGG INTO AN EMPTY ROOM.
IT'S STILL BREATHING.
CAREFUL. WE CRUSHED THE MECHANICAL CONTROLS. BUT ITS ANIMAL PARTS ARE STILL FUNCTIONING.
I GASPED AS THE CREATURE LET OUT A GROAN.
UNNNNNNGGH
WE'VE GOT TO GET OUT OF HERE. WHICH WAY?
I'M ALL TURNED AROUND.
NO WORRIES.
WHAT DO YOU MEAN, NO WORRIES?
I MEAN YOU DON'T HAVE TO WORRY ABOUT IT.

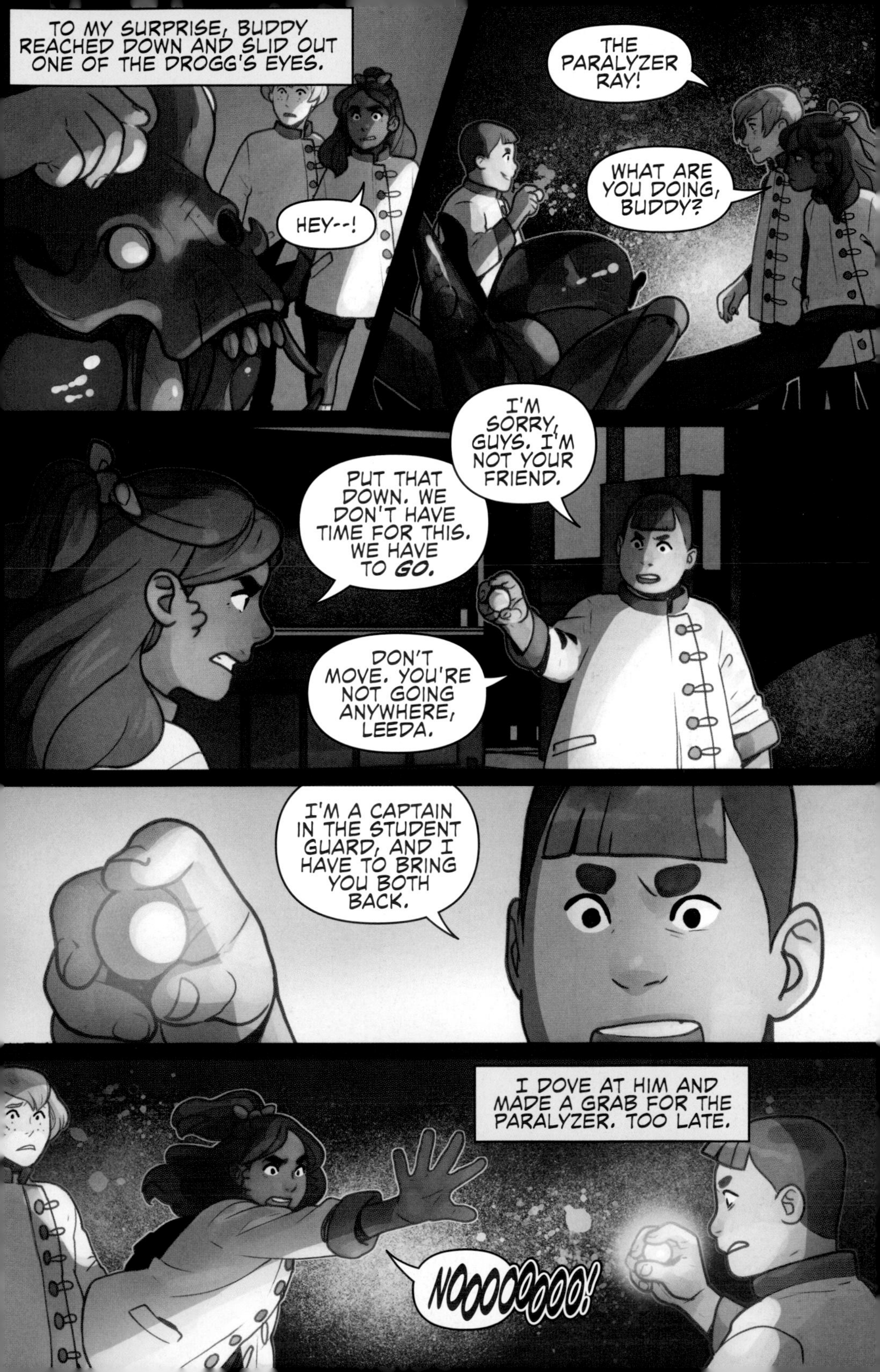
TO MY SURPRISE, BUDDY REACHED DOWN AND SLID OUT ONE OF THE DROGG'S EYES.
HEY--!
THE PARALYZER RAY!
WHAT ARE YOU DOING, BUDDY?
PUT THAT DOWN. WE DON'T HAVE TIME FOR THIS. WE HAVE TO GO.
I'M SORRY, GUYS. I'M NOT YOUR FRIEND.
DON'T MOVE. YOU'RE NOT GOING ANYWHERE, LEEDA.
I'M A CAPTAIN IN THE STUDENT GUARD, AND I HAVE TO BRING YOU BOTH BACK.
I DOVE AT HIM AND MADE A GRAB FOR THE PARALYZER. TOO LATE.
NOOOOOOOO!

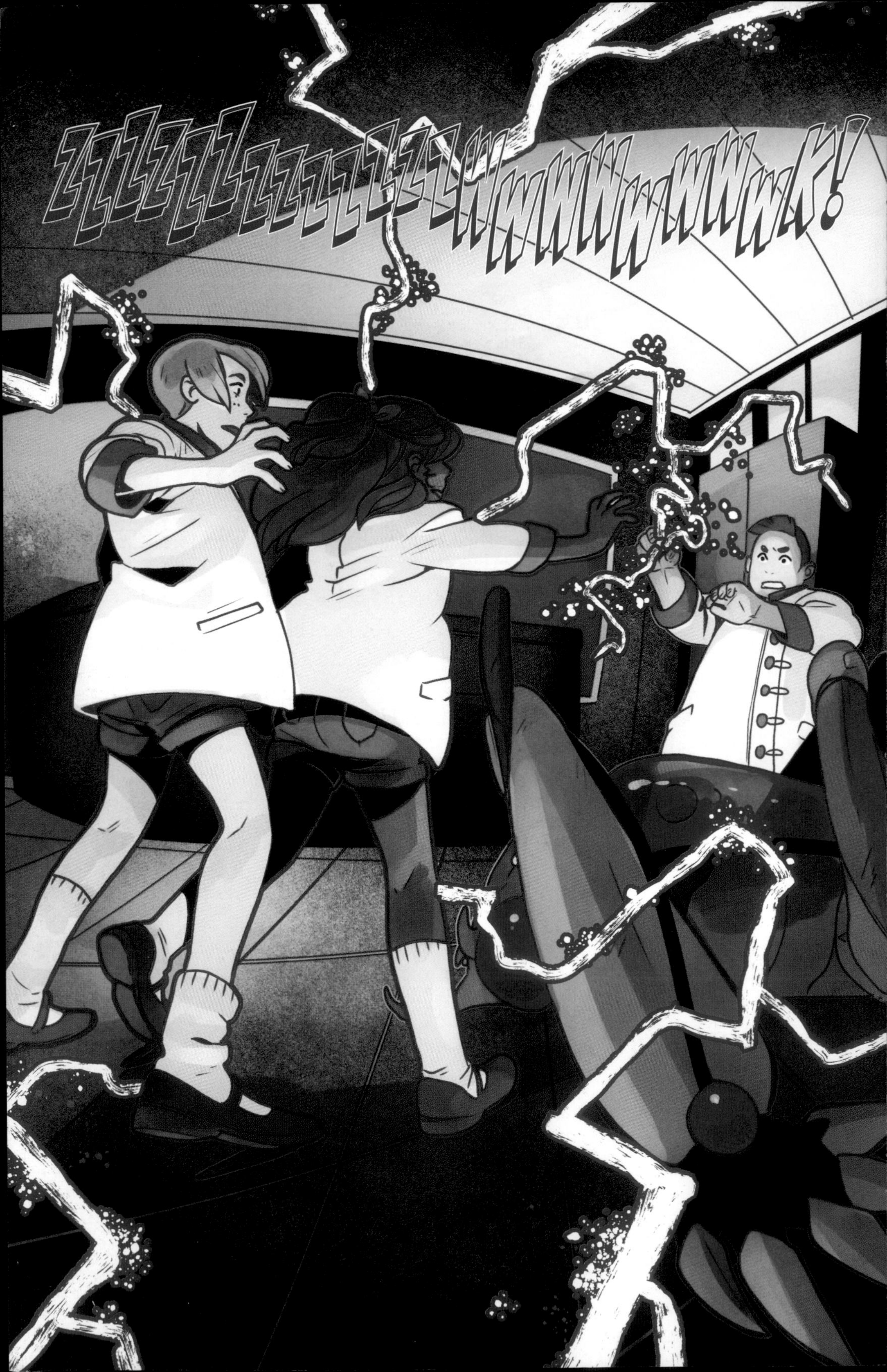
ZZZZZZZZZZZZZZWWWWWWWWWWWK!

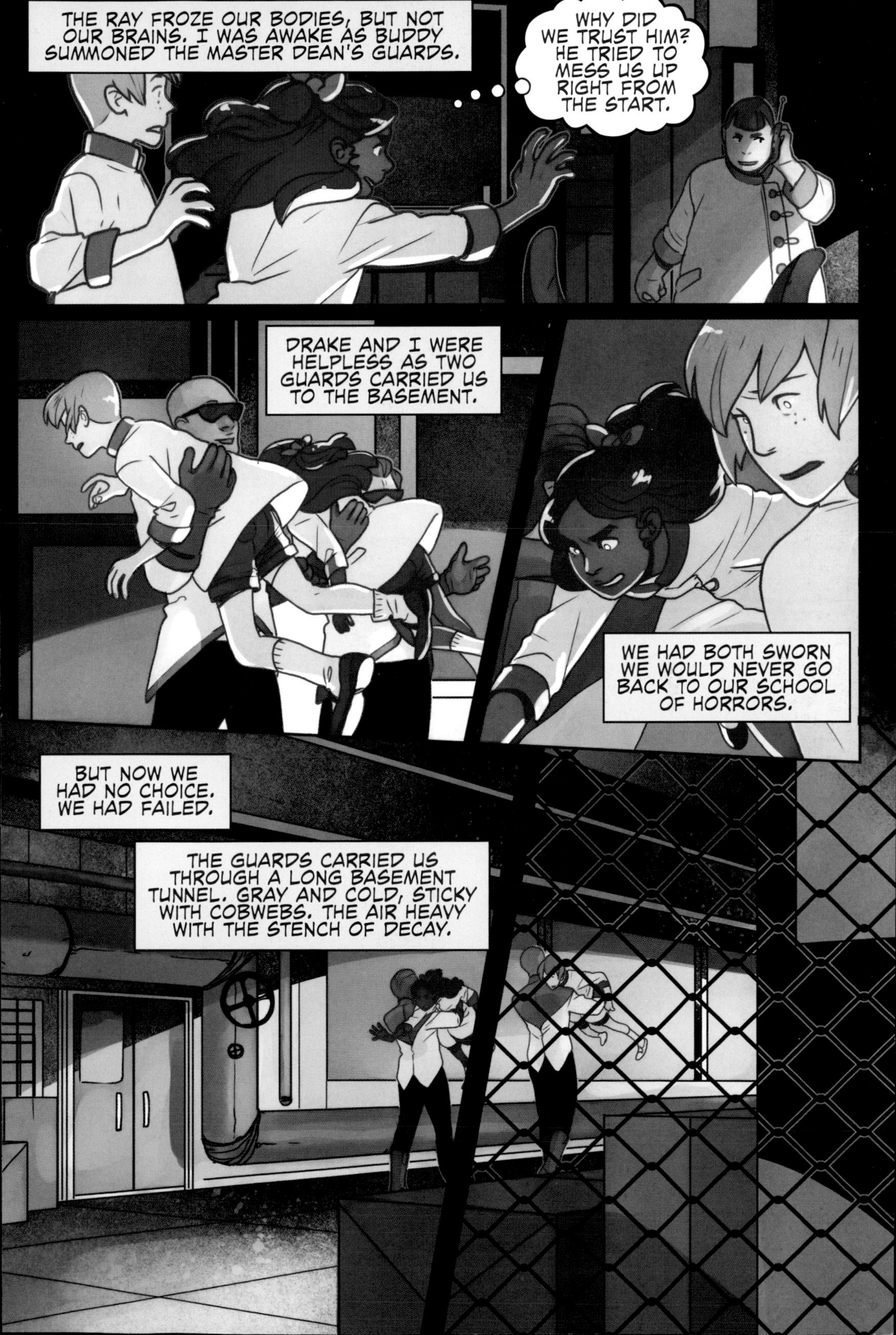
THE RAY FROZE OUR BODIES, BUT NOT OUR BRAINS. I WAS AWAKE AS BUDDY SUMMONED THE MASTER DEAN'S GUARDS.
WHY DID WE TRUST HIM? HE TRIED TO MESS US UP RIGHT FROM THE START.
DRAKE AND I WERE HELPLESS AS TWO GUARDS CARRIED US TO THE BASEMENT.
WE HAD BOTH SWORN WE WOULD NEVER GO BACK TO OUR SCHOOL OF HORRORS.
BUT NOW WE HAD NO CHOICE. WE HAD FAILED.
THE GUARDS CARRIED US THROUGH A LONG BASEMENT TUNNEL. GRAY AND COLD, STICKY WITH COBWEBS. THE AIR HEAVY WITH THE STENCH OF DECAY.

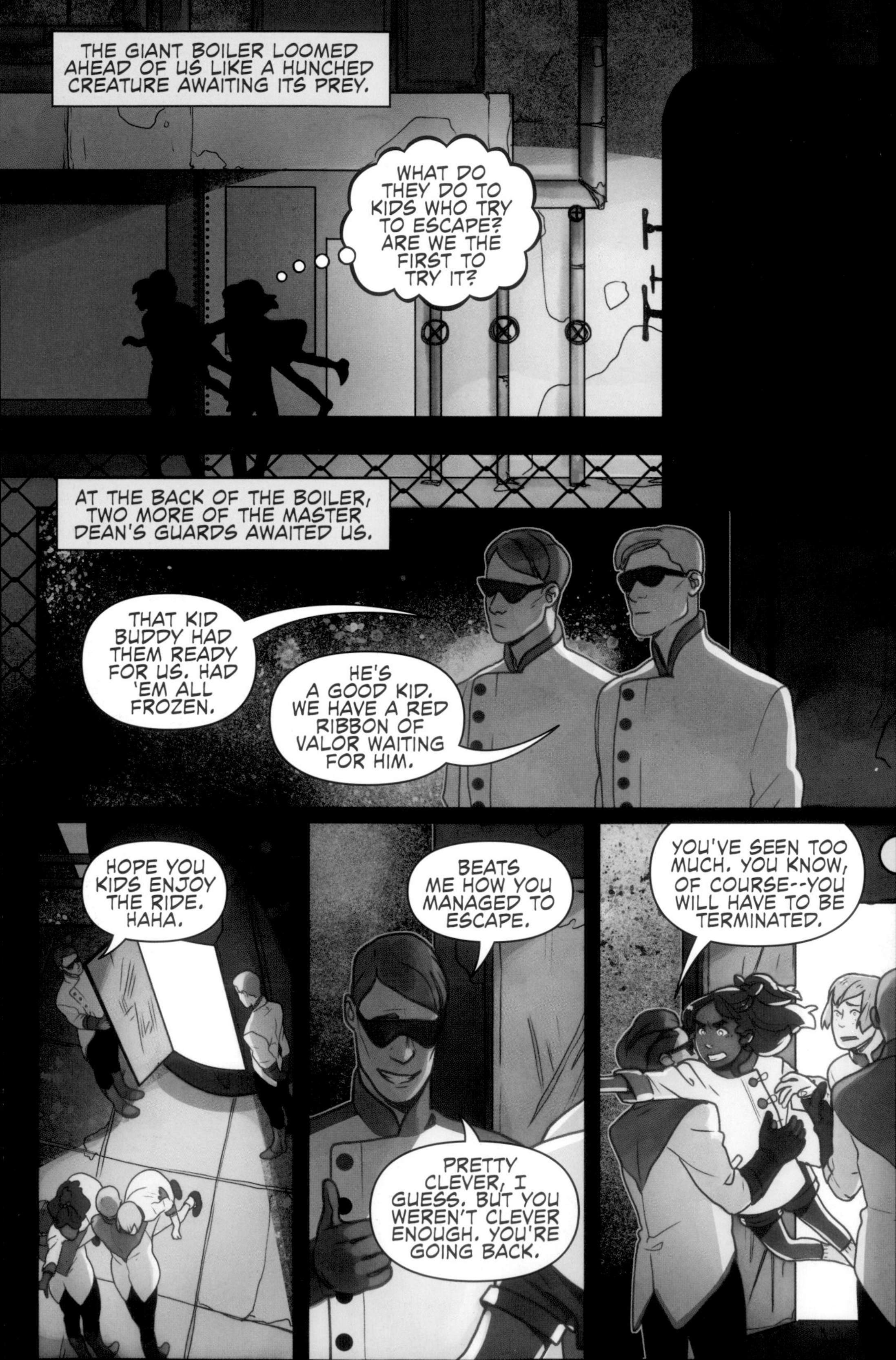
THE GIANT BOILER LOOMED AHEAD OF US LIKE A HUNCHED CREATURE AWAITING ITS PREY.
WHAT DO THEY DO TO KIDS WHO TRY TO ESCAPE? ARE WE THE FIRST TO TRY IT?
AT THE BACK OF THE BOILER, TWO MORE OF THE MASTER DEAN'S GUARDS AWAITED US.
THAT KID BUDDY HAD THEM READY FOR US. HAD 'EM ALL FROZEN.
HE'S A GOOD KID. WE HAVE A RED RIBBON OF VALOR WAITING FOR HIM.
HOPE YOU KIDS ENJOY THE RIDE. HAHA.
BEATS ME HOW YOU MANAGED TO ESCAPE.
PRETTY CLEVER, I GUESS. BUT YOU WEREN'T CLEVER ENOUGH. YOU'RE GOING BACK.
YOU'VE SEEN TOO MUCH. YOU KNOW, OF COURSE--YOU WILL HAVE TO BE TERMINATED.

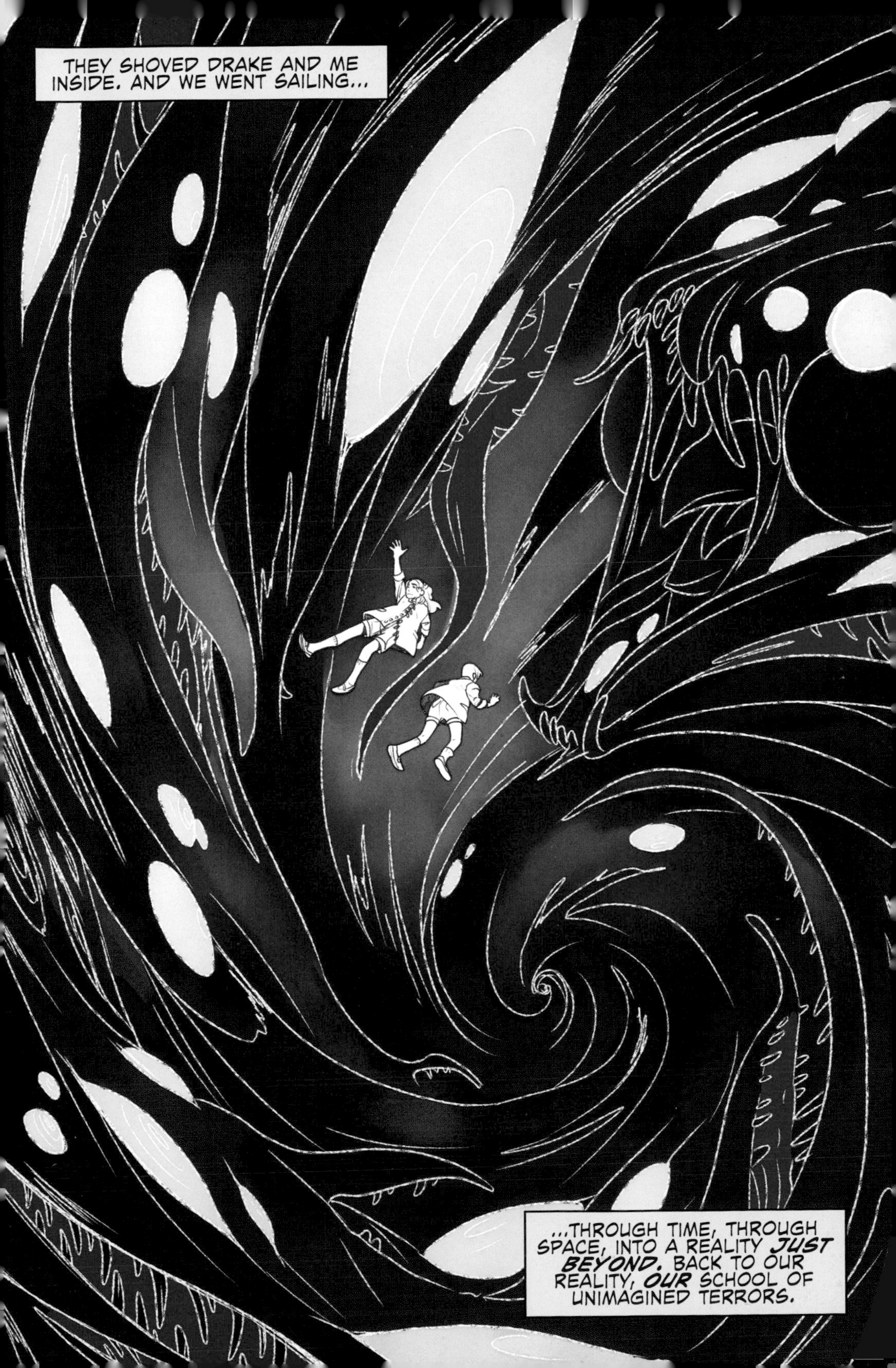
THEY SHOVED DRAKE AND ME INSIDE. AND WE WENT SAILING...
...THROUGH TIME, THROUGH SPACE, INTO A REALITY *JUST BEYOND.* BACK TO OUR REALITY, *OUR* SCHOOL OF UNIMAGINED TERRORS.

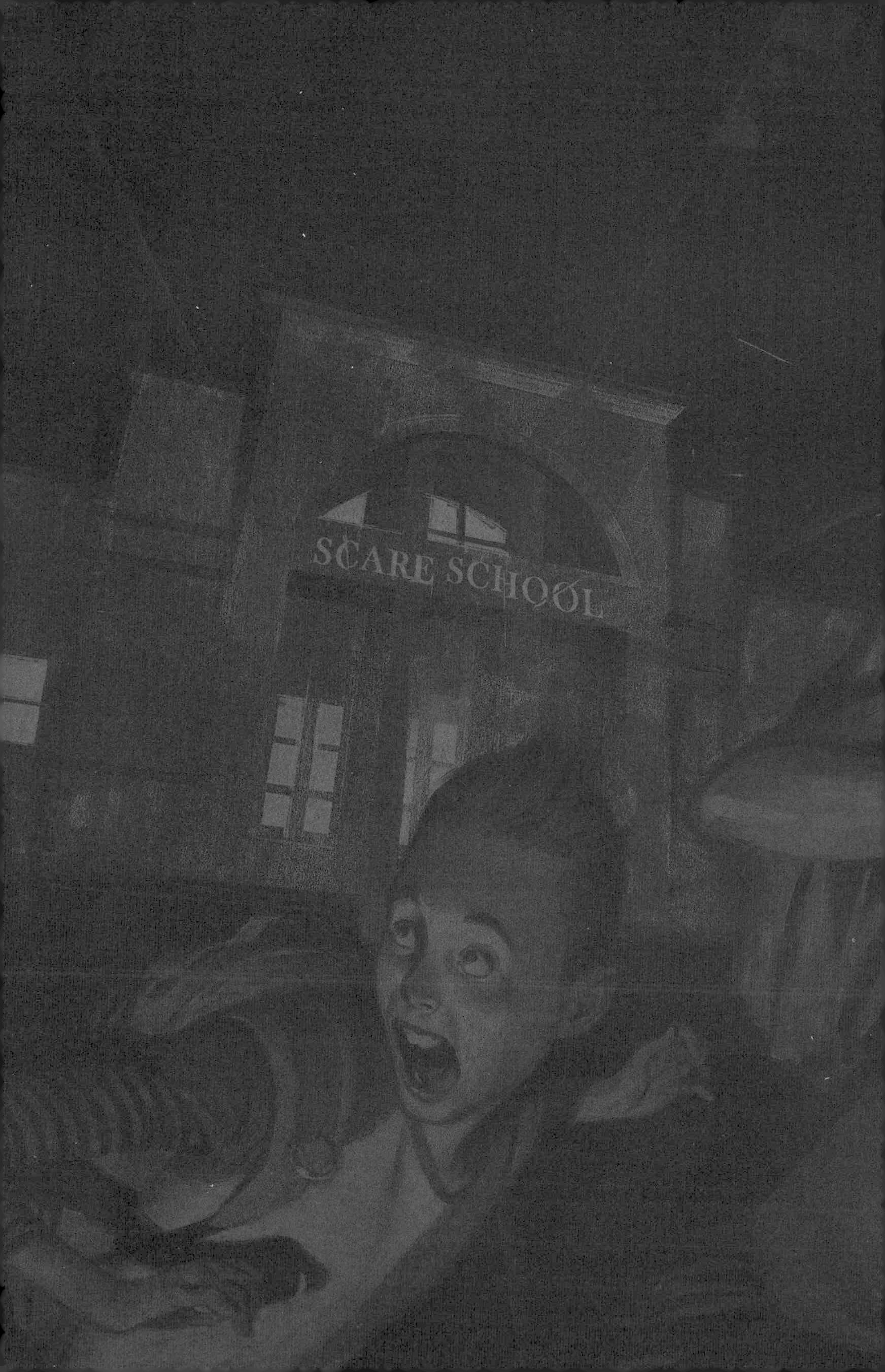
SCARE SCHOOL

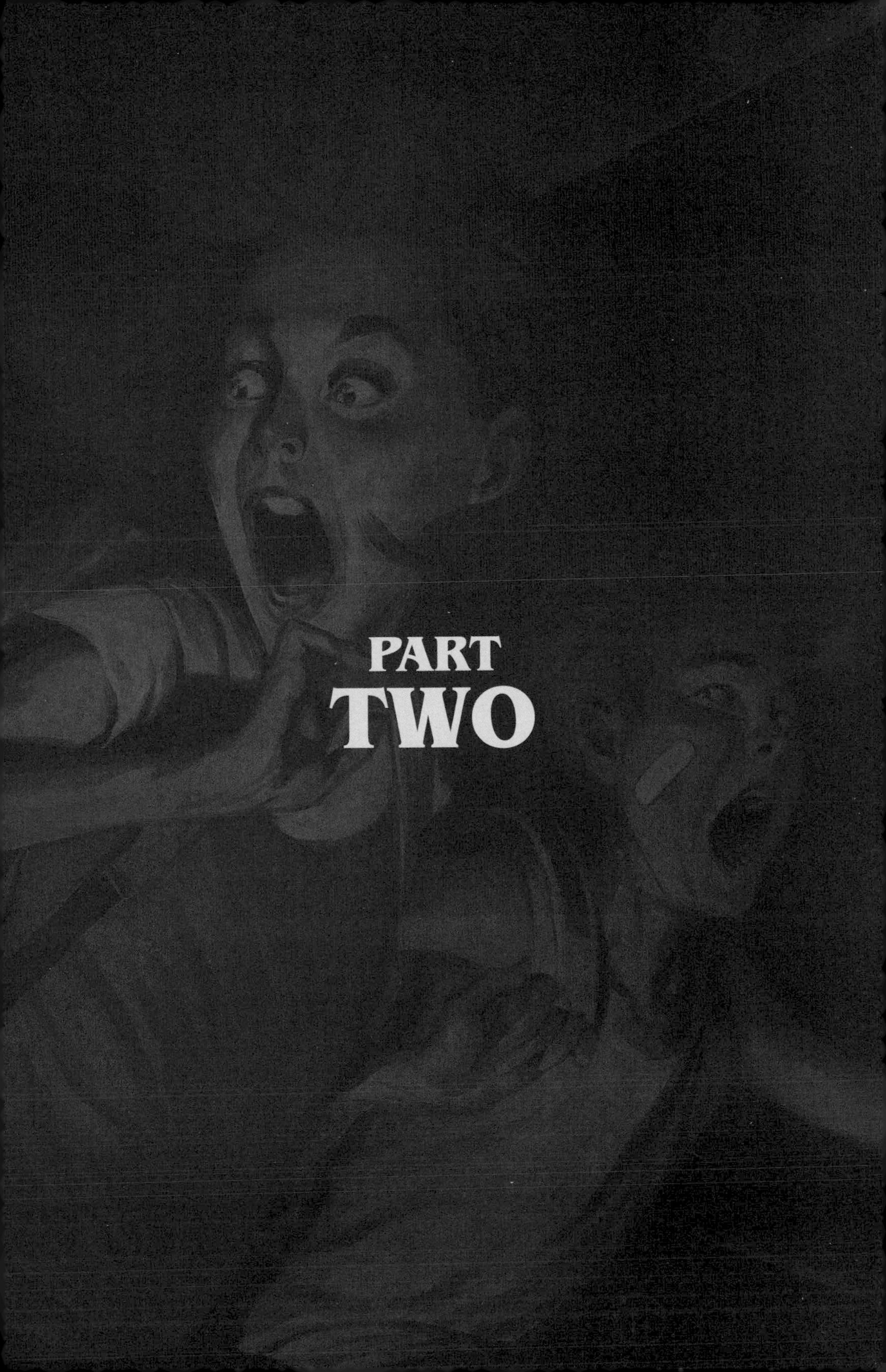

PART TWO

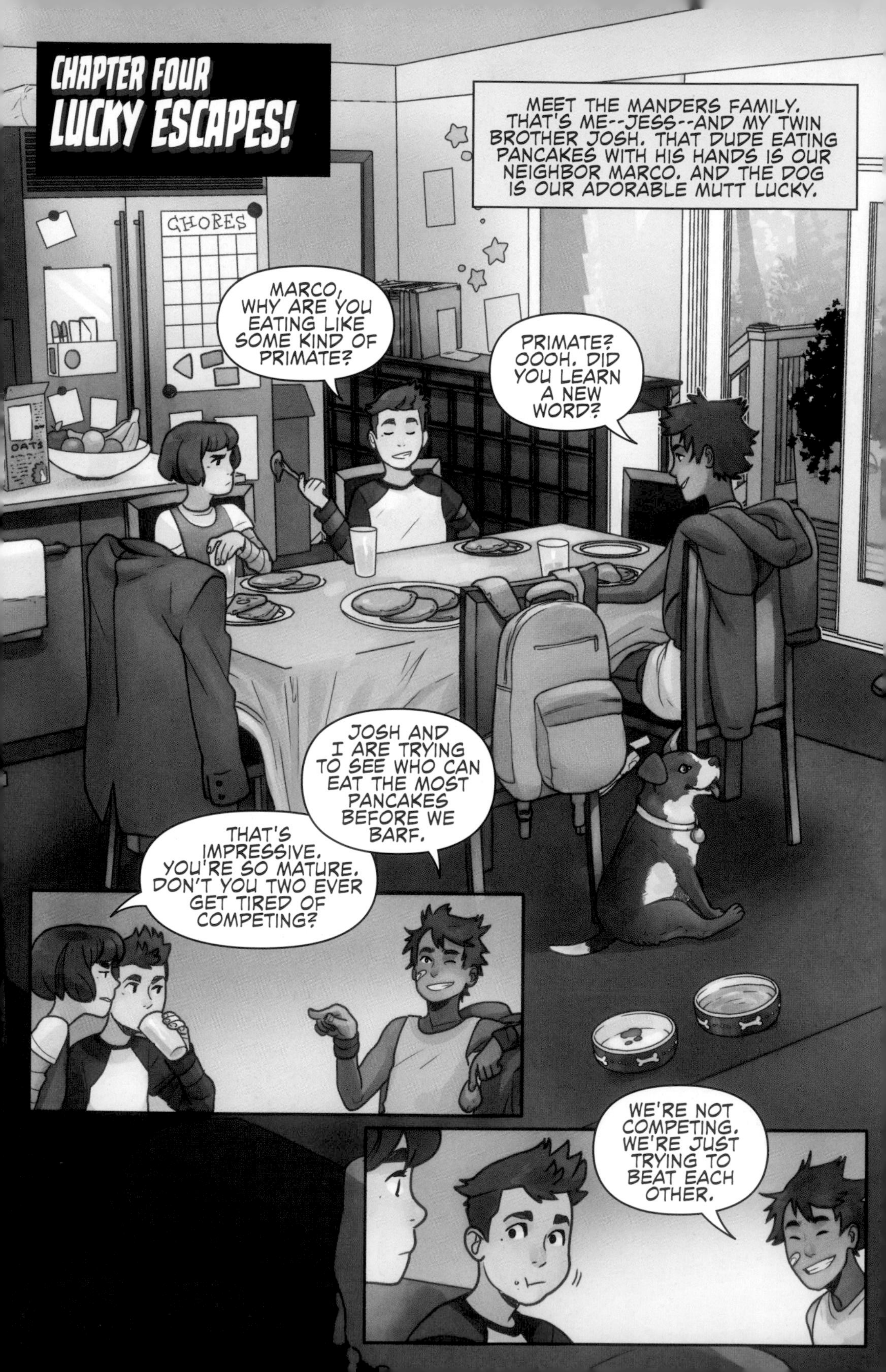
CHAPTER FOUR
LUCKY ESCAPES!
MEET THE MANDERS FAMILY. THAT'S ME--JESS--AND MY TWIN BROTHER JOSH. THAT DUDE EATING PANCAKES WITH HIS HANDS IS OUR NEIGHBOR MARCO. AND THE DOG IS OUR ADORABLE MUTT LUCKY.
CHORES
OATS
MARCO, WHY ARE YOU EATING LIKE SOME KIND OF PRIMATE?
PRIMATE? OOOH. DID YOU LEARN A NEW WORD?
JOSH AND I ARE TRYING TO SEE WHO CAN EAT THE MOST PANCAKES BEFORE WE BARF.
THAT'S IMPRESSIVE. YOU'RE SO MATURE. DON'T YOU TWO EVER GET TIRED OF COMPETING?
WE'RE NOT COMPETING. WE'RE JUST TRYING TO BEAT EACH OTHER.

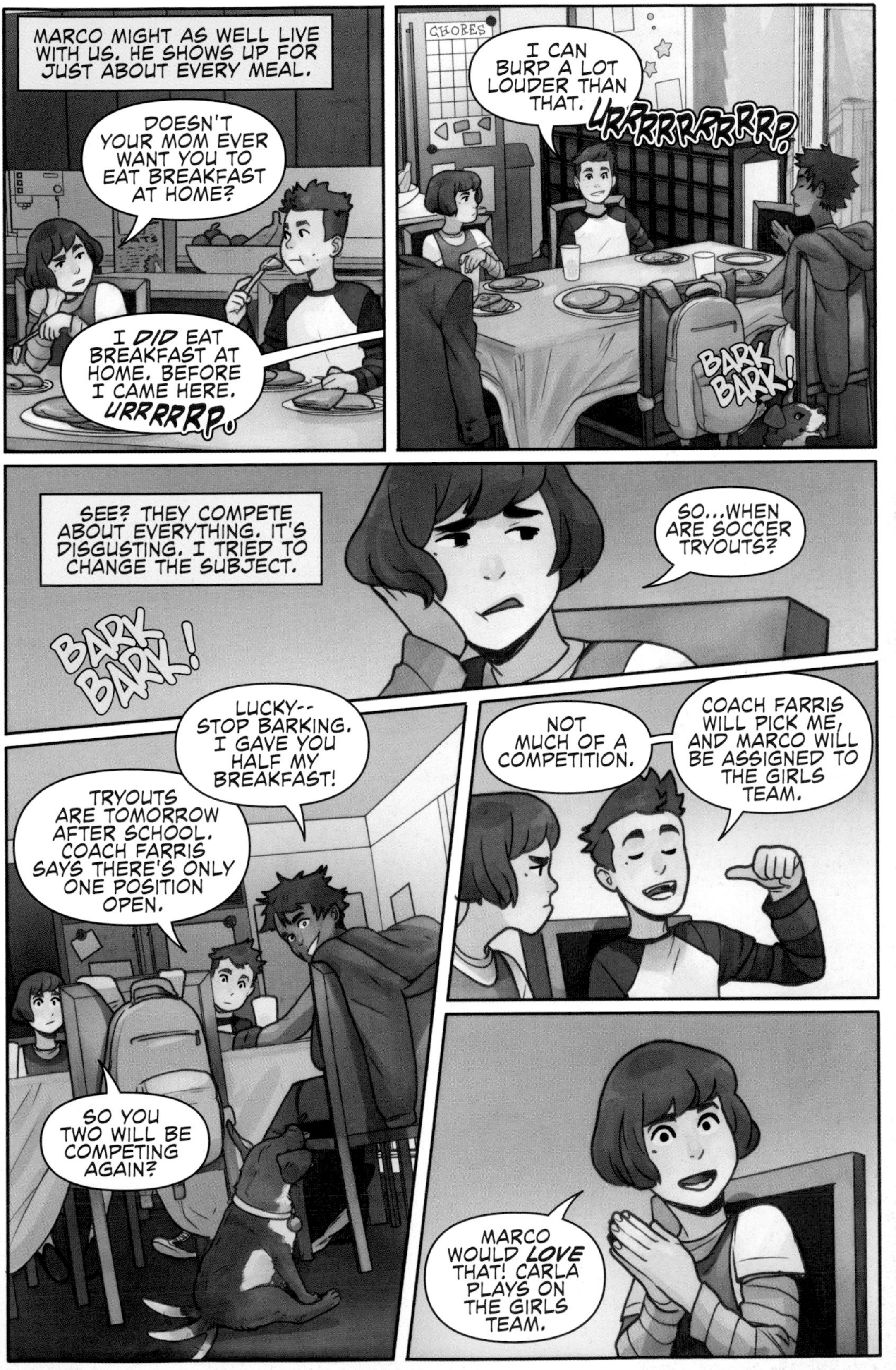
MARCO MIGHT AS WELL LIVE WITH US. HE SHOWS UP FOR JUST ABOUT EVERY MEAL.
DOESN'T YOUR MOM EVER WANT YOU TO EAT BREAKFAST AT HOME?
I *DID* EAT BREAKFAST AT HOME. BEFORE I CAME HERE. URRRRRP.
I CAN BURP A LOT LOUDER THAN THAT. URRRRRRRRRP!
BARK BARK!
SEE? THEY COMPETE ABOUT EVERYTHING. IT'S DISGUSTING. I TRIED TO CHANGE THE SUBJECT.
SO...WHEN ARE SOCCER TRYOUTS?
BARK BARK!
LUCKY-- STOP BARKING. I GAVE YOU HALF MY BREAKFAST!
TRYOUTS ARE TOMORROW AFTER SCHOOL. COACH FARRIS SAYS THERE'S ONLY ONE POSITION OPEN.
SO YOU TWO WILL BE COMPETING AGAIN?
NOT MUCH OF A COMPETITION.
COACH FARRIS WILL PICK ME, AND MARCO WILL BE ASSIGNED TO THE GIRLS TEAM.
MARCO WOULD *LOVE* THAT! CARLA PLAYS ON THE GIRLS TEAM.

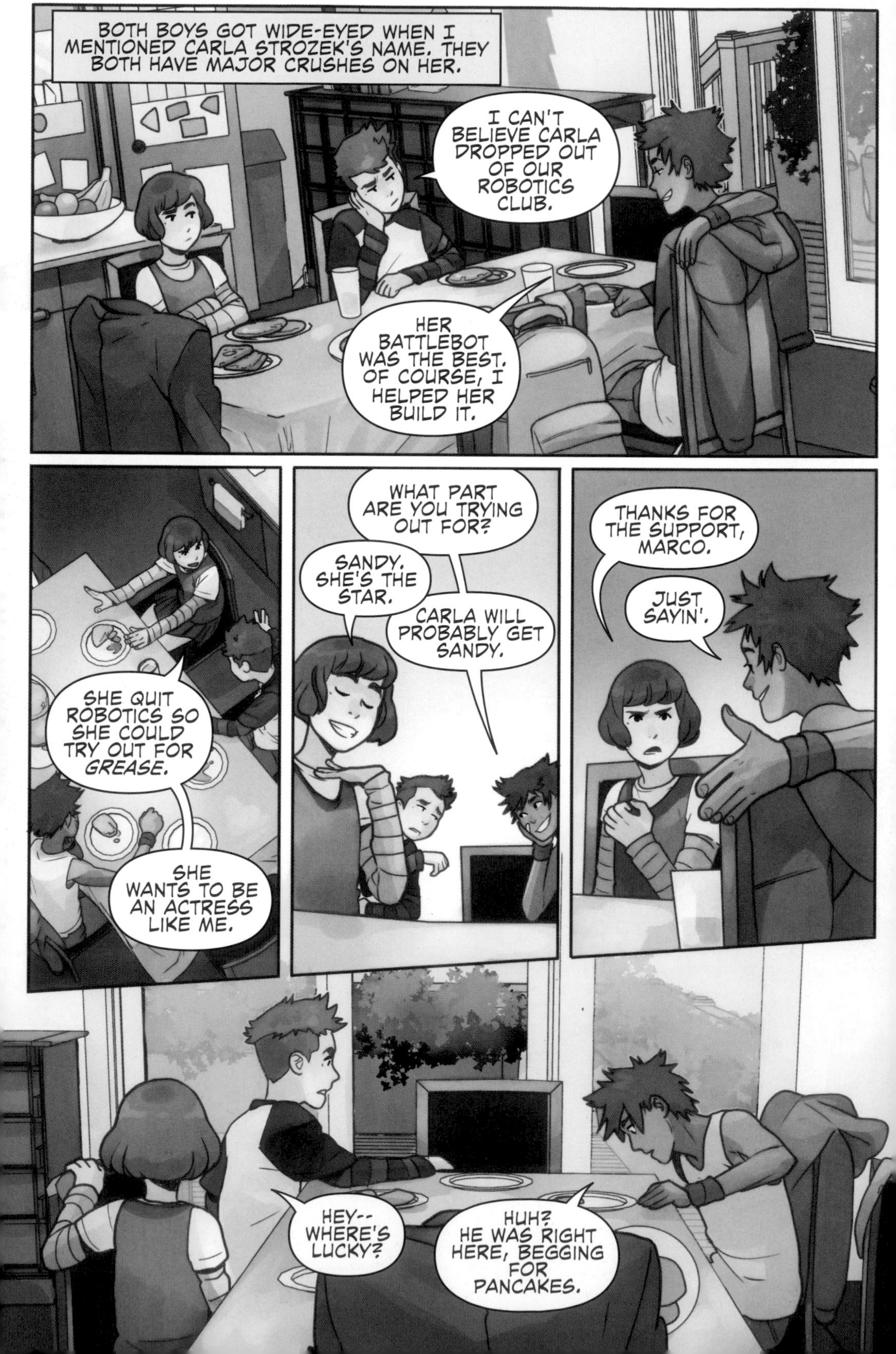
BOTH BOYS GOT WIDE-EYED WHEN I MENTIONED CARLA STROZEK'S NAME. THEY BOTH HAVE MAJOR CRUSHES ON HER.
I CAN'T BELIEVE CARLA DROPPED OUT OF OUR ROBOTICS CLUB.
HER BATTLEBOT WAS THE BEST. OF COURSE, I HELPED HER BUILD IT.
SHE QUIT ROBOTICS SO SHE COULD TRY OUT FOR *GREASE.*
SHE WANTS TO BE AN ACTRESS LIKE ME.
WHAT PART ARE YOU TRYING OUT FOR?
SANDY. SHE'S THE STAR.
CARLA WILL PROBABLY GET SANDY.
THANKS FOR THE SUPPORT, MARCO.
JUST SAYIN'.
HEY--WHERE'S LUCKY?
HUH? HE WAS RIGHT HERE, BEGGING FOR PANCAKES.

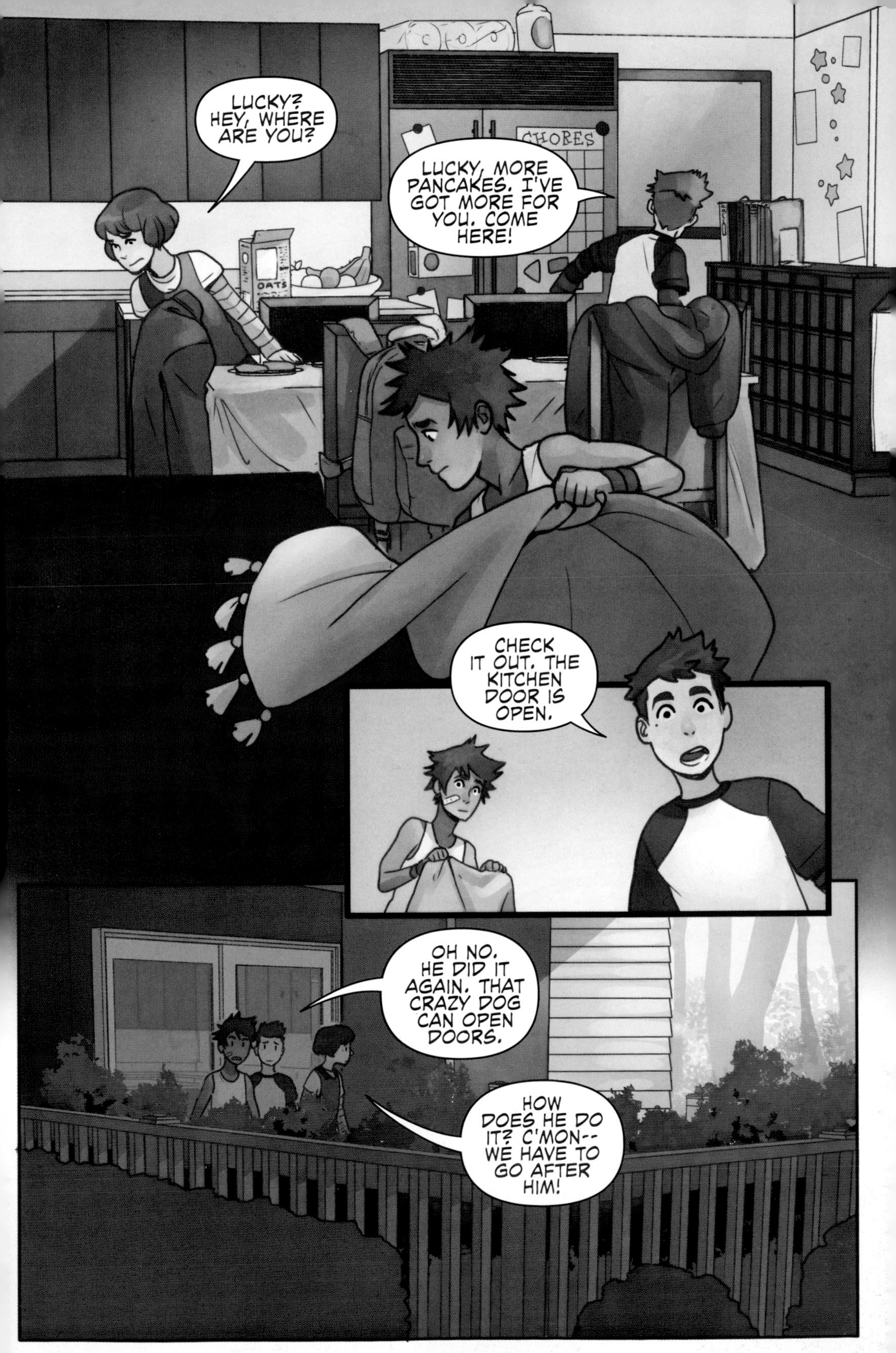
LUCKY? HEY, WHERE ARE YOU?
LUCKY, MORE PANCAKES. I'VE GOT MORE FOR YOU. COME HERE!
CHORES
OATS
CHECK IT OUT. THE KITCHEN DOOR IS OPEN.
OH NO. HE DID IT AGAIN. THAT CRAZY DOG CAN OPEN DOORS.
HOW DOES HE DO IT? C'MON-- WE HAVE TO GO AFTER HIM!

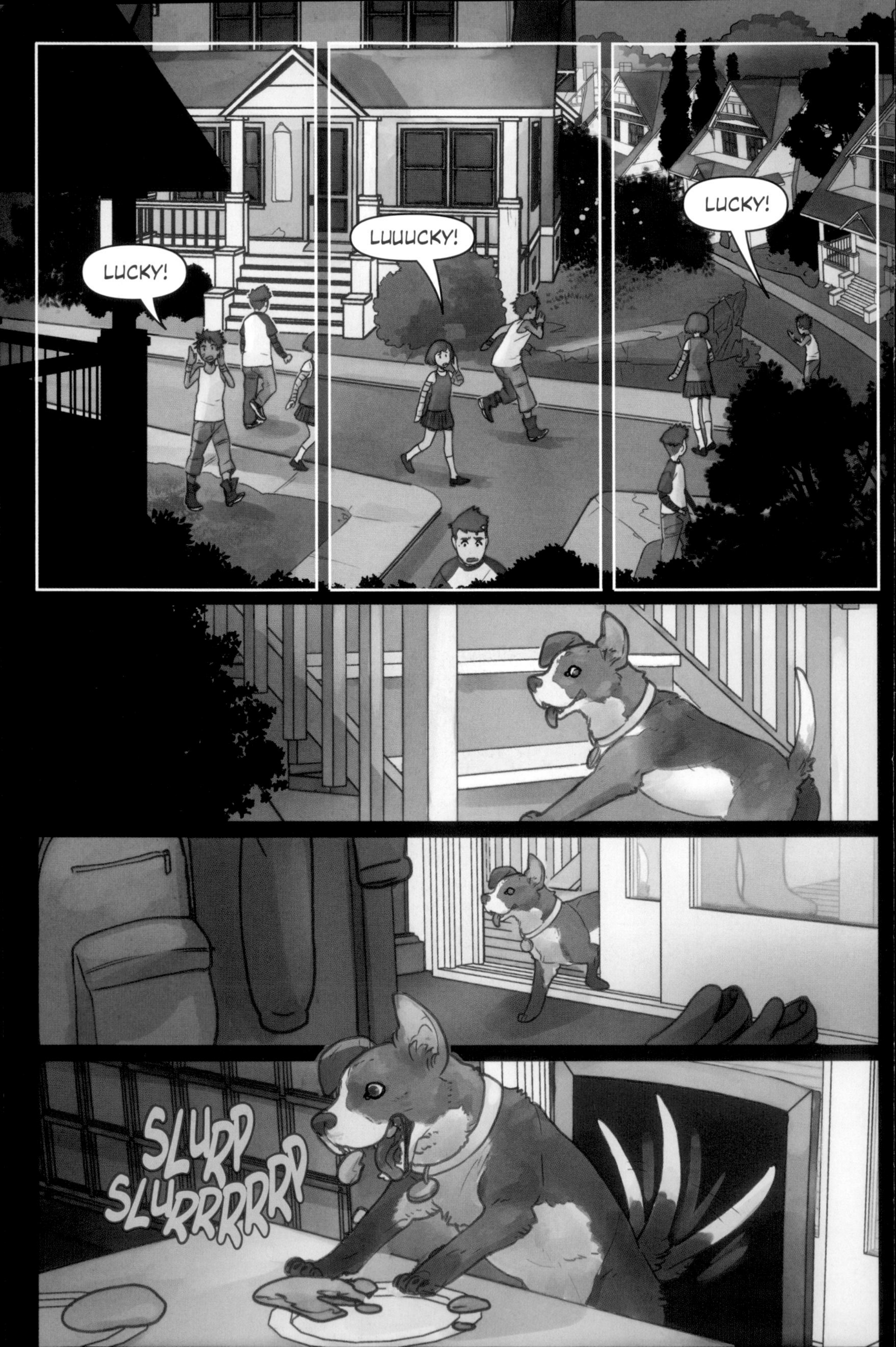
LUCKY!
LUUUCKY!
LUCKY!
SLURP
SLURRRRRP

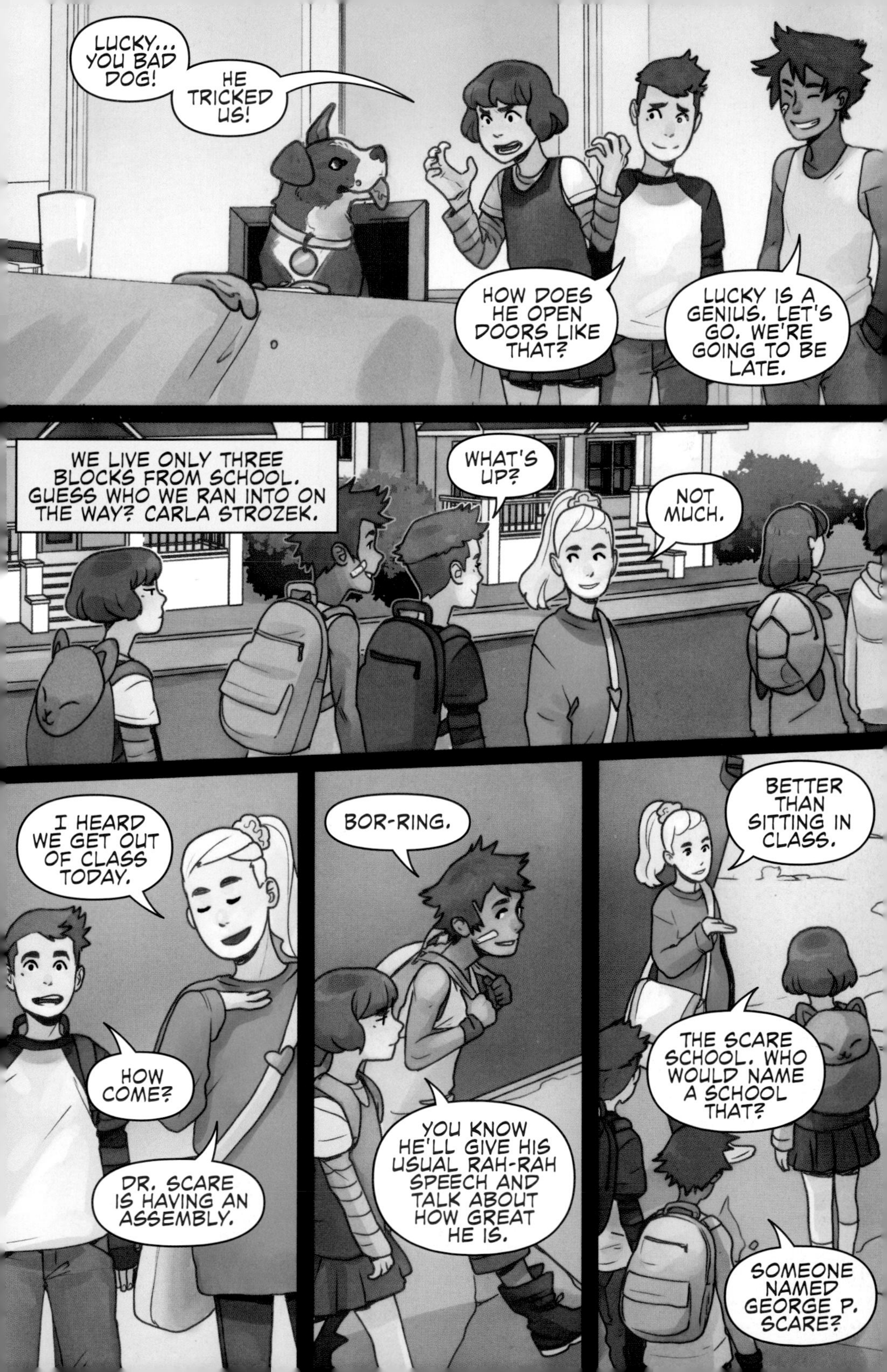
LUCKY... YOU BAD DOG!
HE TRICKED US!
HOW DOES HE OPEN DOORS LIKE THAT?
LUCKY IS A GENIUS. LET'S GO. WE'RE GOING TO BE LATE.
WE LIVE ONLY THREE BLOCKS FROM SCHOOL. GUESS WHO WE RAN INTO ON THE WAY? CARLA STROZEK.
WHAT'S UP?
NOT MUCH.
I HEARD WE GET OUT OF CLASS TODAY.
HOW COME?
DR. SCARE IS HAVING AN ASSEMBLY.
BOR-RING.
YOU KNOW HE'LL GIVE HIS USUAL RAH-RAH SPEECH AND TALK ABOUT HOW GREAT HE IS.
BETTER THAN SITTING IN CLASS.
THE SCARE SCHOOL. WHO WOULD NAME A SCHOOL THAT?
SOMEONE NAMED GEORGE P. SCARE?

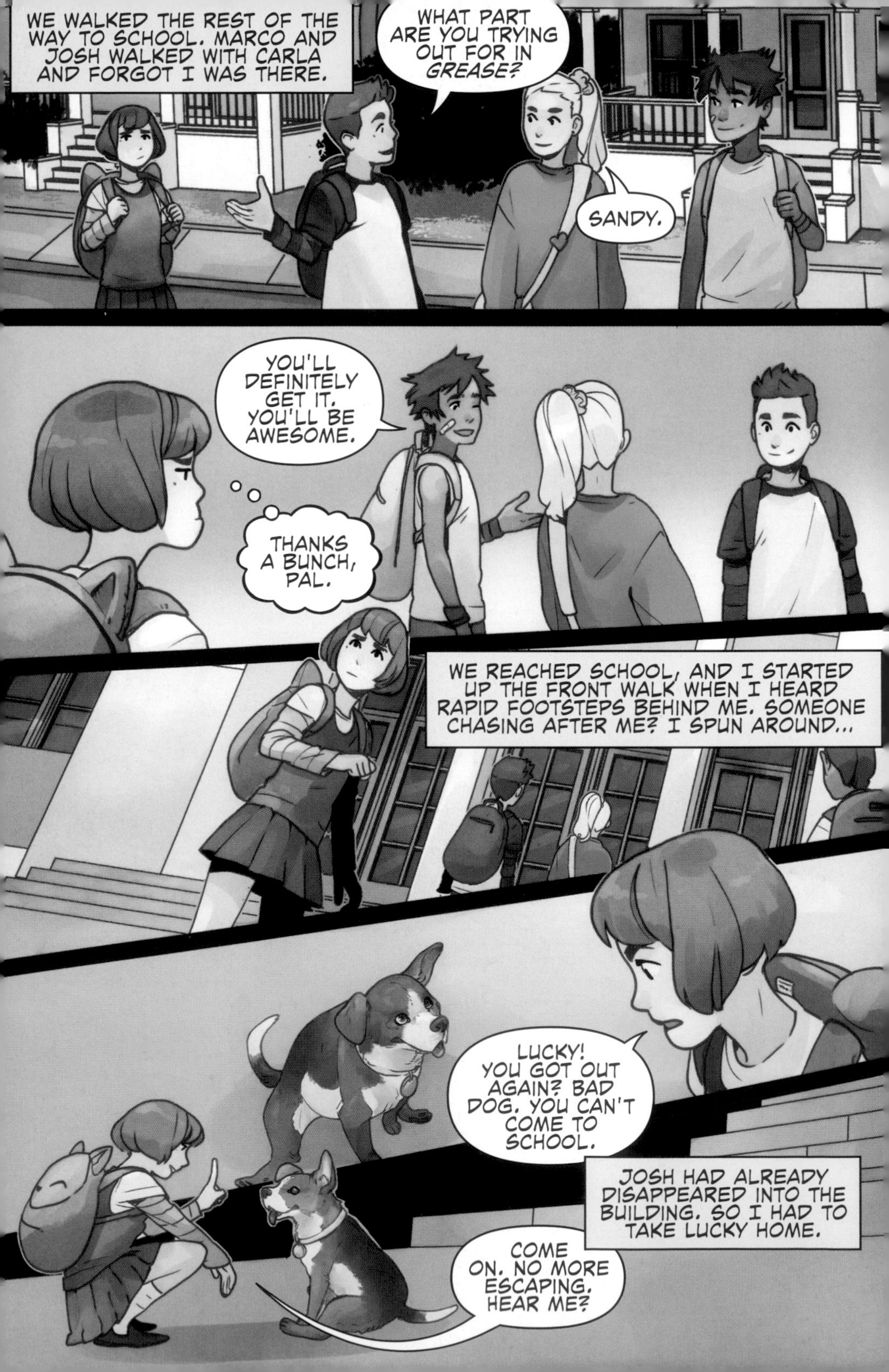
WE WALKED THE REST OF THE WAY TO SCHOOL. MARCO AND JOSH WALKED WITH CARLA AND FORGOT I WAS THERE.
WHAT PART ARE YOU TRYING OUT FOR IN GREASE?
SANDY.
YOU'LL DEFINITELY GET IT. YOU'LL BE AWESOME.
THANKS A BUNCH, PAL.
WE REACHED SCHOOL, AND I STARTED UP THE FRONT WALK WHEN I HEARD RAPID FOOTSTEPS BEHIND ME. SOMEONE CHASING AFTER ME? I SPUN AROUND...
LUCKY! YOU GOT OUT AGAIN? BAD DOG. YOU CAN'T COME TO SCHOOL.
JOSH HAD ALREADY DISAPPEARED INTO THE BUILDING. SO I HAD TO TAKE LUCKY HOME.
COME ON. NO MORE ESCAPING. HEAR ME?

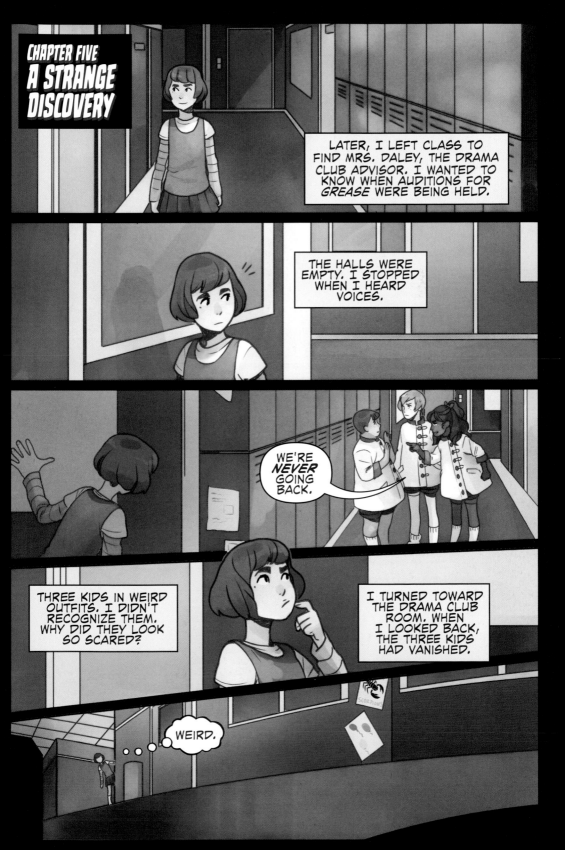

CHAPTER FIVE
A STRANGE DISCOVERY

LATER, I LEFT CLASS TO FIND MRS. DALEY, THE DRAMA CLUB ADVISOR. I WANTED TO KNOW WHEN AUDITIONS FOR *GREASE* WERE BEING HELD.

THE HALLS WERE EMPTY. I STOPPED WHEN I HEARD VOICES.

WE'RE *NEVER* GOING BACK.

THREE KIDS IN WEIRD OUTFITS. I DIDN'T RECOGNIZE THEM. WHY DID THEY LOOK SO SCARED?

I TURNED TOWARD THE DRAMA CLUB ROOM. WHEN I LOOKED BACK, THE THREE KIDS HAD VANISHED.

WEIRD.

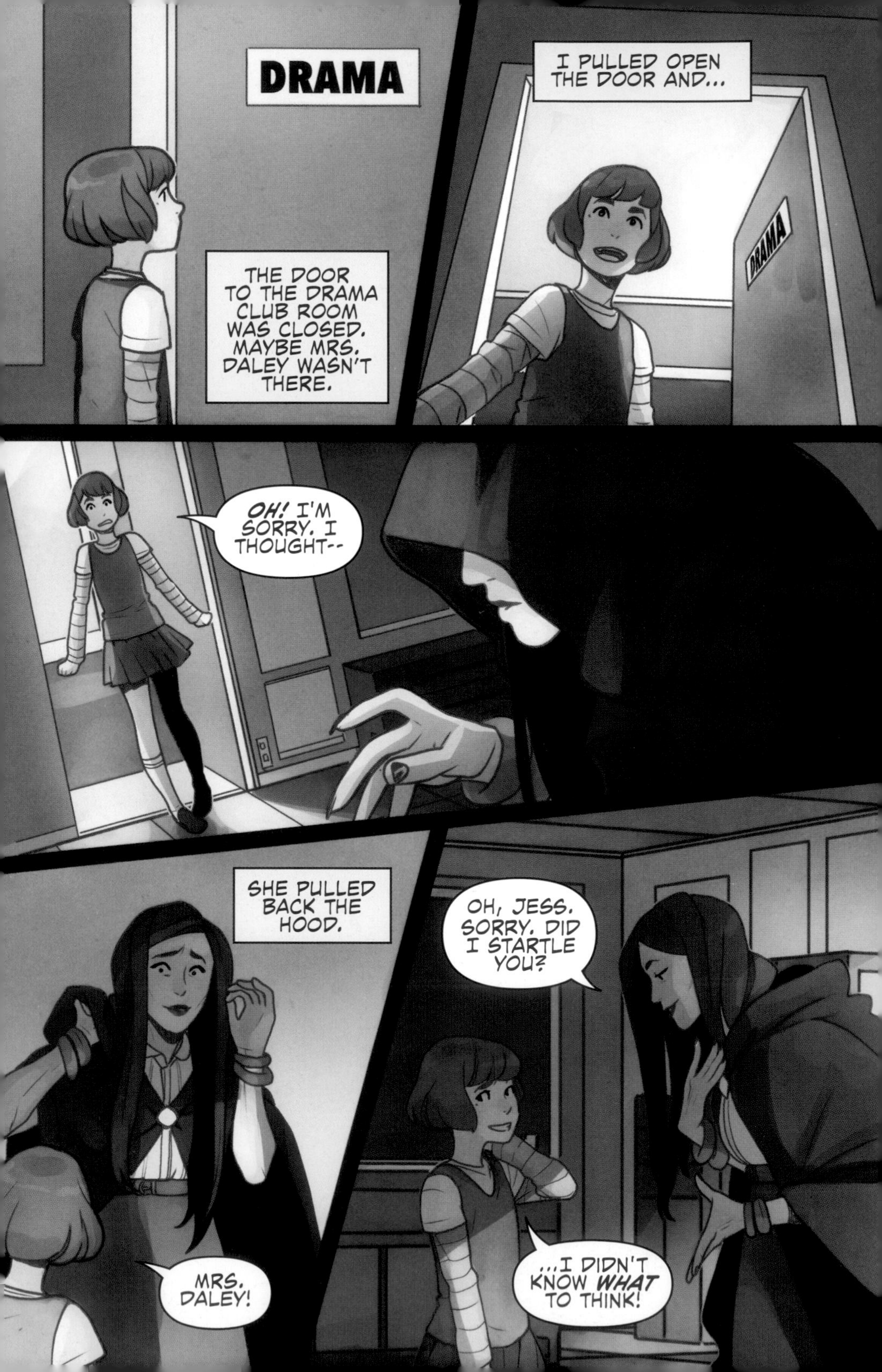
DRAMA
THE DOOR TO THE DRAMA CLUB ROOM WAS CLOSED. MAYBE MRS. DALEY WASN'T THERE.
I PULLED OPEN THE DOOR AND...
DRAMA
OH! I'M SORRY. I THOUGHT--
SHE PULLED BACK THE HOOD.
MRS. DALEY!
OH, JESS. SORRY. DID I STARTLE YOU?
...I DIDN'T KNOW *WHAT* TO THINK!

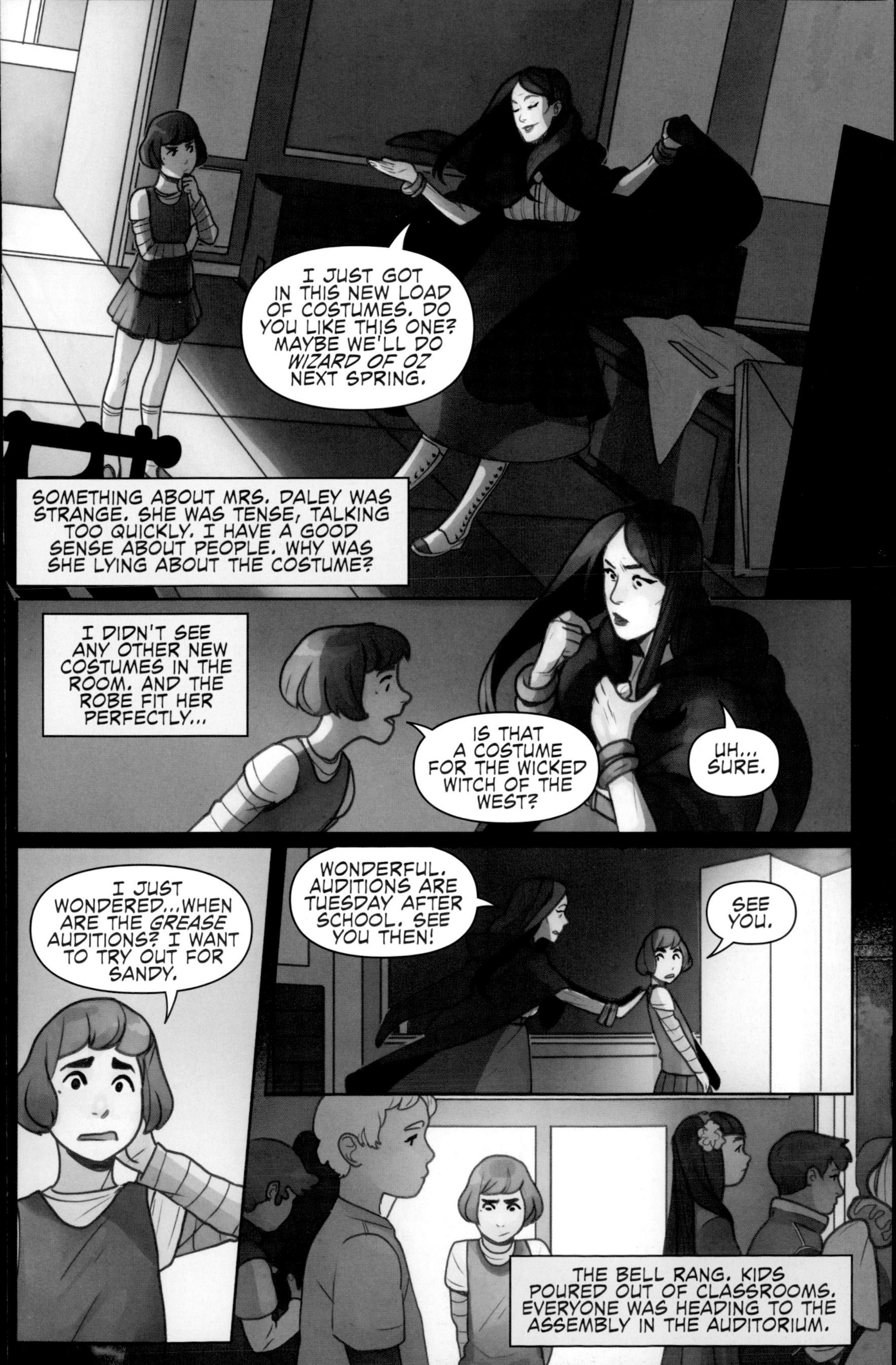
I JUST GOT IN THIS NEW LOAD OF COSTUMES. DO YOU LIKE THIS ONE? MAYBE WE'LL DO *WIZARD OF OZ* NEXT SPRING.
SOMETHING ABOUT MRS. DALEY WAS STRANGE. SHE WAS TENSE, TALKING TOO QUICKLY. I HAVE A GOOD SENSE ABOUT PEOPLE. WHY WAS SHE LYING ABOUT THE COSTUME?
I DIDN'T SEE ANY OTHER NEW COSTUMES IN THE ROOM. AND THE ROBE FIT HER PERFECTLY...
IS THAT A COSTUME FOR THE WICKED WITCH OF THE WEST?
UH... SURE.
I JUST WONDERED...WHEN ARE THE *GREASE* AUDITIONS? I WANT TO TRY OUT FOR SANDY.
WONDERFUL. AUDITIONS ARE TUESDAY AFTER SCHOOL. SEE YOU THEN!
SEE YOU.
THE BELL RANG. KIDS POURED OUT OF CLASSROOMS. EVERYONE WAS HEADING TO THE ASSEMBLY IN THE AUDITORIUM.

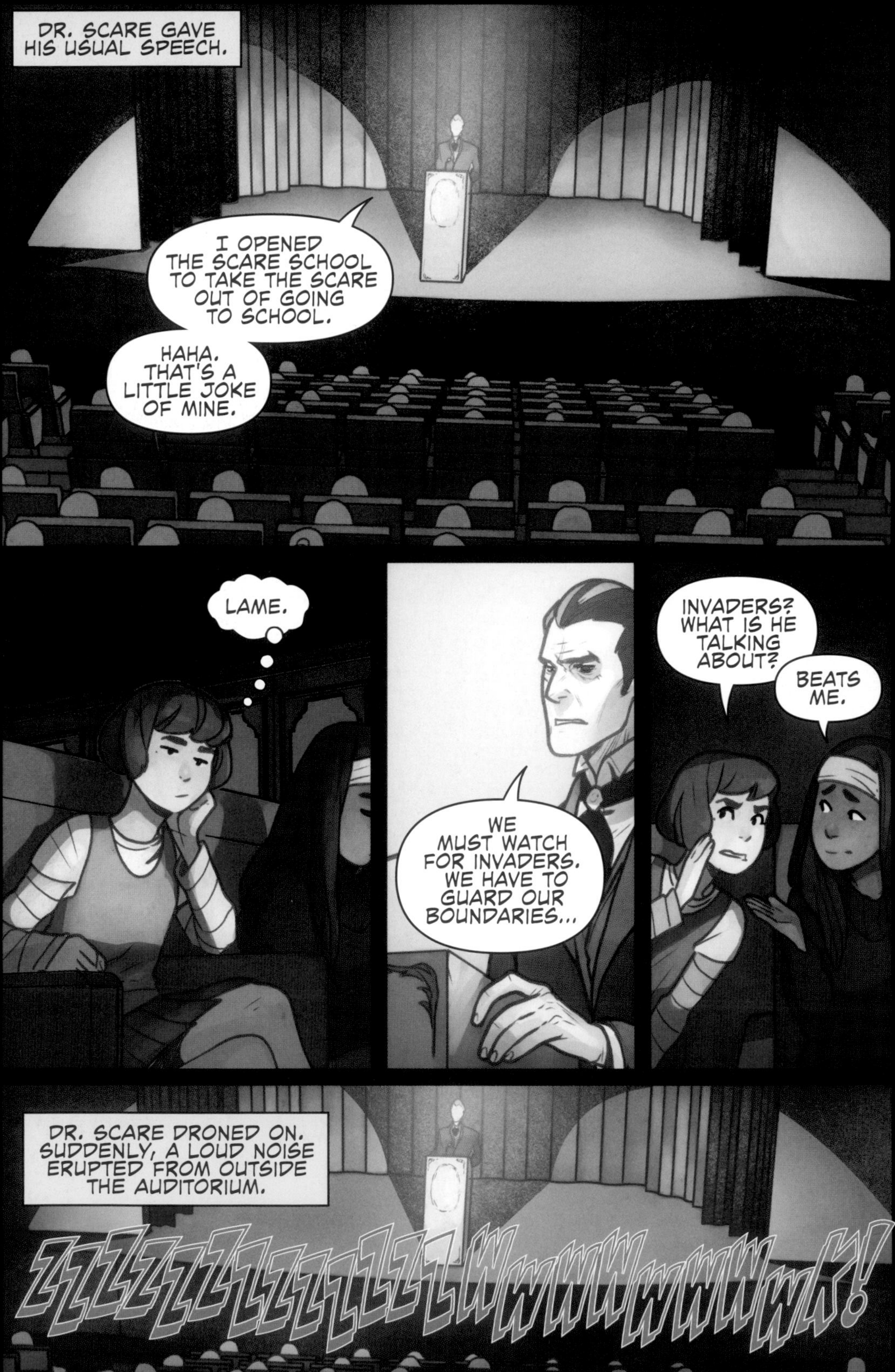
DR. SCARE GAVE HIS USUAL SPEECH.
I OPENED THE SCARE SCHOOL TO TAKE THE SCARE OUT OF GOING TO SCHOOL.
HAHA. THAT'S A LITTLE JOKE OF MINE.
LAME.
WE MUST WATCH FOR INVADERS. WE HAVE TO GUARD OUR BOUNDARIES...
INVADERS? WHAT IS HE TALKING ABOUT?
BEATS ME.
DR. SCARE DRONED ON. SUDDENLY, A LOUD NOISE ERUPTED FROM OUTSIDE THE AUDITORIUM.
ZZZZZZZZZZZZZZZZZZZZZWWWWWWWWWWWWWWWWWAAAAAAAAAAA!

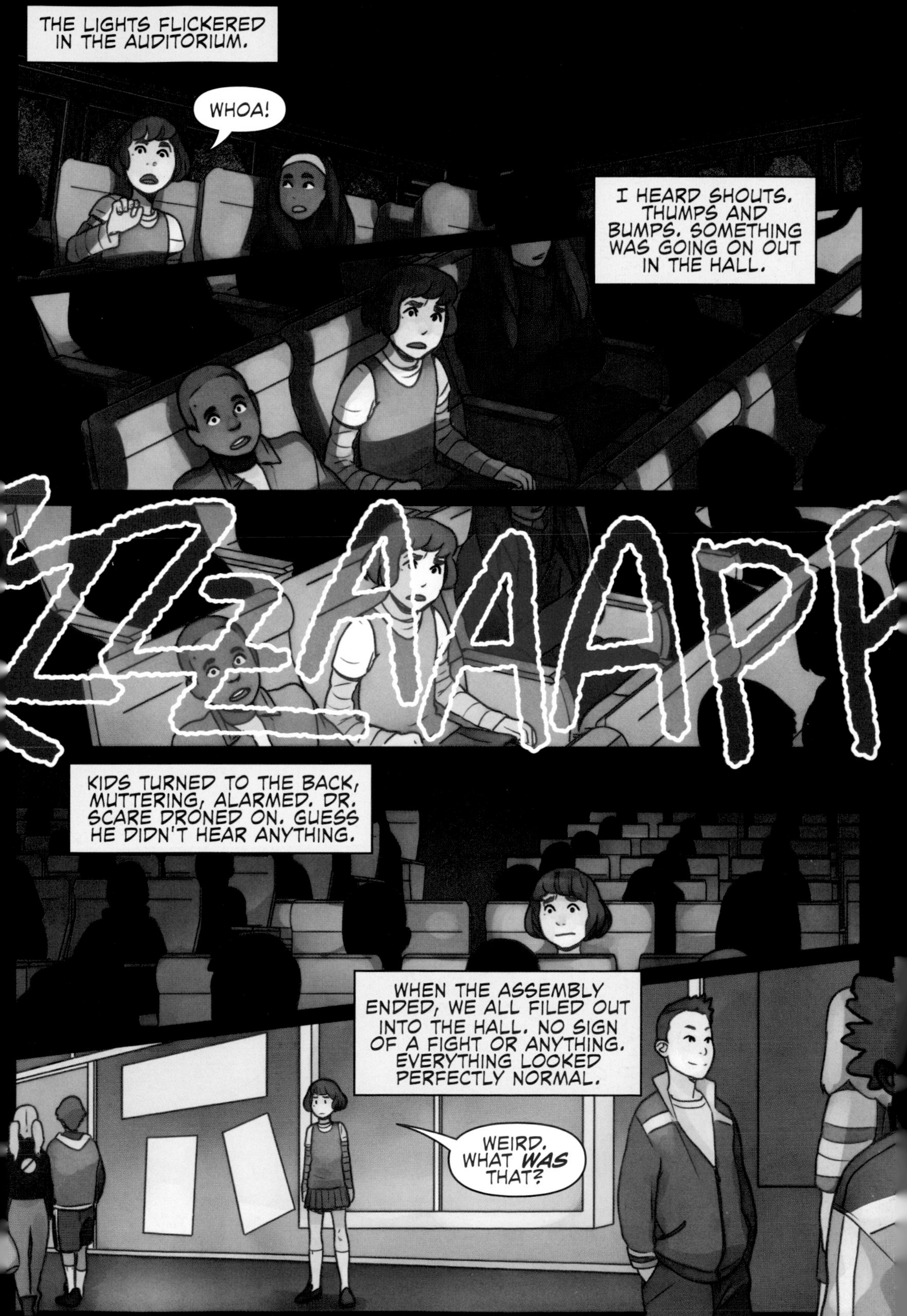
THE LIGHTS FLICKERED IN THE AUDITORIUM.
WHOA!
I HEARD SHOUTS. THUMPS AND BUMPS. SOMETHING WAS GOING ON OUT IN THE HALL.
ZZZAAAPP
KIDS TURNED TO THE BACK, MUTTERING, ALARMED. DR. SCARE DRONED ON. GUESS HE DIDN'T HEAR ANYTHING.
WHEN THE ASSEMBLY ENDED, WE ALL FILED OUT INTO THE HALL. NO SIGN OF A FIGHT OR ANYTHING. EVERYTHING LOOKED PERFECTLY NORMAL.
WEIRD. WHAT ***WAS*** THAT?

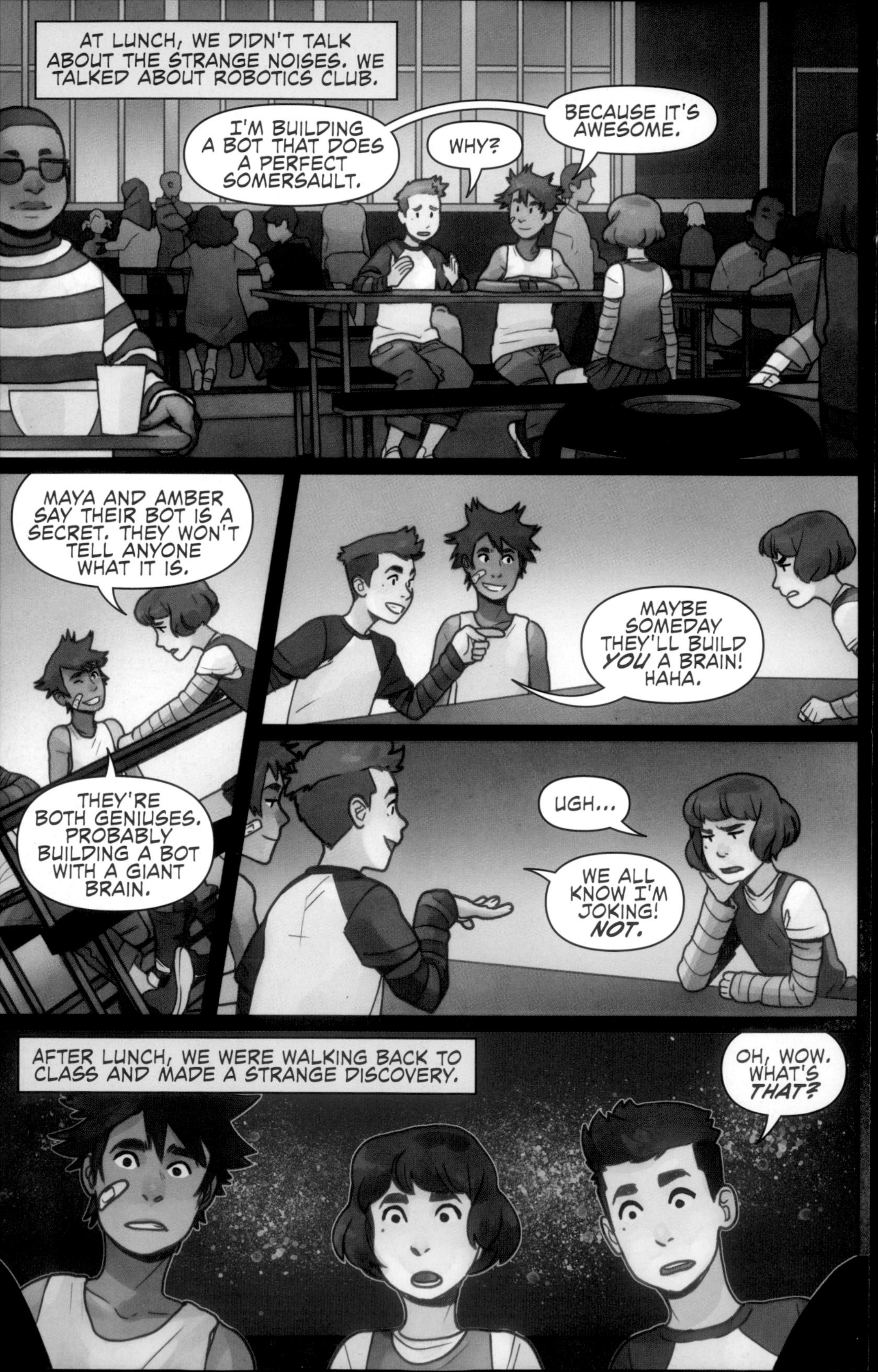
AT LUNCH, WE DIDN'T TALK ABOUT THE STRANGE NOISES. WE TALKED ABOUT ROBOTICS CLUB.
I'M BUILDING A BOT THAT DOES A PERFECT SOMERSAULT.
WHY?
BECAUSE IT'S AWESOME.
MAYA AND AMBER SAY THEIR BOT IS A SECRET. THEY WON'T TELL ANYONE WHAT IT IS.
THEY'RE BOTH GENIUSES. PROBABLY BUILDING A BOT WITH A GIANT BRAIN.
MAYBE SOMEDAY THEY'LL BUILD *YOU* A BRAIN! HAHA.
UGH...
WE ALL KNOW I'M JOKING! ***NOT.***
AFTER LUNCH, WE WERE WALKING BACK TO CLASS AND MADE A STRANGE DISCOVERY.
OH, WOW. WHAT'S ***THAT?***

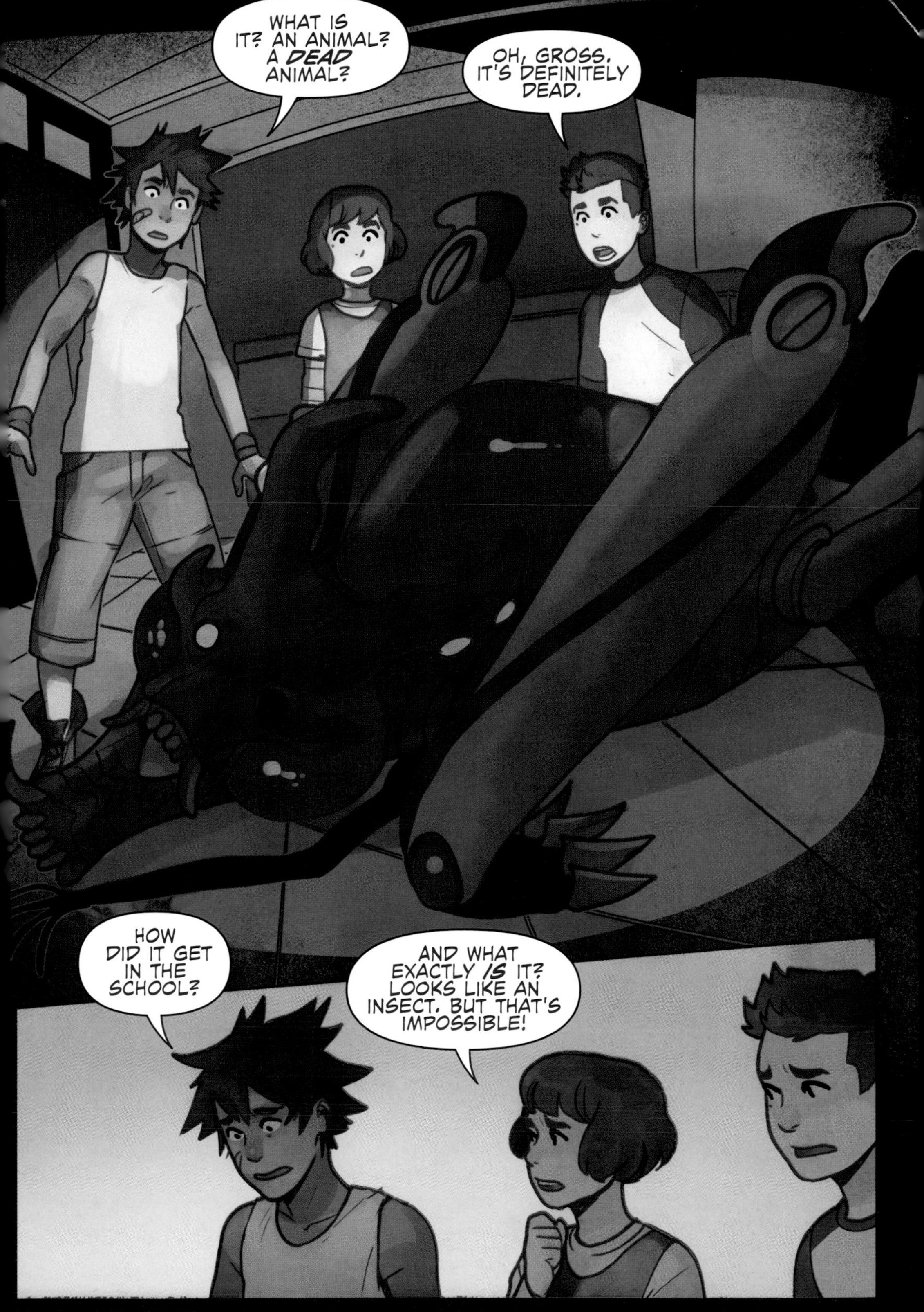
WHAT IS IT? AN ANIMAL? A DEAD ANIMAL?
OH, GROSS. IT'S DEFINITELY DEAD.
HOW DID IT GET IN THE SCHOOL?
AND WHAT EXACTLY IS IT? LOOKS LIKE AN INSECT. BUT THAT'S IMPOSSIBLE!

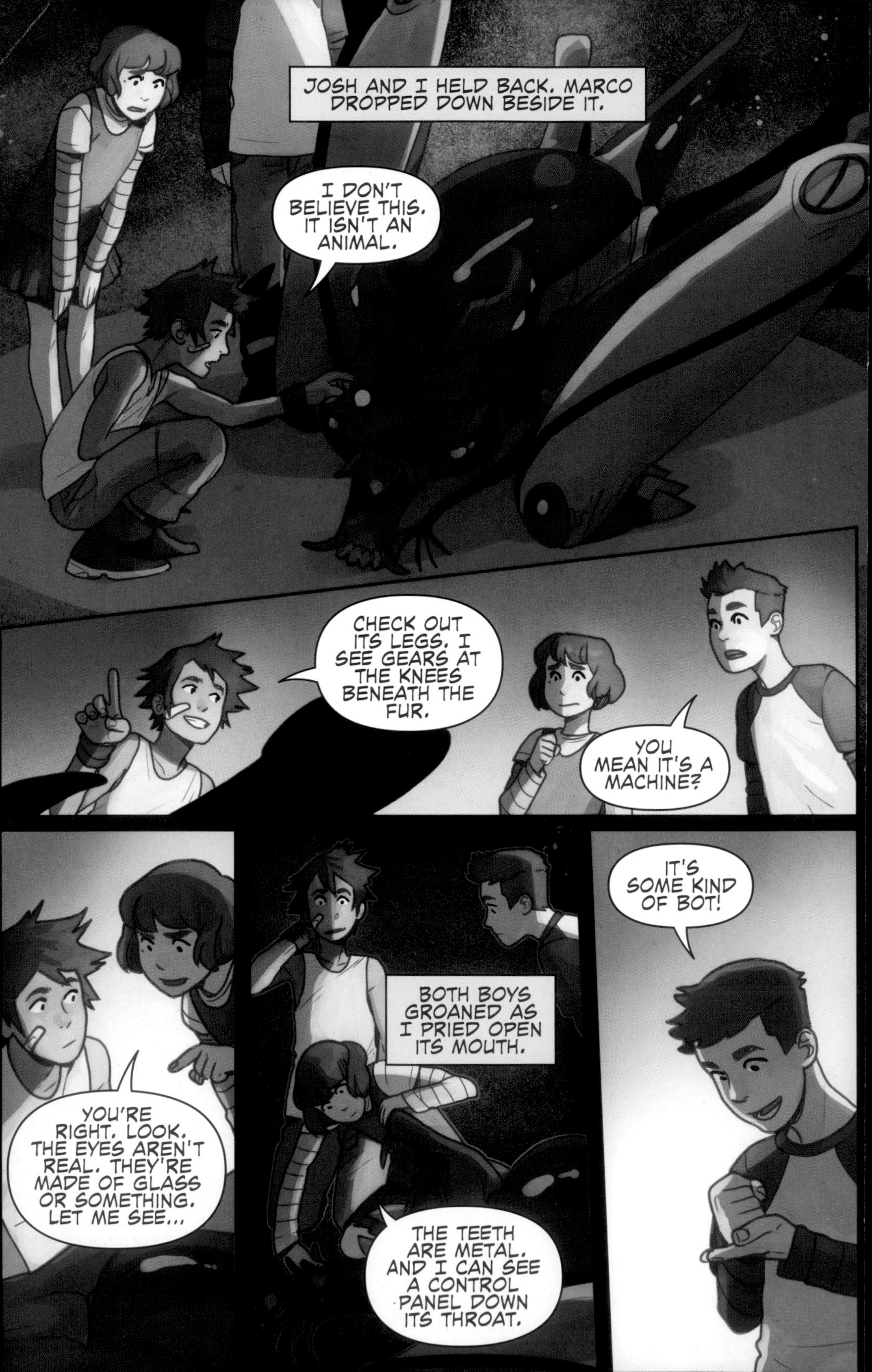
JOSH AND I HELD BACK. MARCO DROPPED DOWN BESIDE IT.
I DON'T BELIEVE THIS. IT ISN'T AN ANIMAL.
CHECK OUT ITS LEGS. I SEE GEARS AT THE KNEES BENEATH THE FUR.
YOU MEAN IT'S A MACHINE?
YOU'RE RIGHT. LOOK. THE EYES AREN'T REAL. THEY'RE MADE OF GLASS OR SOMETHING. LET ME SEE...
BOTH BOYS GROANED AS I PRIED OPEN ITS MOUTH.
THE TEETH ARE METAL. AND I CAN SEE A CONTROL PANEL DOWN ITS THROAT.
IT'S SOME KIND OF BOT!

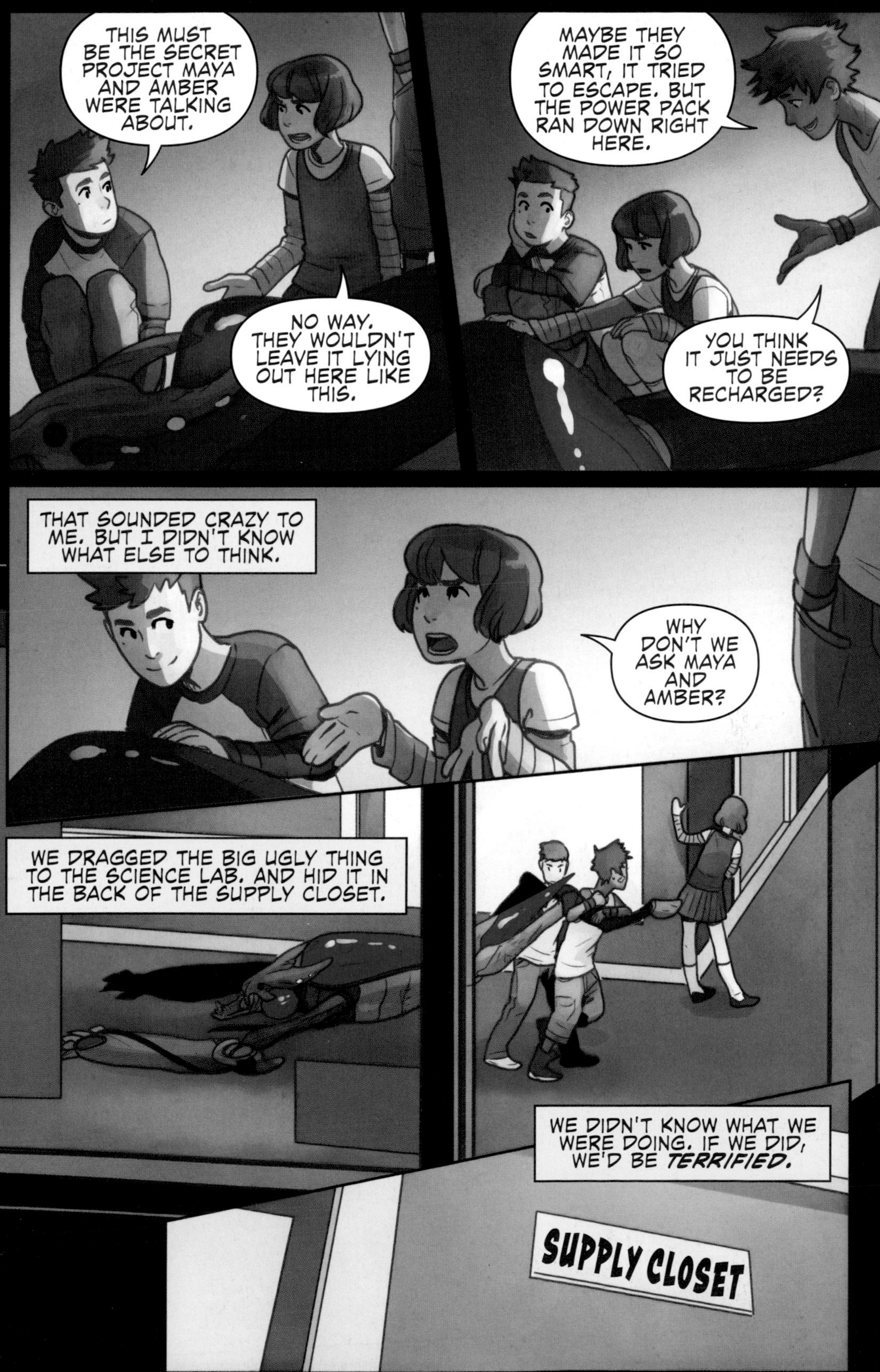
THIS MUST BE THE SECRET PROJECT MAYA AND AMBER WERE TALKING ABOUT.
NO WAY. THEY WOULDN'T LEAVE IT LYING OUT HERE LIKE THIS.
MAYBE THEY MADE IT SO SMART, IT TRIED TO ESCAPE. BUT THE POWER PACK RAN DOWN RIGHT HERE.
YOU THINK IT JUST NEEDS TO BE RECHARGED?
THAT SOUNDED CRAZY TO ME. BUT I DIDN'T KNOW WHAT ELSE TO THINK.
WHY DON'T WE ASK MAYA AND AMBER?
WE DRAGGED THE BIG UGLY THING TO THE SCIENCE LAB. AND HID IT IN THE BACK OF THE SUPPLY CLOSET.
WE DIDN'T KNOW WHAT WE WERE DOING. IF WE DID, WE'D BE *TERRIFIED*.
SUPPLY CLOSET

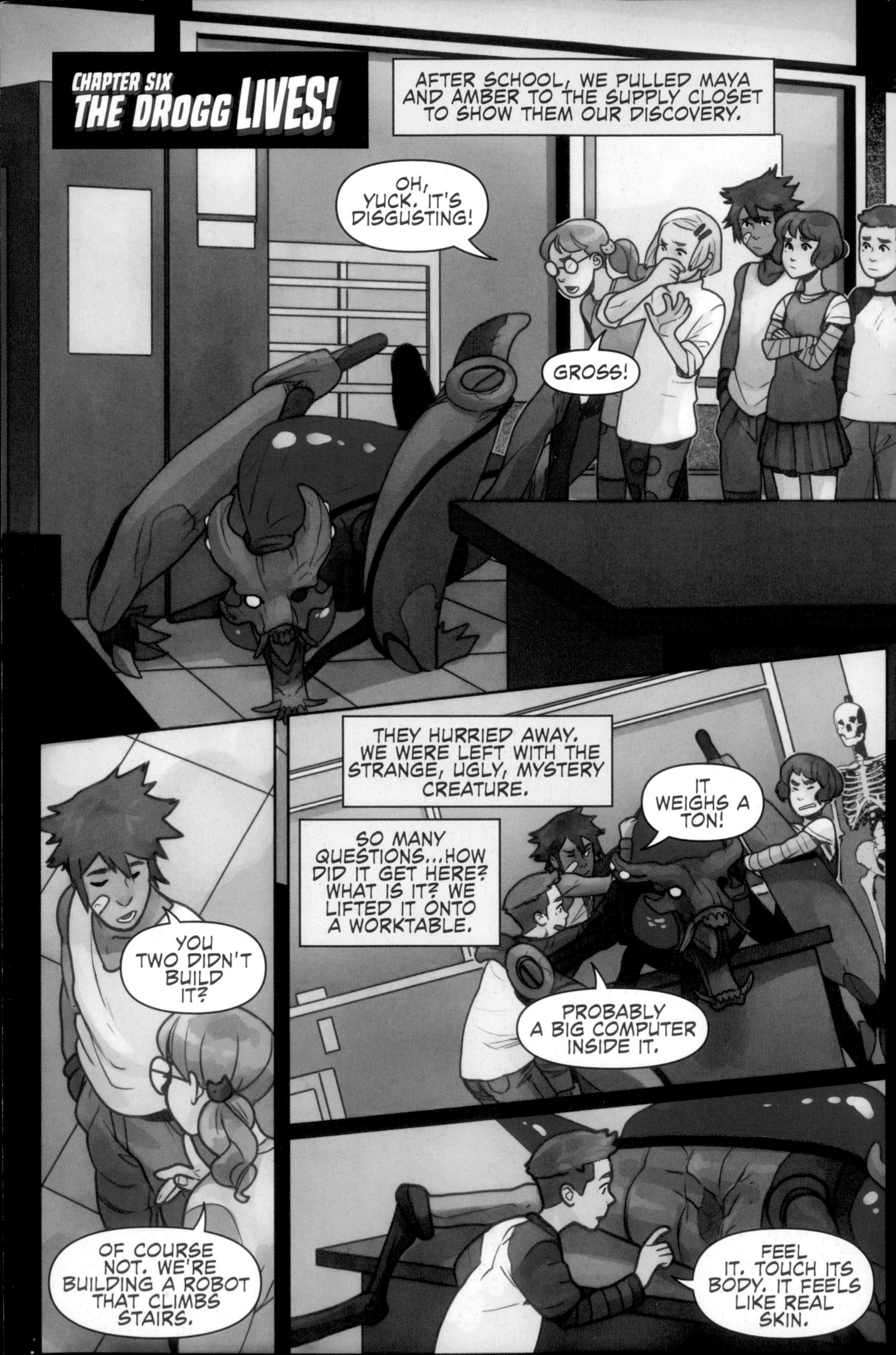
CHAPTER SIX
THE DROGG LIVES!
AFTER SCHOOL, WE PULLED MAYA AND AMBER TO THE SUPPLY CLOSET TO SHOW THEM OUR DISCOVERY.
OH, YUCK. IT'S DISGUSTING!
GROSS!
YOU TWO DIDN'T BUILD IT?
OF COURSE NOT. WE'RE BUILDING A ROBOT THAT CLIMBS STAIRS.
THEY HURRIED AWAY. WE WERE LEFT WITH THE STRANGE, UGLY, MYSTERY CREATURE.
SO MANY QUESTIONS...HOW DID IT GET HERE? WHAT IS IT? WE LIFTED IT ONTO A WORKTABLE.
IT WEIGHS A TON!
PROBABLY A BIG COMPUTER INSIDE IT.
FEEL IT. TOUCH ITS BODY. IT FEELS LIKE REAL SKIN.

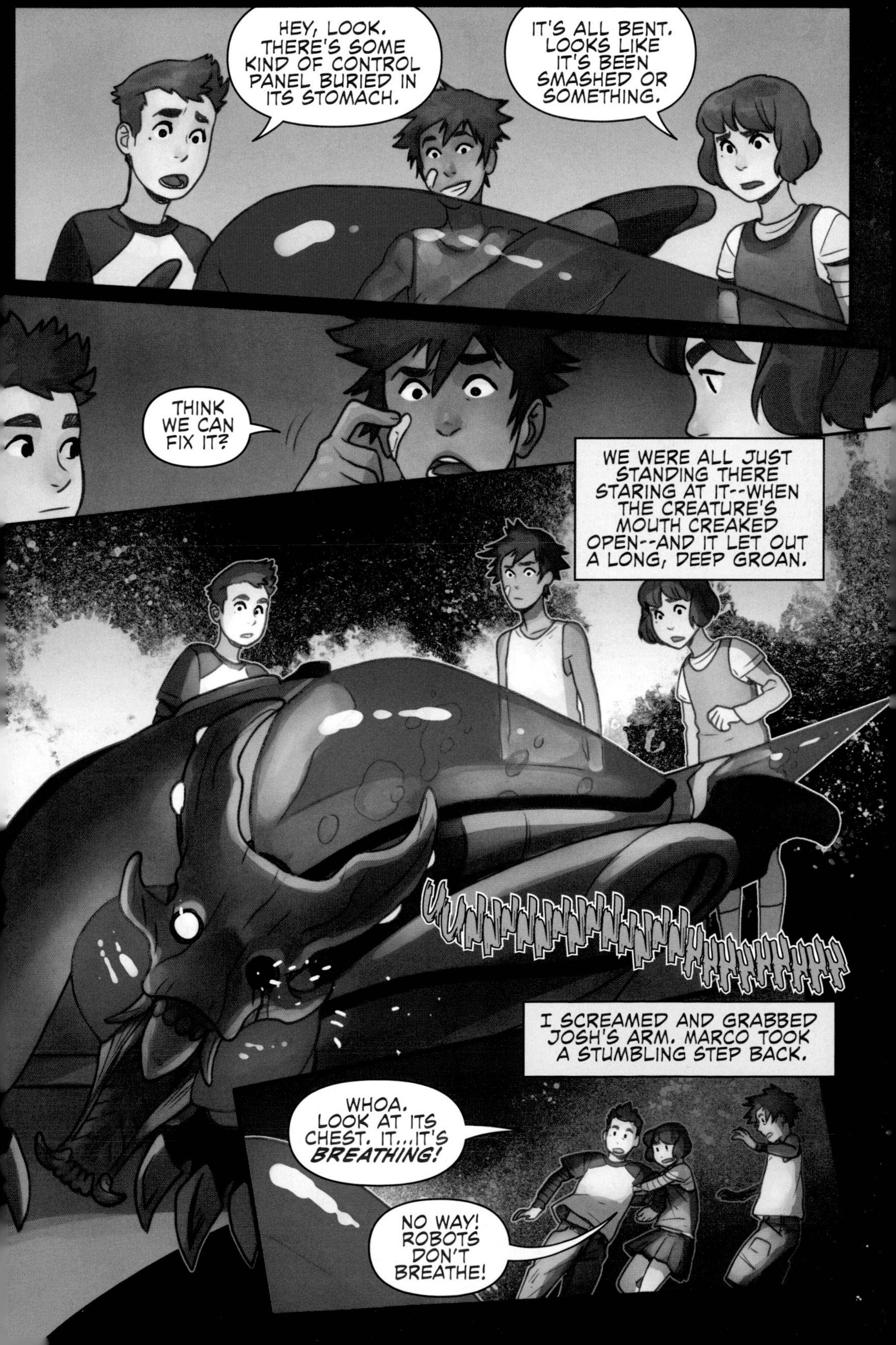
HEY, LOOK. THERE'S SOME KIND OF CONTROL PANEL BURIED IN ITS STOMACH.
IT'S ALL BENT. LOOKS LIKE IT'S BEEN SMASHED OR SOMETHING.
THINK WE CAN FIX IT?
WE WERE ALL JUST STANDING THERE STARING AT IT--WHEN THE CREATURE'S MOUTH CREAKED OPEN--AND IT LET OUT A LONG, DEEP GROAN.
UUNNNNNNNNNNNNNNNNNHHHHHHHHH
I SCREAMED AND GRABBED JOSH'S ARM. MARCO TOOK A STUMBLING STEP BACK.
WHOA. LOOK AT ITS CHEST. IT...IT'S *BREATHING!*
NO WAY! ROBOTS DON'T BREATHE!

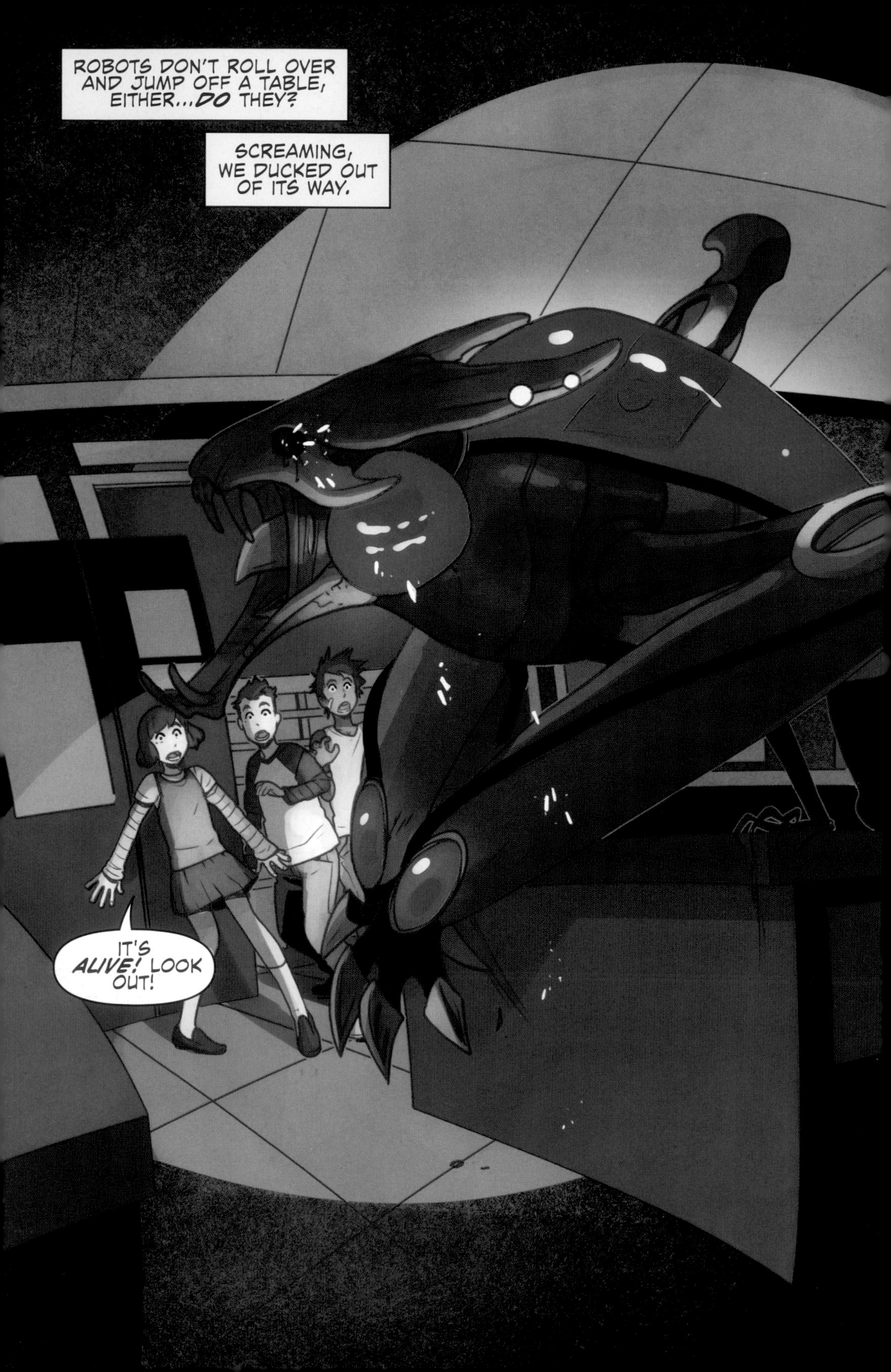
ROBOTS DON'T ROLL OVER AND JUMP OFF A TABLE, EITHER...DO THEY?
SCREAMING, WE DUCKED OUT OF ITS WAY.
IT'S ALIVE! LOOK OUT!

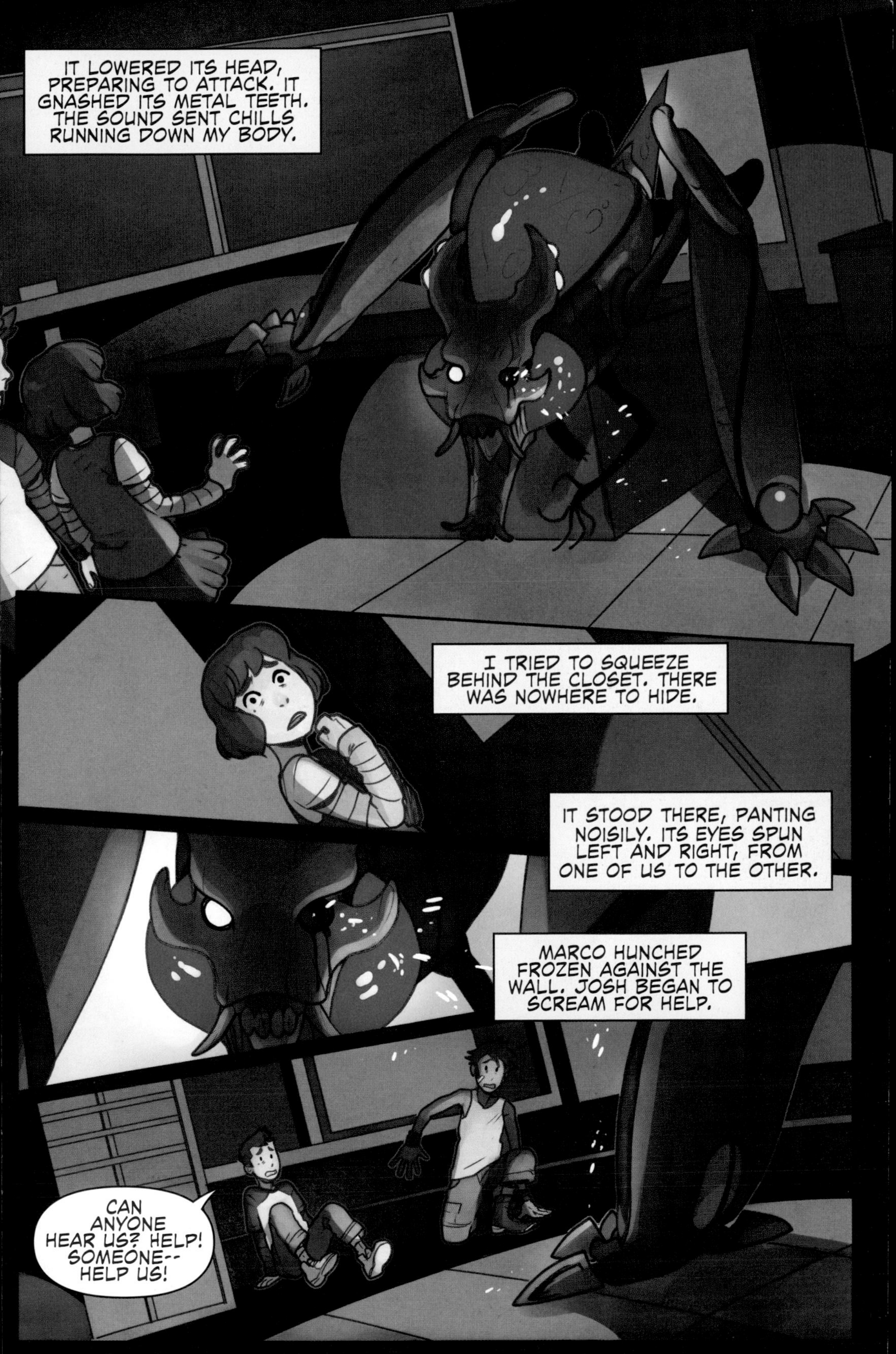
IT LOWERED ITS HEAD, PREPARING TO ATTACK. IT GNASHED ITS METAL TEETH. THE SOUND SENT CHILLS RUNNING DOWN MY BODY.
I TRIED TO SQUEEZE BEHIND THE CLOSET. THERE WAS NOWHERE TO HIDE.
IT STOOD THERE, PANTING NOISILY. ITS EYES SPUN LEFT AND RIGHT, FROM ONE OF US TO THE OTHER.
MARCO HUNCHED FROZEN AGAINST THE WALL. JOSH BEGAN TO SCREAM FOR HELP.
CAN ANYONE HEAR US? HELP! SOMEONE-- HELP US!

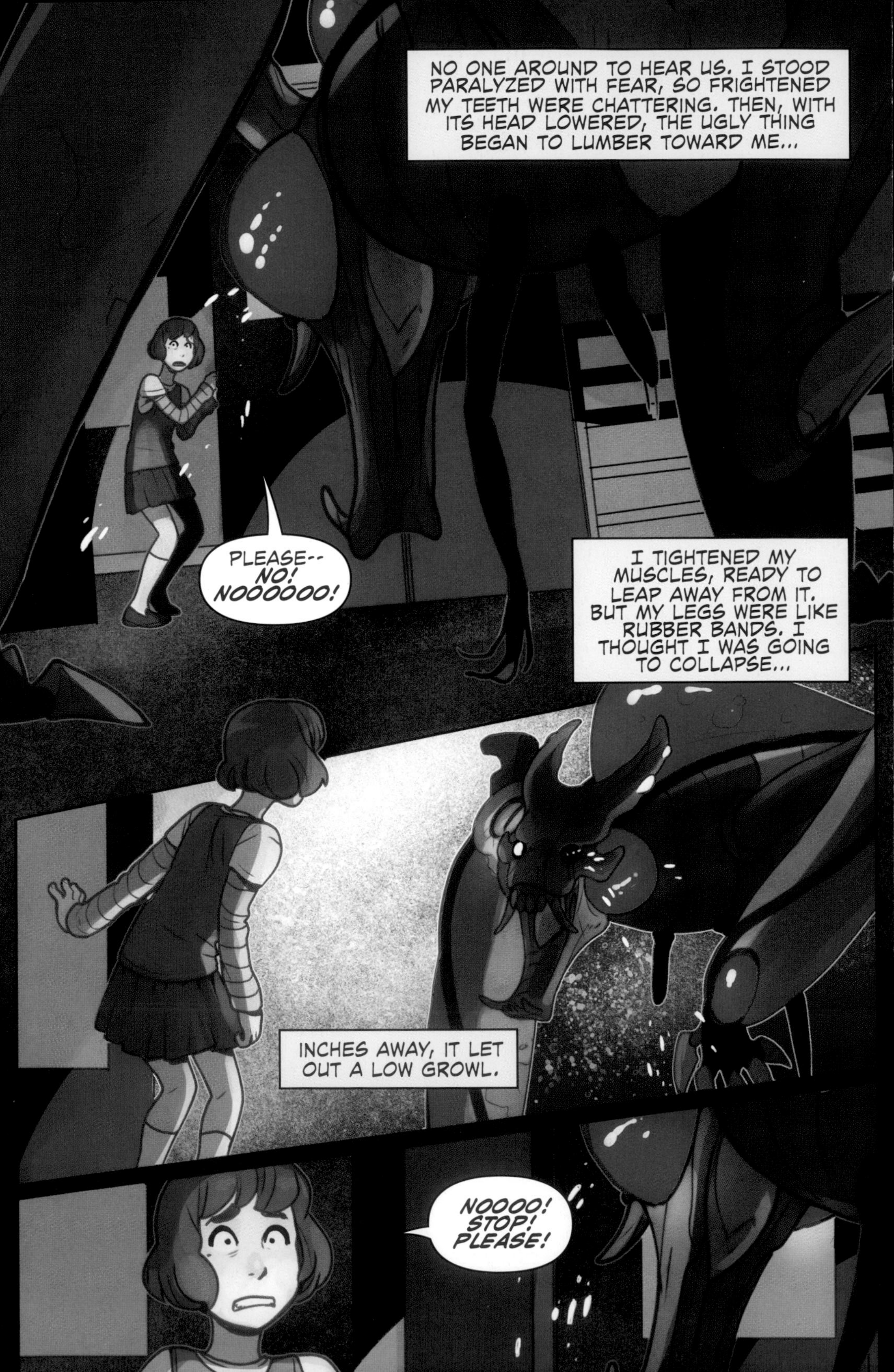
NO ONE AROUND TO HEAR US. I STOOD PARALYZED WITH FEAR, SO FRIGHTENED MY TEETH WERE CHATTERING. THEN, WITH ITS HEAD LOWERED, THE UGLY THING BEGAN TO LUMBER TOWARD ME...
PLEASE-- NO! NOOOOOO!
I TIGHTENED MY MUSCLES, READY TO LEAP AWAY FROM IT. BUT MY LEGS WERE LIKE RUBBER BANDS. I THOUGHT I WAS GOING TO COLLAPSE...
INCHES AWAY, IT LET OUT A LOW GROWL.
NOOOO! STOP! PLEASE!

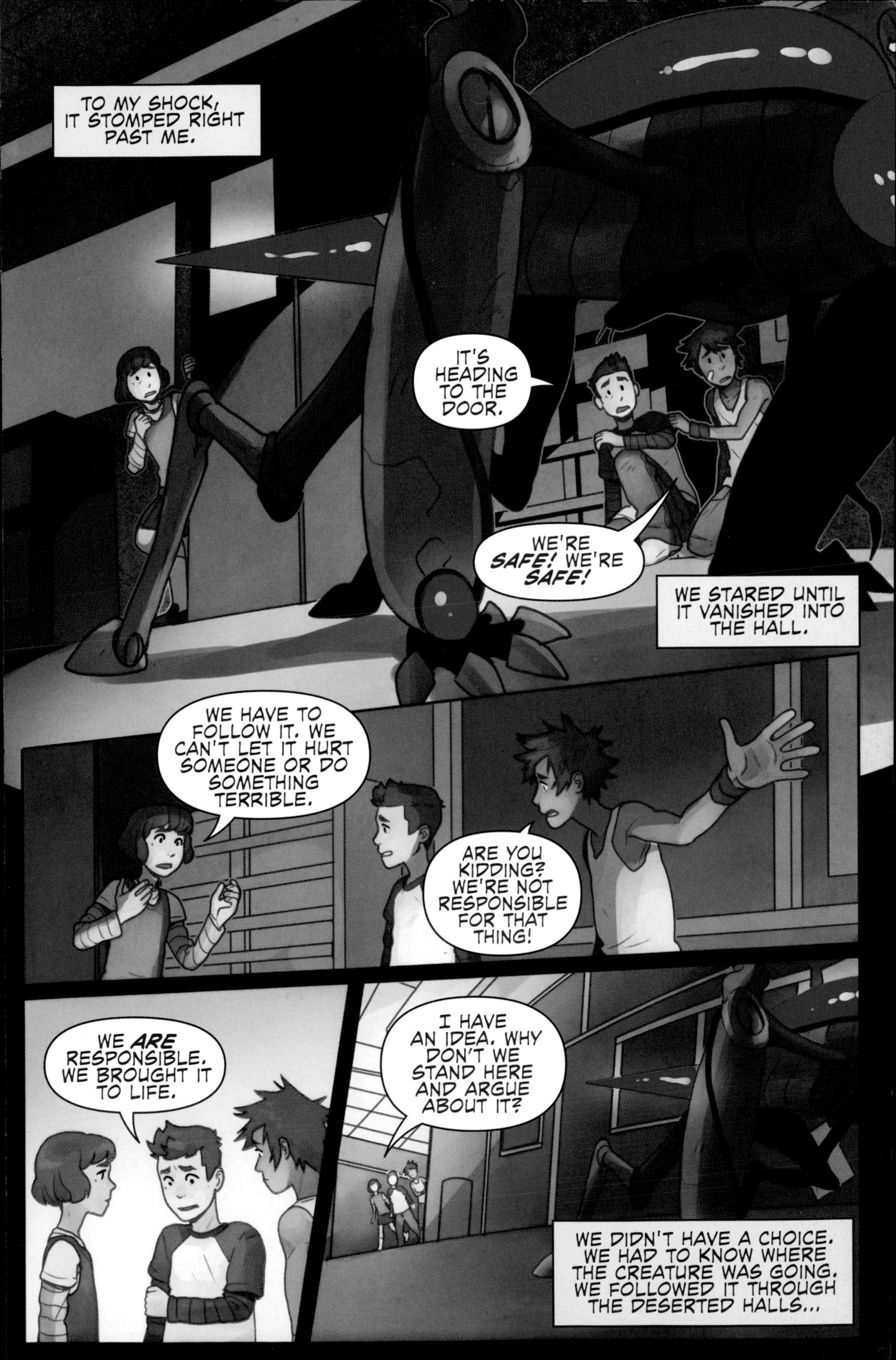
TO MY SHOCK, IT STOMPED RIGHT PAST ME.
IT'S HEADING TO THE DOOR.
WE'RE SAFE! WE'RE SAFE!
WE STARED UNTIL IT VANISHED INTO THE HALL.
WE HAVE TO FOLLOW IT. WE CAN'T LET IT HURT SOMEONE OR DO SOMETHING TERRIBLE.
ARE YOU KIDDING? WE'RE NOT RESPONSIBLE FOR THAT THING!
WE ARE RESPONSIBLE. WE BROUGHT IT TO LIFE.
I HAVE AN IDEA. WHY DON'T WE STAND HERE AND ARGUE ABOUT IT?
WE DIDN'T HAVE A CHOICE. WE HAD TO KNOW WHERE THE CREATURE WAS GOING. WE FOLLOWED IT THROUGH THE DESERTED HALLS...

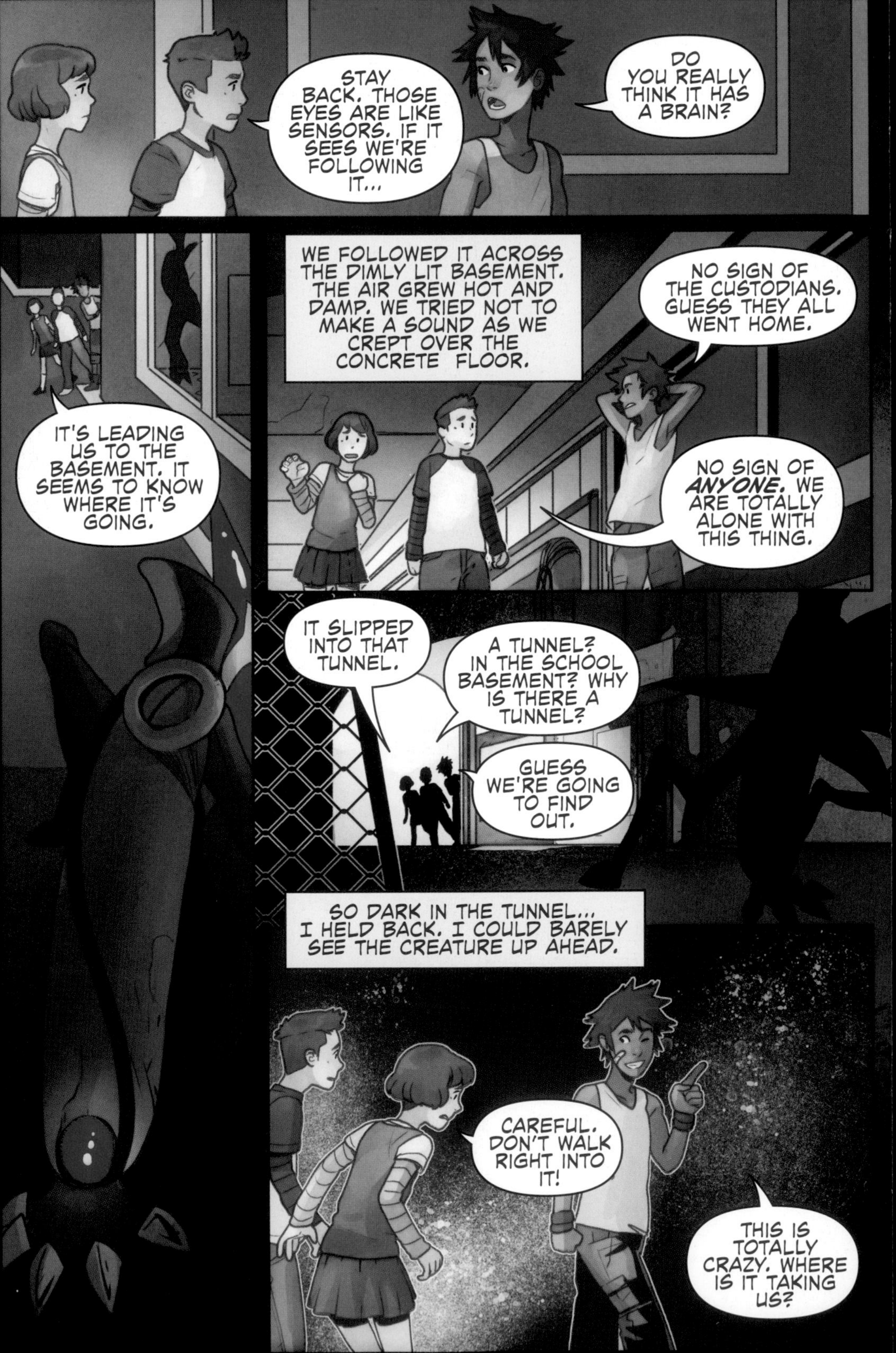
STAY BACK. THOSE EYES ARE LIKE SENSORS. IF IT SEES WE'RE FOLLOWING IT...
DO YOU REALLY THINK IT HAS A BRAIN?
IT'S LEADING US TO THE BASEMENT. IT SEEMS TO KNOW WHERE IT'S GOING.
WE FOLLOWED IT ACROSS THE DIMLY LIT BASEMENT. THE AIR GREW HOT AND DAMP. WE TRIED NOT TO MAKE A SOUND AS WE CREPT OVER THE CONCRETE FLOOR.
NO SIGN OF THE CUSTODIANS. GUESS THEY ALL WENT HOME.
NO SIGN OF *ANYONE.* WE ARE TOTALLY ALONE WITH THIS THING.
IT SLIPPED INTO THAT TUNNEL.
A TUNNEL? IN THE SCHOOL BASEMENT? WHY IS THERE A TUNNEL?
GUESS WE'RE GOING TO FIND OUT.
SO DARK IN THE TUNNEL... I HELD BACK. I COULD BARELY SEE THE CREATURE UP AHEAD.
CAREFUL. DON'T WALK RIGHT INTO IT!
THIS IS TOTALLY CRAZY. WHERE IS IT TAKING US?

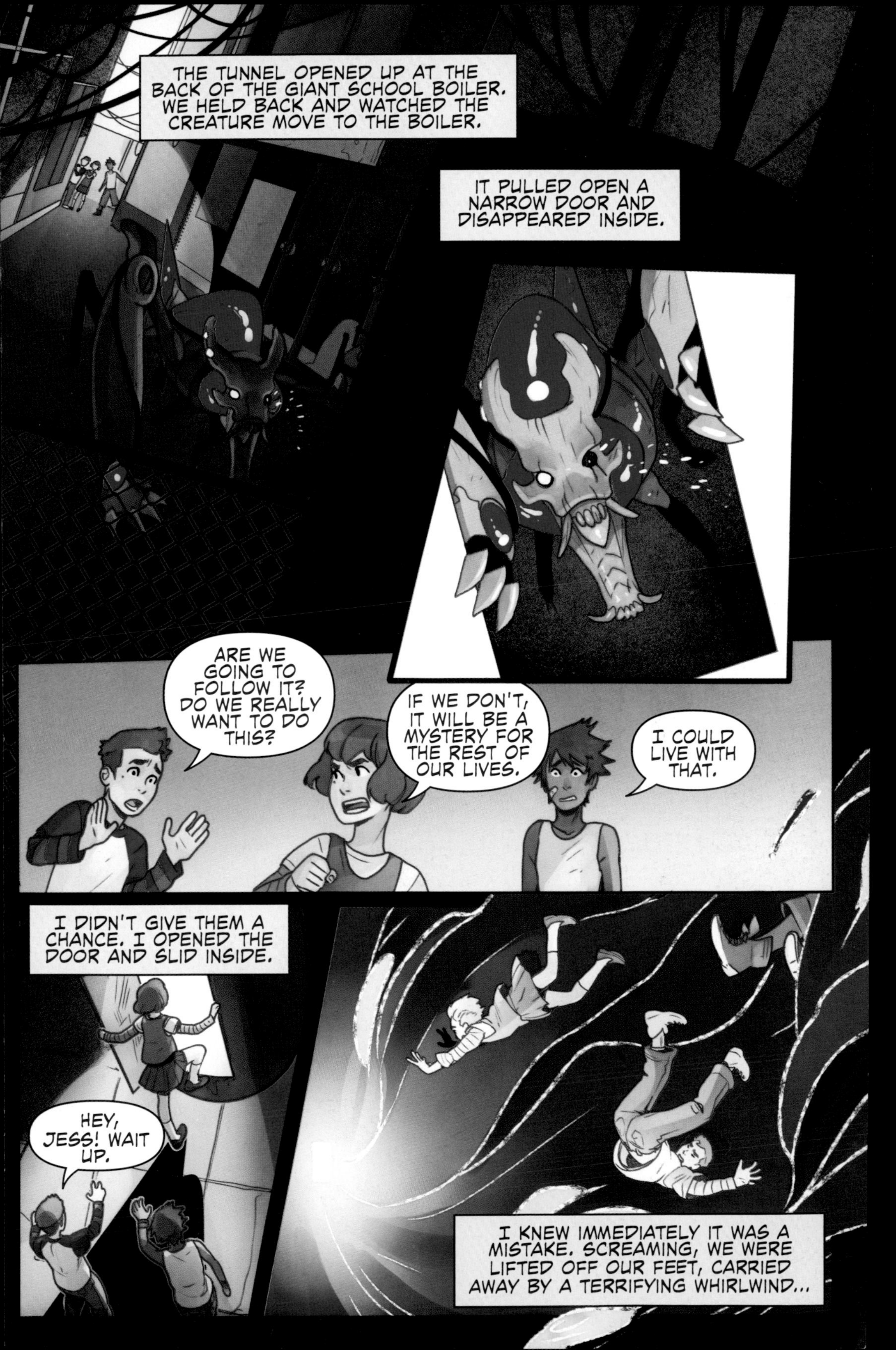
THE TUNNEL OPENED UP AT THE BACK OF THE GIANT SCHOOL BOILER. WE HELD BACK AND WATCHED THE CREATURE MOVE TO THE BOILER.
IT PULLED OPEN A NARROW DOOR AND DISAPPEARED INSIDE.
ARE WE GOING TO FOLLOW IT? DO WE REALLY WANT TO DO THIS?
IF WE DON'T, IT WILL BE A MYSTERY FOR THE REST OF OUR LIVES.
I COULD LIVE WITH THAT.
I DIDN'T GIVE THEM A CHANCE. I OPENED THE DOOR AND SLID INSIDE.
HEY, JESS! WAIT UP.
I KNEW IMMEDIATELY IT WAS A MISTAKE. SCREAMING, WE WERE LIFTED OFF OUR FEET, CARRIED AWAY BY A TERRIFYING WHIRLWIND...

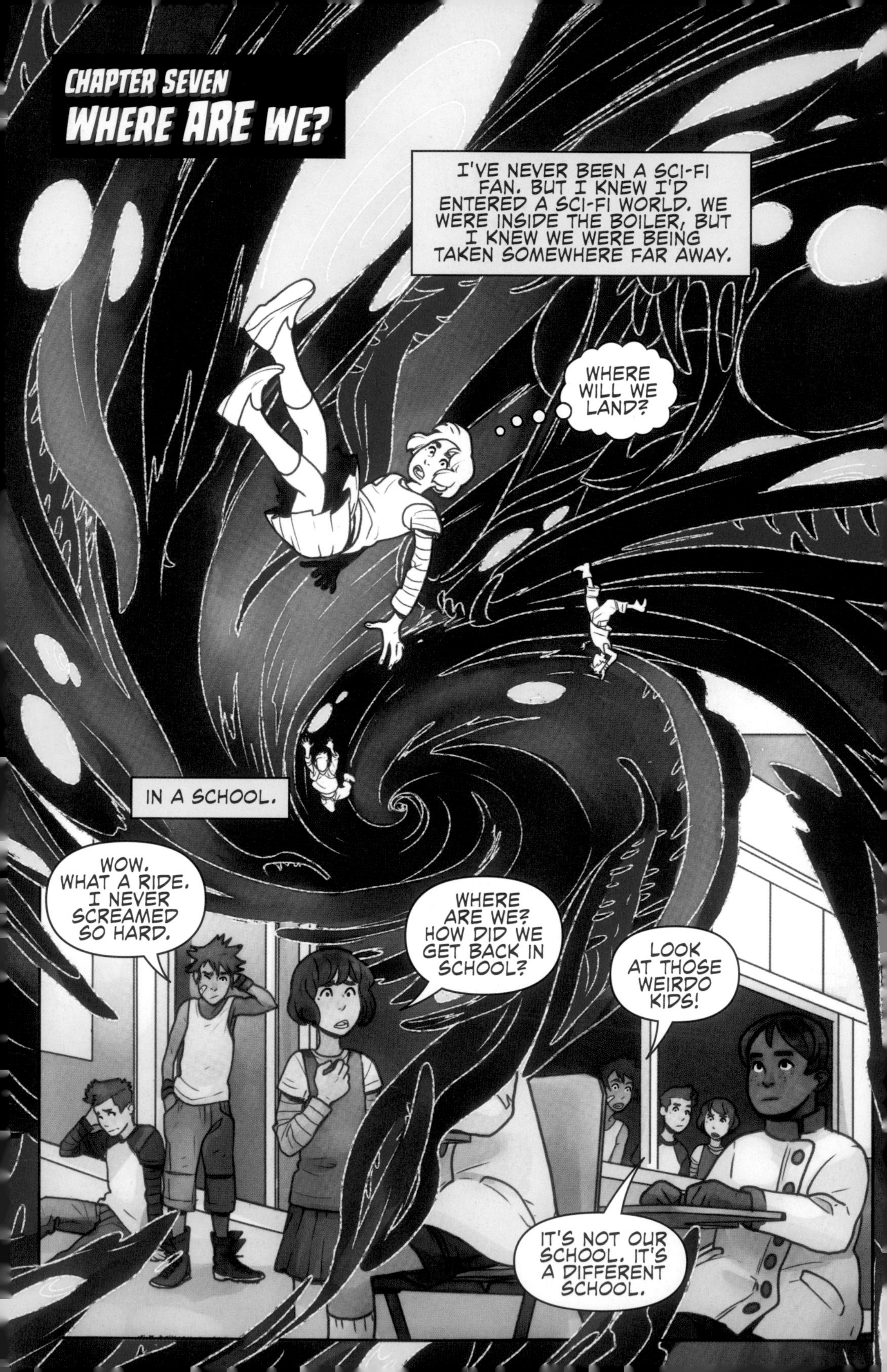
CHAPTER SEVEN
WHERE ARE WE?
I'VE NEVER BEEN A SCI-FI FAN. BUT I KNEW I'D ENTERED A SCI-FI WORLD. WE WERE INSIDE THE BOILER, BUT I KNEW WE WERE BEING TAKEN SOMEWHERE FAR AWAY.
WHERE WILL WE LAND?
IN A SCHOOL.
WOW. WHAT A RIDE. I NEVER SCREAMED SO HARD.
WHERE ARE WE? HOW DID WE GET BACK IN SCHOOL?
LOOK AT THOSE WEIRDO KIDS!
IT'S NOT OUR SCHOOL. IT'S A DIFFERENT SCHOOL.

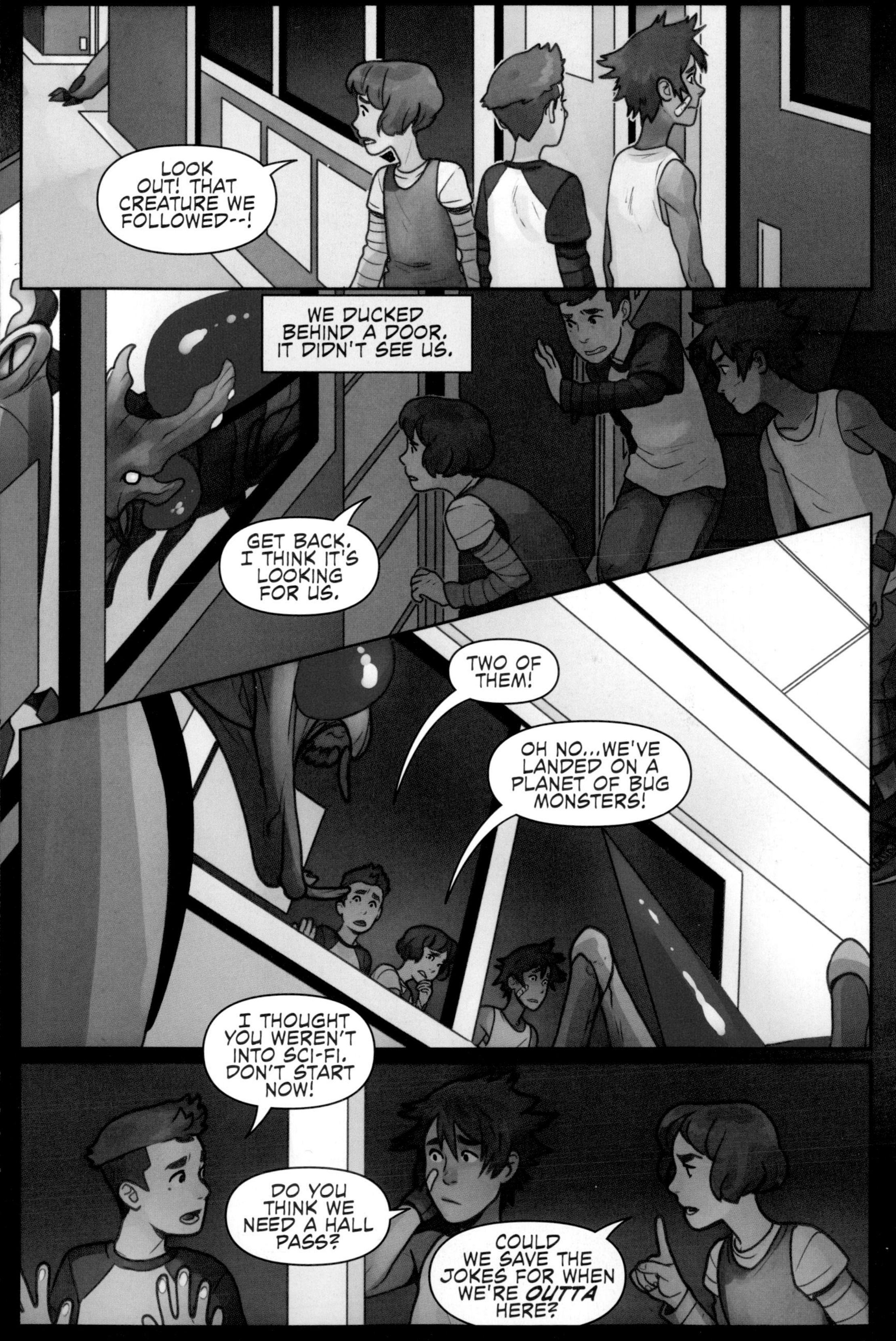
LOOK OUT! THAT CREATURE WE FOLLOWED--!
WE DUCKED BEHIND A DOOR. IT DIDN'T SEE US.
GET BACK. I THINK IT'S LOOKING FOR US.
TWO OF THEM!
OH NO...WE'VE LANDED ON A PLANET OF BUG MONSTERS!
I THOUGHT YOU WEREN'T INTO SCI-FI. DON'T START NOW!
DO YOU THINK WE NEED A HALL PASS?
COULD WE SAVE THE JOKES FOR WHEN WE'RE *OUTTA* HERE?

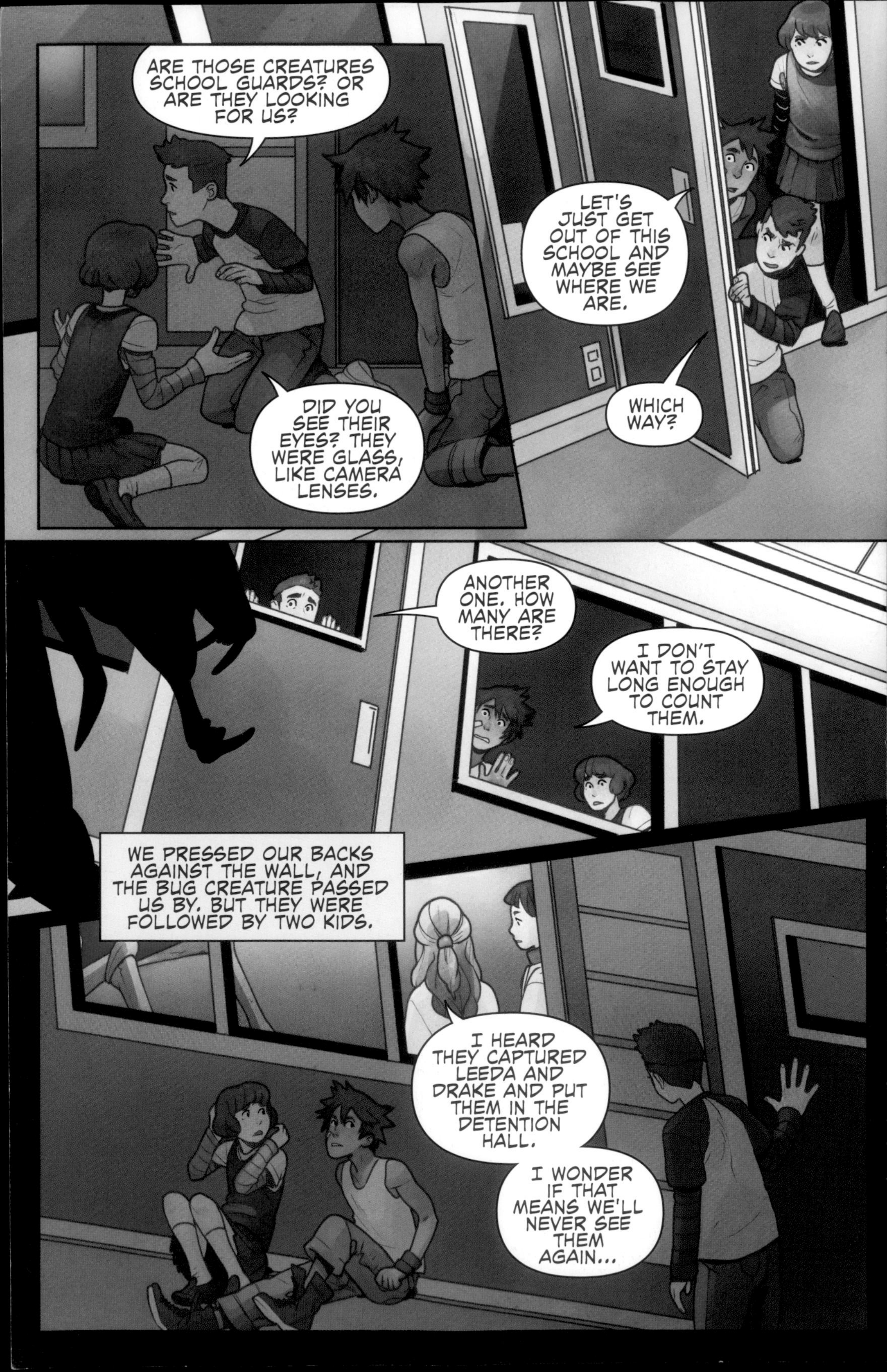
ARE THOSE CREATURES SCHOOL GUARDS? OR ARE THEY LOOKING FOR US?
DID YOU SEE THEIR EYES? THEY WERE GLASS, LIKE CAMERA LENSES.
LET'S JUST GET OUT OF THIS SCHOOL AND MAYBE SEE WHERE WE ARE.
WHICH WAY?
ANOTHER ONE. HOW MANY ARE THERE?
I DON'T WANT TO STAY LONG ENOUGH TO COUNT THEM.
WE PRESSED OUR BACKS AGAINST THE WALL, AND THE BUG CREATURE PASSED US BY. BUT THEY WERE FOLLOWED BY TWO KIDS.
I HEARD THEY CAPTURED LEEDA AND DRAKE AND PUT THEM IN THE DETENTION HALL.
I WONDER IF THAT MEANS WE'LL NEVER SEE THEM AGAIN...

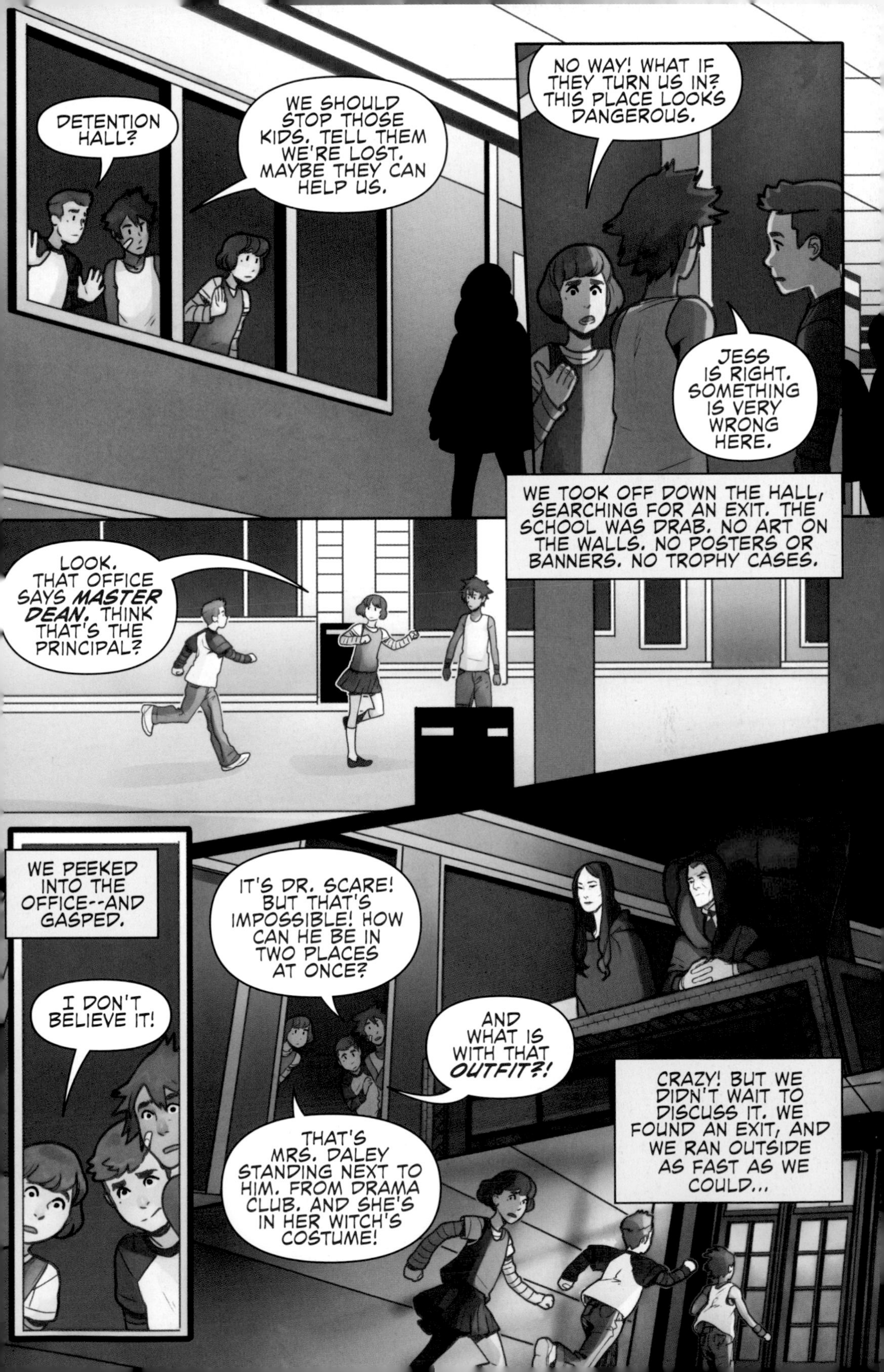
DETENTION HALL?
WE SHOULD STOP THOSE KIDS. TELL THEM WE'RE LOST. MAYBE THEY CAN HELP US.
NO WAY! WHAT IF THEY TURN US IN? THIS PLACE LOOKS DANGEROUS.
JESS IS RIGHT. SOMETHING IS VERY WRONG HERE.
WE TOOK OFF DOWN THE HALL, SEARCHING FOR AN EXIT. THE SCHOOL WAS DRAB. NO ART ON THE WALLS. NO POSTERS OR BANNERS. NO TROPHY CASES.
LOOK. THAT OFFICE SAYS MASTER DEAN. THINK THAT'S THE PRINCIPAL?
WE PEEKED INTO THE OFFICE--AND GASPED.
I DON'T BELIEVE IT!
IT'S DR. SCARE! BUT THAT'S IMPOSSIBLE! HOW CAN HE BE IN TWO PLACES AT ONCE?
AND WHAT IS WITH THAT OUTFIT?!
THAT'S MRS. DALEY STANDING NEXT TO HIM. FROM DRAMA CLUB. AND SHE'S IN HER WITCH'S COSTUME!
CRAZY! BUT WE DIDN'T WAIT TO DISCUSS IT. WE FOUND AN EXIT, AND WE RAN OUTSIDE AS FAST AS WE COULD...

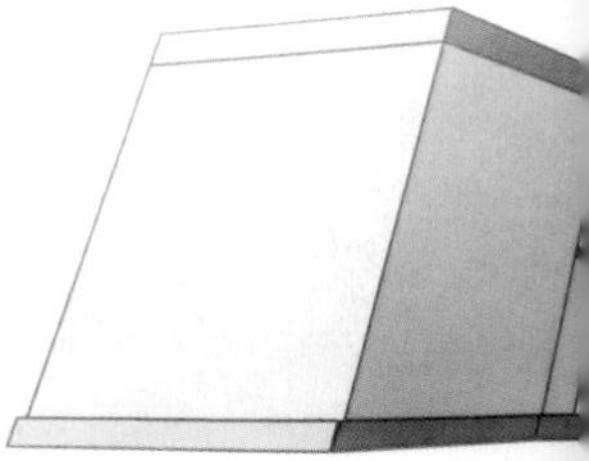

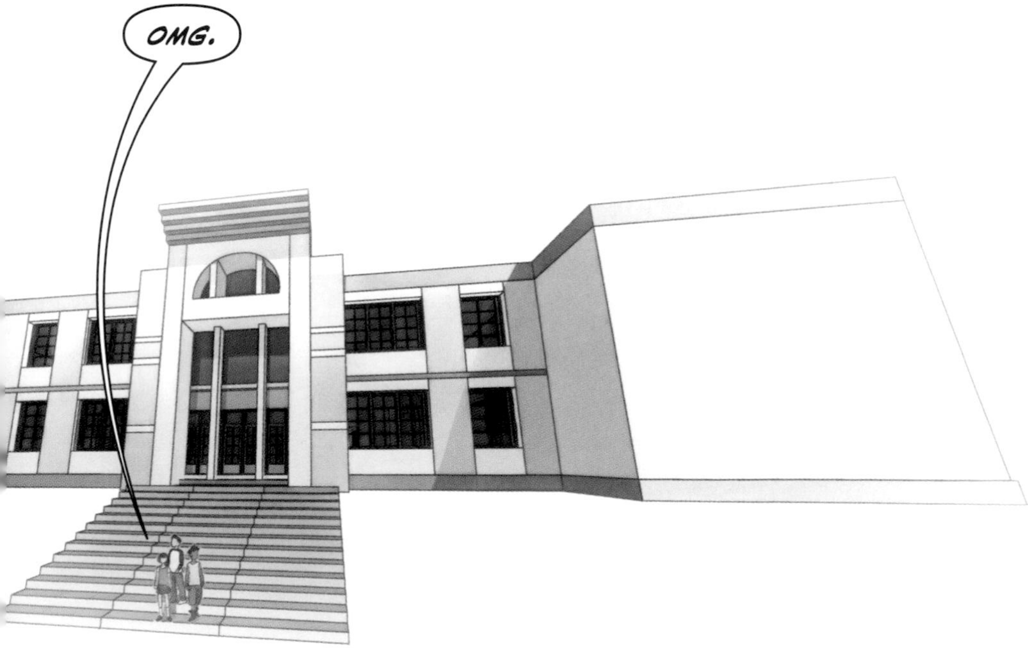
OMG.

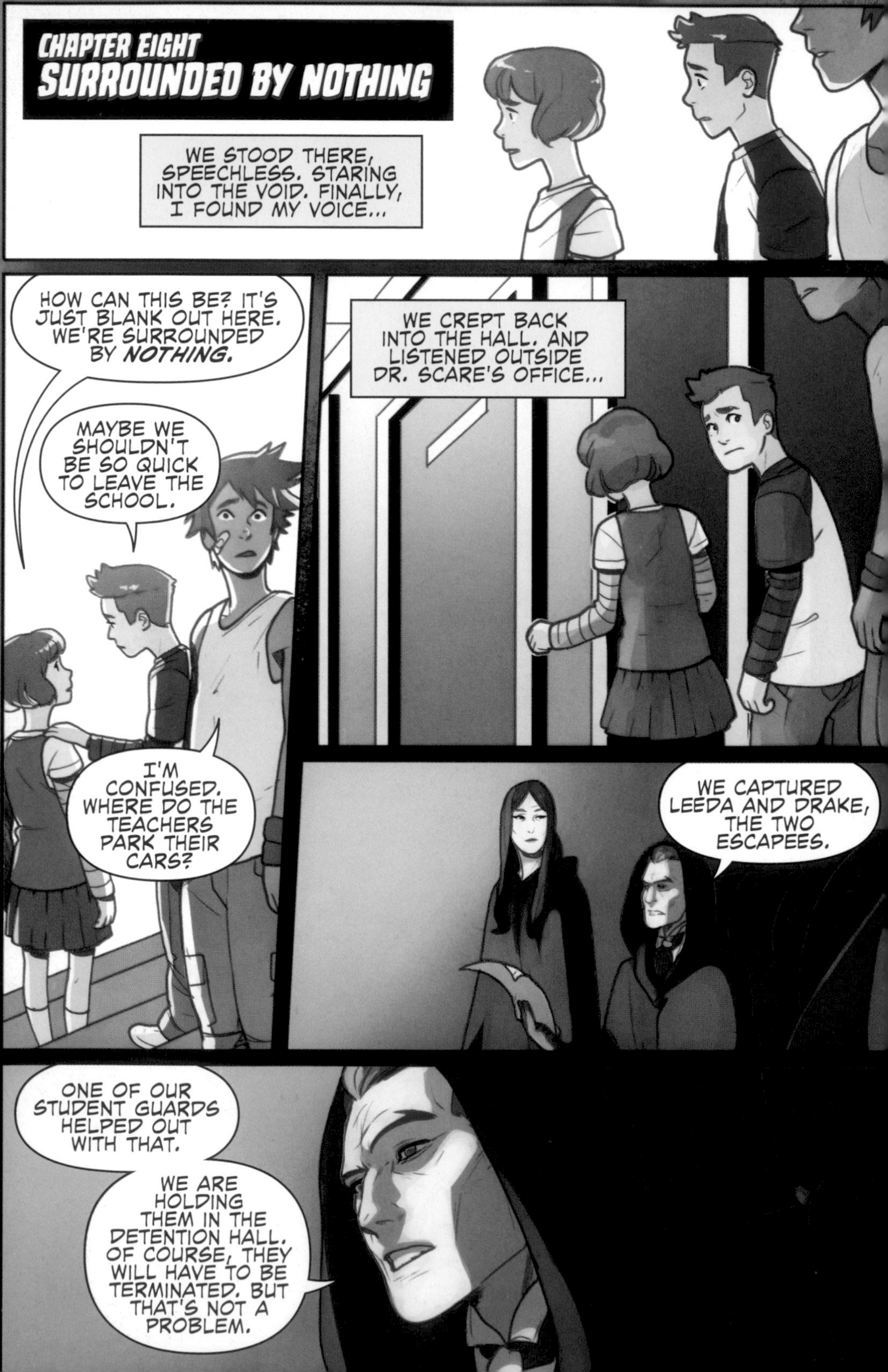
CHAPTER EIGHT
SURROUNDED BY NOTHING
WE STOOD THERE, SPEECHLESS. STARING INTO THE VOID. FINALLY, I FOUND MY VOICE...
HOW CAN THIS BE? IT'S JUST BLANK OUT HERE. WE'RE SURROUNDED BY NOTHING.
MAYBE WE SHOULDN'T BE SO QUICK TO LEAVE THE SCHOOL.
I'M CONFUSED. WHERE DO THE TEACHERS PARK THEIR CARS?
WE CREPT BACK INTO THE HALL. AND LISTENED OUTSIDE DR. SCARE'S OFFICE...
WE CAPTURED LEEDA AND DRAKE, THE TWO ESCAPEES.
ONE OF OUR STUDENT GUARDS HELPED OUT WITH THAT.
WE ARE HOLDING THEM IN THE DETENTION HALL. OF COURSE, THEY WILL HAVE TO BE TERMINATED. BUT THAT'S NOT A PROBLEM.

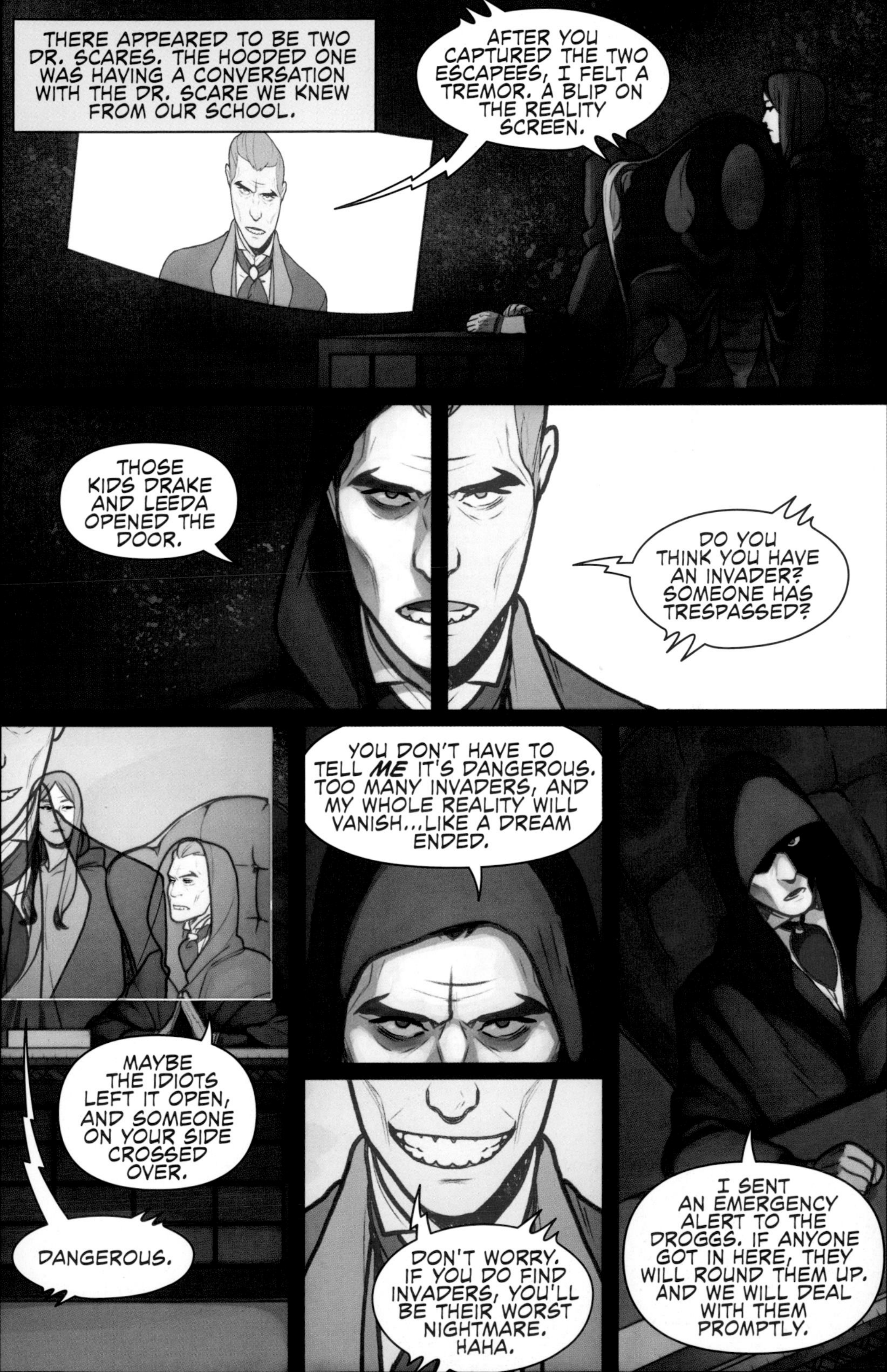

THERE APPEARED TO BE TWO DR. SCARES. THE HOODED ONE WAS HAVING A CONVERSATION WITH THE DR. SCARE WE KNEW FROM OUR SCHOOL.
AFTER YOU CAPTURED THE TWO ESCAPEES, I FELT A TREMOR. A BLIP ON THE REALITY SCREEN.
THOSE KIDS DRAKE AND LEEDA OPENED THE DOOR.
DO YOU THINK YOU HAVE AN INVADER? SOMEONE HAS TRESPASSED?
MAYBE THE IDIOTS LEFT IT OPEN, AND SOMEONE ON YOUR SIDE CROSSED OVER.
DANGEROUS.
YOU DON'T HAVE TO TELL *ME* IT'S DANGEROUS. TOO MANY INVADERS, AND MY WHOLE REALITY WILL VANISH...LIKE A DREAM ENDED.
DON'T WORRY. IF YOU DO FIND INVADERS, YOU'LL BE THEIR WORST NIGHTMARE. HAHA.
I SENT AN EMERGENCY ALERT TO THE DROGGS. IF ANYONE GOT IN HERE, THEY WILL ROUND THEM UP. AND WE WILL DEAL WITH THEM PROMPTLY.

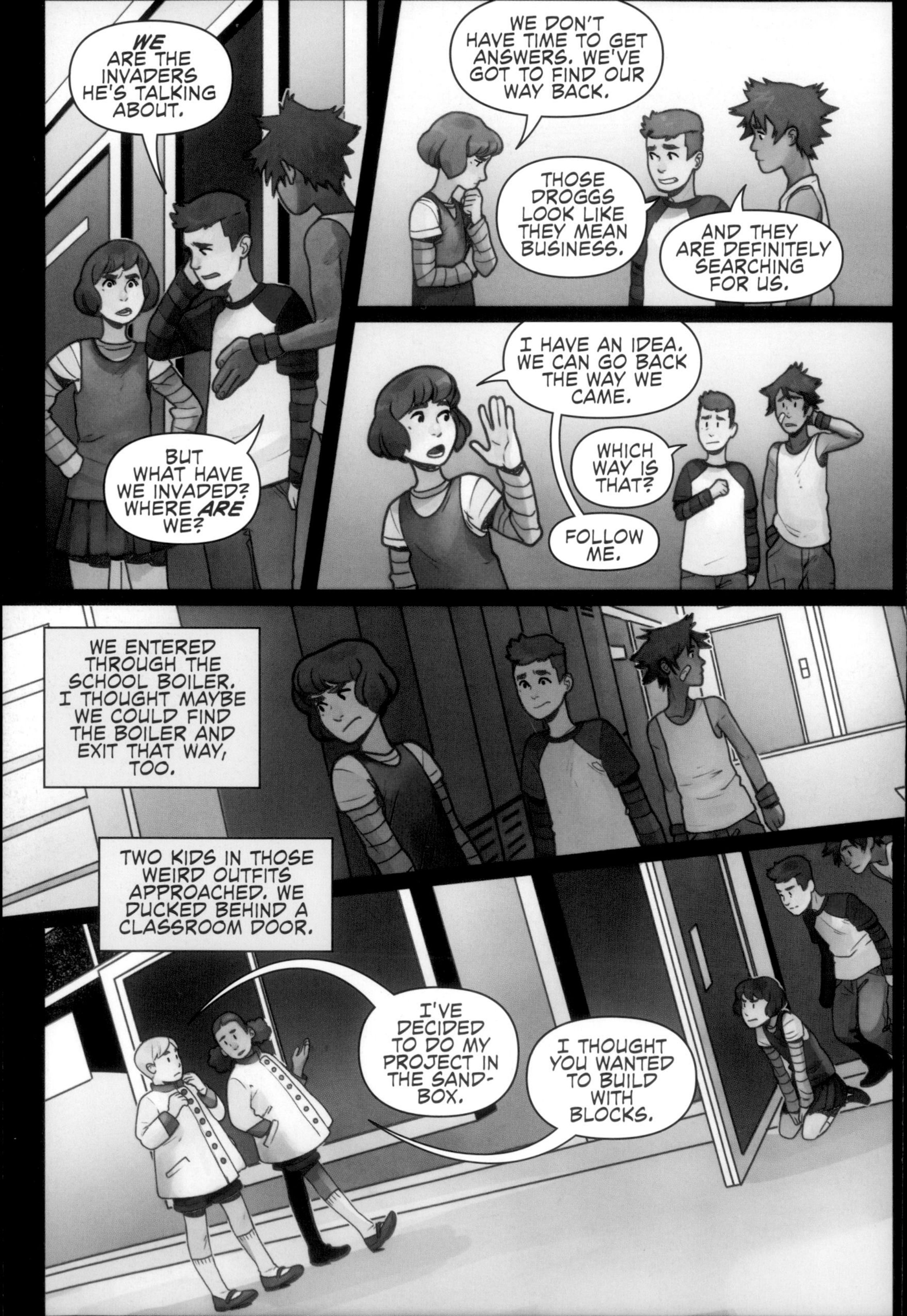
WE ARE THE INVADERS HE'S TALKING ABOUT.
BUT WHAT HAVE WE INVADED? WHERE ARE WE?
WE DON'T HAVE TIME TO GET ANSWERS. WE'VE GOT TO FIND OUR WAY BACK.
THOSE DROGGS LOOK LIKE THEY MEAN BUSINESS.
AND THEY ARE DEFINITELY SEARCHING FOR US.
I HAVE AN IDEA. WE CAN GO BACK THE WAY WE CAME.
WHICH WAY IS THAT?
FOLLOW ME.
WE ENTERED THROUGH THE SCHOOL BOILER. I THOUGHT MAYBE WE COULD FIND THE BOILER AND EXIT THAT WAY, TOO.
TWO KIDS IN THOSE WEIRD OUTFITS APPROACHED. WE DUCKED BEHIND A CLASSROOM DOOR.
I'VE DECIDED TO DO MY PROJECT IN THE SAND-BOX.
I THOUGHT YOU WANTED TO BUILD WITH BLOCKS.

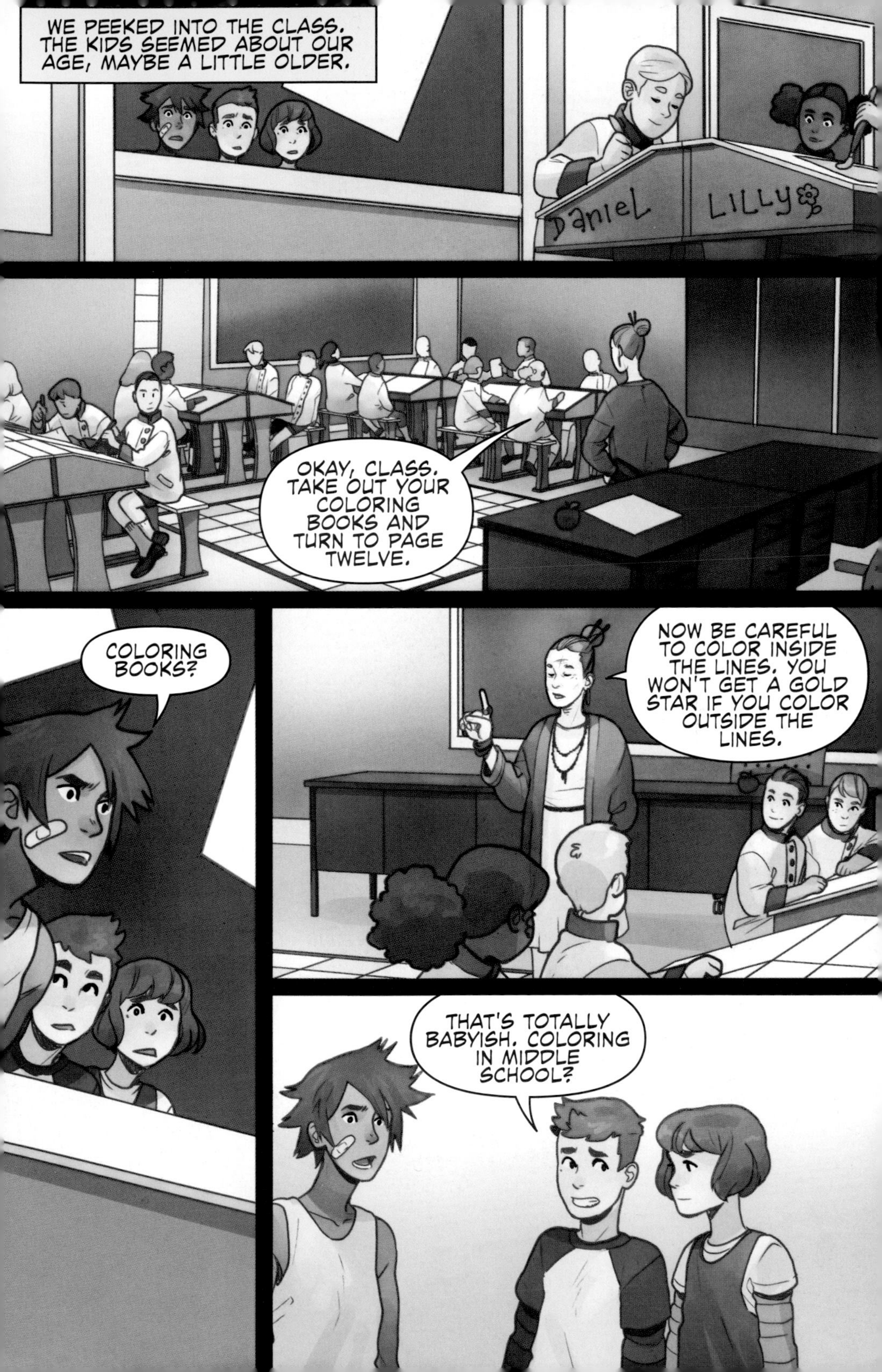

WE PEEKED INTO THE CLASS. THE KIDS SEEMED ABOUT OUR AGE, MAYBE A LITTLE OLDER.
DanieL
LILLY
OKAY, CLASS. TAKE OUT YOUR COLORING BOOKS AND TURN TO PAGE TWELVE.
COLORING BOOKS?
NOW BE CAREFUL TO COLOR INSIDE THE LINES. YOU WON'T GET A GOLD STAR IF YOU COLOR OUTSIDE THE LINES.
THAT'S TOTALLY BABYISH. COLORING IN MIDDLE SCHOOL?

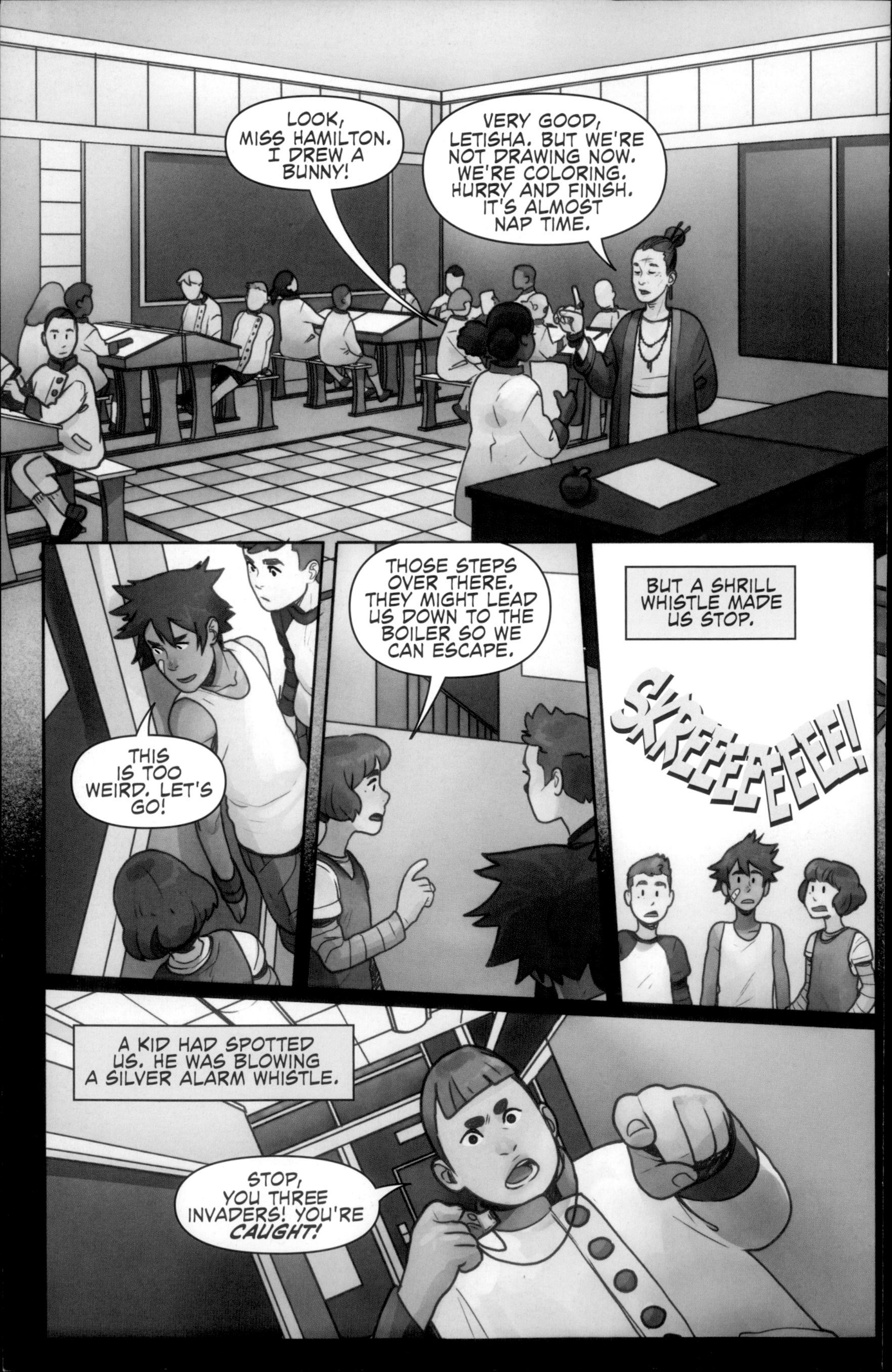
LOOK, MISS HAMILTON. I DREW A BUNNY!
VERY GOOD, LETISHA. BUT WE'RE NOT DRAWING NOW. WE'RE COLORING. HURRY AND FINISH. IT'S ALMOST NAP TIME.
THIS IS TOO WEIRD. LET'S GO!
THOSE STEPS OVER THERE. THEY MIGHT LEAD US DOWN TO THE BOILER SO WE CAN ESCAPE.
BUT A SHRILL WHISTLE MADE US STOP.
SKREEEEEEEEE!
A KID HAD SPOTTED US. HE WAS BLOWING A SILVER ALARM WHISTLE.
STOP, YOU THREE INVADERS! YOU'RE *CAUGHT!*

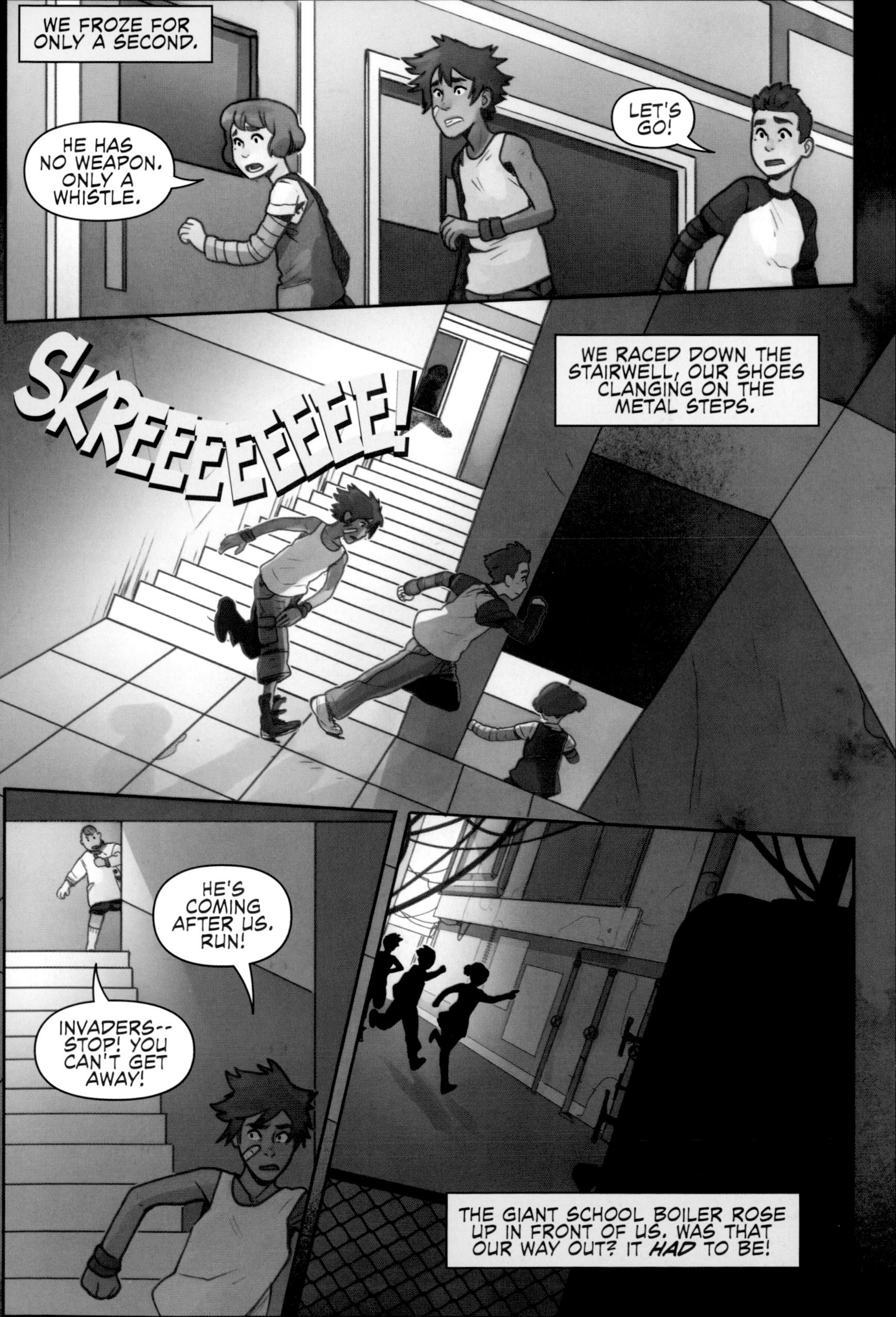

WE FROZE FOR ONLY A SECOND.
HE HAS NO WEAPON. ONLY A WHISTLE.
LET'S GO!
SKREEEEEEEEE!
WE RACED DOWN THE STAIRWELL, OUR SHOES CLANGING ON THE METAL STEPS.
HE'S COMING AFTER US. RUN!
INVADERS-- STOP! YOU CAN'T GET AWAY!
THE GIANT SCHOOL BOILER ROSE UP IN FRONT OF US. WAS THAT OUR WAY OUT? IT *HAD* TO BE!

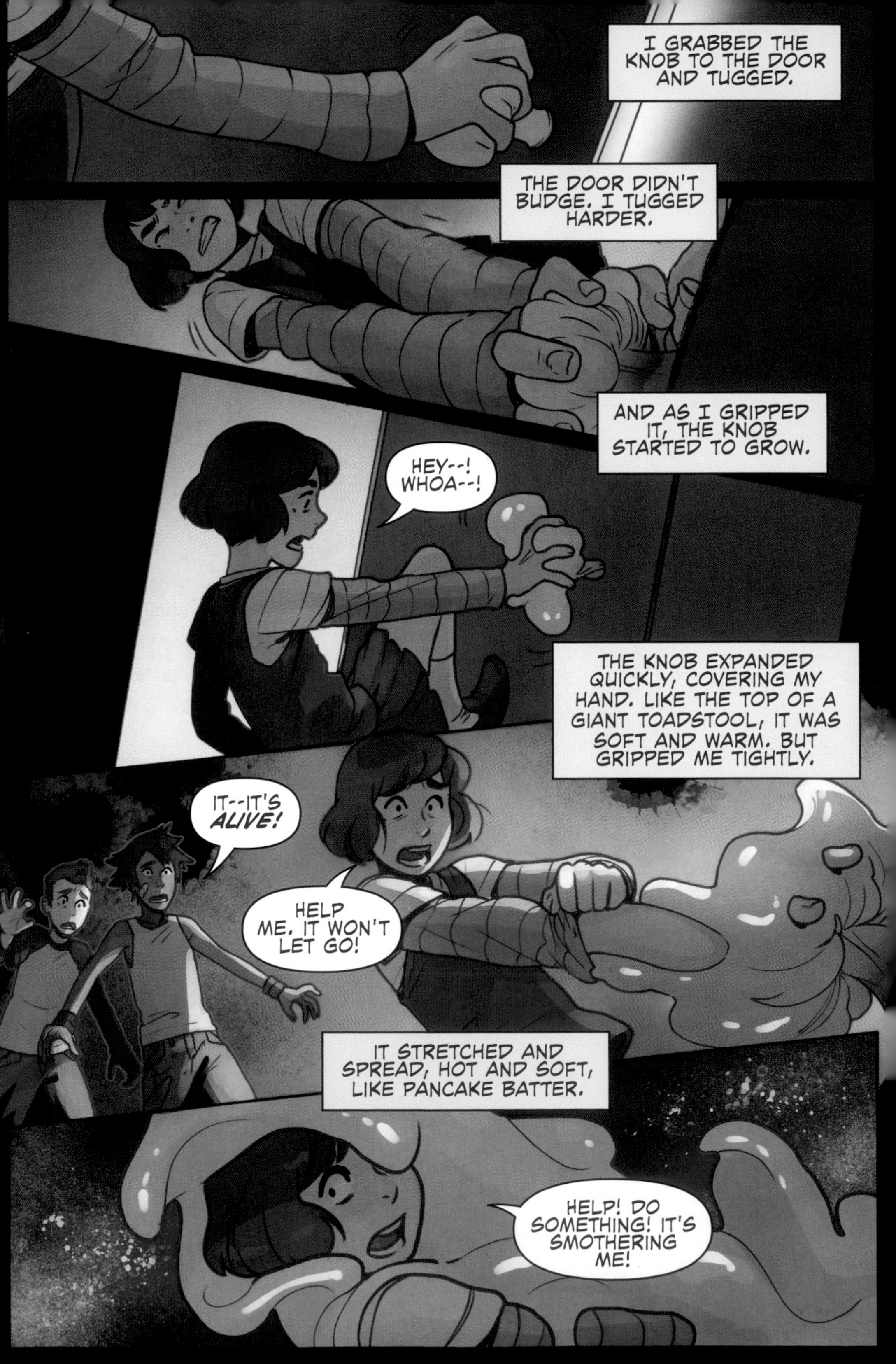
I GRABBED THE KNOB TO THE DOOR AND TUGGED.
THE DOOR DIDN'T BUDGE. I TUGGED HARDER.
AND AS I GRIPPED IT, THE KNOB STARTED TO GROW.
HEY--! WHOA--!
THE KNOB EXPANDED QUICKLY, COVERING MY HAND. LIKE THE TOP OF A GIANT TOADSTOOL, IT WAS SOFT AND WARM. BUT GRIPPED ME TIGHTLY.
IT--IT'S *ALIVE!*
HELP ME. IT WON'T LET GO!
IT STRETCHED AND SPREAD, HOT AND SOFT, LIKE PANCAKE BATTER.
HELP! DO SOMETHING! IT'S SMOTHERING ME!

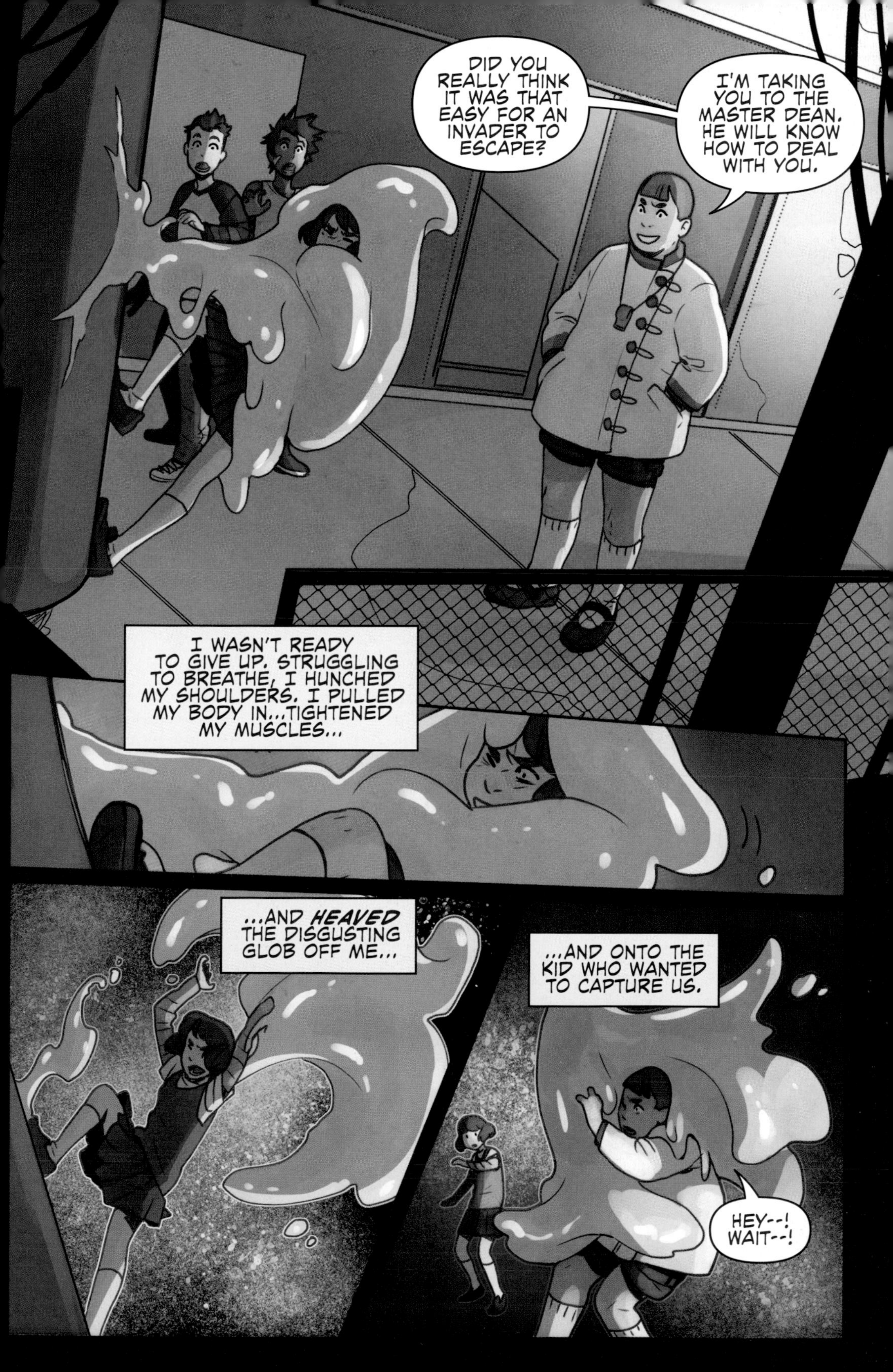
DID YOU REALLY THINK IT WAS THAT EASY FOR AN INVADER TO ESCAPE?
I'M TAKING YOU TO THE MASTER DEAN. HE WILL KNOW HOW TO DEAL WITH YOU.
I WASN'T READY TO GIVE UP. STRUGGLING TO BREATHE, I HUNCHED MY SHOULDERS. I PULLED MY BODY IN...TIGHTENED MY MUSCLES...
...AND HEAVED THE DISGUSTING GLOB OFF ME...
...AND ONTO THE KID WHO WANTED TO CAPTURE US.
HEY--! WAIT--!

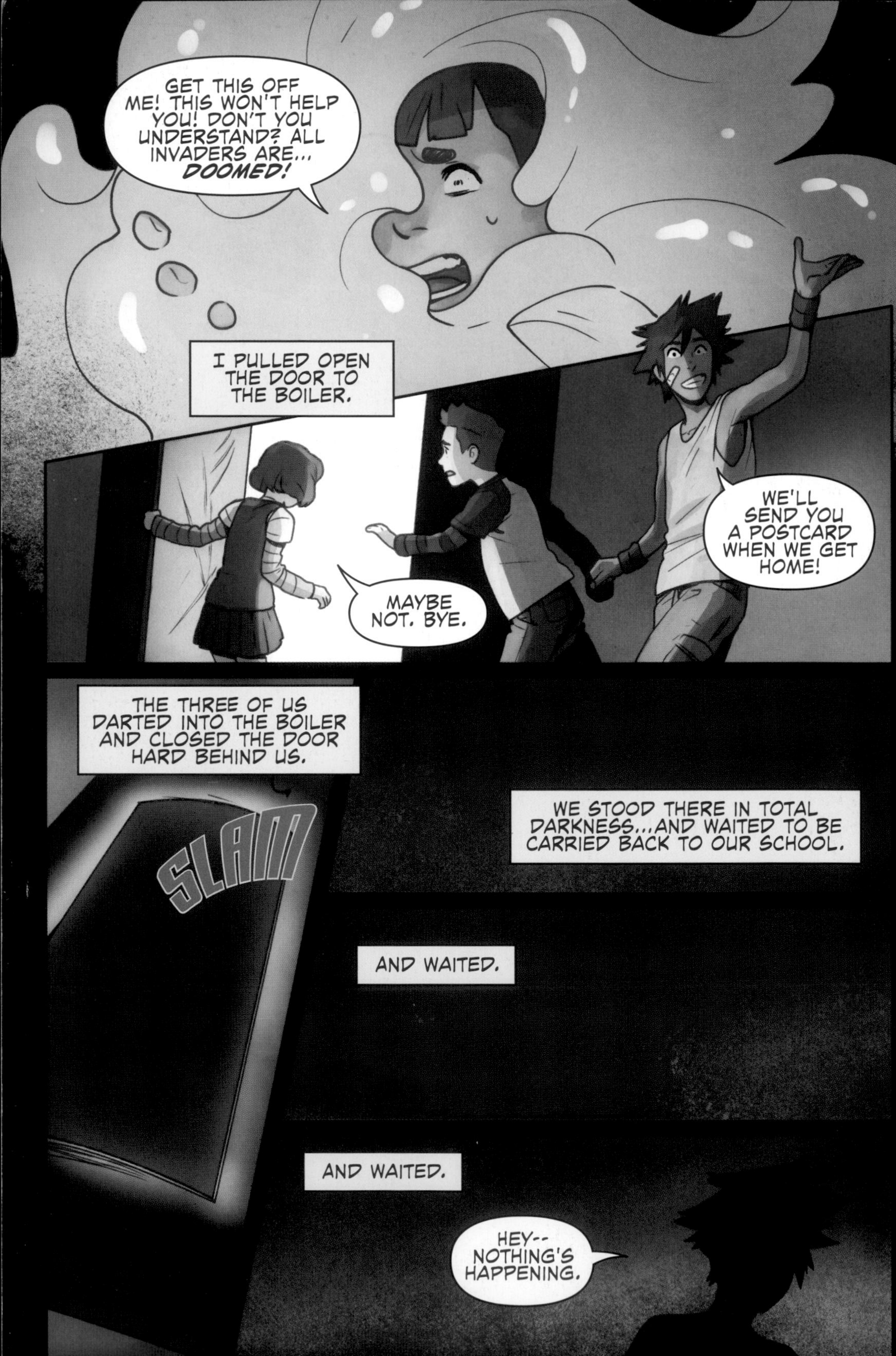
GET THIS OFF ME! THIS WON'T HELP YOU! DON'T YOU UNDERSTAND? ALL INVADERS ARE... DOOMED!
I PULLED OPEN THE DOOR TO THE BOILER.
WE'LL SEND YOU A POSTCARD WHEN WE GET HOME!
MAYBE NOT. BYE.
THE THREE OF US DARTED INTO THE BOILER AND CLOSED THE DOOR HARD BEHIND US.
SLAM
WE STOOD THERE IN TOTAL DARKNESS...AND WAITED TO BE CARRIED BACK TO OUR SCHOOL.
AND WAITED.
AND WAITED.
HEY-- NOTHING'S HAPPENING.

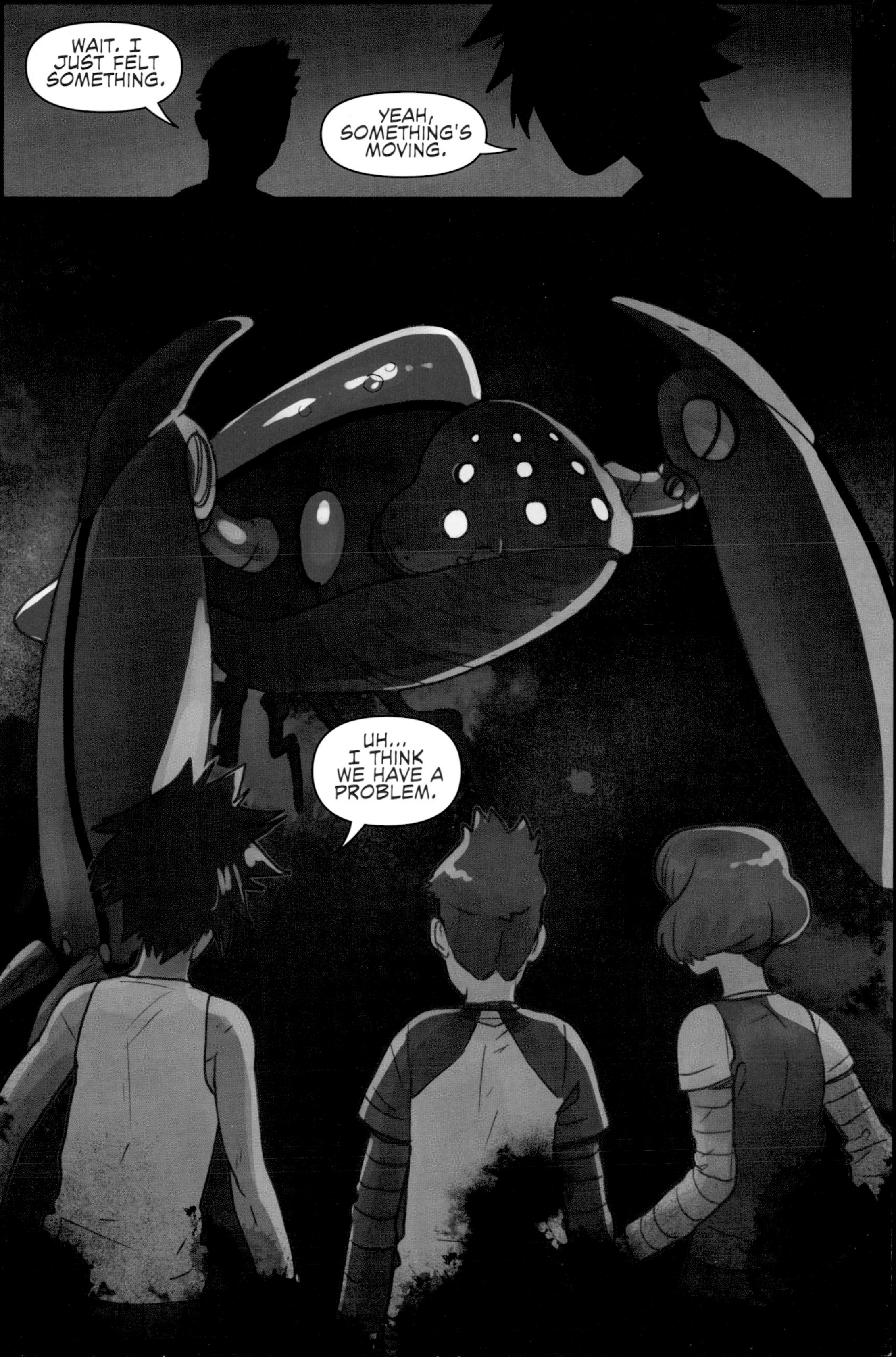

WAIT. I JUST FELT SOMETHING.
YEAH, SOMETHING'S MOVING.
UH... I THINK WE HAVE A PROBLEM.

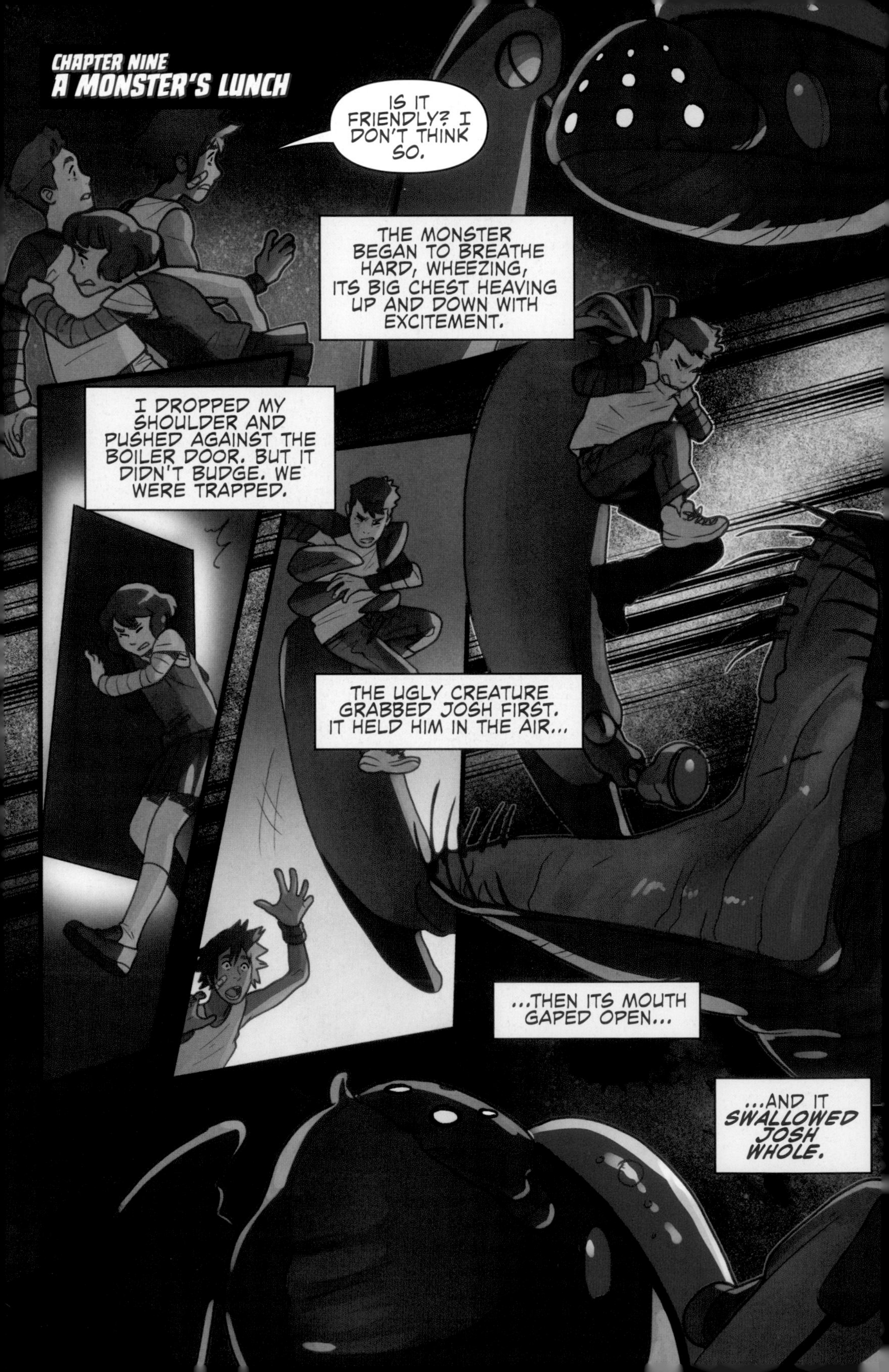
CHAPTER NINE
A MONSTER'S LUNCH
IS IT FRIENDLY? I DON'T THINK SO.
THE MONSTER BEGAN TO BREATHE HARD, WHEEZING, ITS BIG CHEST HEAVING UP AND DOWN WITH EXCITEMENT.
I DROPPED MY SHOULDER AND PUSHED AGAINST THE BOILER DOOR. BUT IT DIDN'T BUDGE. WE WERE TRAPPED.
THE UGLY CREATURE GRABBED JOSH FIRST. IT HELD HIM IN THE AIR...
...THEN ITS MOUTH GAPED OPEN...
...AND IT *SWALLOWED JOSH WHOLE*.

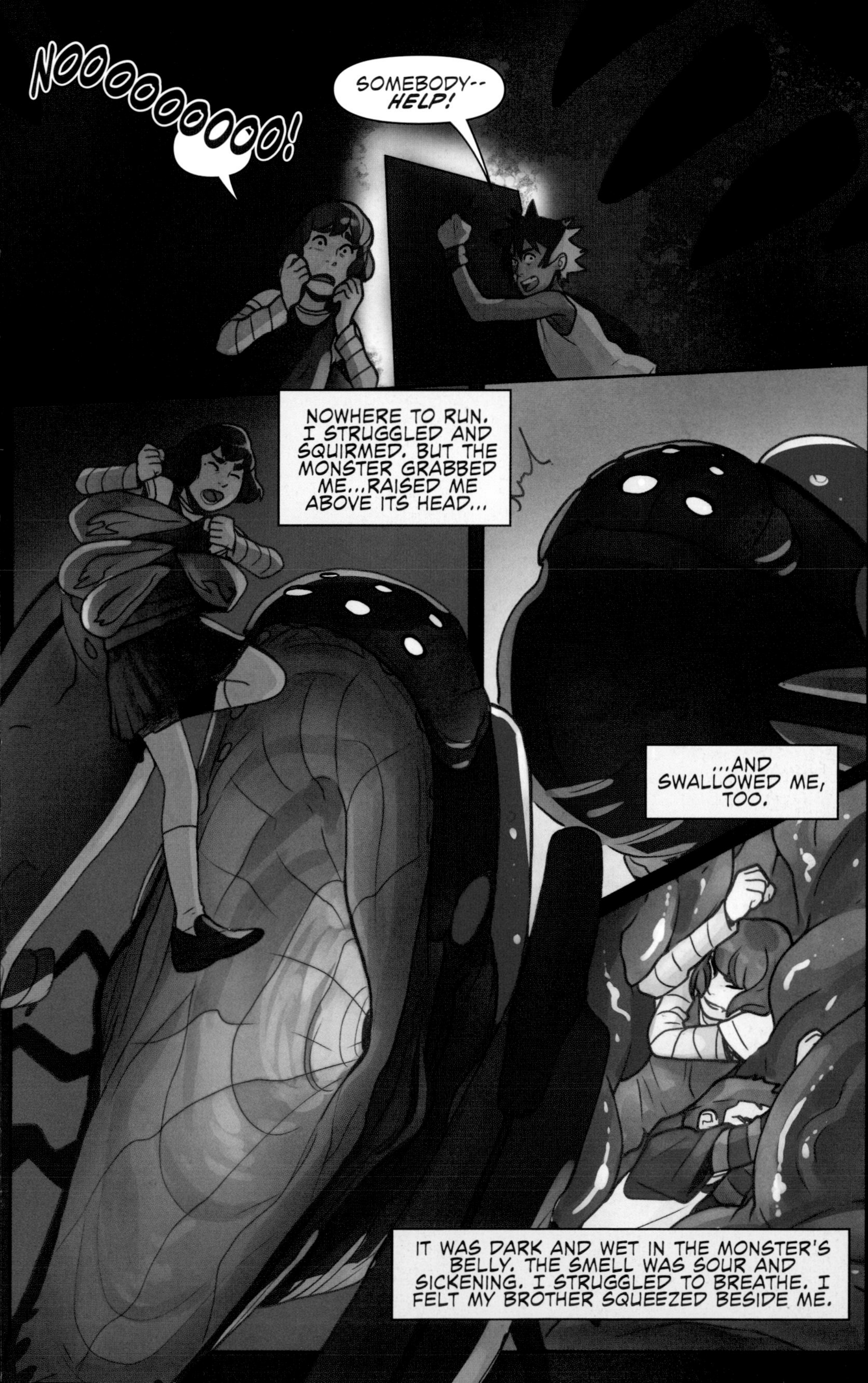
NOOOOOOOOOO!
SOMEBODY-- HELP!
NOWHERE TO RUN. I STRUGGLED AND SQUIRMED. BUT THE MONSTER GRABBED ME...RAISED ME ABOVE ITS HEAD...
...AND SWALLOWED ME, TOO.
IT WAS DARK AND WET IN THE MONSTER'S BELLY. THE SMELL WAS SOUR AND SICKENING. I STRUGGLED TO BREATHE. I FELT MY BROTHER SQUEEZED BESIDE ME.

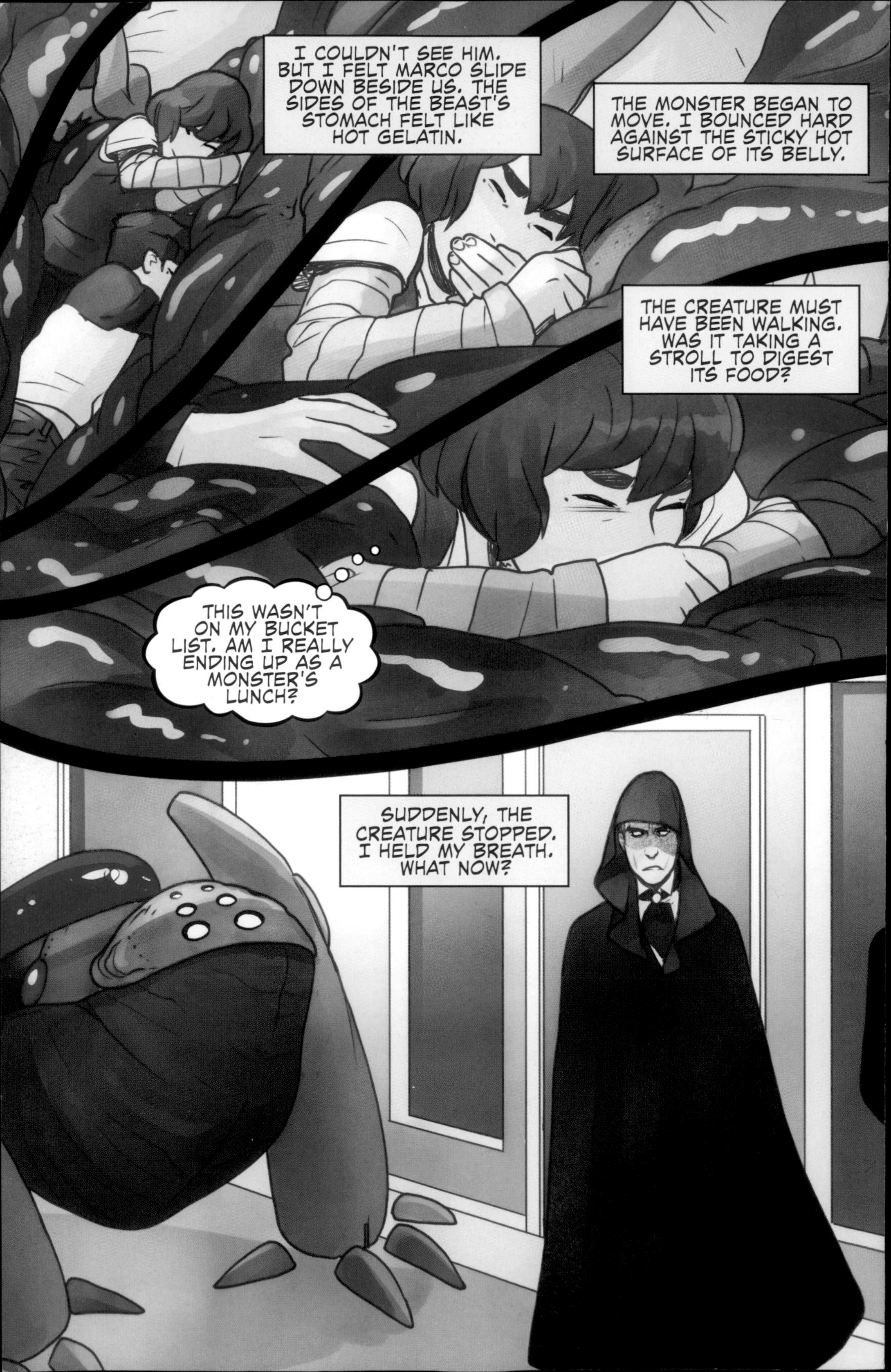
I COULDN'T SEE HIM. BUT I FELT MARCO SLIDE DOWN BESIDE US. THE SIDES OF THE BEAST'S STOMACH FELT LIKE HOT GELATIN.
THE MONSTER BEGAN TO MOVE. I BOUNCED HARD AGAINST THE STICKY HOT SURFACE OF ITS BELLY.
THE CREATURE MUST HAVE BEEN WALKING. WAS IT TAKING A STROLL TO DIGEST ITS FOOD?
THIS WASN'T ON MY BUCKET LIST. AM I REALLY ENDING UP AS A MONSTER'S LUNCH?
SUDDENLY, THE CREATURE STOPPED. I HELD MY BREATH. WHAT NOW?

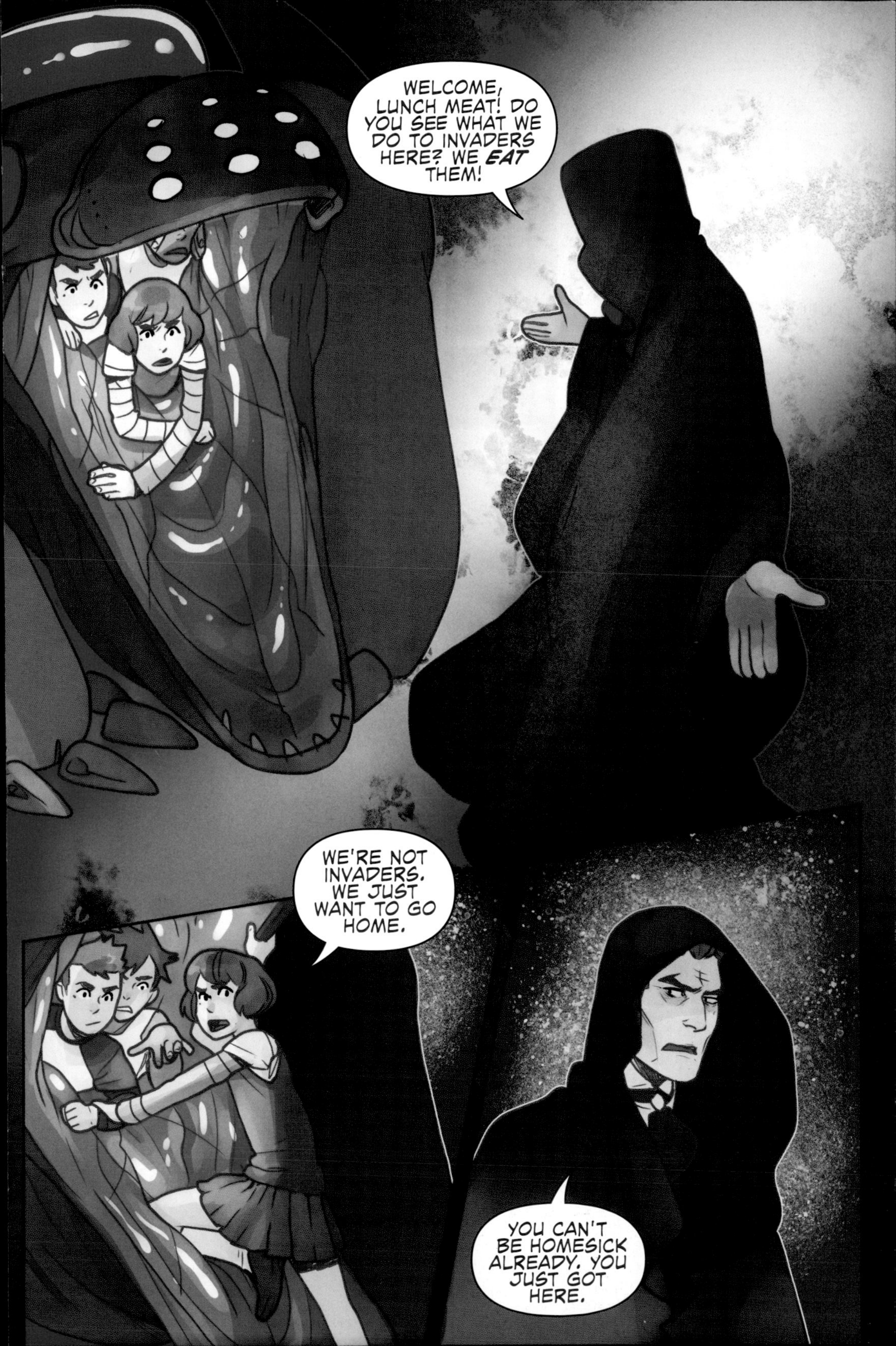
WELCOME, LUNCH MEAT! DO YOU SEE WHAT WE DO TO INVADERS HERE? WE *EAT* THEM!
WE'RE NOT INVADERS. WE JUST WANT TO GO HOME.
YOU CAN'T BE HOMESICK ALREADY. YOU JUST GOT HERE.

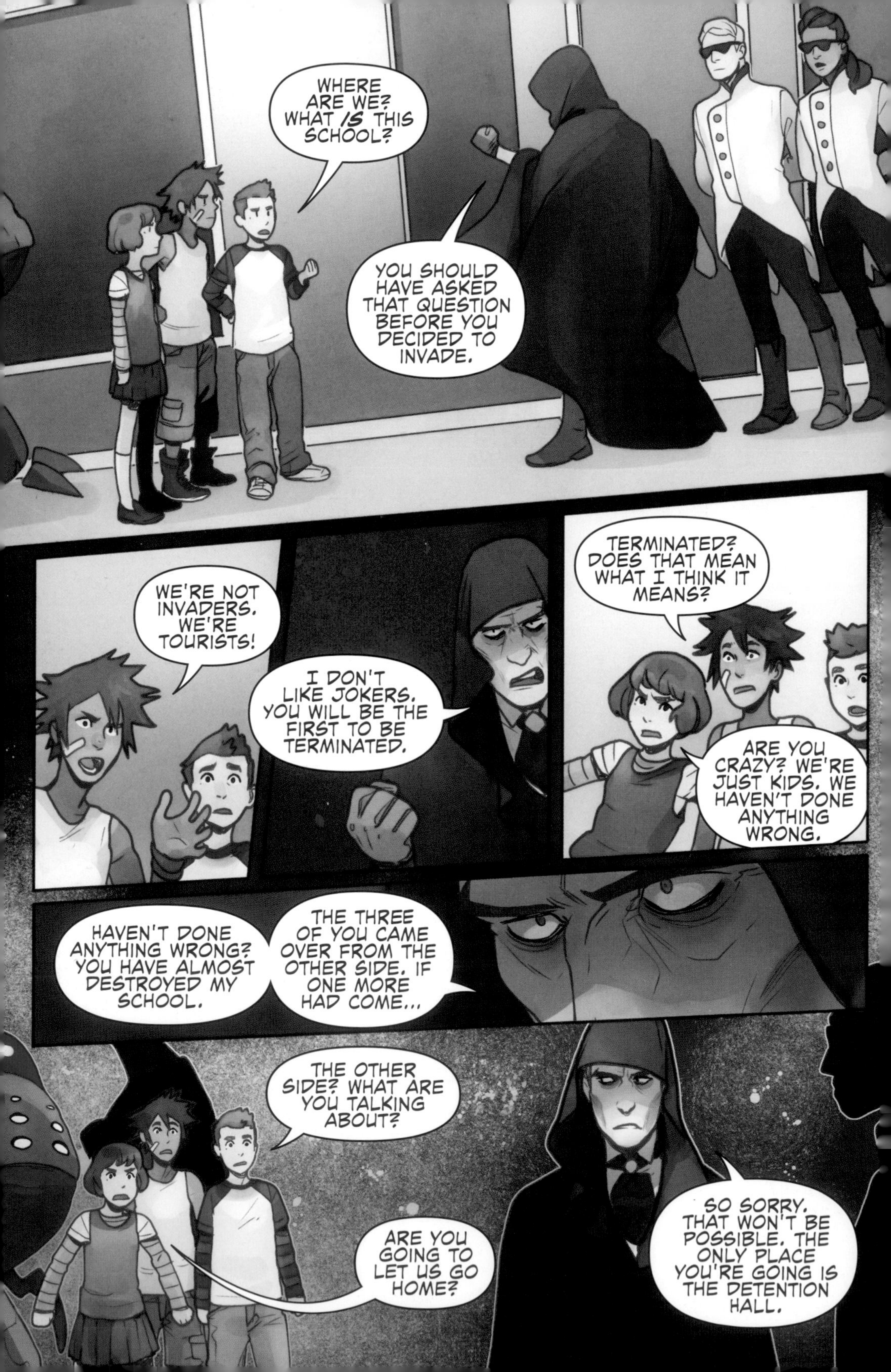
WHERE ARE WE? WHAT IS THIS SCHOOL?
YOU SHOULD HAVE ASKED THAT QUESTION BEFORE YOU DECIDED TO INVADE.
WE'RE NOT INVADERS. WE'RE TOURISTS!
I DON'T LIKE JOKERS. YOU WILL BE THE FIRST TO BE TERMINATED.
TERMINATED? DOES THAT MEAN WHAT I THINK IT MEANS?
ARE YOU CRAZY? WE'RE JUST KIDS. WE HAVEN'T DONE ANYTHING WRONG.
HAVEN'T DONE ANYTHING WRONG? YOU HAVE ALMOST DESTROYED MY SCHOOL.
THE THREE OF YOU CAME OVER FROM THE OTHER SIDE. IF ONE MORE HAD COME...
THE OTHER SIDE? WHAT ARE YOU TALKING ABOUT?
ARE YOU GOING TO LET US GO HOME?
SO SORRY. THAT WON'T BE POSSIBLE. THE ONLY PLACE YOU'RE GOING IS THE DETENTION HALL.

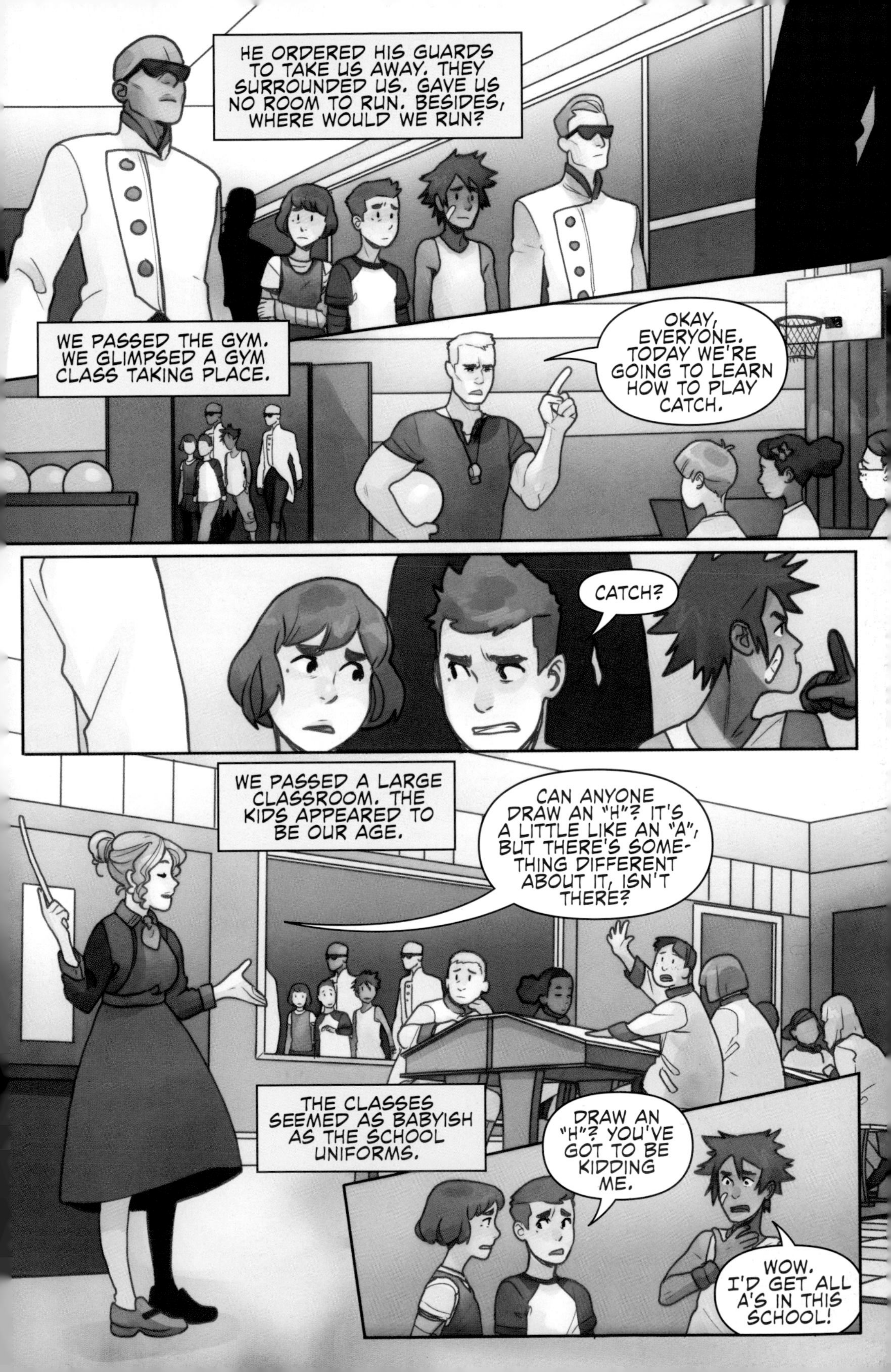
HE ORDERED HIS GUARDS TO TAKE US AWAY. THEY SURROUNDED US. GAVE US NO ROOM TO RUN. BESIDES, WHERE WOULD WE RUN?
WE PASSED THE GYM. WE GLIMPSED A GYM CLASS TAKING PLACE.
OKAY, EVERYONE. TODAY WE'RE GOING TO LEARN HOW TO PLAY CATCH.
CATCH?
WE PASSED A LARGE CLASSROOM. THE KIDS APPEARED TO BE OUR AGE.
CAN ANYONE DRAW AN "H"? IT'S A LITTLE LIKE AN "A", BUT THERE'S SOMETHING DIFFERENT ABOUT IT, ISN'T THERE?
THE CLASSES SEEMED AS BABYISH AS THE SCHOOL UNIFORMS.
DRAW AN "H"? YOU'VE GOT TO BE KIDDING ME.
WOW. I'D GET ALL A'S IN THIS SCHOOL!

CHAPTER TEN
TERMINATED

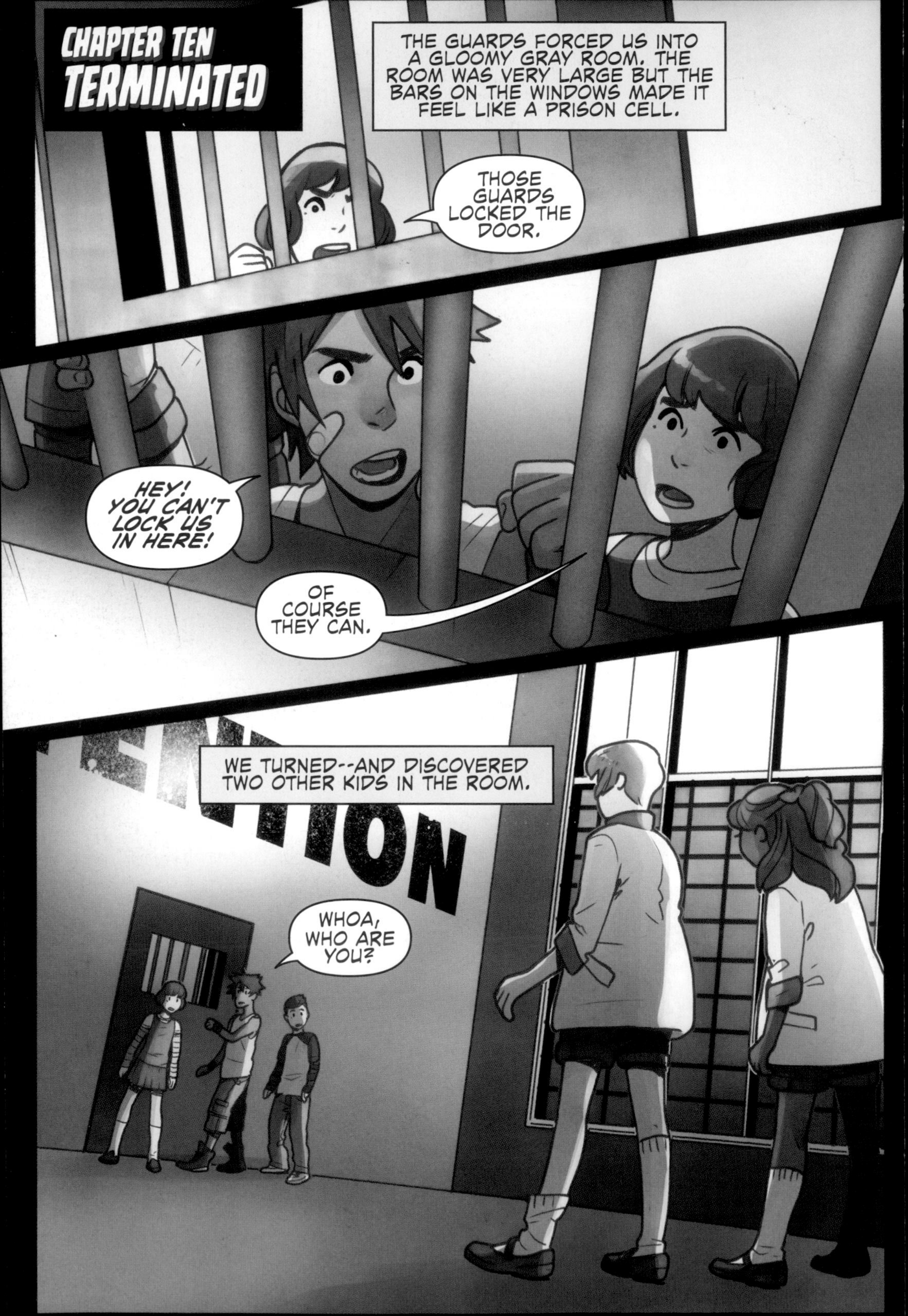
THE GUARDS FORCED US INTO A GLOOMY GRAY ROOM. THE ROOM WAS VERY LARGE BUT THE BARS ON THE WINDOWS MADE IT FEEL LIKE A PRISON CELL.
THOSE GUARDS LOCKED THE DOOR.
HEY! YOU CAN'T LOCK US IN HERE!
OF COURSE THEY CAN.
WE TURNED--AND DISCOVERED TWO OTHER KIDS IN THE ROOM.
WHOA, WHO ARE YOU?

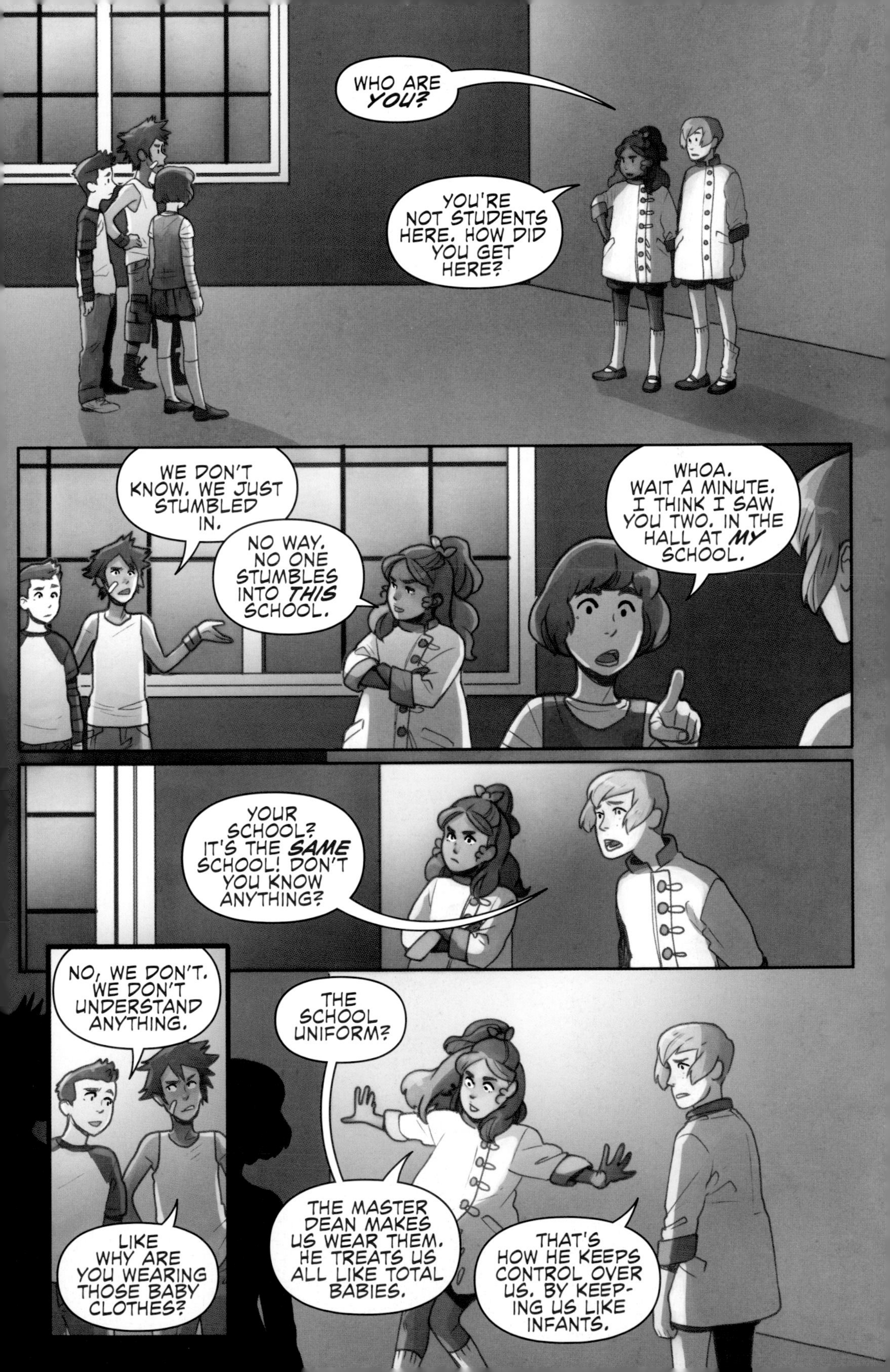
WHO ARE *YOU?*
YOU'RE NOT STUDENTS HERE. HOW DID YOU GET HERE?
WE DON'T KNOW. WE JUST STUMBLED IN.
NO WAY. NO ONE STUMBLES INTO *THIS* SCHOOL.
WHOA. WAIT A MINUTE. I THINK I SAW YOU TWO. IN THE HALL AT *MY* SCHOOL.
YOUR SCHOOL? IT'S THE *SAME* SCHOOL! DON'T YOU KNOW ANYTHING?
NO, WE DON'T. WE DON'T UNDERSTAND ANYTHING.
LIKE WHY ARE YOU WEARING THOSE BABY CLOTHES?
THE SCHOOL UNIFORM?
THE MASTER DEAN MAKES US WEAR THEM. HE TREATS US ALL LIKE TOTAL BABIES.
THAT'S HOW HE KEEPS CONTROL OVER US, BY KEEP-ING US LIKE INFANTS.

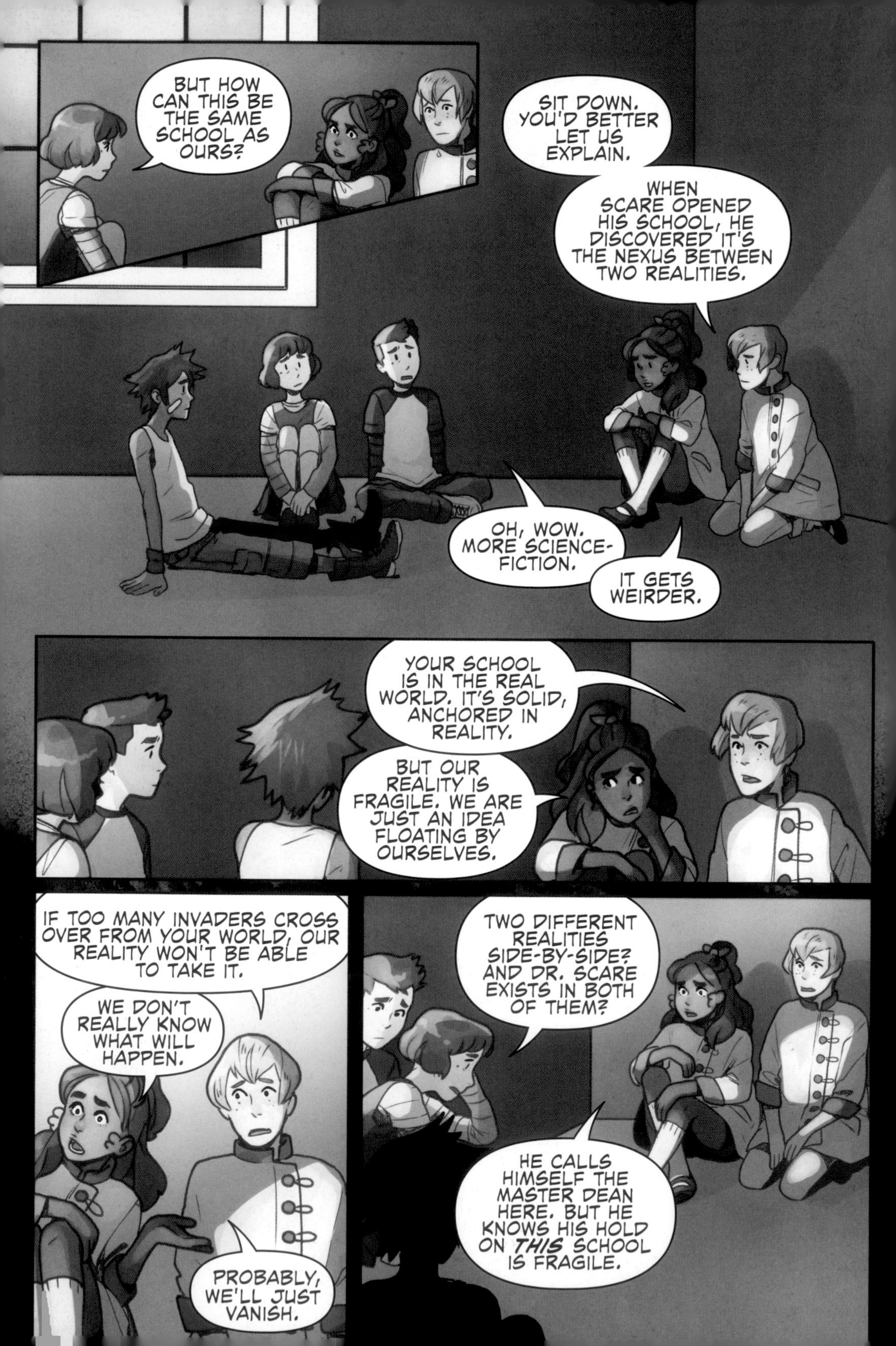
BUT HOW CAN THIS BE THE SAME SCHOOL AS OURS?
SIT DOWN. YOU'D BETTER LET US EXPLAIN.
WHEN SCARE OPENED HIS SCHOOL, HE DISCOVERED IT'S THE NEXUS BETWEEN TWO REALITIES.
OH, WOW. MORE SCIENCE-FICTION.
IT GETS WEIRDER.
YOUR SCHOOL IS IN THE REAL WORLD. IT'S SOLID, ANCHORED IN REALITY.
BUT OUR REALITY IS FRAGILE. WE ARE JUST AN IDEA FLOATING BY OURSELVES.
IF TOO MANY INVADERS CROSS OVER FROM YOUR WORLD, OUR REALITY WON'T BE ABLE TO TAKE IT.
WE DON'T REALLY KNOW WHAT WILL HAPPEN.
PROBABLY, WE'LL JUST VANISH.
TWO DIFFERENT REALITIES SIDE-BY-SIDE? AND DR. SCARE EXISTS IN BOTH OF THEM?
HE CALLS HIMSELF THE MASTER DEAN HERE. BUT HE KNOWS HIS HOLD ON THIS SCHOOL IS FRAGILE.

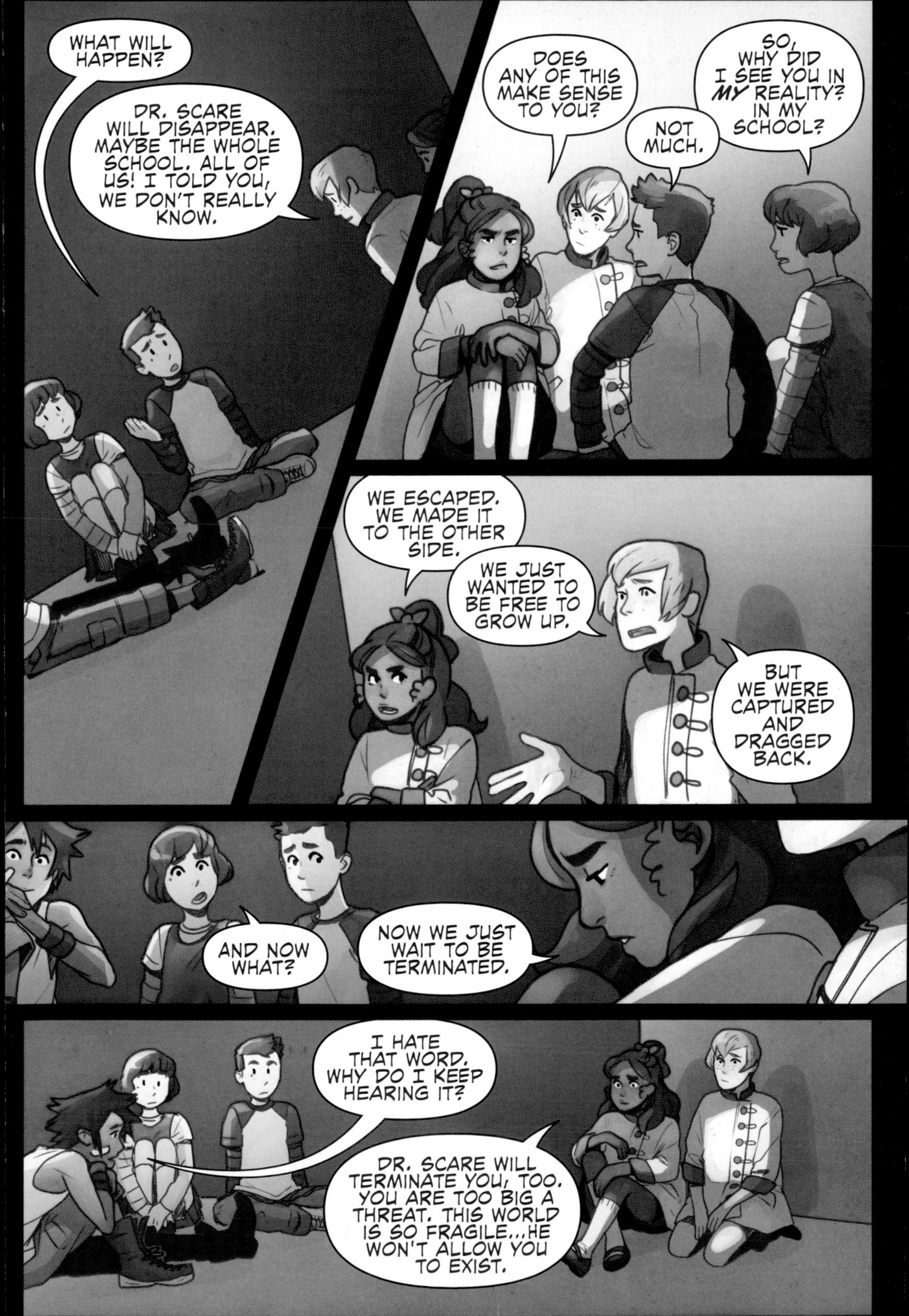
WHAT WILL HAPPEN?
DR. SCARE WILL DISAPPEAR. MAYBE THE WHOLE SCHOOL. ALL OF US! I TOLD YOU, WE DON'T REALLY KNOW.
DOES ANY OF THIS MAKE SENSE TO YOU?
NOT MUCH.
SO, WHY DID I SEE YOU IN *MY* REALITY? IN MY SCHOOL?
WE ESCAPED. WE MADE IT TO THE OTHER SIDE.
WE JUST WANTED TO BE FREE TO GROW UP.
BUT WE WERE CAPTURED AND DRAGGED BACK.
AND NOW WHAT?
NOW WE JUST WAIT TO BE TERMINATED.
I HATE THAT WORD. WHY DO I KEEP HEARING IT?
DR. SCARE WILL TERMINATE YOU, TOO. YOU ARE TOO BIG A THREAT. THIS WORLD IS SO FRAGILE...HE WON'T ALLOW YOU TO EXIST.

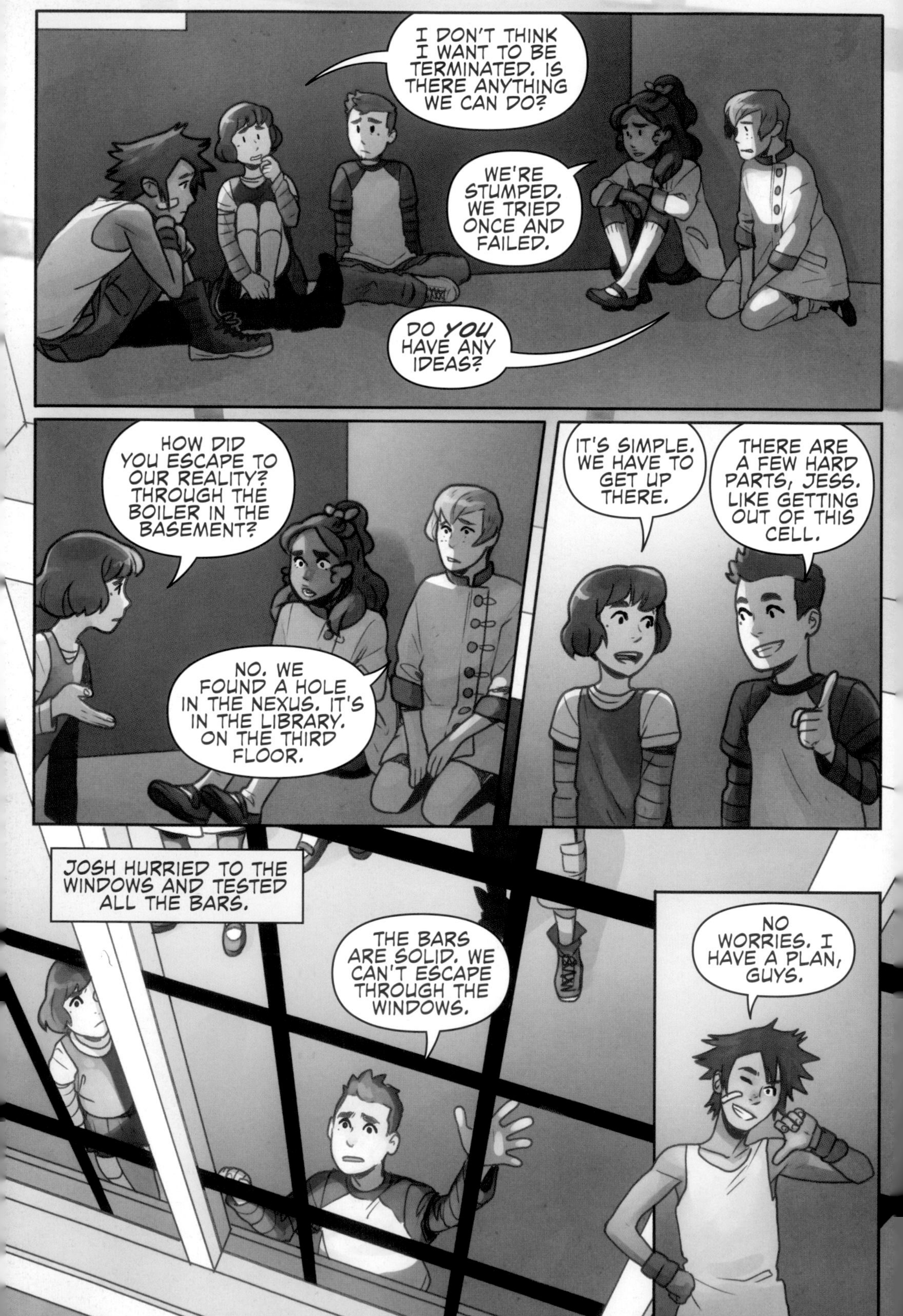
I DON'T THINK I WANT TO BE TERMINATED. IS THERE ANYTHING WE CAN DO?
WE'RE STUMPED. WE TRIED ONCE AND FAILED.
DO *YOU* HAVE ANY IDEAS?
HOW DID YOU ESCAPE TO OUR REALITY? THROUGH THE BOILER IN THE BASEMENT?
NO. WE FOUND A HOLE IN THE NEXUS. IT'S IN THE LIBRARY. ON THE THIRD FLOOR.
IT'S SIMPLE. WE HAVE TO GET UP THERE.
THERE ARE A FEW HARD PARTS, JESS. LIKE GETTING OUT OF THIS CELL.
JOSH HURRIED TO THE WINDOWS AND TESTED ALL THE BARS.
THE BARS ARE SOLID. WE CAN'T ESCAPE THROUGH THE WINDOWS.
NO WORRIES. I HAVE A PLAN, GUYS.

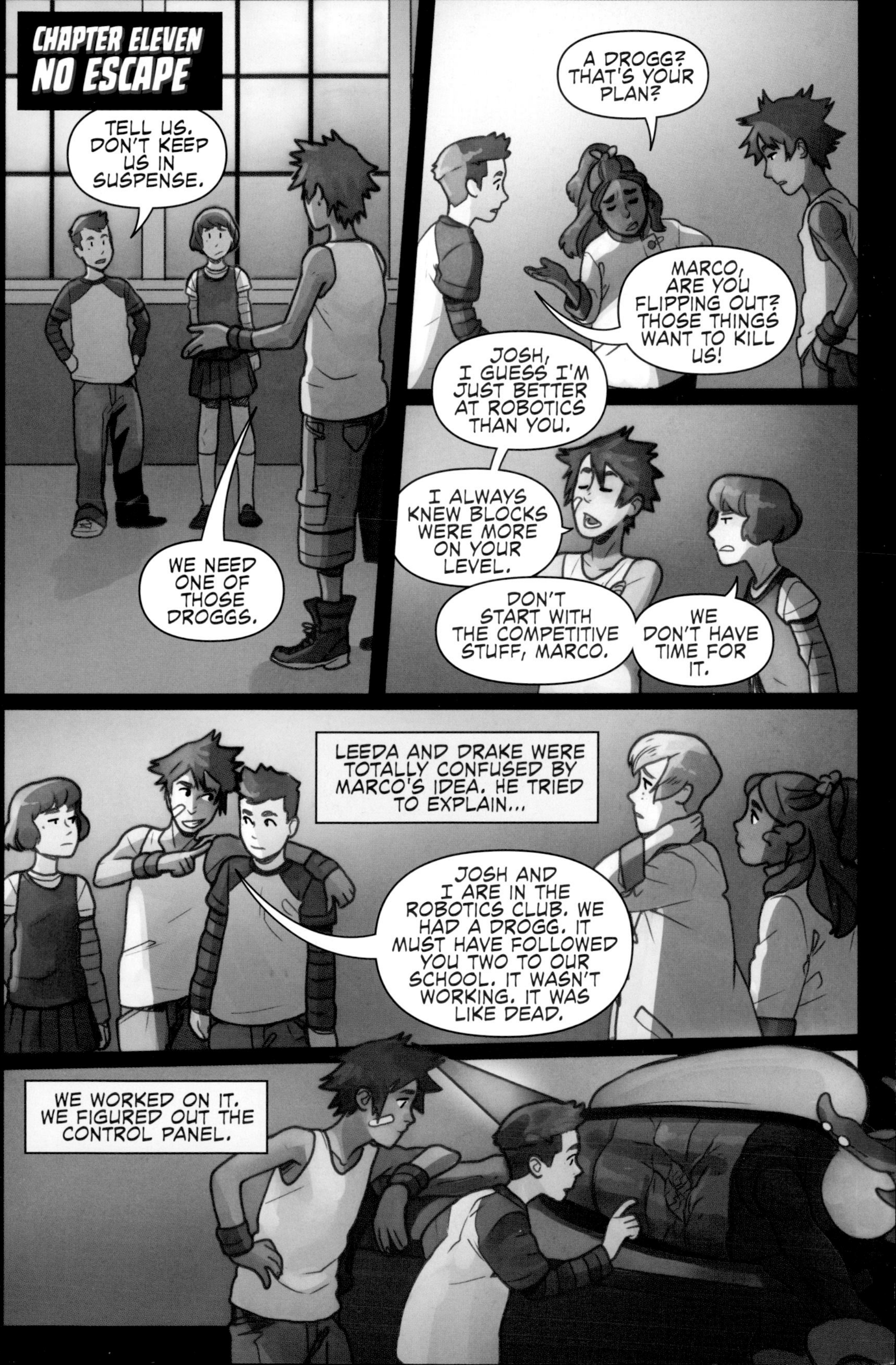
CHAPTER ELEVEN
NO ESCAPE
TELL US. DON'T KEEP US IN SUSPENSE.
WE NEED ONE OF THOSE DROGGS.
A DROGG? THAT'S YOUR PLAN?
MARCO, ARE YOU FLIPPING OUT? THOSE THINGS WANT TO KILL US!
JOSH, I GUESS I'M JUST BETTER AT ROBOTICS THAN YOU.
I ALWAYS KNEW BLOCKS WERE MORE ON YOUR LEVEL.
DON'T START WITH THE COMPETITIVE STUFF, MARCO.
WE DON'T HAVE TIME FOR IT.
LEEDA AND DRAKE WERE TOTALLY CONFUSED BY MARCO'S IDEA. HE TRIED TO EXPLAIN...
JOSH AND I ARE IN THE ROBOTICS CLUB. WE HAD A DROGG. IT MUST HAVE FOLLOWED YOU TWO TO OUR SCHOOL. IT WASN'T WORKING. IT WAS LIKE DEAD.
WE WORKED ON IT. WE FIGURED OUT THE CONTROL PANEL.

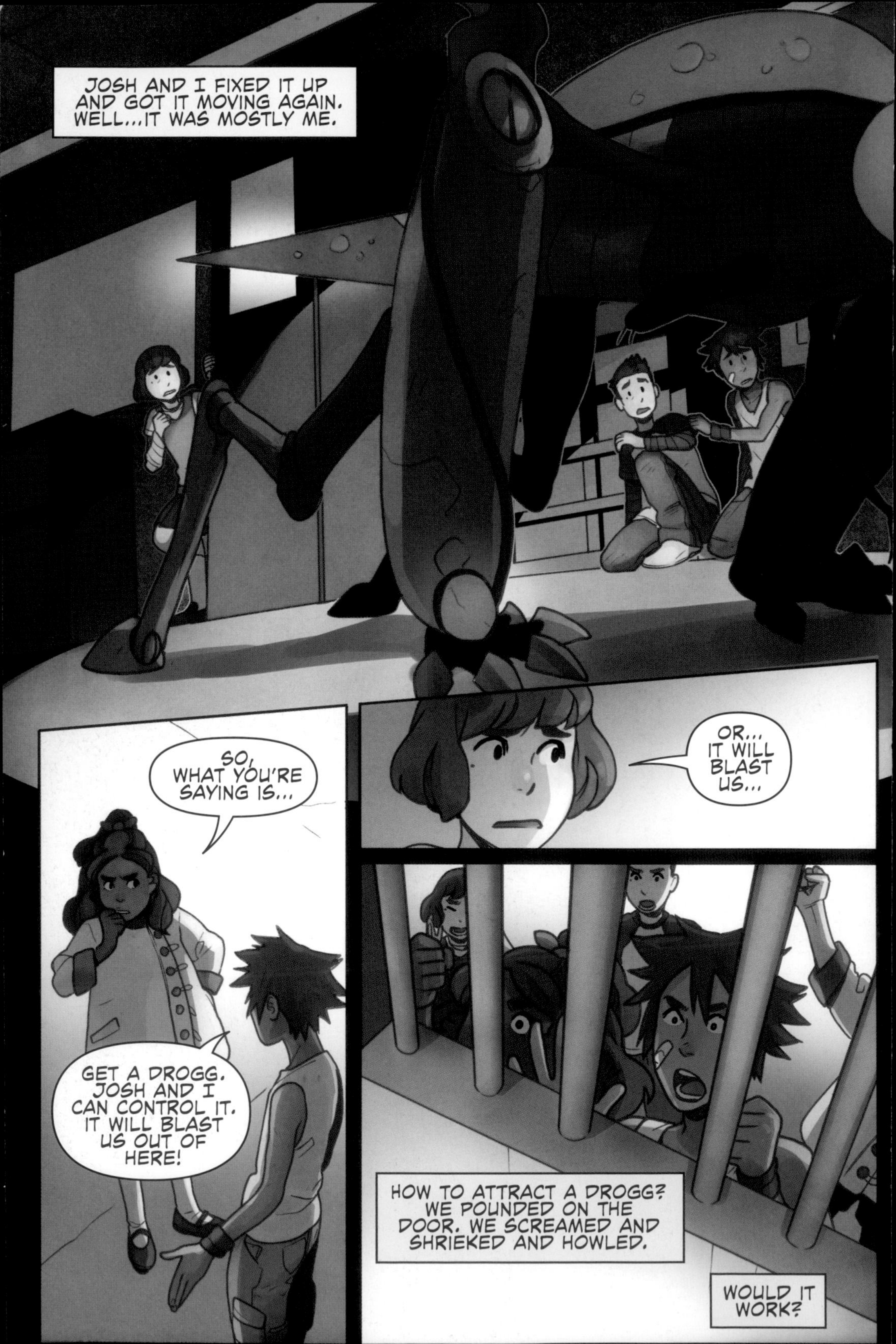
JOSH AND I FIXED IT UP AND GOT IT MOVING AGAIN. WELL...IT WAS MOSTLY ME.
SO, WHAT YOU'RE SAYING IS...
OR... IT WILL BLAST US...
GET A DROGG. JOSH AND I CAN CONTROL IT. IT WILL BLAST US OUT OF HERE!
HOW TO ATTRACT A DROGG? WE POUNDED ON THE DOOR. WE SCREAMED AND SHRIEKED AND HOWLED.
WOULD IT WORK?

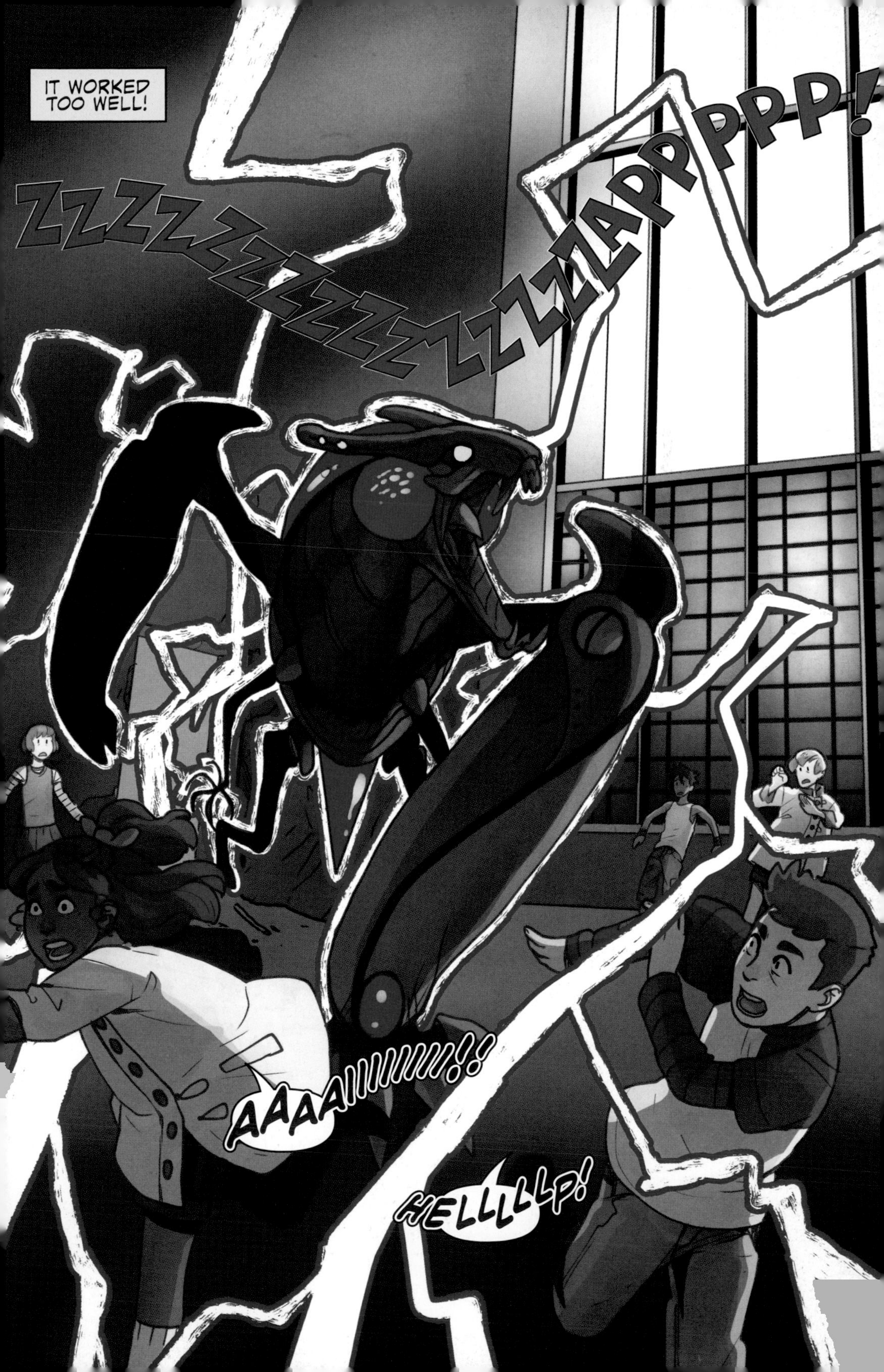
IT WORKED TOO WELL!
ZZZZZZZZZZZZZZZZZZAPPPPPP!
AAAAIIIIIIIIII!!
HELLLLLP!

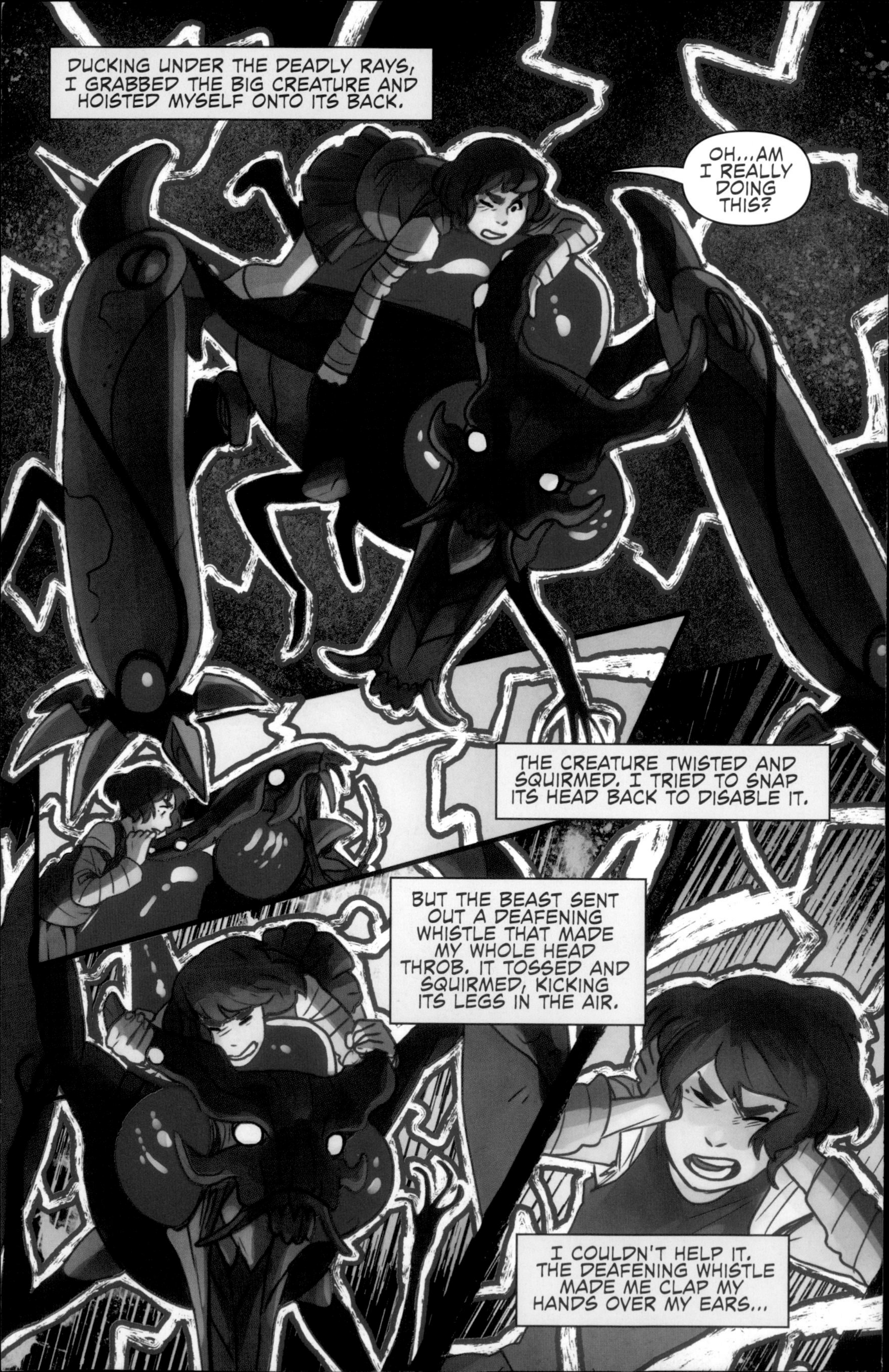
DUCKING UNDER THE DEADLY RAYS, I GRABBED THE BIG CREATURE AND HOISTED MYSELF ONTO ITS BACK.
OH...AM I REALLY DOING THIS?
THE CREATURE TWISTED AND SQUIRMED. I TRIED TO SNAP ITS HEAD BACK TO DISABLE IT.
BUT THE BEAST SENT OUT A DEAFENING WHISTLE THAT MADE MY WHOLE HEAD THROB. IT TOSSED AND SQUIRMED, KICKING ITS LEGS IN THE AIR.
I COULDN'T HELP IT. THE DEAFENING WHISTLE MADE ME CLAP MY HANDS OVER MY EARS...

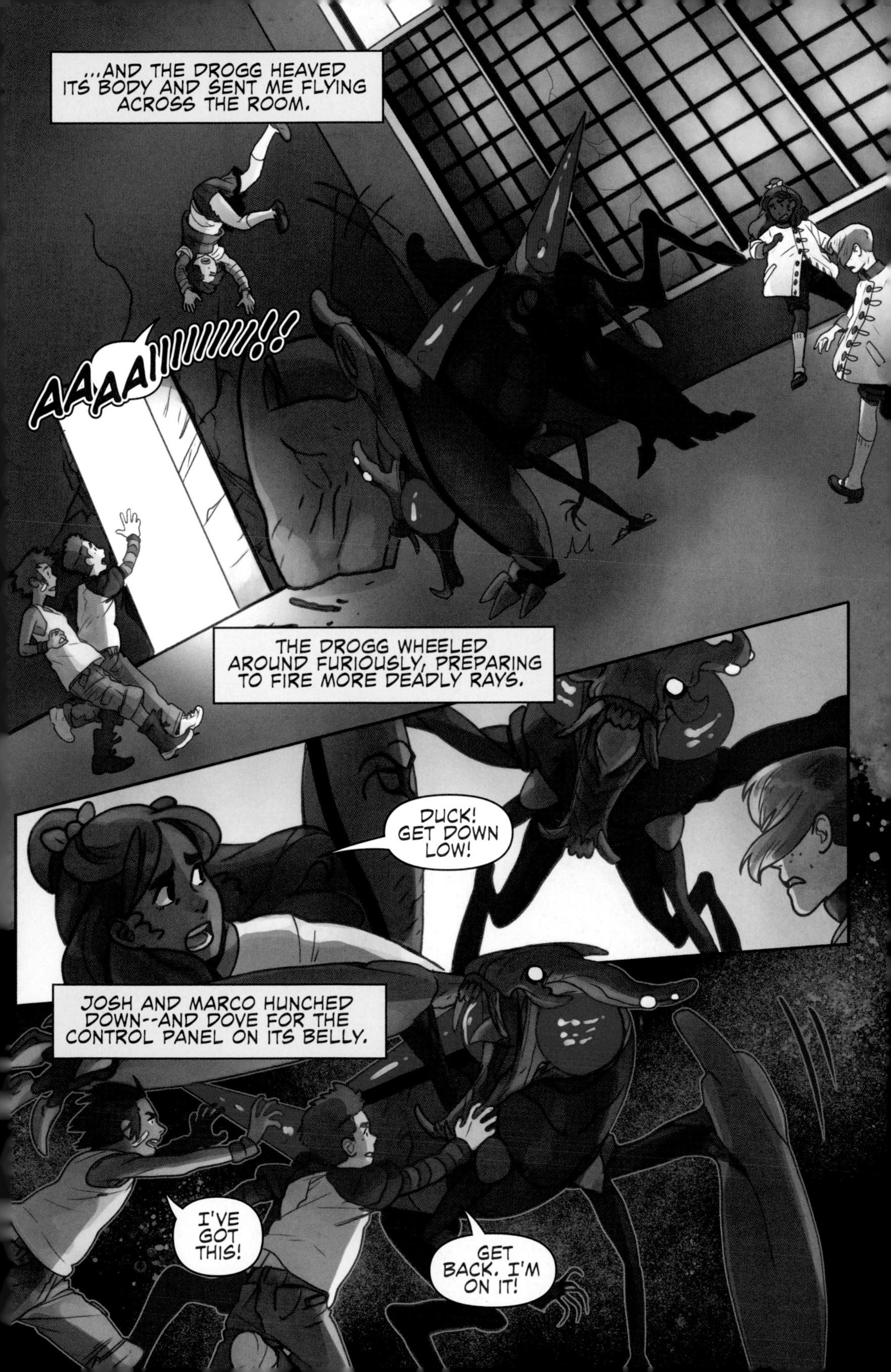
...AND THE DROGG HEAVED ITS BODY AND SENT ME FLYING ACROSS THE ROOM.
AAAAIIIIIIIII!!
THE DROGG WHEELED AROUND FURIOUSLY, PREPARING TO FIRE MORE DEADLY RAYS.
DUCK! GET DOWN LOW!
JOSH AND MARCO HUNCHED DOWN--AND DOVE FOR THE CONTROL PANEL ON ITS BELLY.
I'VE GOT THIS!
GET BACK. I'M ON IT!

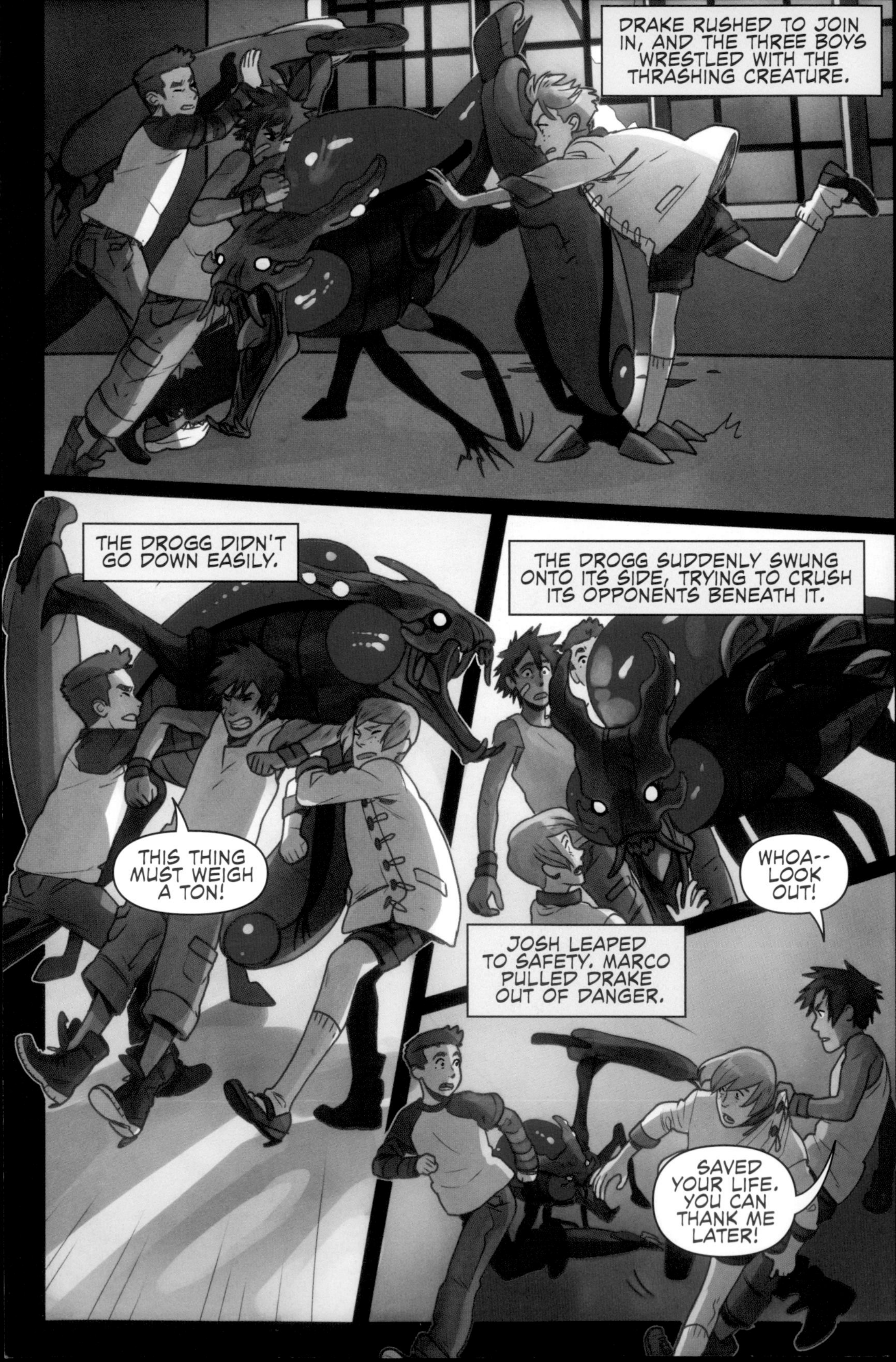
DRAKE RUSHED TO JOIN IN, AND THE THREE BOYS WRESTLED WITH THE THRASHING CREATURE.
THE DROGG DIDN'T GO DOWN EASILY.
THIS THING MUST WEIGH A TON!
THE DROGG SUDDENLY SWUNG ONTO ITS SIDE, TRYING TO CRUSH ITS OPPONENTS BENEATH IT.
WHOA--LOOK OUT!
JOSH LEAPED TO SAFETY. MARCO PULLED DRAKE OUT OF DANGER.
SAVED YOUR LIFE. YOU CAN THANK ME LATER!

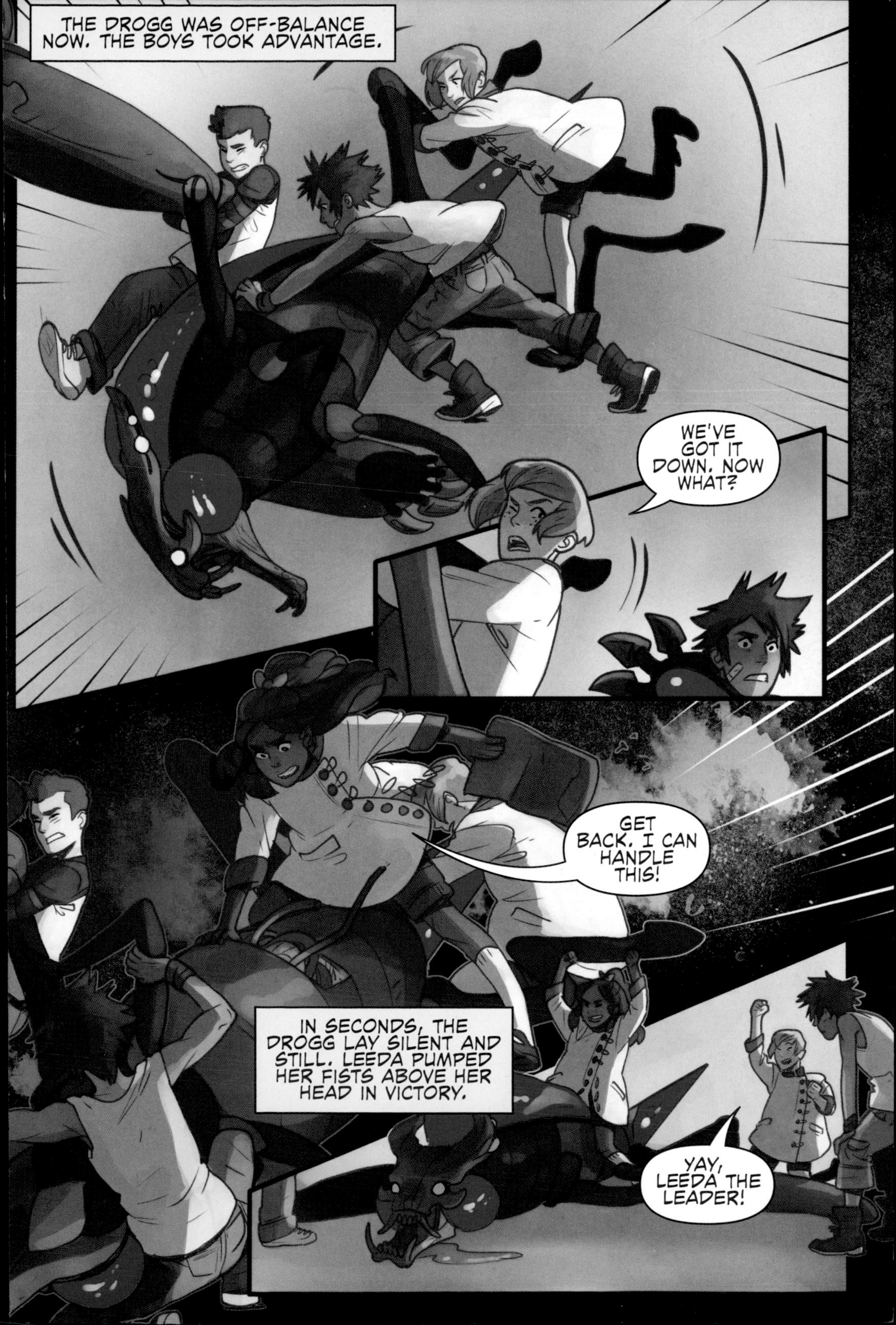
THE DROGG WAS OFF-BALANCE NOW. THE BOYS TOOK ADVANTAGE.
WE'VE GOT IT DOWN. NOW WHAT?
GET BACK. I CAN HANDLE THIS!
IN SECONDS, THE DROGG LAY SILENT AND STILL. LEEDA PUMPED HER FISTS ABOVE HER HEAD IN VICTORY.
YAY, LEEDA THE LEADER!

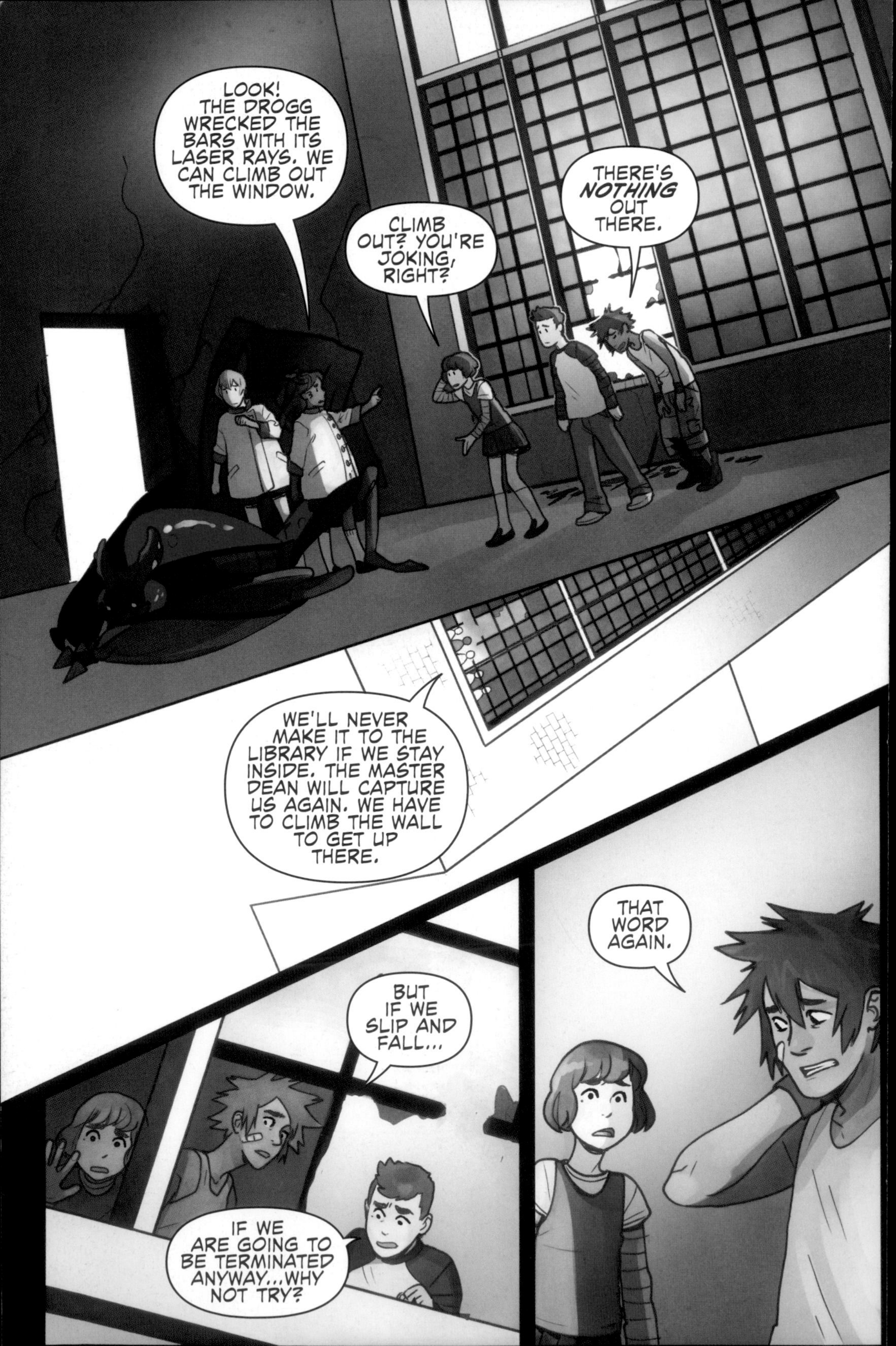
LOOK! THE DROGG WRECKED THE BARS WITH ITS LASER RAYS. WE CAN CLIMB OUT THE WINDOW.
CLIMB OUT? YOU'RE JOKING, RIGHT?
THERE'S *NOTHING* OUT THERE.
WE'LL NEVER MAKE IT TO THE LIBRARY IF WE STAY INSIDE. THE MASTER DEAN WILL CAPTURE US AGAIN. WE HAVE TO CLIMB THE WALL TO GET UP THERE.
BUT IF WE SLIP AND FALL...
IF WE ARE GOING TO BE TERMINATED ANYWAY...WHY NOT TRY?
THAT WORD AGAIN.

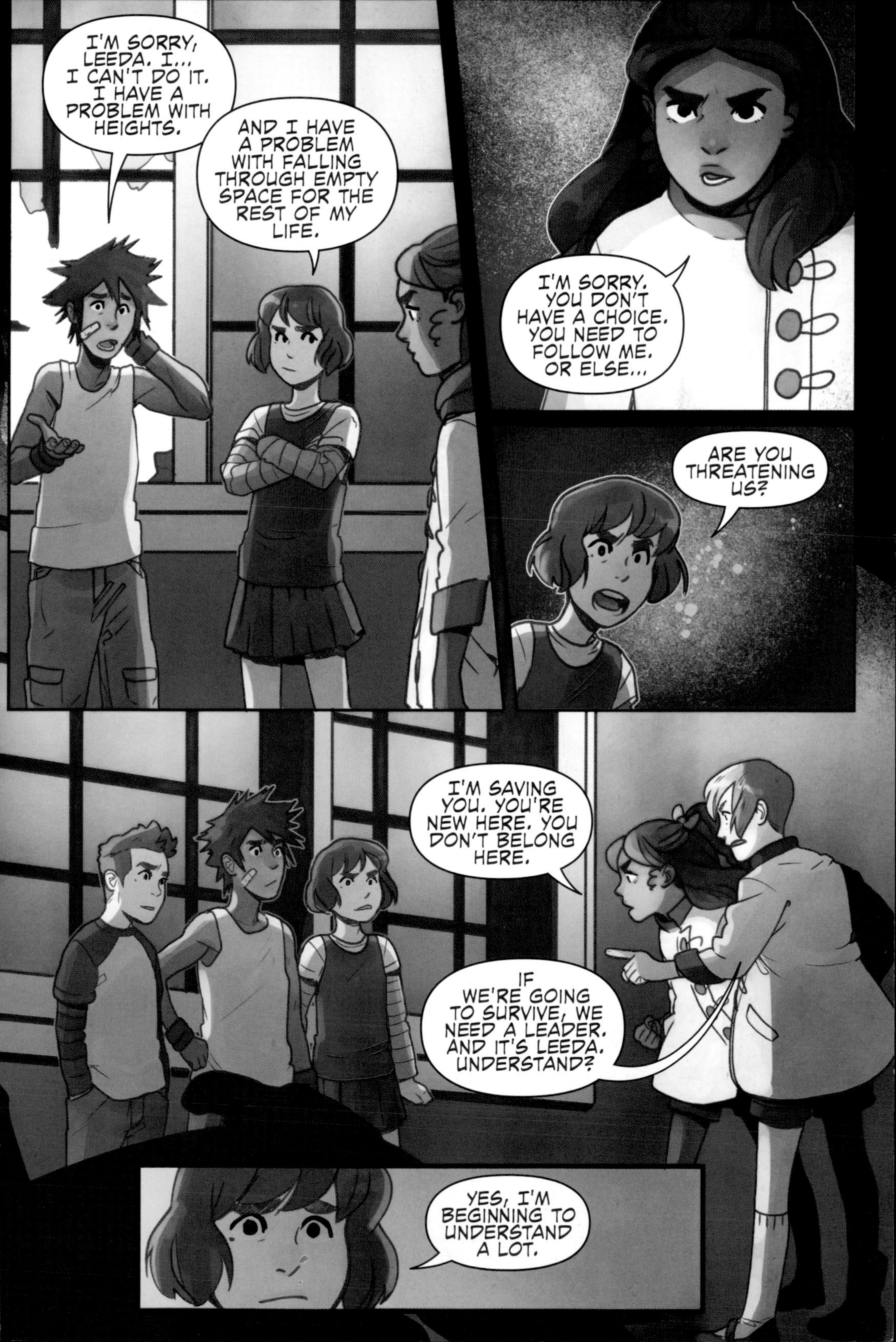
I'M SORRY, LEEDA. I... I CAN'T DO IT. I HAVE A PROBLEM WITH HEIGHTS.
AND I HAVE A PROBLEM WITH FALLING THROUGH EMPTY SPACE FOR THE REST OF MY LIFE.
I'M SORRY. YOU DON'T HAVE A CHOICE. YOU NEED TO FOLLOW ME. OR ELSE...
ARE YOU THREATENING US?
I'M SAVING YOU. YOU'RE NEW HERE. YOU DON'T BELONG HERE.
IF WE'RE GOING TO SURVIVE, WE NEED A LEADER. AND IT'S LEEDA. UNDERSTAND?
YES, I'M BEGINNING TO UNDERSTAND A LOT.

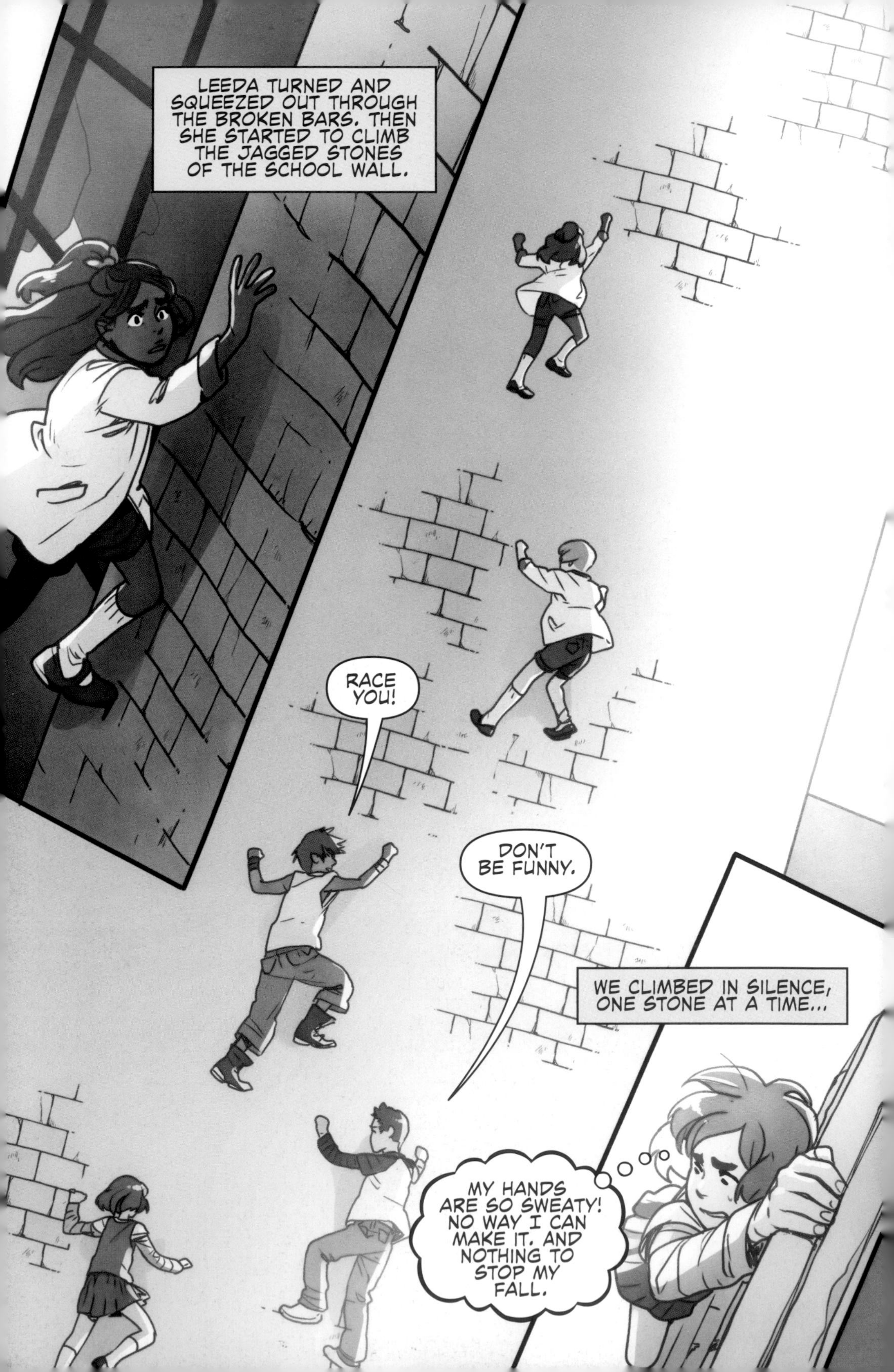
LEEDA TURNED AND SQUEEZED OUT THROUGH THE BROKEN BARS. THEN SHE STARTED TO CLIMB THE JAGGED STONES OF THE SCHOOL WALL.
RACE YOU!
DON'T BE FUNNY.
WE CLIMBED IN SILENCE, ONE STONE AT A TIME...
MY HANDS ARE SO SWEATY! NO WAY I CAN MAKE IT. AND NOTHING TO STOP MY FALL.

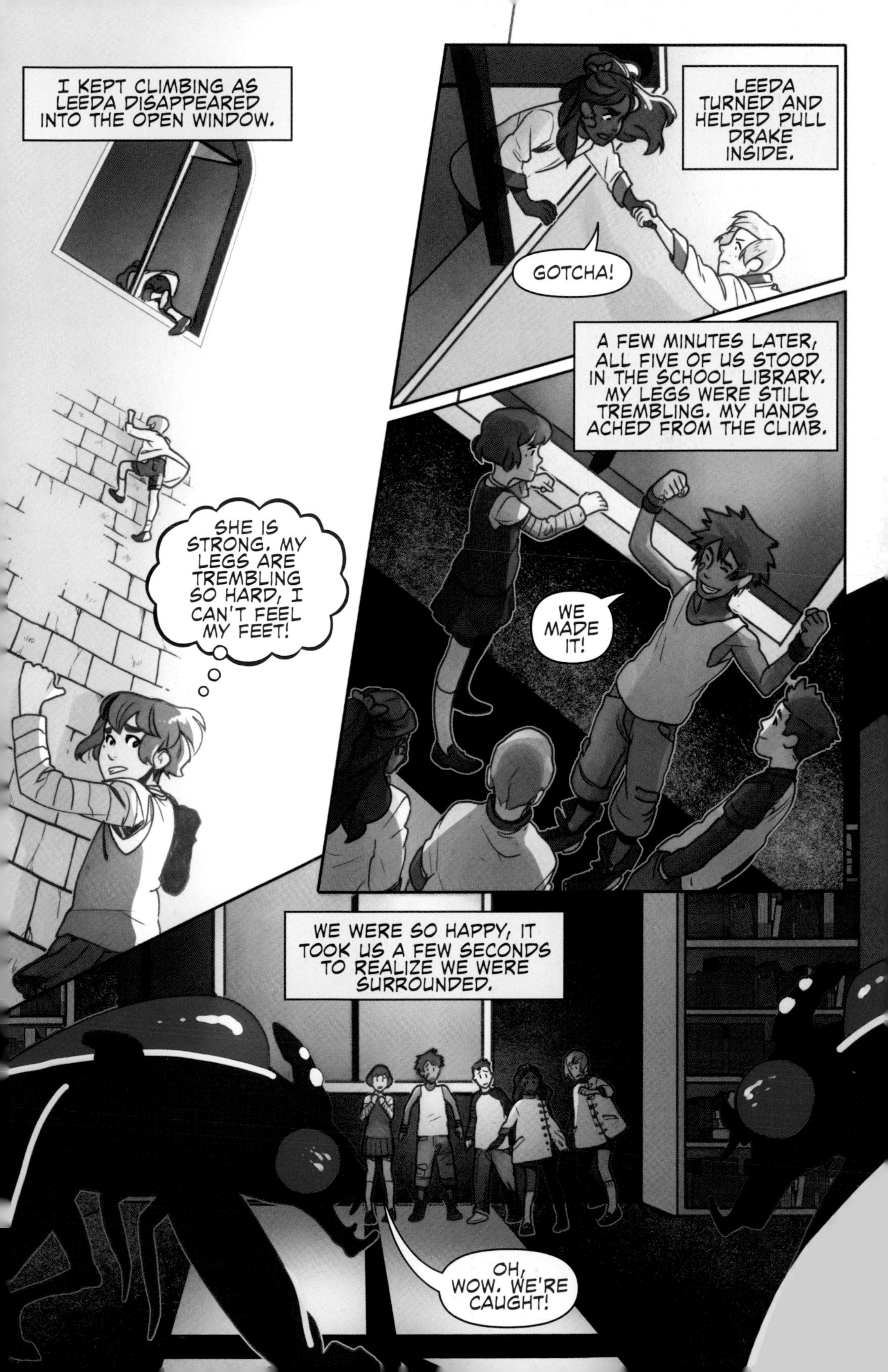
I KEPT CLIMBING AS LEEDA DISAPPEARED INTO THE OPEN WINDOW.
LEEDA TURNED AND HELPED PULL DRAKE INSIDE.
GOTCHA!
SHE IS STRONG. MY LEGS ARE TREMBLING SO HARD, I CAN'T FEEL MY FEET!
A FEW MINUTES LATER, ALL FIVE OF US STOOD IN THE SCHOOL LIBRARY. MY LEGS WERE STILL TREMBLING. MY HANDS ACHED FROM THE CLIMB.
WE MADE IT!
WE WERE SO HAPPY, IT TOOK US A FEW SECONDS TO REALIZE WE WERE SURROUNDED.
OH, WOW. WE'RE CAUGHT!

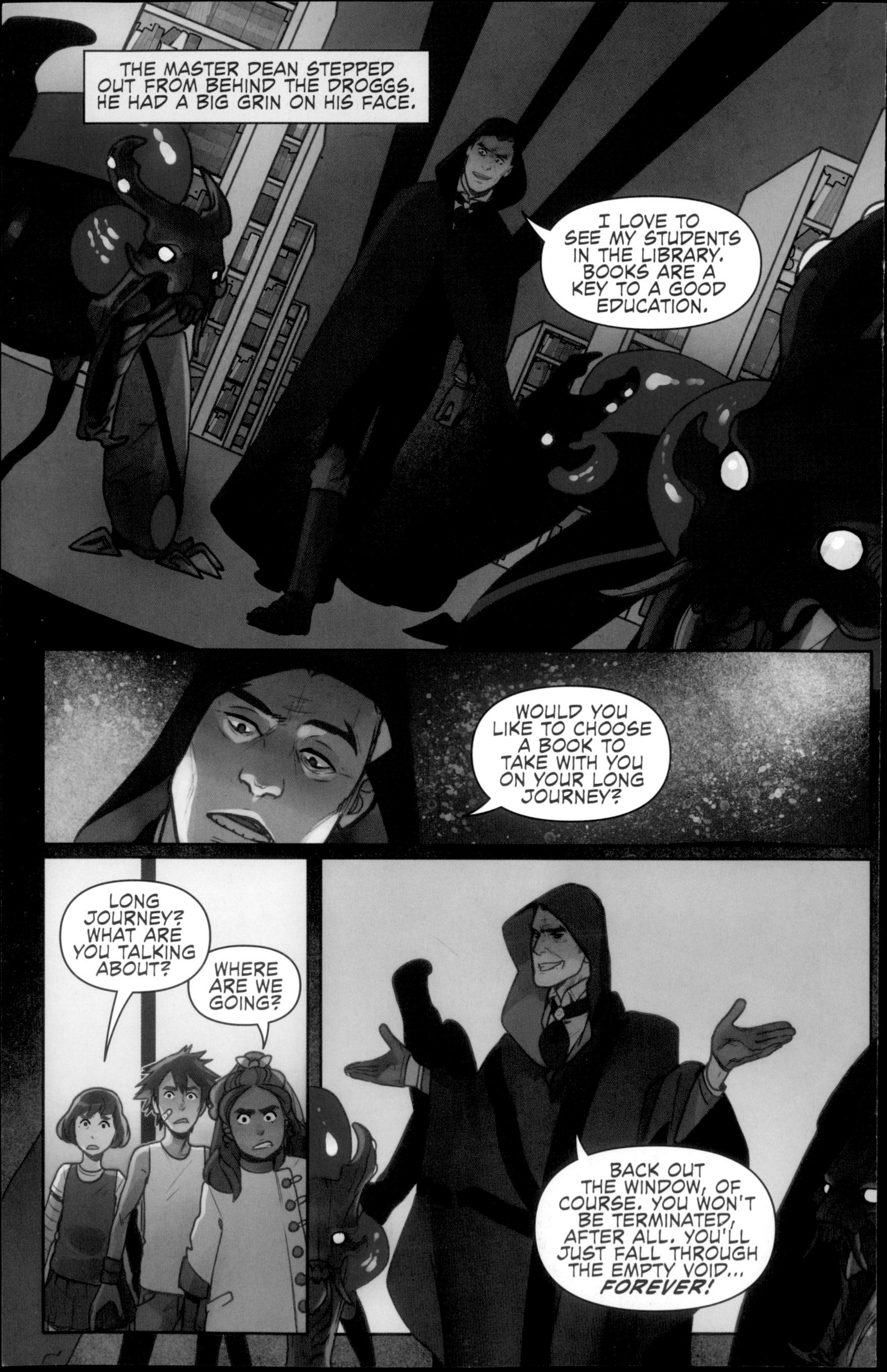
THE MASTER DEAN STEPPED OUT FROM BEHIND THE DROGGS. HE HAD A BIG GRIN ON HIS FACE.
I LOVE TO SEE MY STUDENTS IN THE LIBRARY. BOOKS ARE A KEY TO A GOOD EDUCATION.
WOULD YOU LIKE TO CHOOSE A BOOK TO TAKE WITH YOU ON YOUR LONG JOURNEY?
LONG JOURNEY? WHAT ARE YOU TALKING ABOUT?
WHERE ARE WE GOING?
BACK OUT THE WINDOW, OF COURSE. YOU WON'T BE TERMINATED, AFTER ALL. YOU'LL JUST FALL THROUGH THE EMPTY VOID... FOREVER!

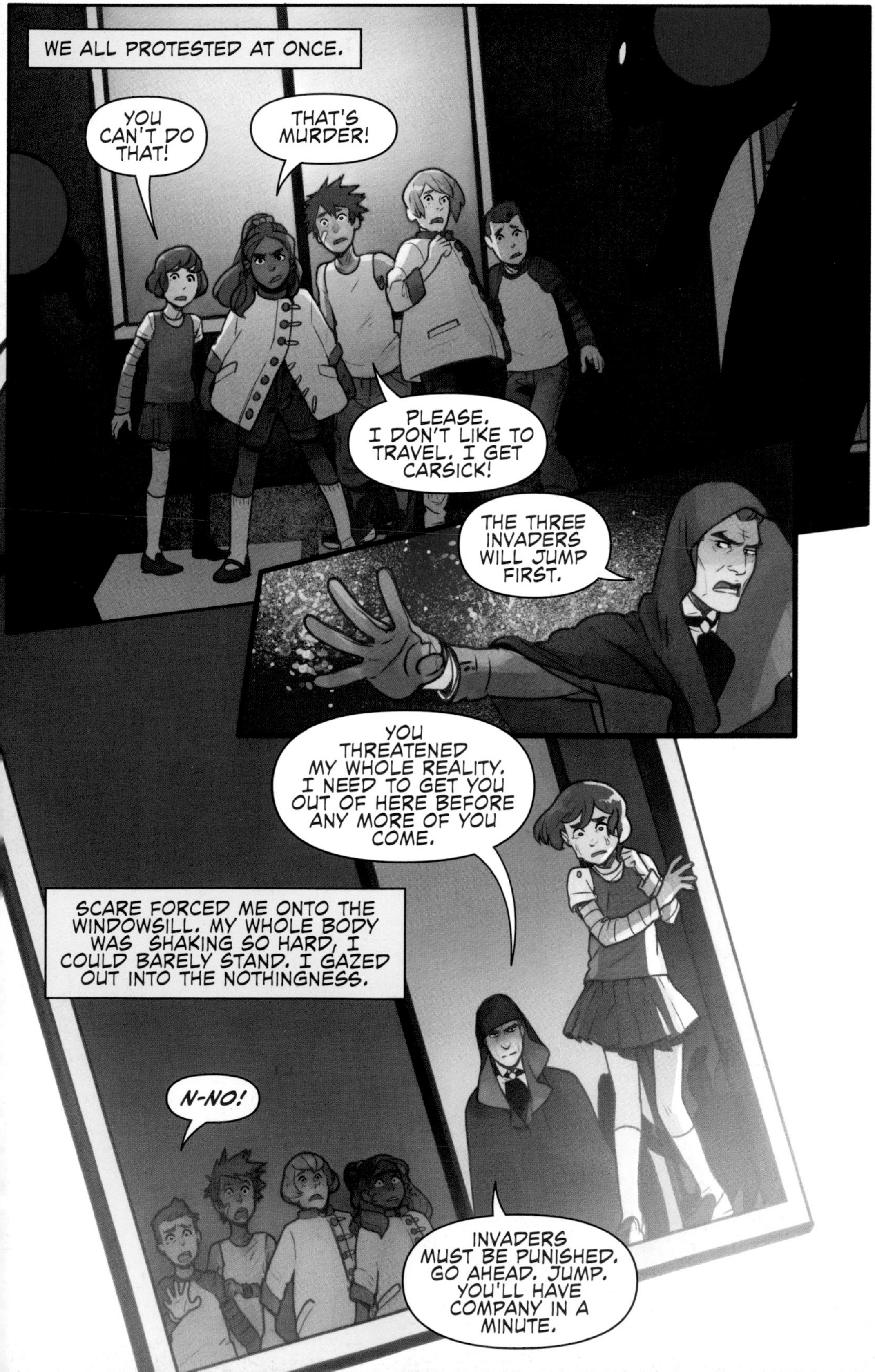
WE ALL PROTESTED AT ONCE.
YOU CAN'T DO THAT!
THAT'S MURDER!
PLEASE. I DON'T LIKE TO TRAVEL. I GET CARSICK!
THE THREE INVADERS WILL JUMP FIRST.
YOU THREATENED MY WHOLE REALITY. I NEED TO GET YOU OUT OF HERE BEFORE ANY MORE OF YOU COME.
SCARE FORCED ME ONTO THE WINDOWSILL. MY WHOLE BODY WAS SHAKING SO HARD, I COULD BARELY STAND. I GAZED OUT INTO THE NOTHINGNESS.
N-NO!
INVADERS MUST BE PUNISHED. GO AHEAD. JUMP. YOU'LL HAVE COMPANY IN A MINUTE.

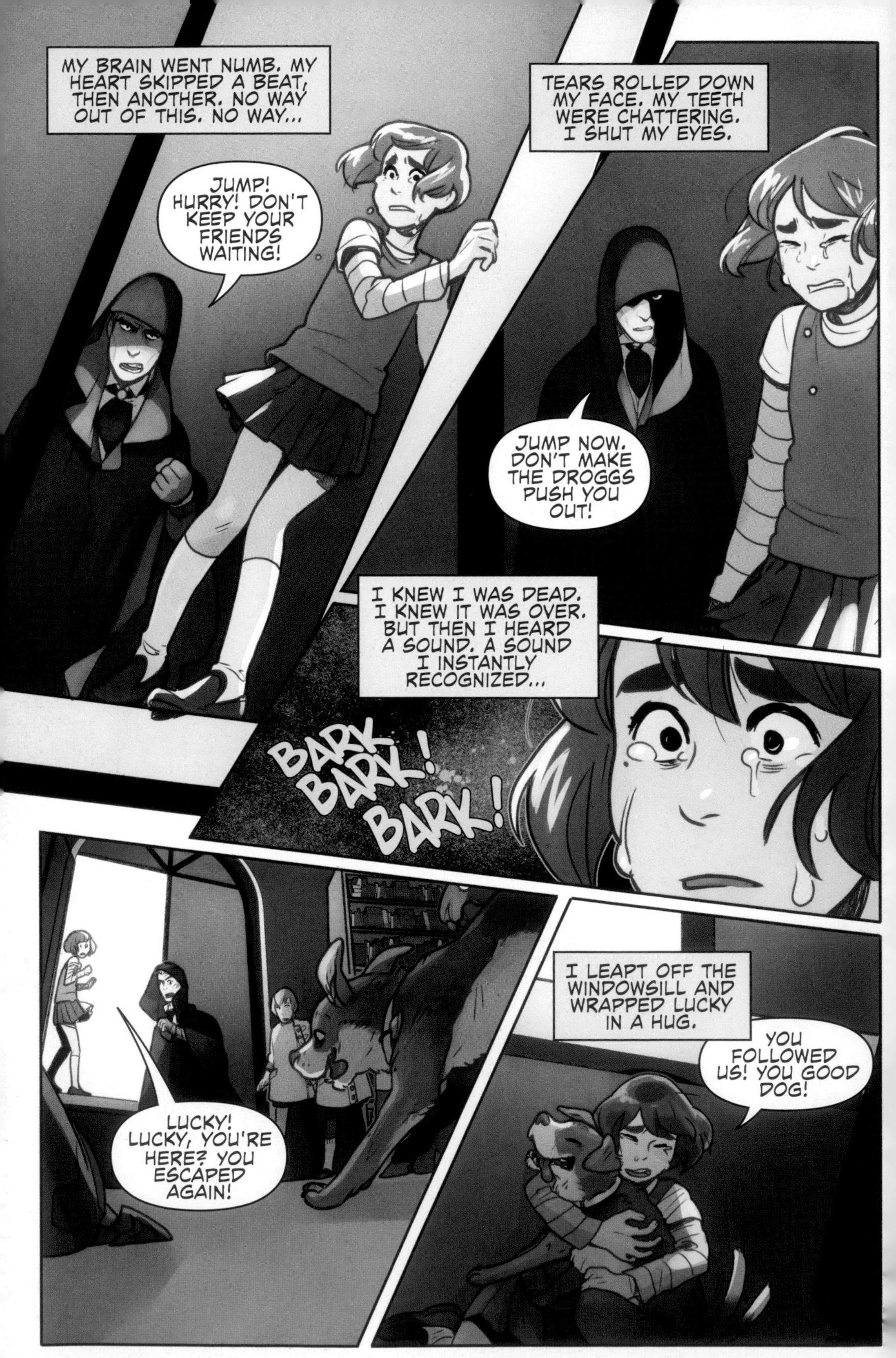
MY BRAIN WENT NUMB. MY HEART SKIPPED A BEAT, THEN ANOTHER. NO WAY OUT OF THIS. NO WAY...
JUMP! HURRY! DON'T KEEP YOUR FRIENDS WAITING!
TEARS ROLLED DOWN MY FACE. MY TEETH WERE CHATTERING. I SHUT MY EYES.
JUMP NOW. DON'T MAKE THE DROGGS PUSH YOU OUT!
I KNEW I WAS DEAD. I KNEW IT WAS OVER. BUT THEN I HEARD A SOUND. A SOUND I INSTANTLY RECOGNIZED...
BARK BARK! BARK!
LUCKY! LUCKY, YOU'RE HERE? YOU ESCAPED AGAIN!
I LEAPT OFF THE WINDOWSILL AND WRAPPED LUCKY IN A HUG.
YOU FOLLOWED US! YOU GOOD DOG!

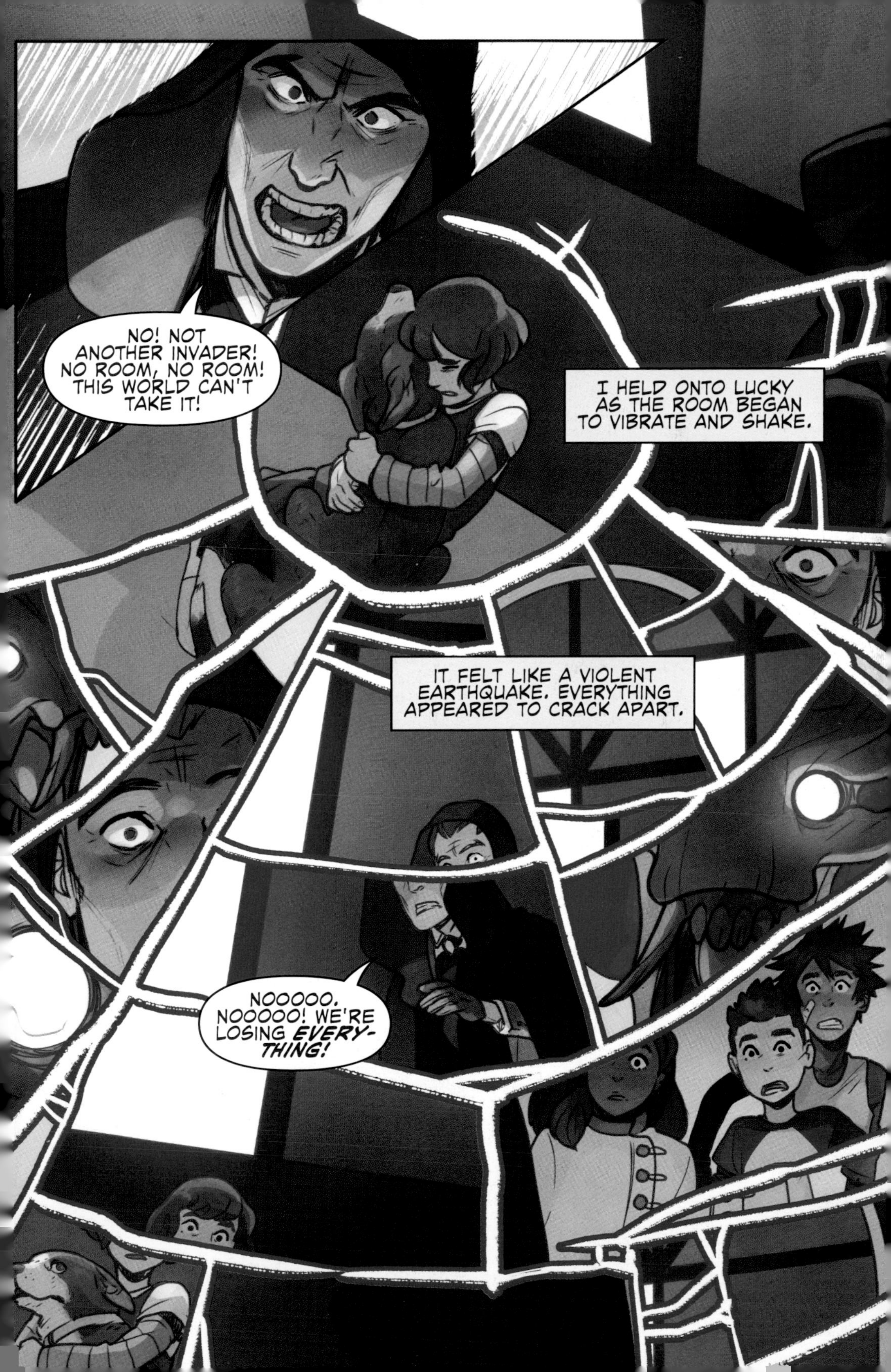
NO! NOT ANOTHER INVADER! NO ROOM, NO ROOM! THIS WORLD CAN'T TAKE IT!
I HELD ONTO LUCKY AS THE ROOM BEGAN TO VIBRATE AND SHAKE.
IT FELT LIKE A VIOLENT EARTHQUAKE. EVERYTHING APPEARED TO CRACK APART.
NOOOOO. NOOOOO! WE'RE LOSING *EVERY-THING!*

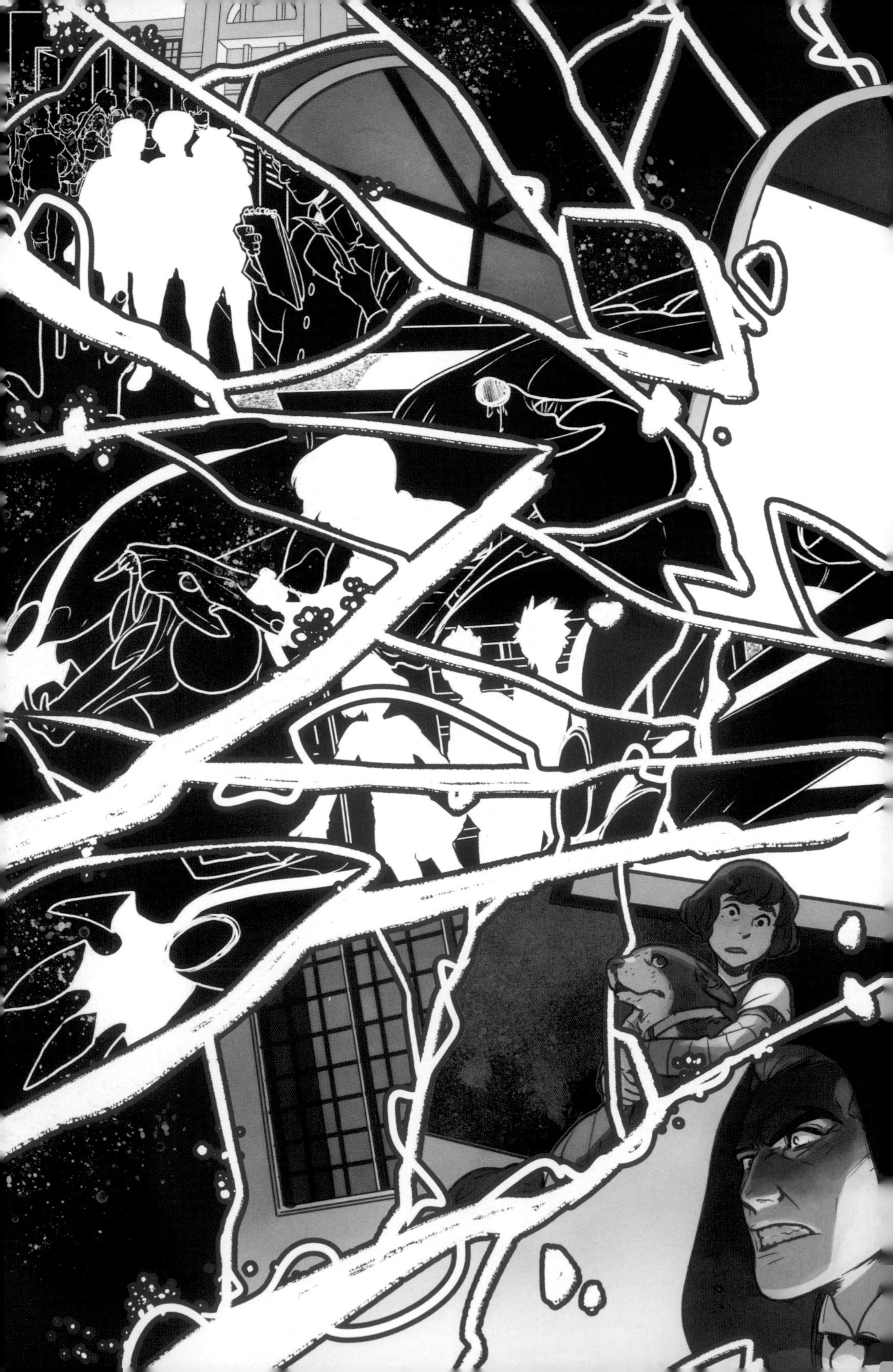

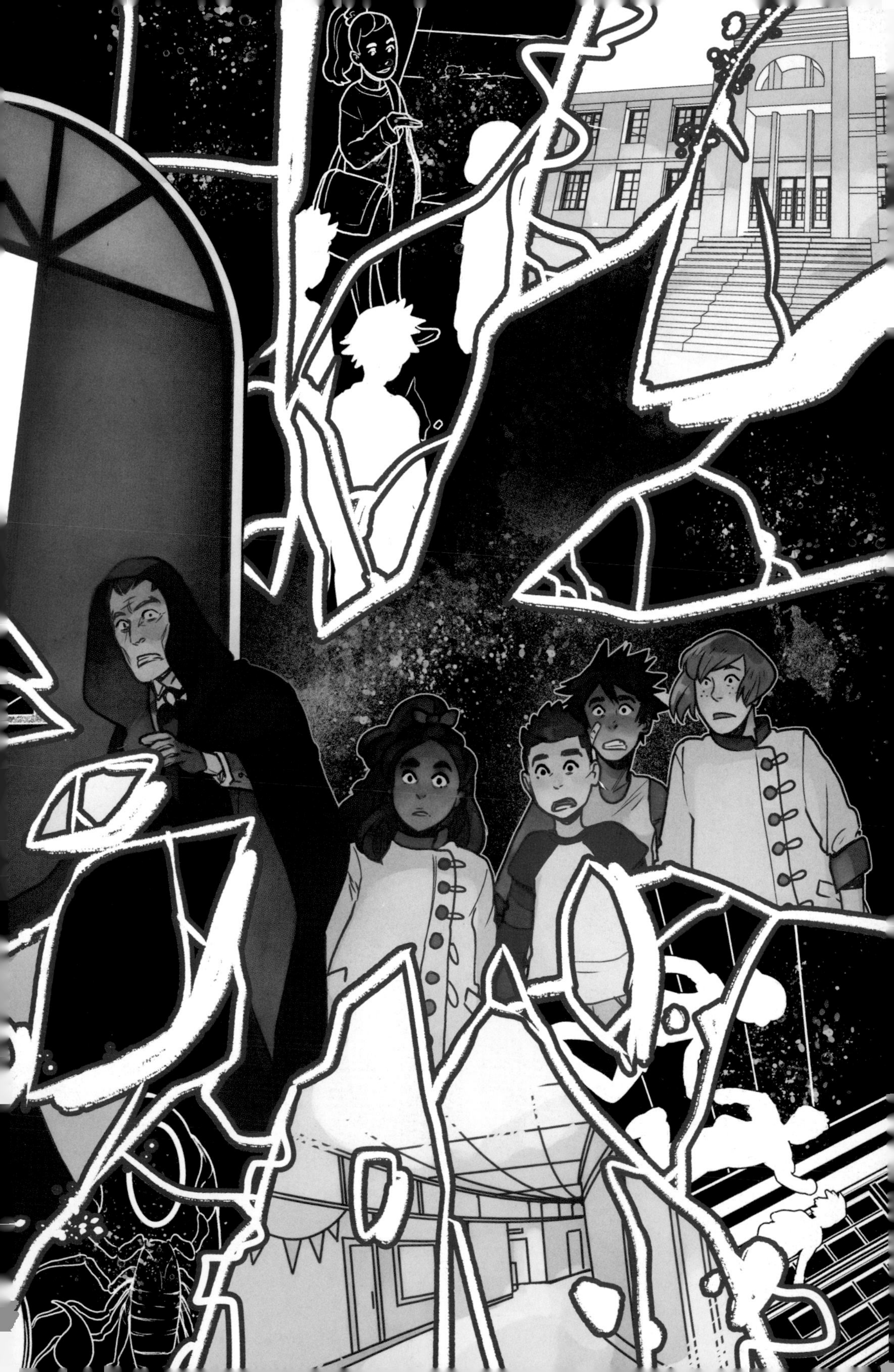

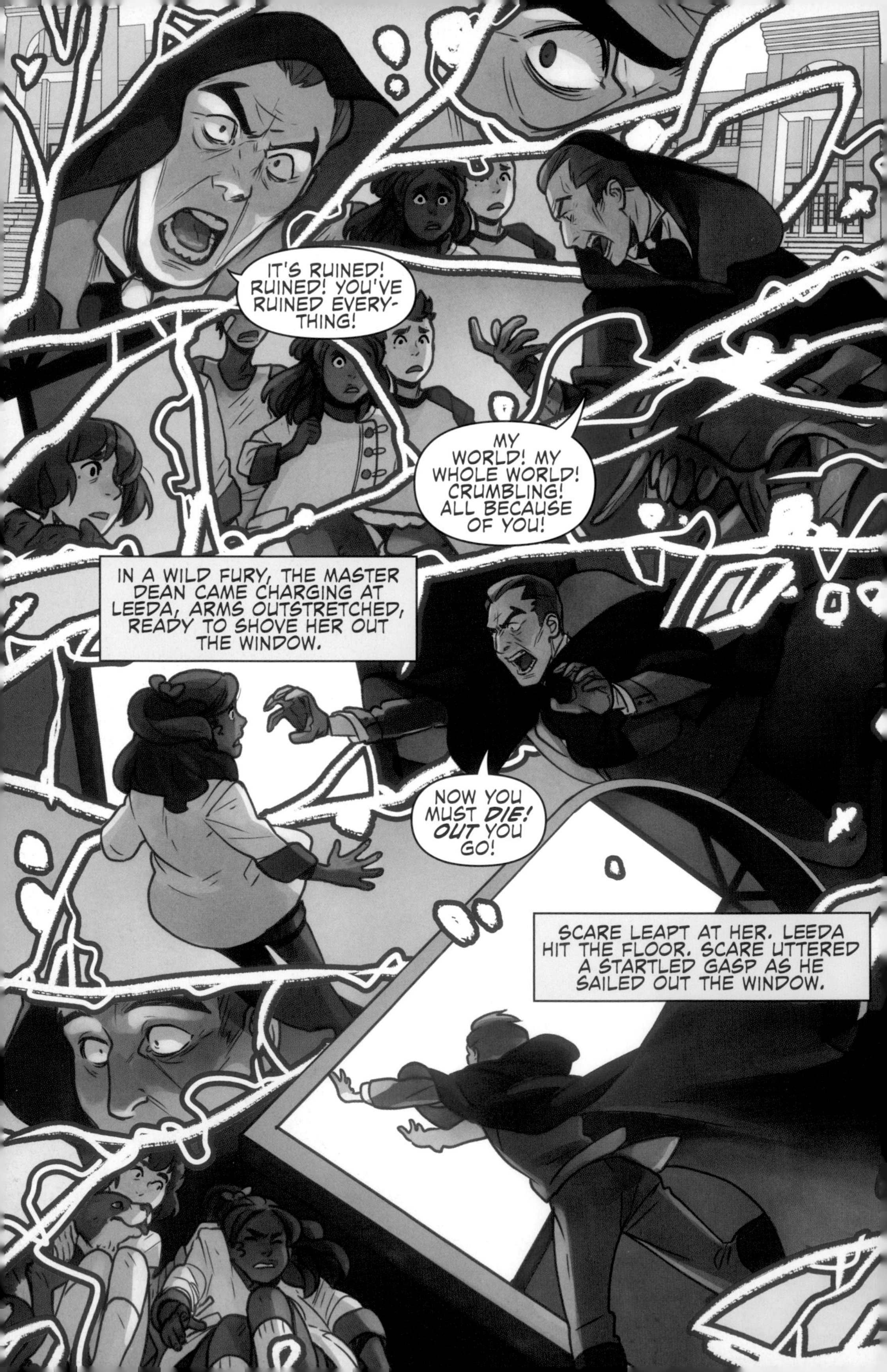
IT'S RUINED! RUINED! YOU'VE RUINED EVERY-THING!
MY WORLD! MY WHOLE WORLD! CRUMBLING! ALL BECAUSE OF YOU!
IN A WILD FURY, THE MASTER DEAN CAME CHARGING AT LEEDA, ARMS OUTSTRETCHED, READY TO SHOVE HER OUT THE WINDOW.
NOW YOU MUST ***DIE! OUT*** YOU GO!
SCARE LEAPT AT HER. LEEDA HIT THE FLOOR. SCARE UTTERED A STARTLED GASP AS HE SAILED OUT THE WINDOW.

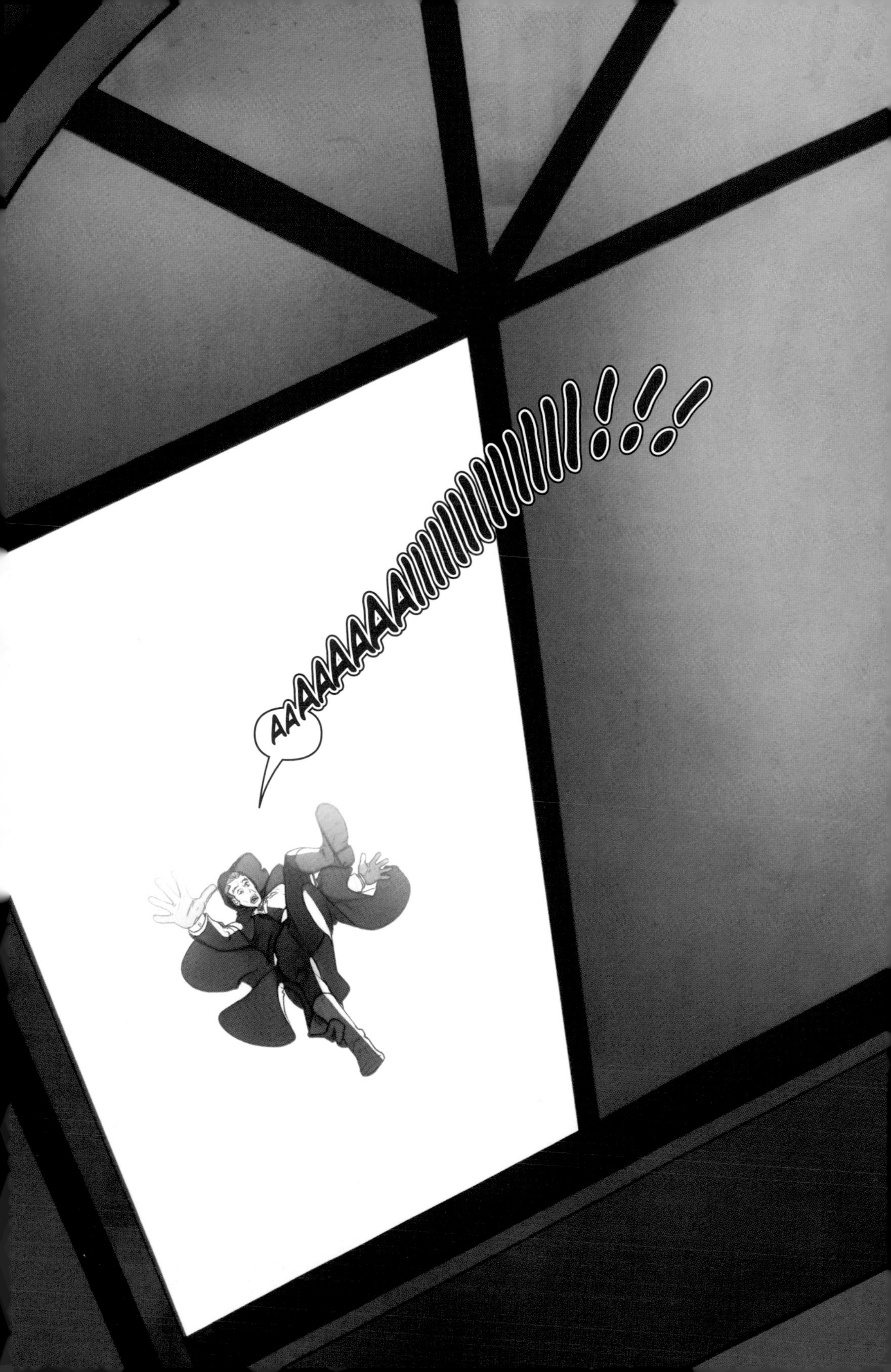
AAAAAAAAAIIIIIIIIIIIII!!!

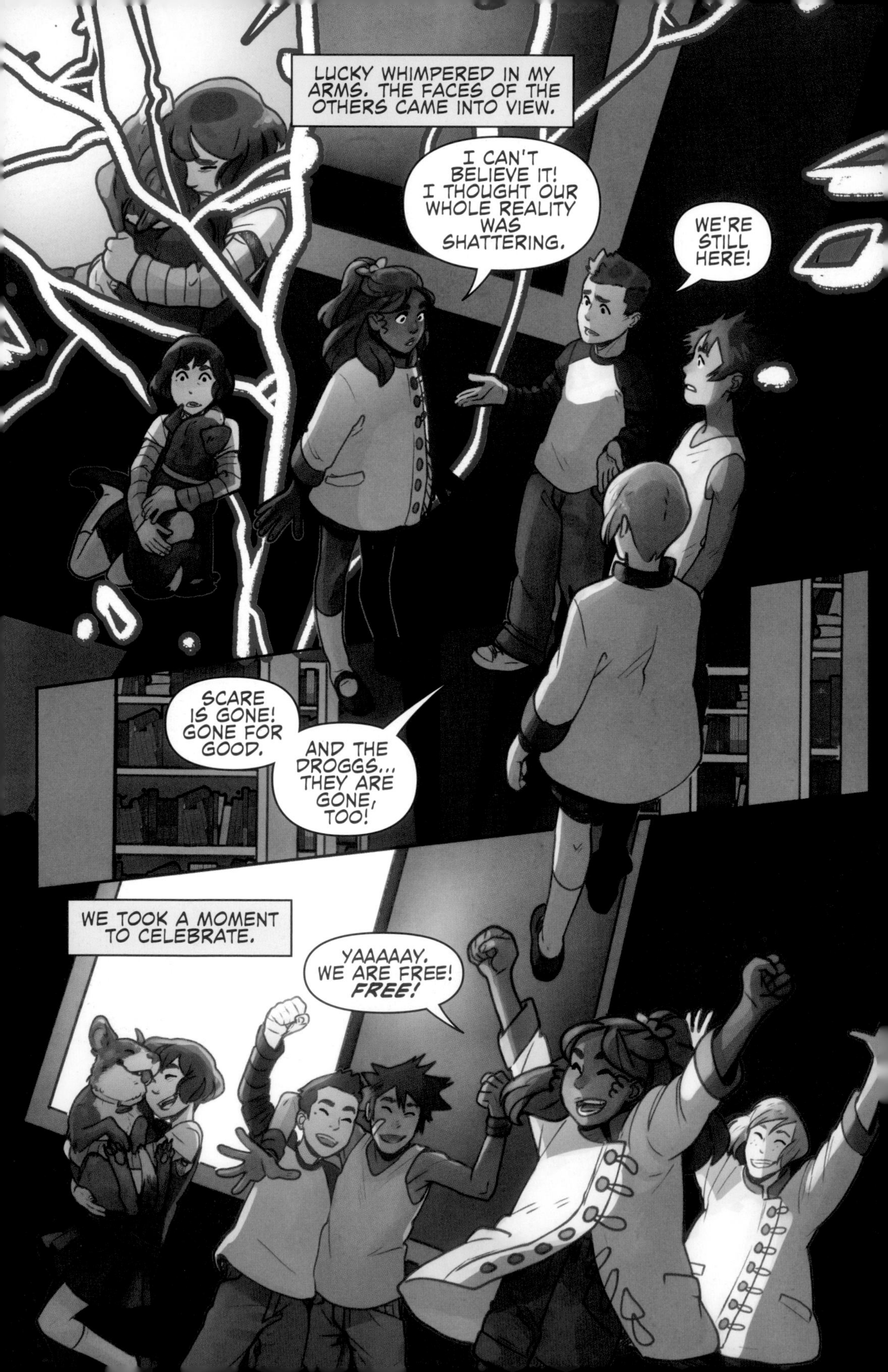
LUCKY WHIMPERED IN MY ARMS. THE FACES OF THE OTHERS CAME INTO VIEW.
I CAN'T BELIEVE IT! I THOUGHT OUR WHOLE REALITY WAS SHATTERING.
WE'RE STILL HERE!
SCARE IS GONE! GONE FOR GOOD.
AND THE DROGGS... THEY ARE GONE, TOO!
WE TOOK A MOMENT TO CELEBRATE.
YAAAAAY. WE ARE FREE! FREE!

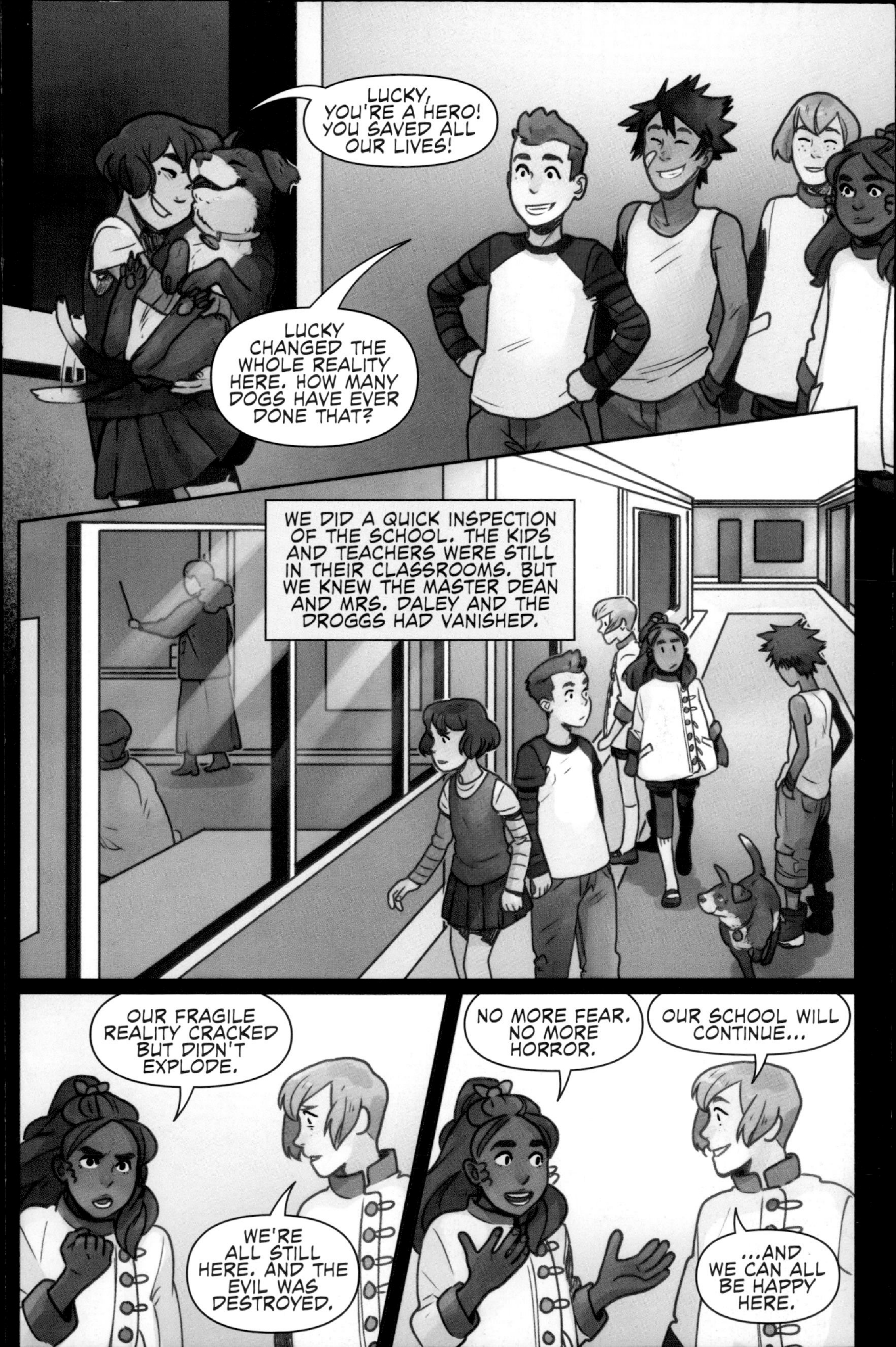
LUCKY, YOU'RE A HERO! YOU SAVED ALL OUR LIVES!
LUCKY CHANGED THE WHOLE REALITY HERE. HOW MANY DOGS HAVE EVER DONE THAT?
WE DID A QUICK INSPECTION OF THE SCHOOL. THE KIDS AND TEACHERS WERE STILL IN THEIR CLASSROOMS. BUT WE KNEW THE MASTER DEAN AND MRS. DALEY AND THE DROGGS HAD VANISHED.
OUR FRAGILE REALITY CRACKED BUT DIDN'T EXPLODE.
WE'RE ALL STILL HERE. AND THE EVIL WAS DESTROYED.
NO MORE FEAR. NO MORE HORROR.
OUR SCHOOL WILL CONTINUE...
...AND WE CAN ALL BE HAPPY HERE.

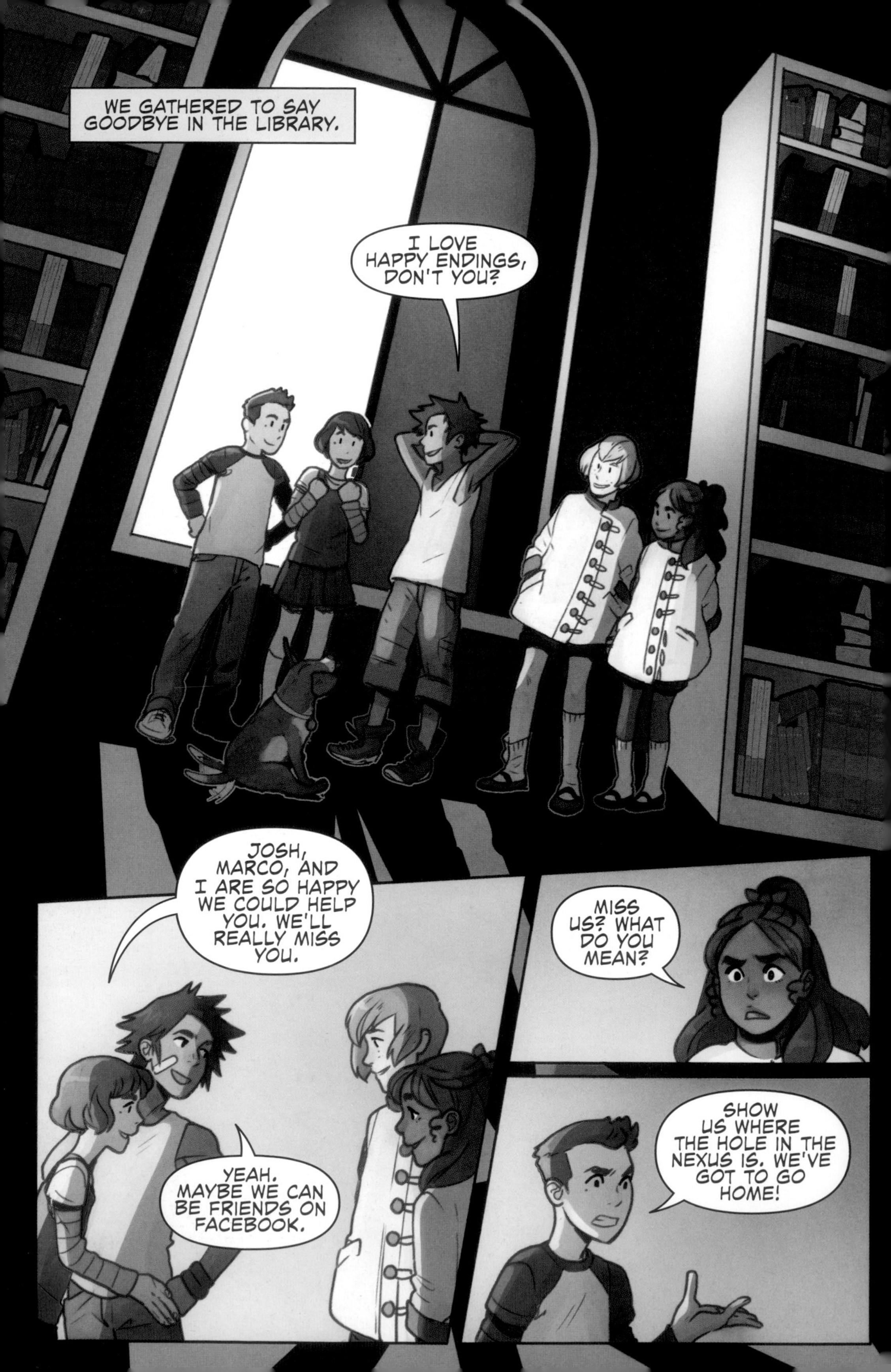
WE GATHERED TO SAY GOODBYE IN THE LIBRARY.
I LOVE HAPPY ENDINGS, DON'T YOU?
JOSH, MARCO, AND I ARE SO HAPPY WE COULD HELP YOU. WE'LL REALLY MISS YOU.
YEAH. MAYBE WE CAN BE FRIENDS ON FACEBOOK.
MISS US? WHAT DO YOU MEAN?
SHOW US WHERE THE HOLE IN THE NEXUS IS. WE'VE GOT TO GO HOME!

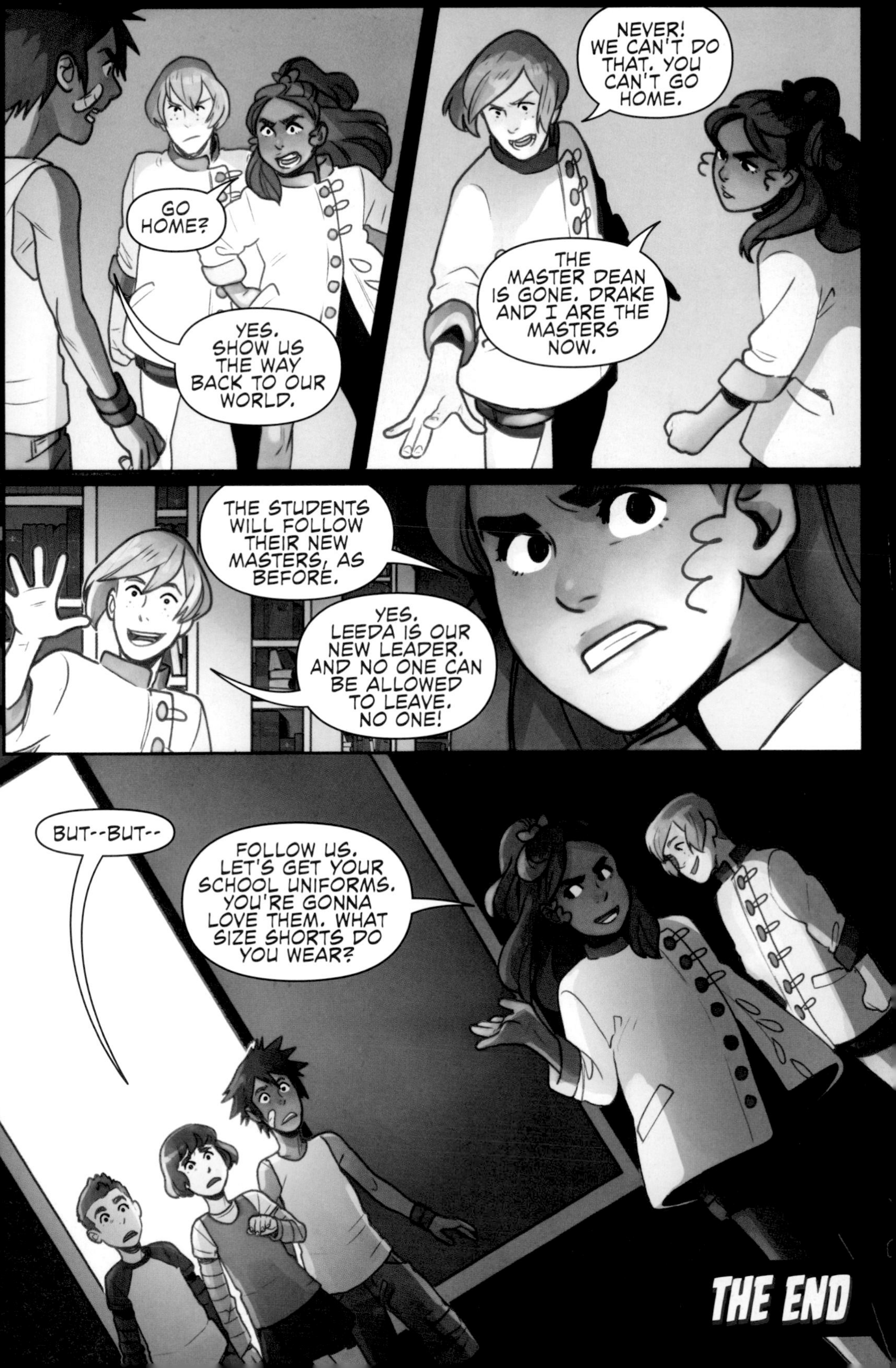
GO HOME?
YES. SHOW US THE WAY BACK TO OUR WORLD.
NEVER! WE CAN'T DO THAT. YOU CAN'T GO HOME.
THE MASTER DEAN IS GONE. DRAKE AND I ARE THE MASTERS NOW.
THE STUDENTS WILL FOLLOW THEIR NEW MASTERS, AS BEFORE.
YES. LEEDA IS OUR NEW LEADER. AND NO ONE CAN BE ALLOWED TO LEAVE. NO ONE!
BUT--BUT--
FOLLOW US. LET'S GET YOUR SCHOOL UNIFORMS. YOU'RE GONNA LOVE THEM. WHAT SIZE SHORTS DO YOU WEAR?
THE END

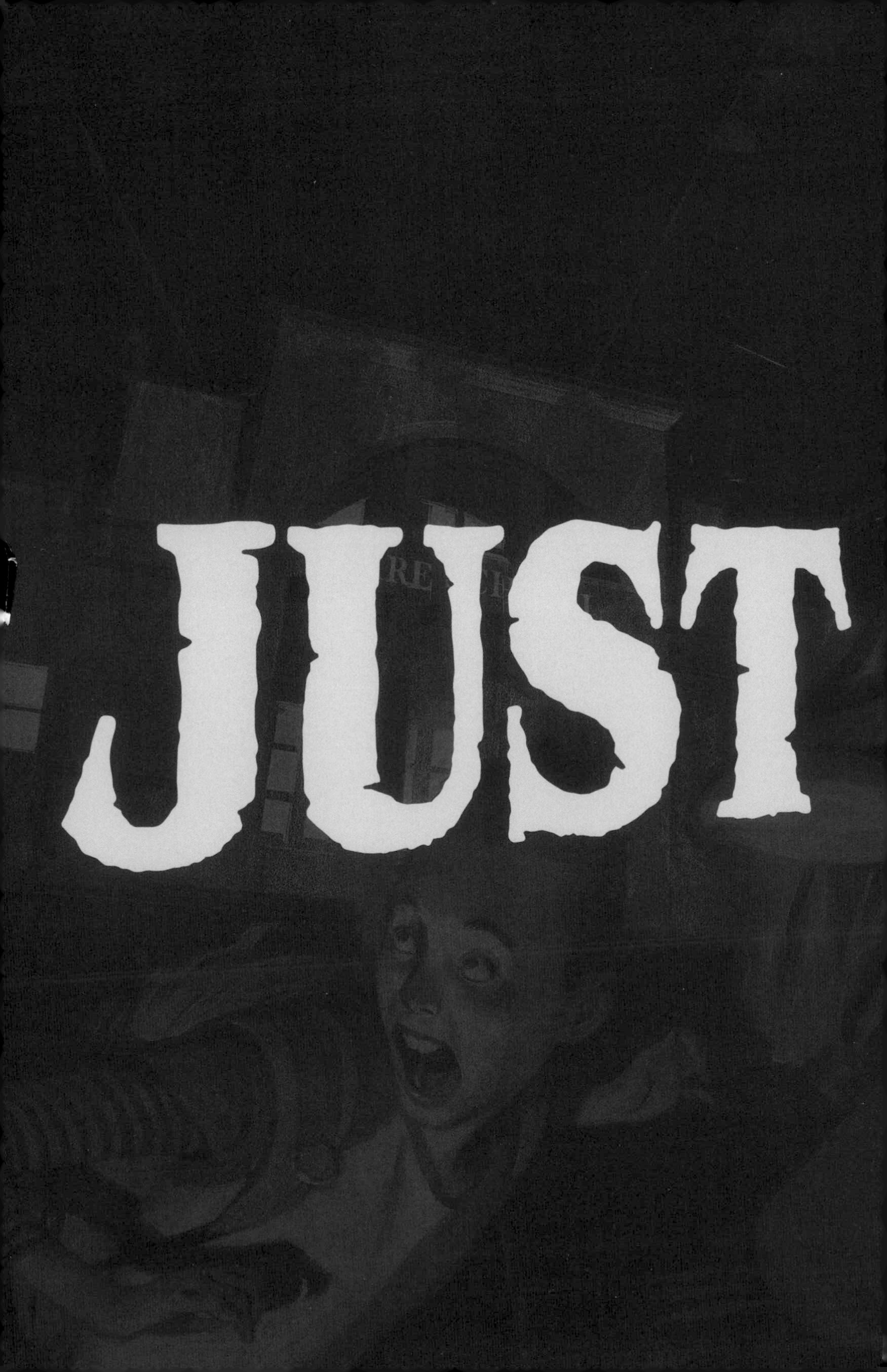
JUST

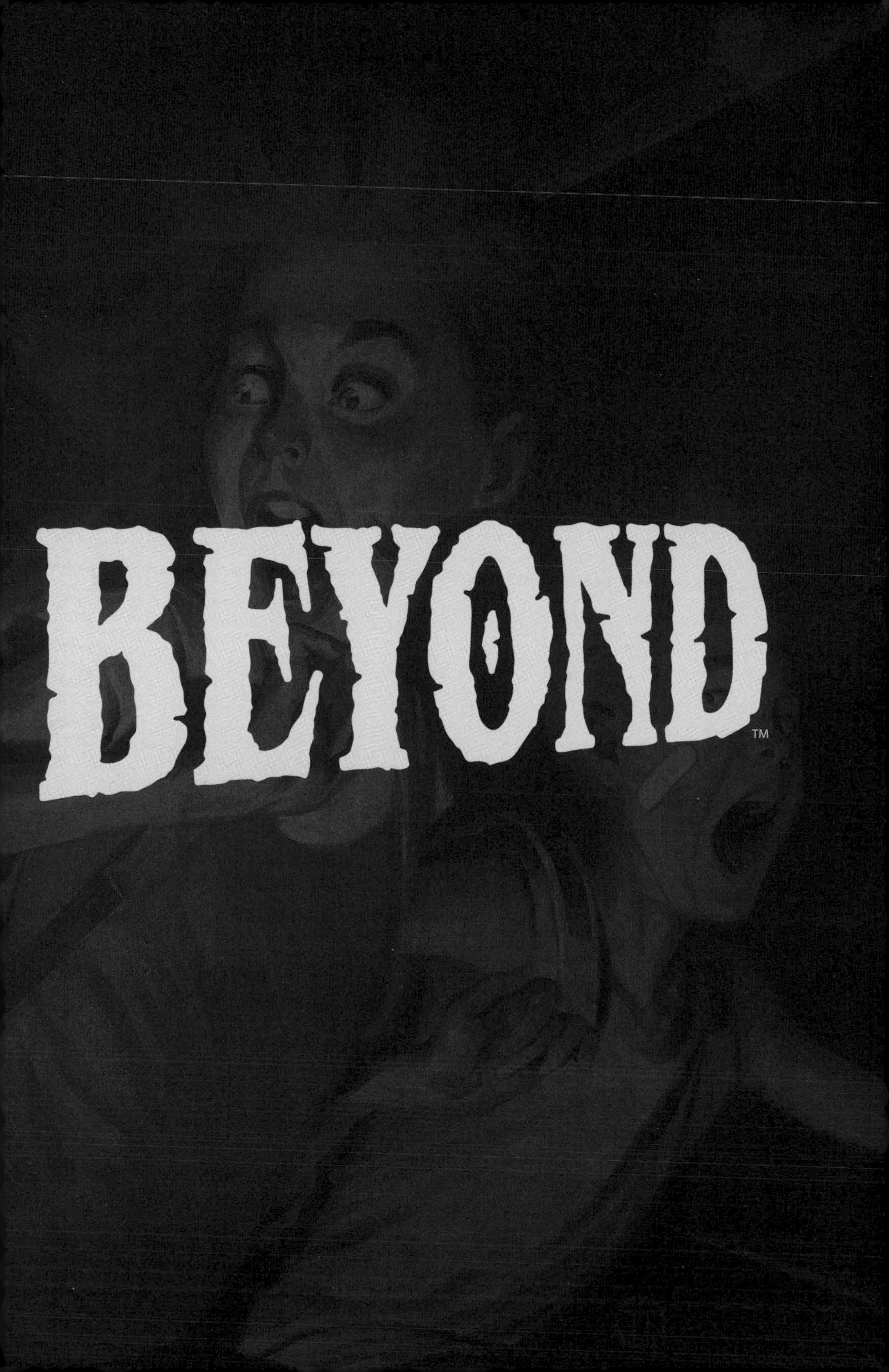
BEYOND™

ABOUT THE
AUTHORS

R.L. Stine

R.L. Stine is one of the best-selling children's authors in history. His *Goosebumps* and *Fear Street* series have sold more than 400 million copies around the world and have been translated into 32 languages. He has had several TV series based on his work, and two feature films, *Goosebumps* (2015) and *Goosebumps 2: Haunted Halloween* (2018) starring Jack Black as R.L. Stine. *Just Beyond* is Stine's first-ever series of original graphic novels. He lives in New York City with his wife Jane, an editor and publisher.

Kelly & Nicole Matthews

Kelly and Nichole Matthews are twin sisters (and totally not four cats in a trench coat) who work as freelance comic book artists and illustrators just north of the Emerald City. They've worked on a number of titles that you may have heard of (and maybe even read!) including *Jim Henson's The Power of the Dark Crystal*, *Pandora's Legacy*, and *Toil & Trouble*. They have an original webcomic, *Maskless*, that you can read for free on Hiveworks.

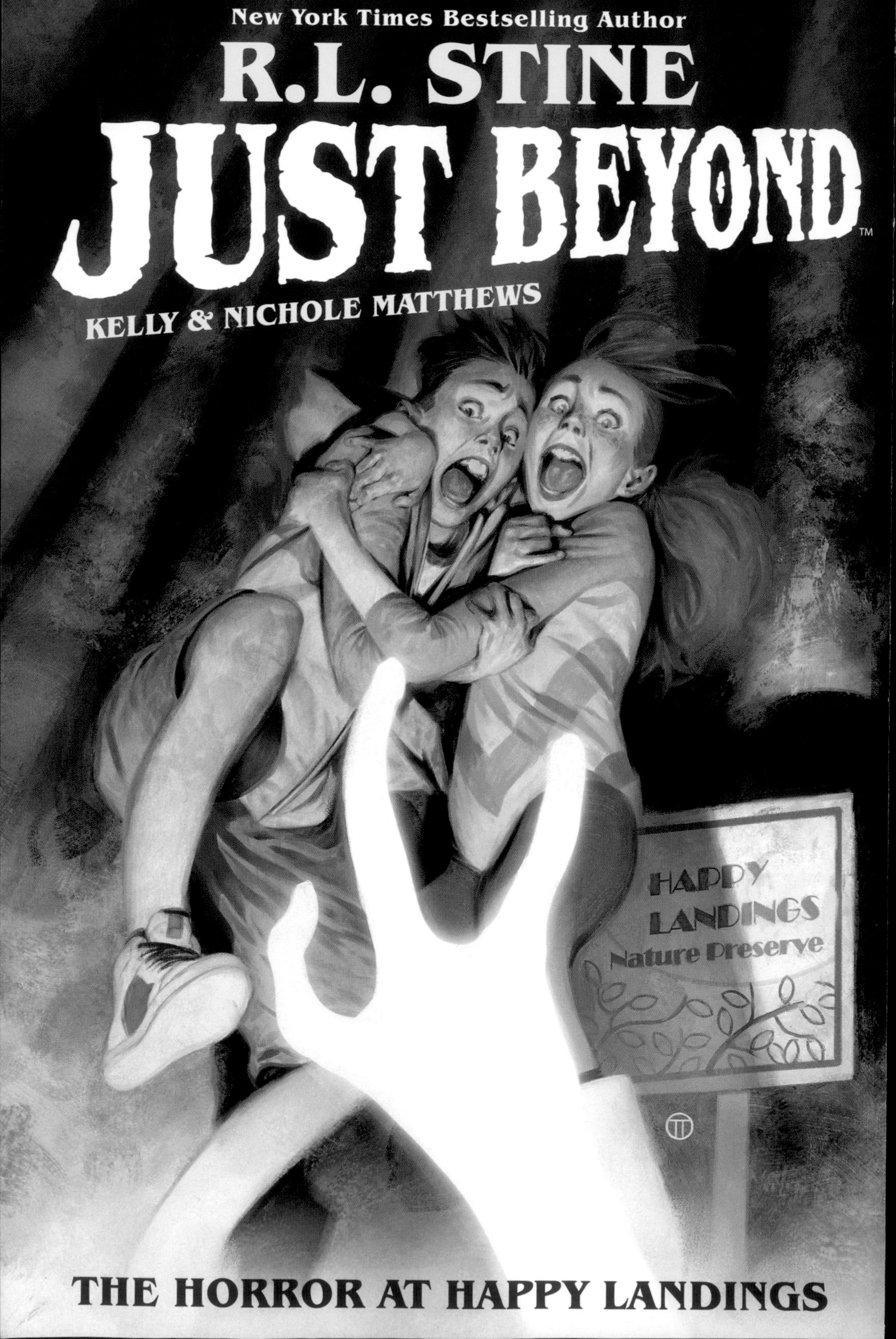
New York Times Bestselling Author
R.L. STINE
JUST BEYOND™
KELLY & NICHOLE MATTHEWS
HAPPY
LANDINGS
Nature Preserve
THE HORROR AT HAPPY LANDINGS

YOUR SCARY SNEAK PEEK!

Written by
R.L. Stine

Illustrated by
Kelly & Nichole Matthews

Lettered by
Mike Fiorentino

Cover by
Julian Totino Tedesco

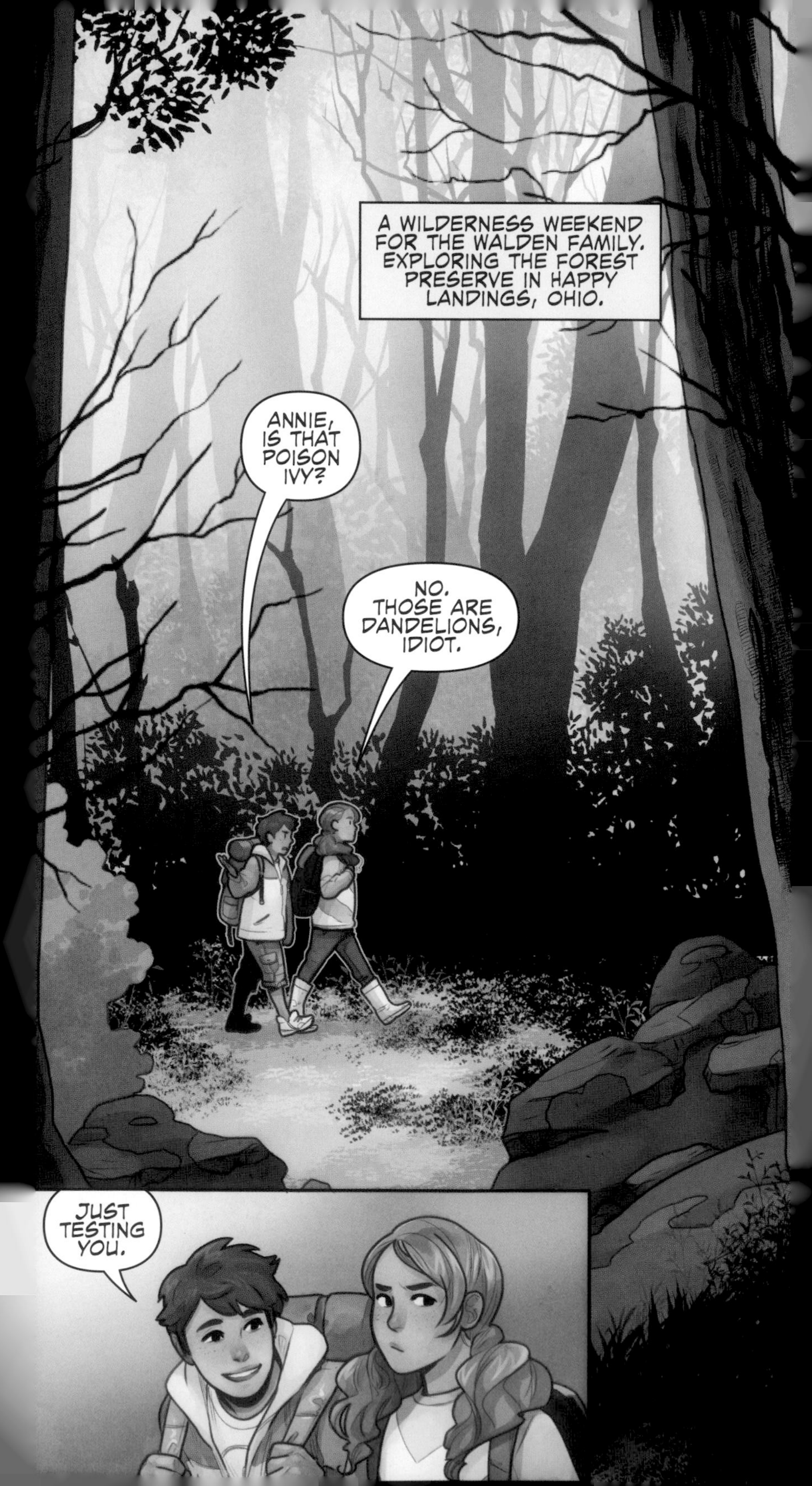
A WILDERNESS WEEKEND FOR THE WALDEN FAMILY. EXPLORING THE FOREST PRESERVE IN HAPPY LANDINGS, OHIO.
ANNIE, IS THAT POISON IVY?
NO. THOSE ARE DANDELIONS, IDIOT.
JUST TESTING YOU.

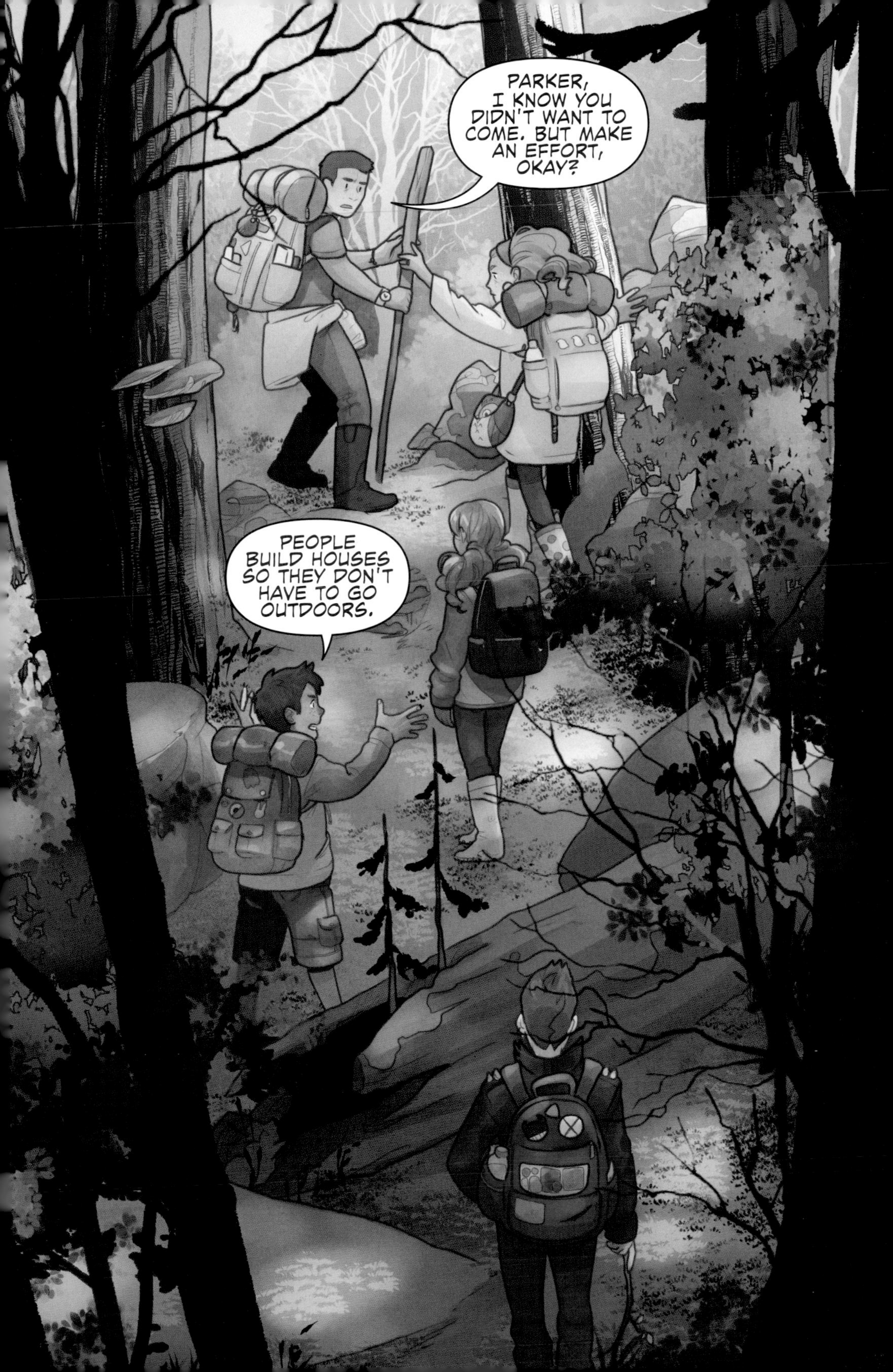
PARKER, I KNOW YOU DIDN'T WANT TO COME. BUT MAKE AN EFFORT, OKAY?
PEOPLE BUILD HOUSES SO THEY DON'T HAVE TO GO OUTDOORS.

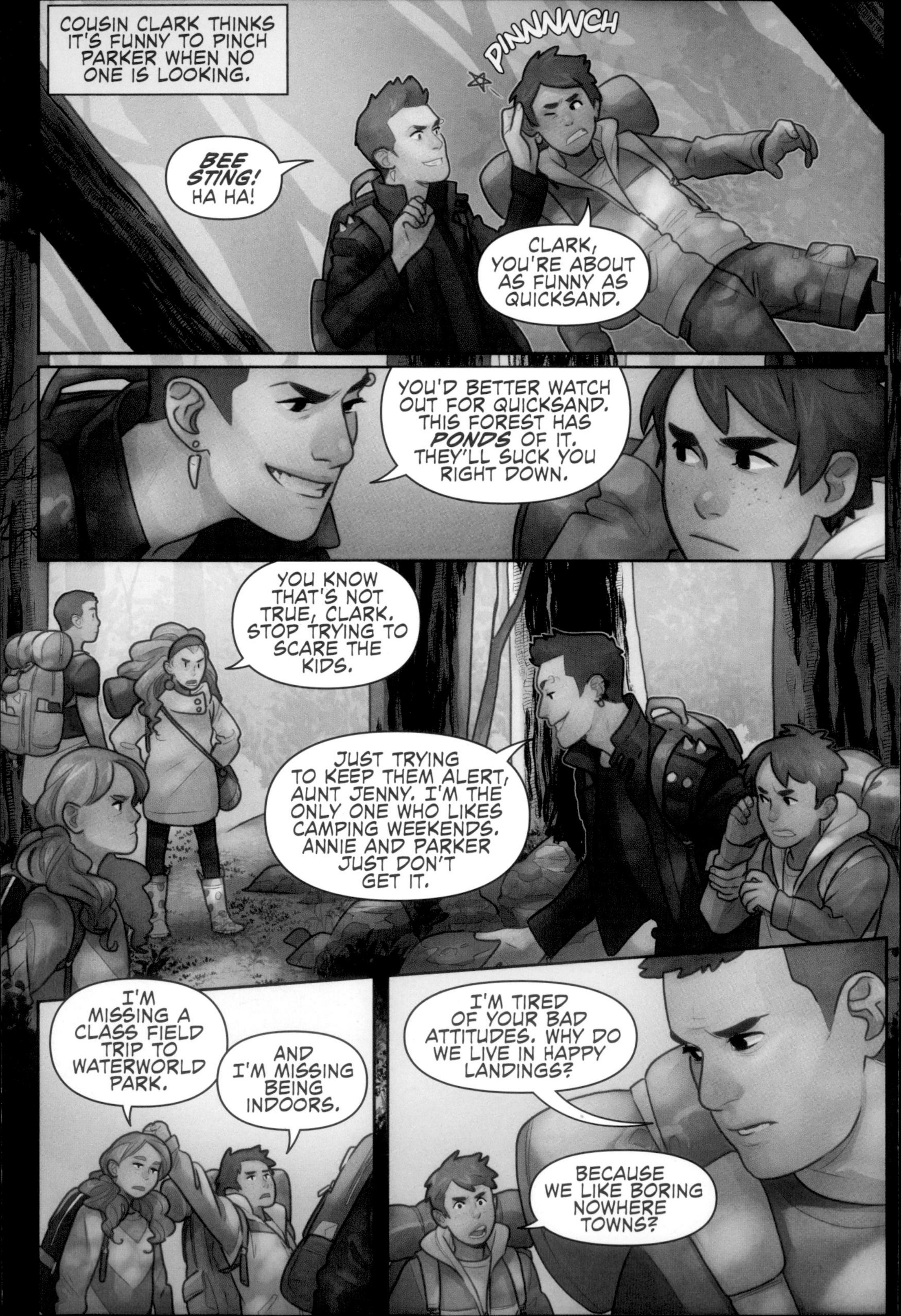
COUSIN CLARK THINKS IT'S FUNNY TO PINCH PARKER WHEN NO ONE IS LOOKING.
PINNNNCH
BEE STING! HA HA!
CLARK, YOU'RE ABOUT AS FUNNY AS QUICKSAND.
YOU'D BETTER WATCH OUT FOR QUICKSAND. THIS FOREST HAS PONDS OF IT. THEY'LL SUCK YOU RIGHT DOWN.
YOU KNOW THAT'S NOT TRUE, CLARK. STOP TRYING TO SCARE THE KIDS.
JUST TRYING TO KEEP THEM ALERT, AUNT JENNY. I'M THE ONLY ONE WHO LIKES CAMPING WEEKENDS. ANNIE AND PARKER JUST DON'T GET IT.
I'M MISSING A CLASS FIELD TRIP TO WATERWORLD PARK.
AND I'M MISSING BEING INDOORS.
I'M TIRED OF YOUR BAD ATTITUDES. WHY DO WE LIVE IN HAPPY LANDINGS?
BECAUSE WE LIKE BORING NOWHERE TOWNS?

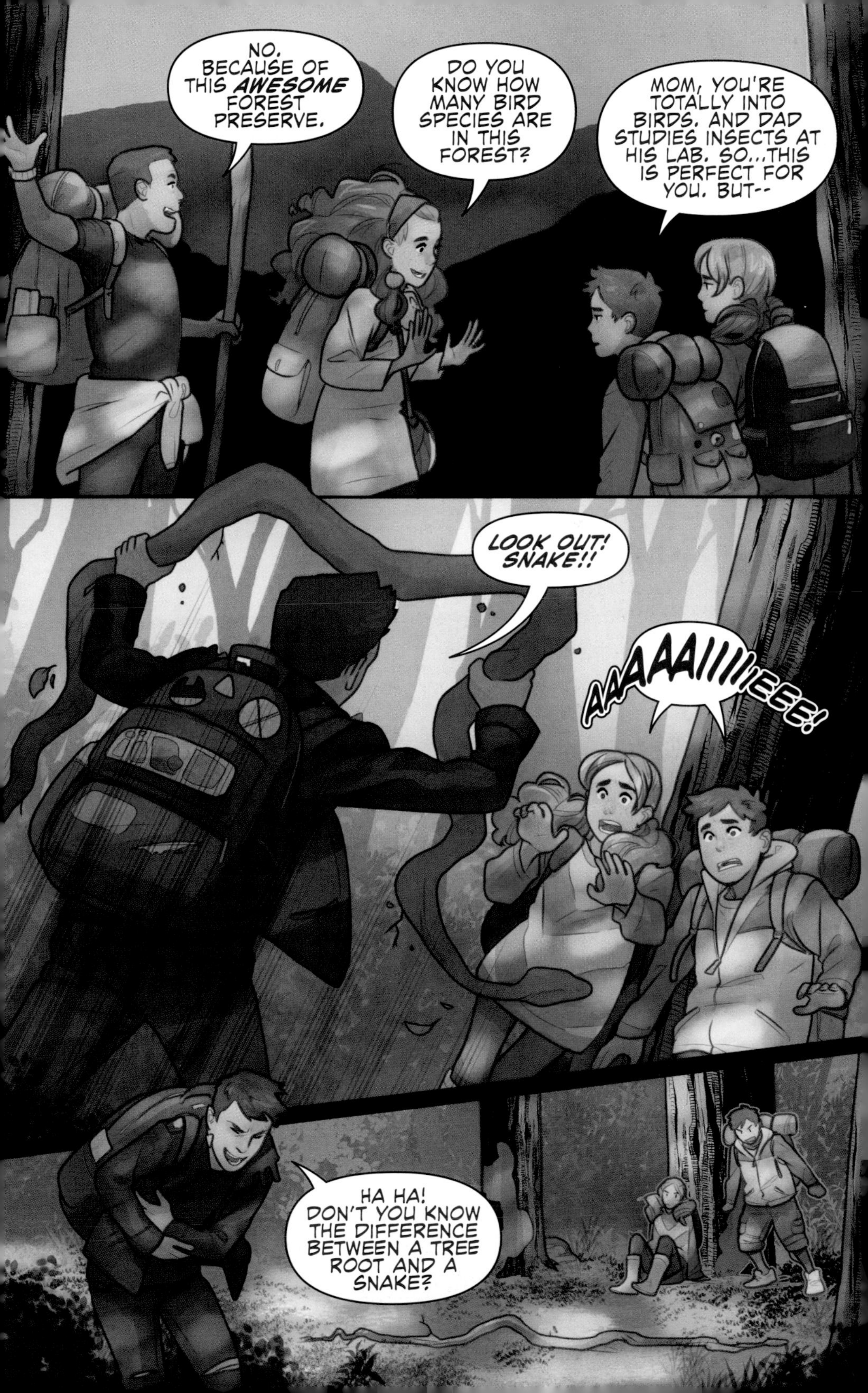
NO. BECAUSE OF THIS AWESOME FOREST PRESERVE.
DO YOU KNOW HOW MANY BIRD SPECIES ARE IN THIS FOREST?
MOM, YOU'RE TOTALLY INTO BIRDS. AND DAD STUDIES INSECTS AT HIS LAB. SO...THIS IS PERFECT FOR YOU. BUT--
LOOK OUT! SNAKE!!
AAAAAIIIIIIEEEE!
HA HA! DON'T YOU KNOW THE DIFFERENCE BETWEEN A TREE ROOT AND A SNAKE?

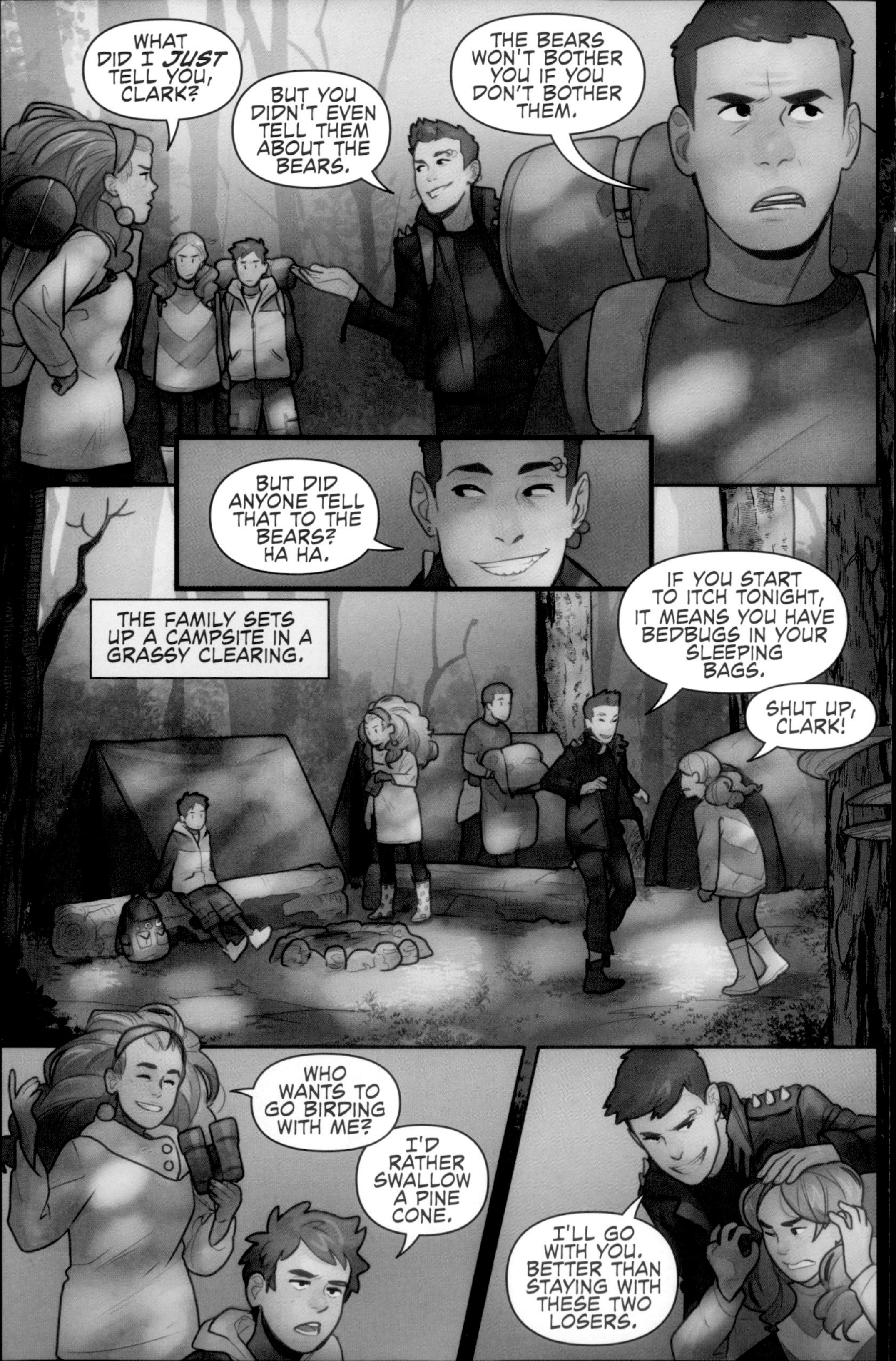
WHAT DID I *JUST* TELL YOU, CLARK?
BUT YOU DIDN'T EVEN TELL THEM ABOUT THE BEARS.
THE BEARS WON'T BOTHER YOU IF YOU DON'T BOTHER THEM.
BUT DID ANYONE TELL THAT TO THE BEARS? HA HA.
THE FAMILY SETS UP A CAMPSITE IN A GRASSY CLEARING.
IF YOU START TO ITCH TONIGHT, IT MEANS YOU HAVE BEDBUGS IN YOUR SLEEPING BAGS.
SHUT UP, CLARK!
WHO WANTS TO GO BIRDING WITH ME?
I'D RATHER SWALLOW A PINE CONE.
I'LL GO WITH YOU. BETTER THAN STAYING WITH THESE TWO LOSERS.

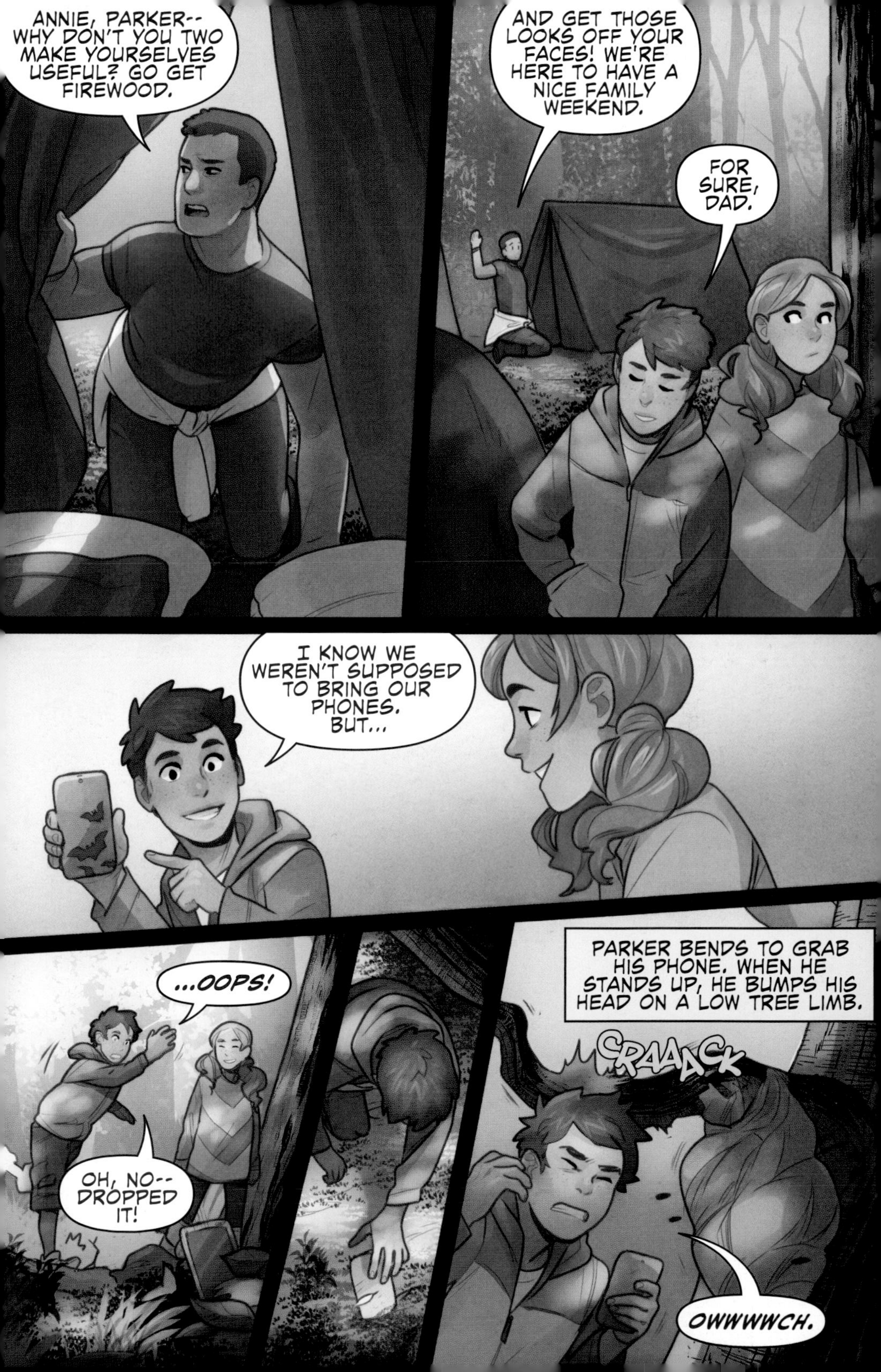
ANNIE, PARKER-- WHY DON'T YOU TWO MAKE YOURSELVES USEFUL? GO GET FIREWOOD.
AND GET THOSE LOOKS OFF YOUR FACES! WE'RE HERE TO HAVE A NICE FAMILY WEEKEND.
FOR SURE, DAD.
I KNOW WE WEREN'T SUPPOSED TO BRING OUR PHONES. BUT...
...OOPS!
OH, NO-- DROPPED IT!
PARKER BENDS TO GRAB HIS PHONE. WHEN HE STANDS UP, HE BUMPS HIS HEAD ON A LOW TREE LIMB.
CRAAACK
OWWWWCH.

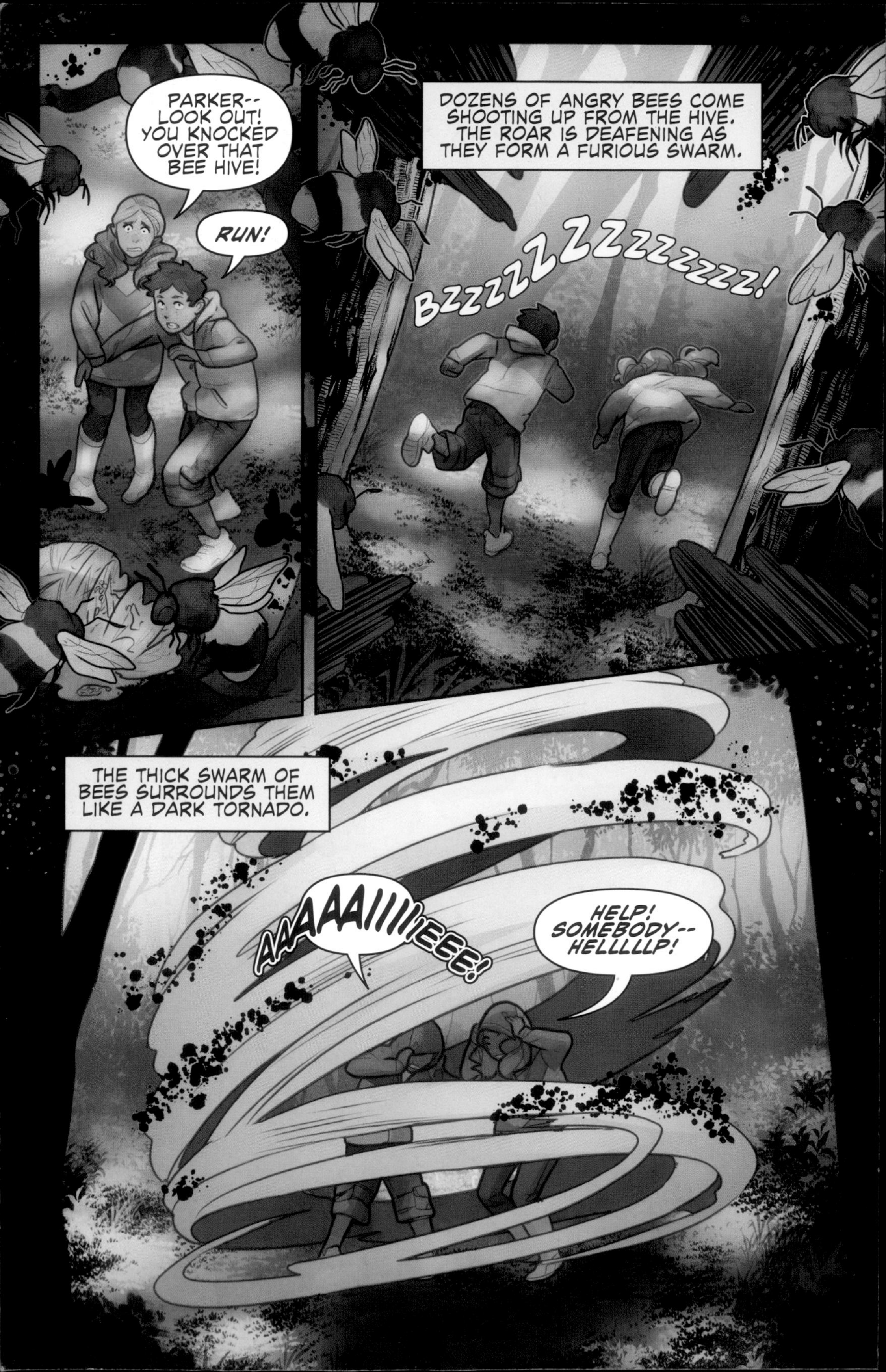
PARKER-- LOOK OUT! YOU KNOCKED OVER THAT BEE HIVE!
RUN!
DOZENS OF ANGRY BEES COME SHOOTING UP FROM THE HIVE. THE ROAR IS DEAFENING AS THEY FORM A FURIOUS SWARM.
BZZZZZZZZZZZZZZZ!
THE THICK SWARM OF BEES SURROUNDS THEM LIKE A DARK TORNADO.
AAAAAIIIIIEEEE!
HELP! SOMEBODY-- HELLLLLP!

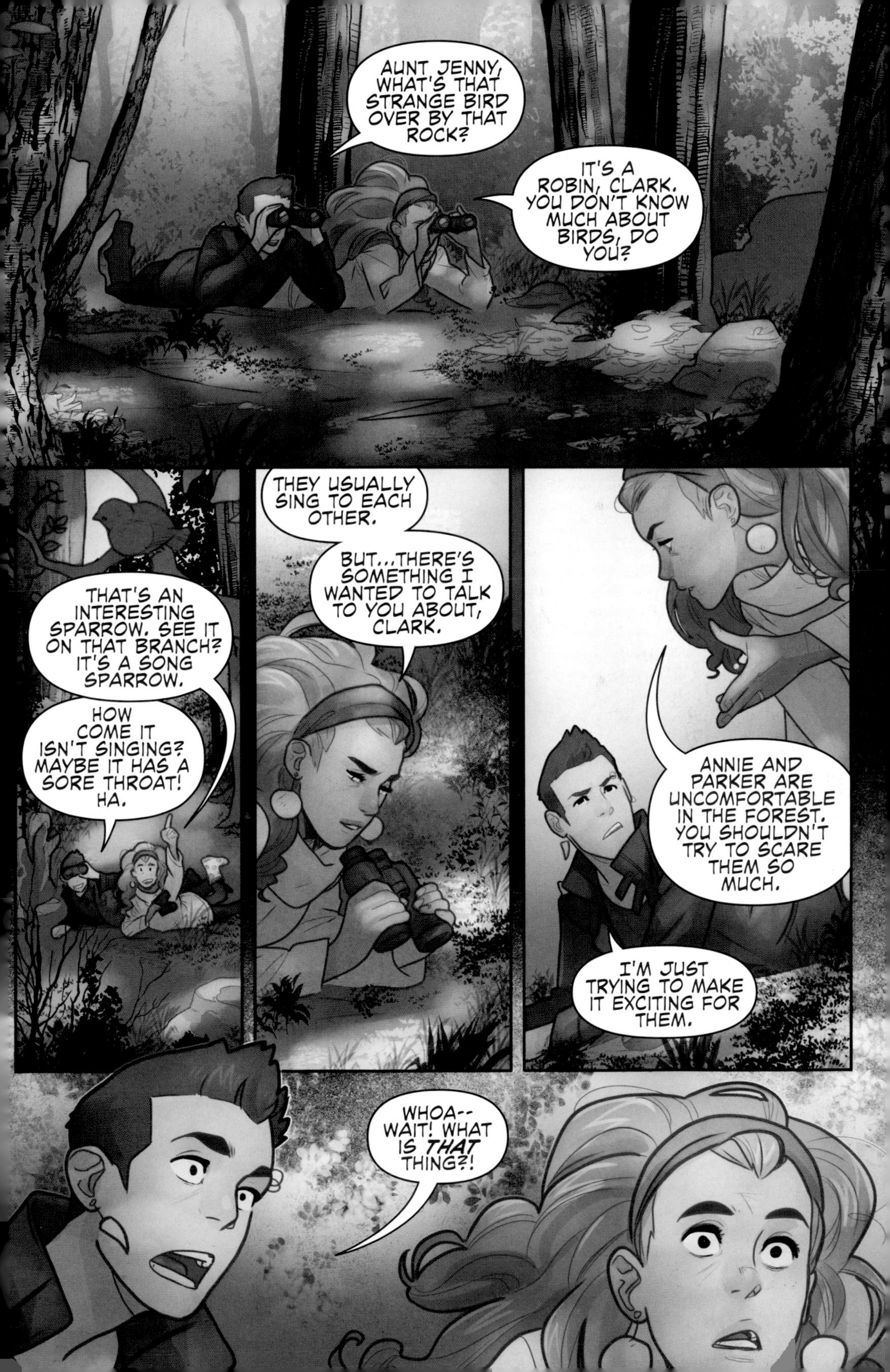
AUNT JENNY, WHAT'S THAT STRANGE BIRD OVER BY THAT ROCK?
IT'S A ROBIN, CLARK. YOU DON'T KNOW MUCH ABOUT BIRDS, DO YOU?
THAT'S AN INTERESTING SPARROW. SEE IT ON THAT BRANCH? IT'S A SONG SPARROW.
HOW COME IT ISN'T SINGING? MAYBE IT HAS A SORE THROAT! HA.
THEY USUALLY SING TO EACH OTHER.
BUT...THERE'S SOMETHING I WANTED TO TALK TO YOU ABOUT, CLARK.
ANNIE AND PARKER ARE UNCOMFORTABLE IN THE FOREST. YOU SHOULDN'T TRY TO SCARE THEM SO MUCH.
I'M JUST TRYING TO MAKE IT EXCITING FOR THEM.
WHOA--WAIT! WHAT IS *THAT* THING?!

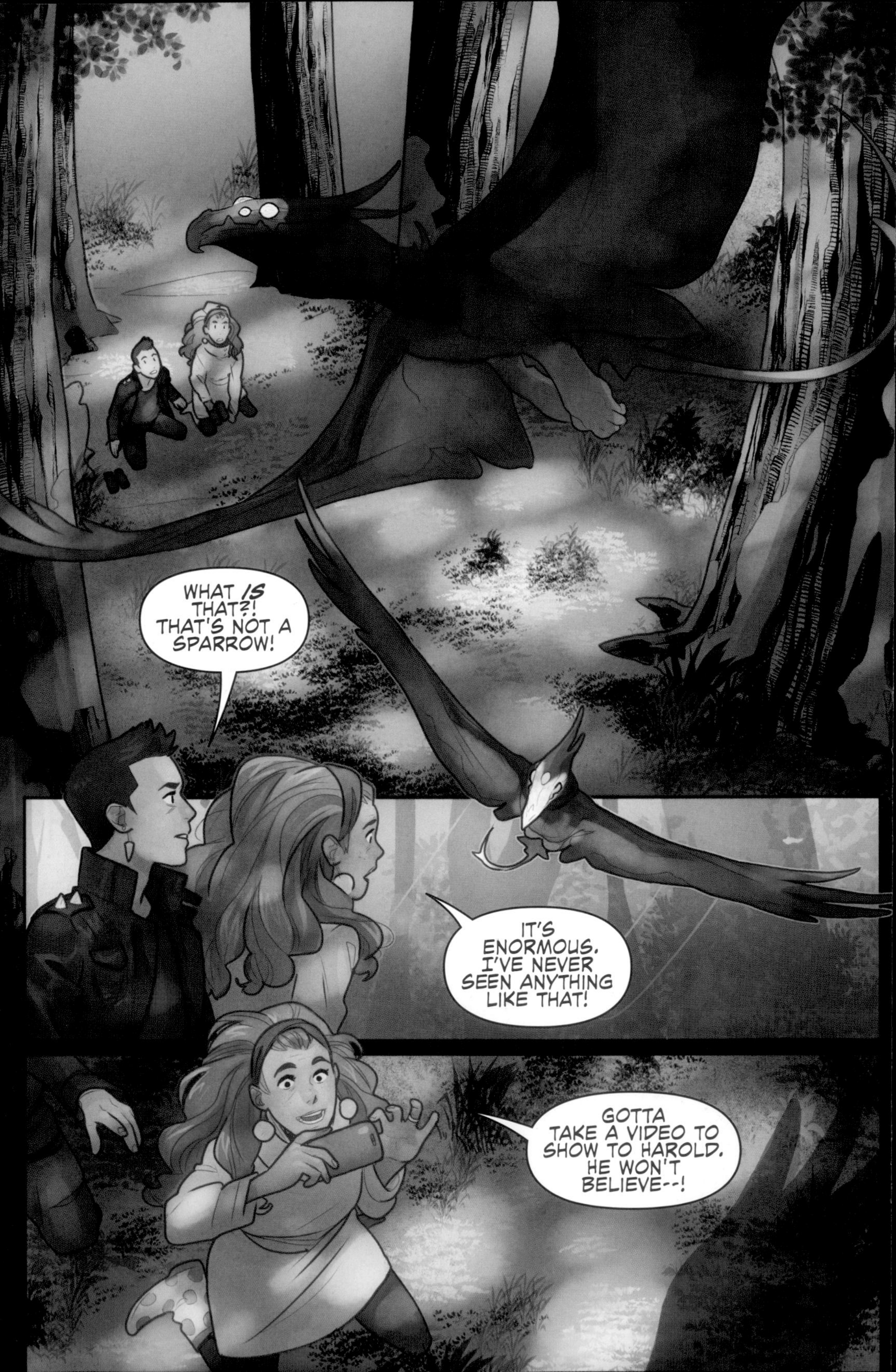
WHAT *IS* THAT?! THAT'S NOT A SPARROW!
IT'S ENORMOUS. I'VE NEVER SEEN ANYTHING LIKE THAT!
GOTTA TAKE A VIDEO TO SHOW TO HAROLD. HE WON'T BELIEVE--!

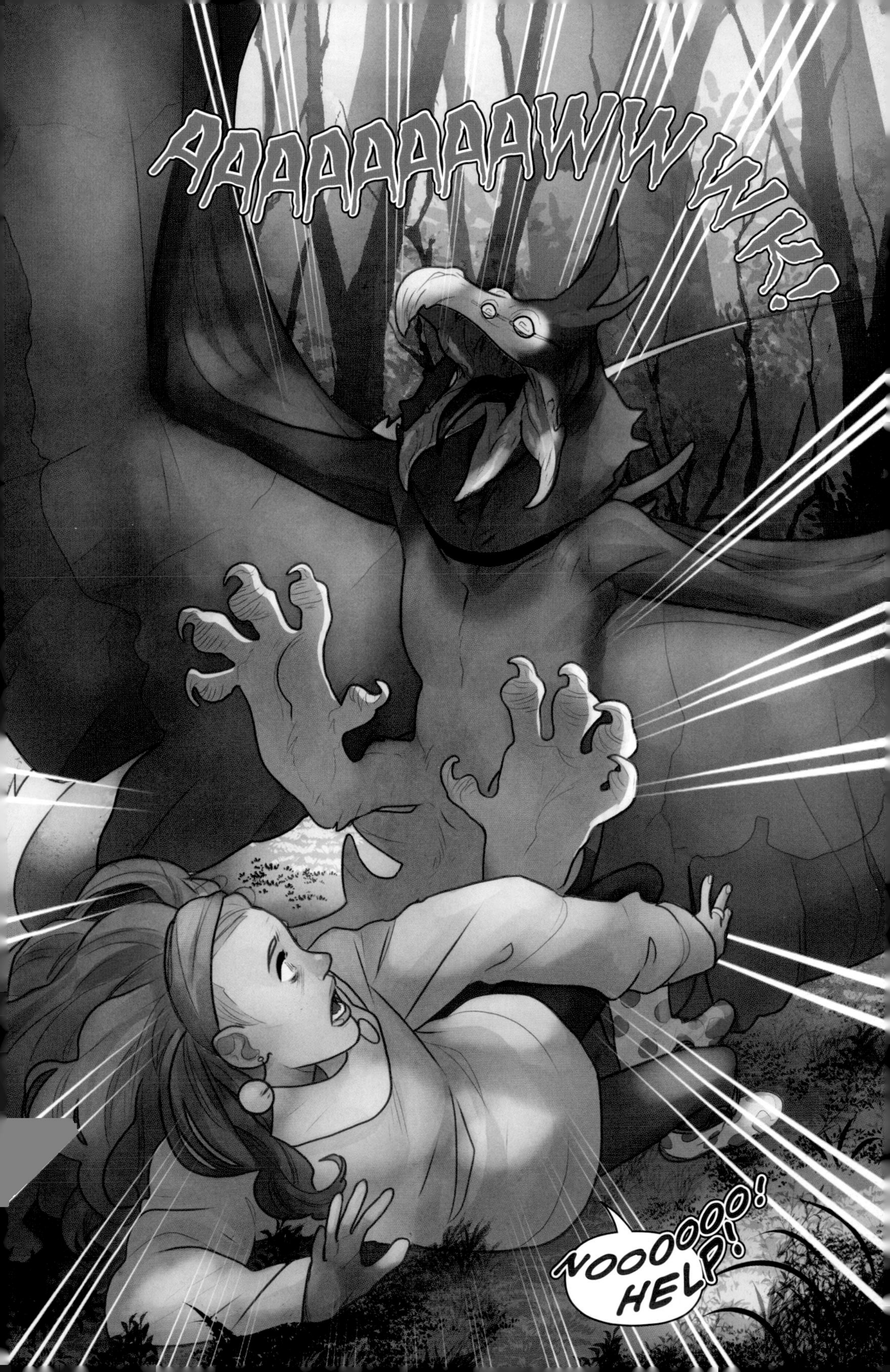
AAAAAAAAWWWK!
NOOOOOOO! HELP!

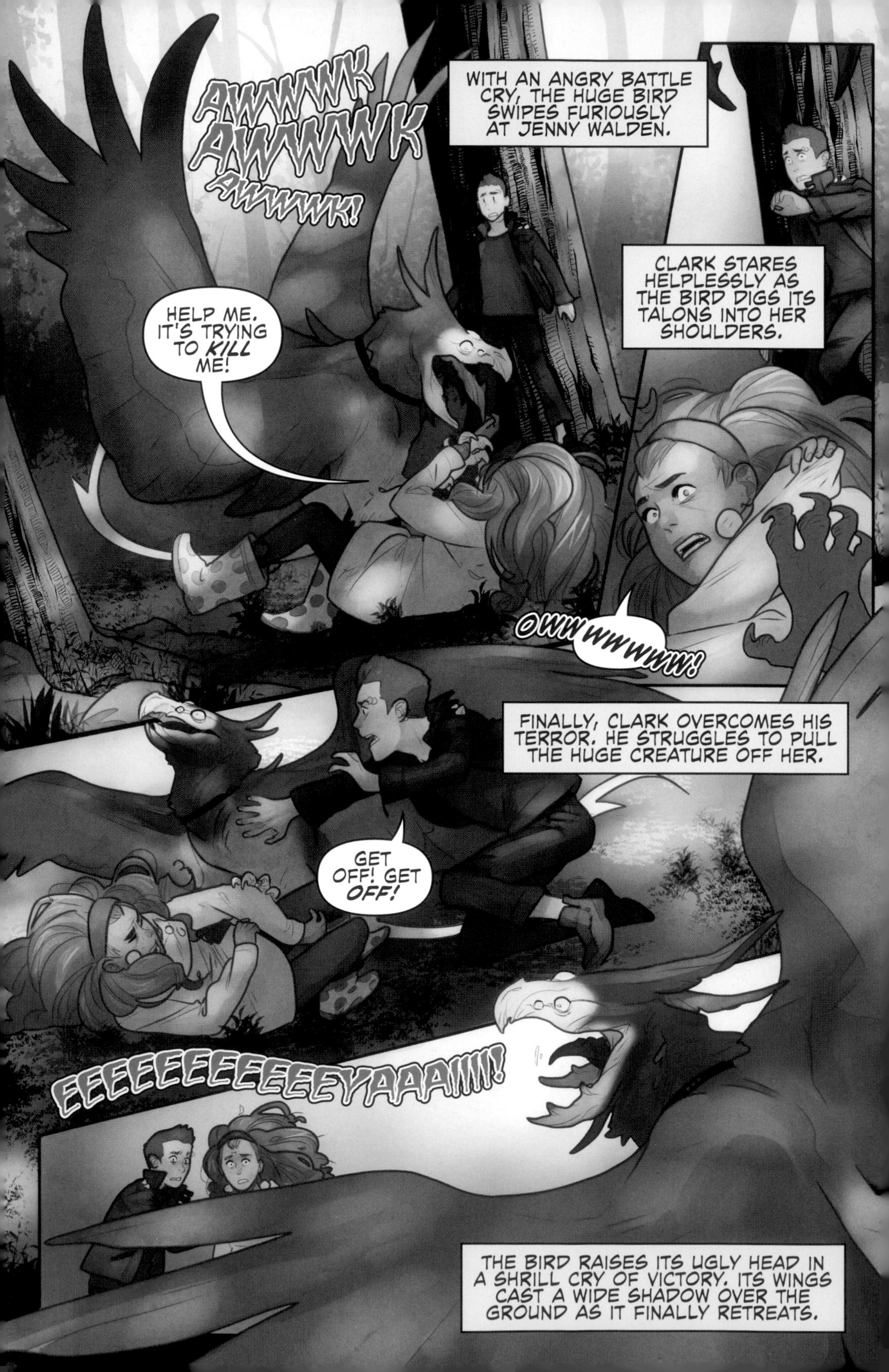
AWWWK AWWWK AWWWK!
WITH AN ANGRY BATTLE CRY, THE HUGE BIRD SWIPES FURIOUSLY AT JENNY WALDEN.
HELP ME. IT'S TRYING TO KILL ME!
CLARK STARES HELPLESSLY AS THE BIRD DIGS ITS TALONS INTO HER SHOULDERS.
OWWWWWWWW!
FINALLY, CLARK OVERCOMES HIS TERROR. HE STRUGGLES TO PULL THE HUGE CREATURE OFF HER.
GET OFF! GET OFF!
EEEEEEEEEEEEEYAAA!!!!!
THE BIRD RAISES ITS UGLY HEAD IN A SHRILL CRY OF VICTORY. ITS WINGS CAST A WIDE SHADOW OVER THE GROUND AS IT FINALLY RETREATS.

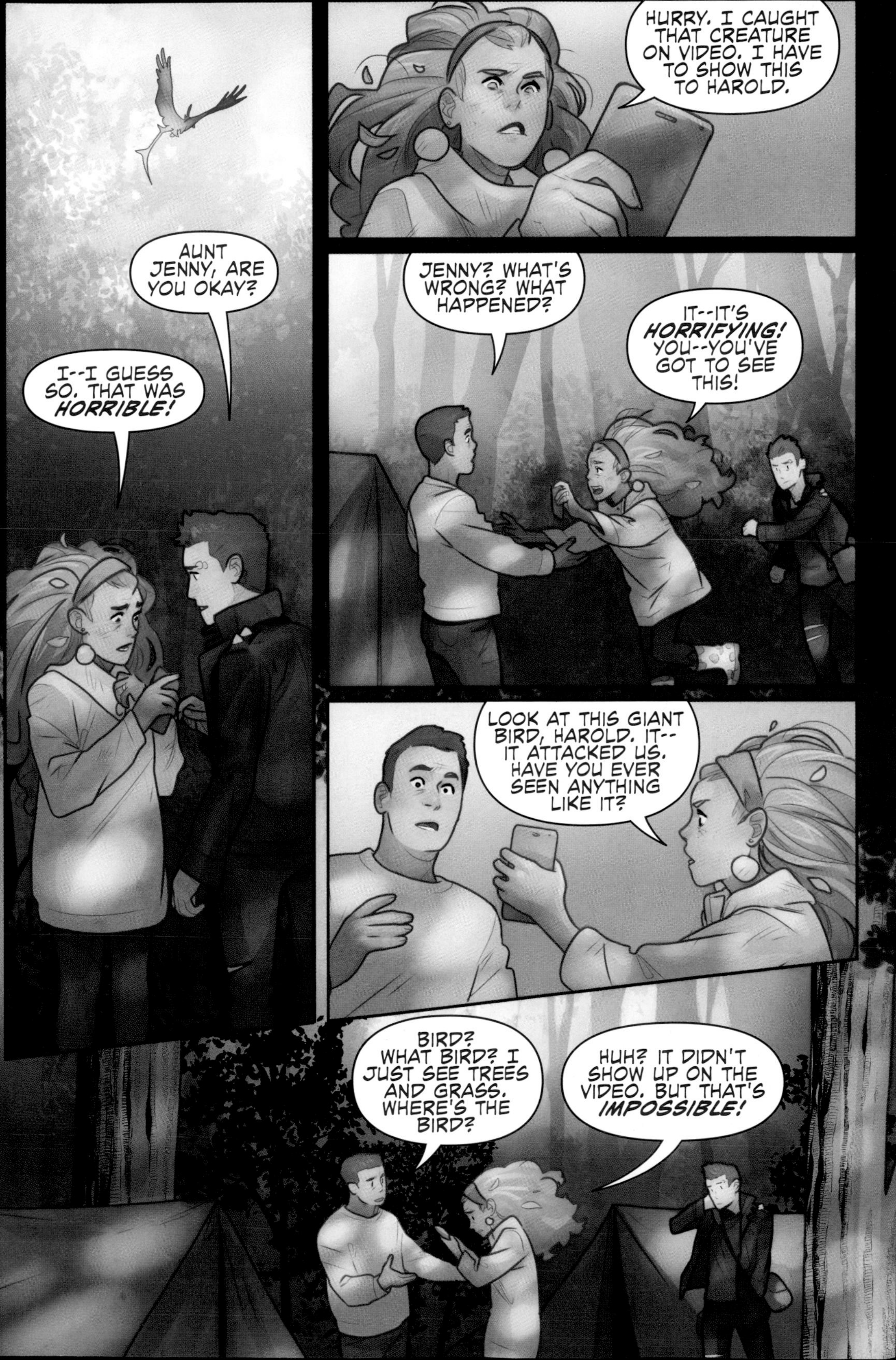
AUNT JENNY, ARE YOU OKAY?
I--I GUESS SO. THAT WAS *HORRIBLE!*
HURRY. I CAUGHT THAT CREATURE ON VIDEO. I HAVE TO SHOW THIS TO HAROLD.
JENNY? WHAT'S WRONG? WHAT HAPPENED?
IT--IT'S *HORRIFYING!* YOU--YOU'VE GOT TO SEE THIS!
LOOK AT THIS GIANT BIRD, HAROLD. IT--IT ATTACKED US. HAVE YOU EVER SEEN ANYTHING LIKE IT?
BIRD? WHAT BIRD? I JUST SEE TREES AND GRASS. WHERE'S THE BIRD?
HUH? IT DIDN'T SHOW UP ON THE VIDEO. BUT THAT'S *IMPOSSIBLE!*

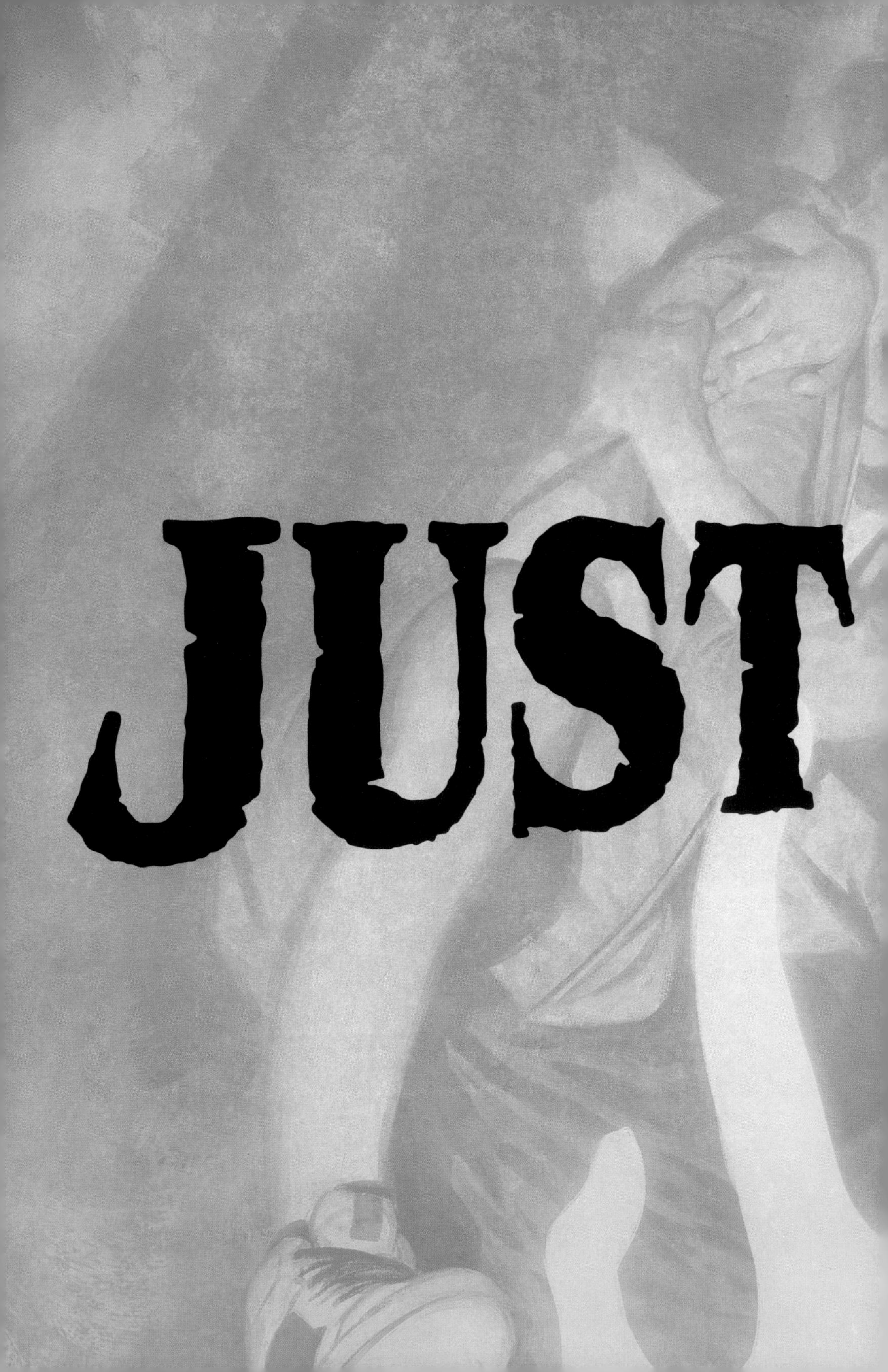
JUST

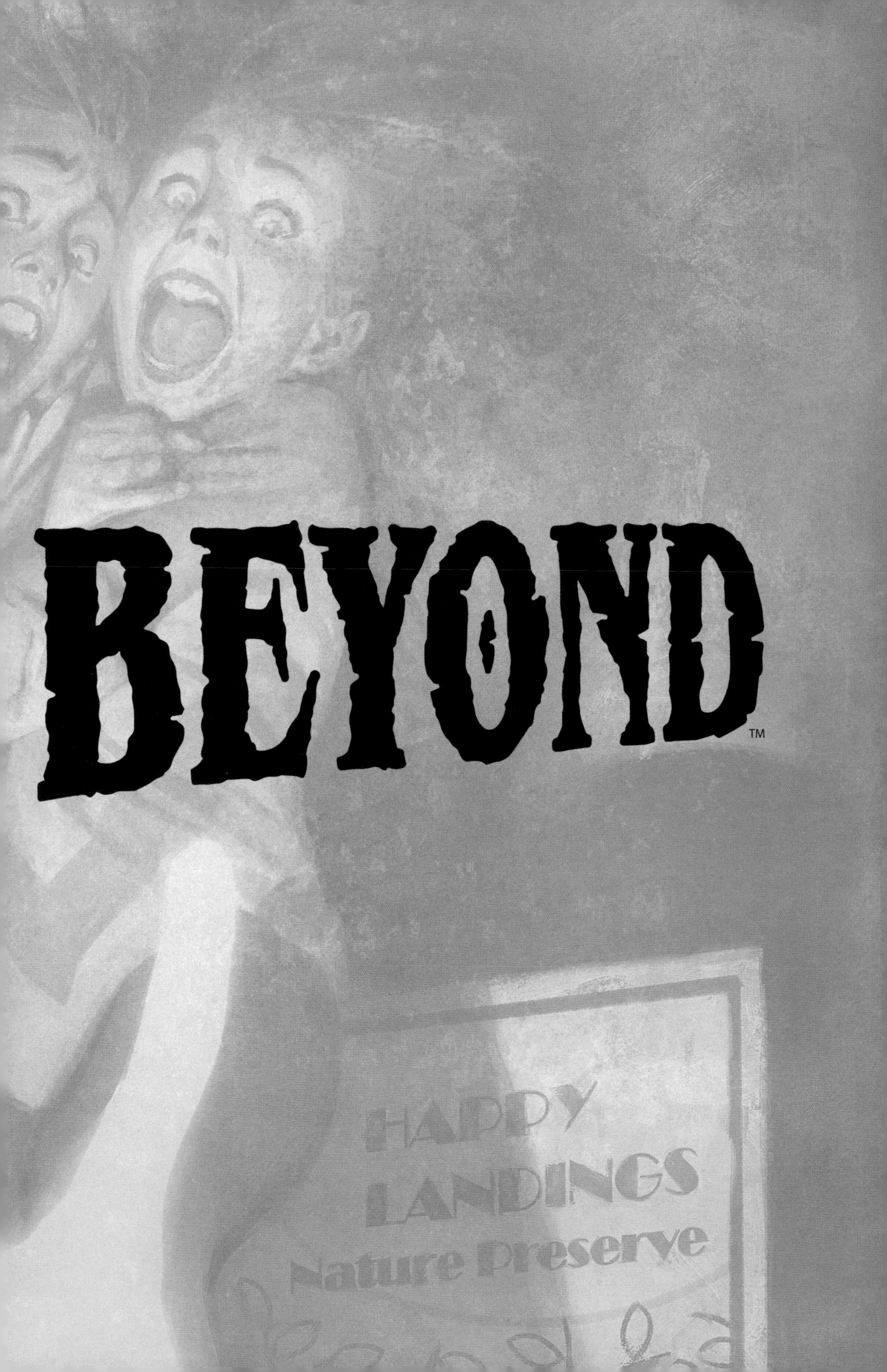
BEYOND™
HAPPY
LANDINGS
Nature Preserve

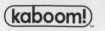

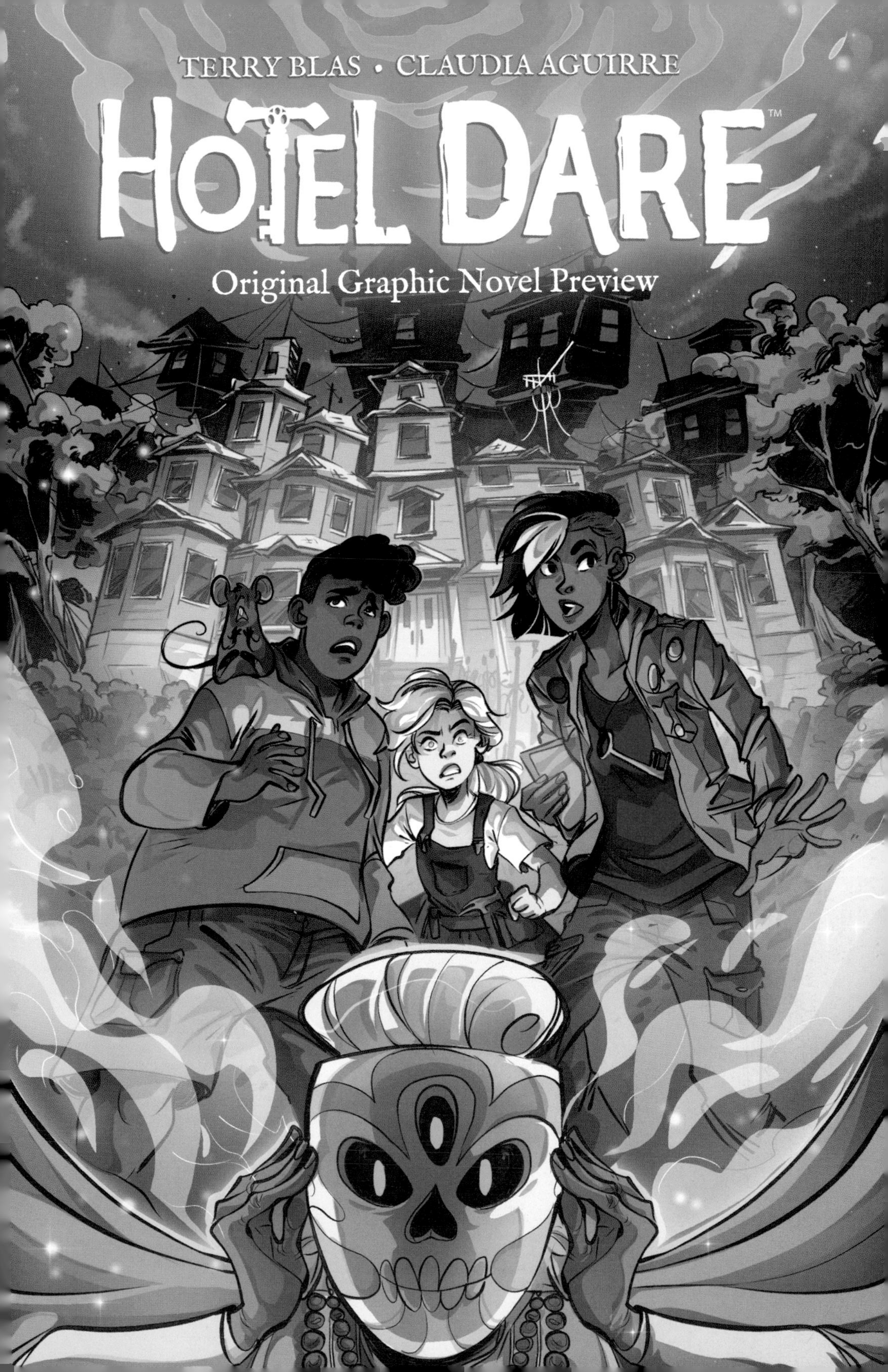
TERRY BLAS • CLAUDIA AGUIRRE
HOTEL DARE™
Original Graphic Novel Preview

Created & Written by
Terry Blas

Illustrated by
Claudia Aguirre

Letters by
Mike Fiorentino

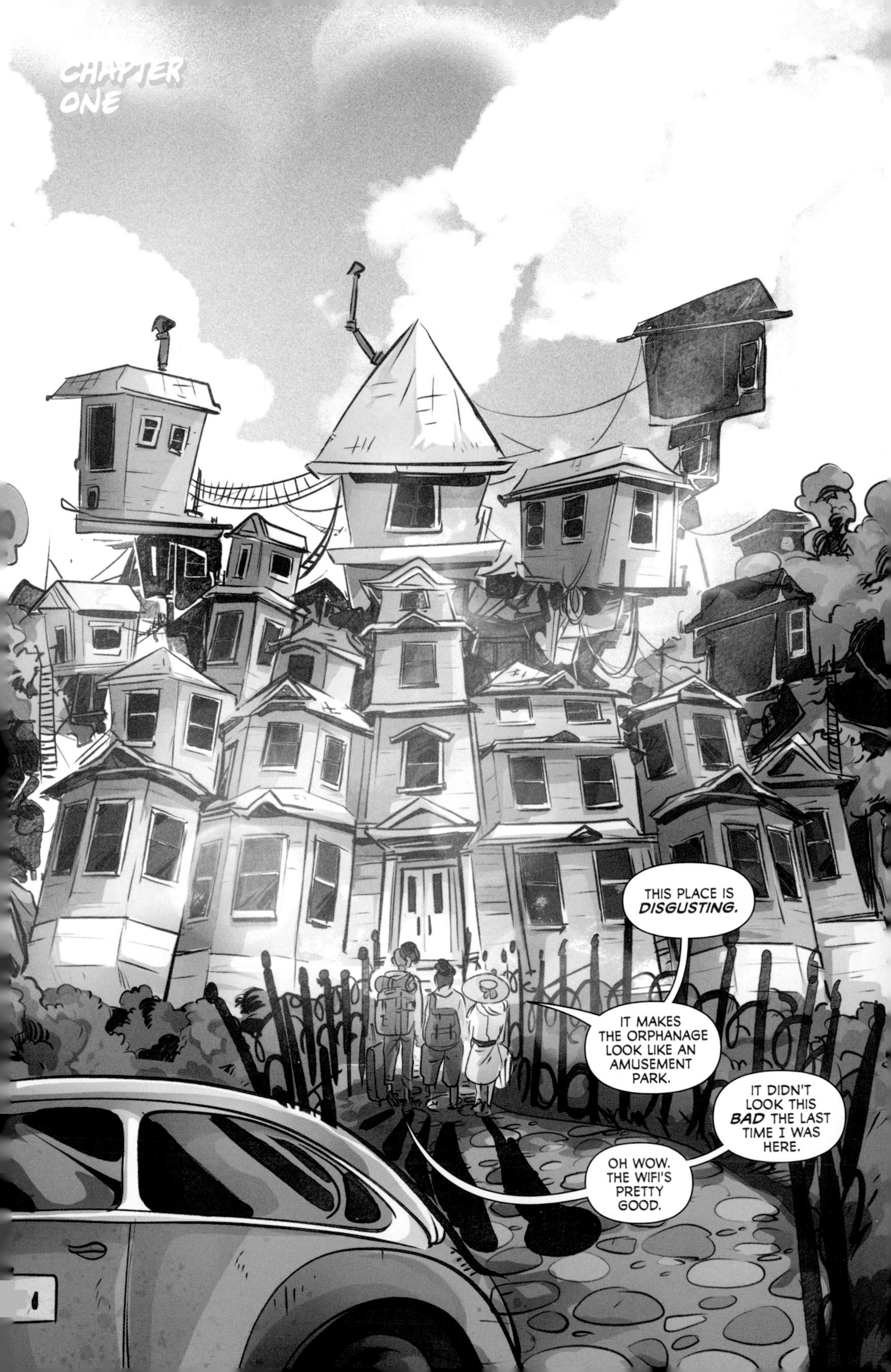
CHAPTER ONE
THIS PLACE IS *DISGUSTING.*
IT MAKES THE ORPHANAGE LOOK LIKE AN AMUSEMENT PARK.
IT DIDN'T LOOK THIS *BAD* THE LAST TIME I WAS HERE.
OH WOW. THE WIFI'S PRETTY GOOD.

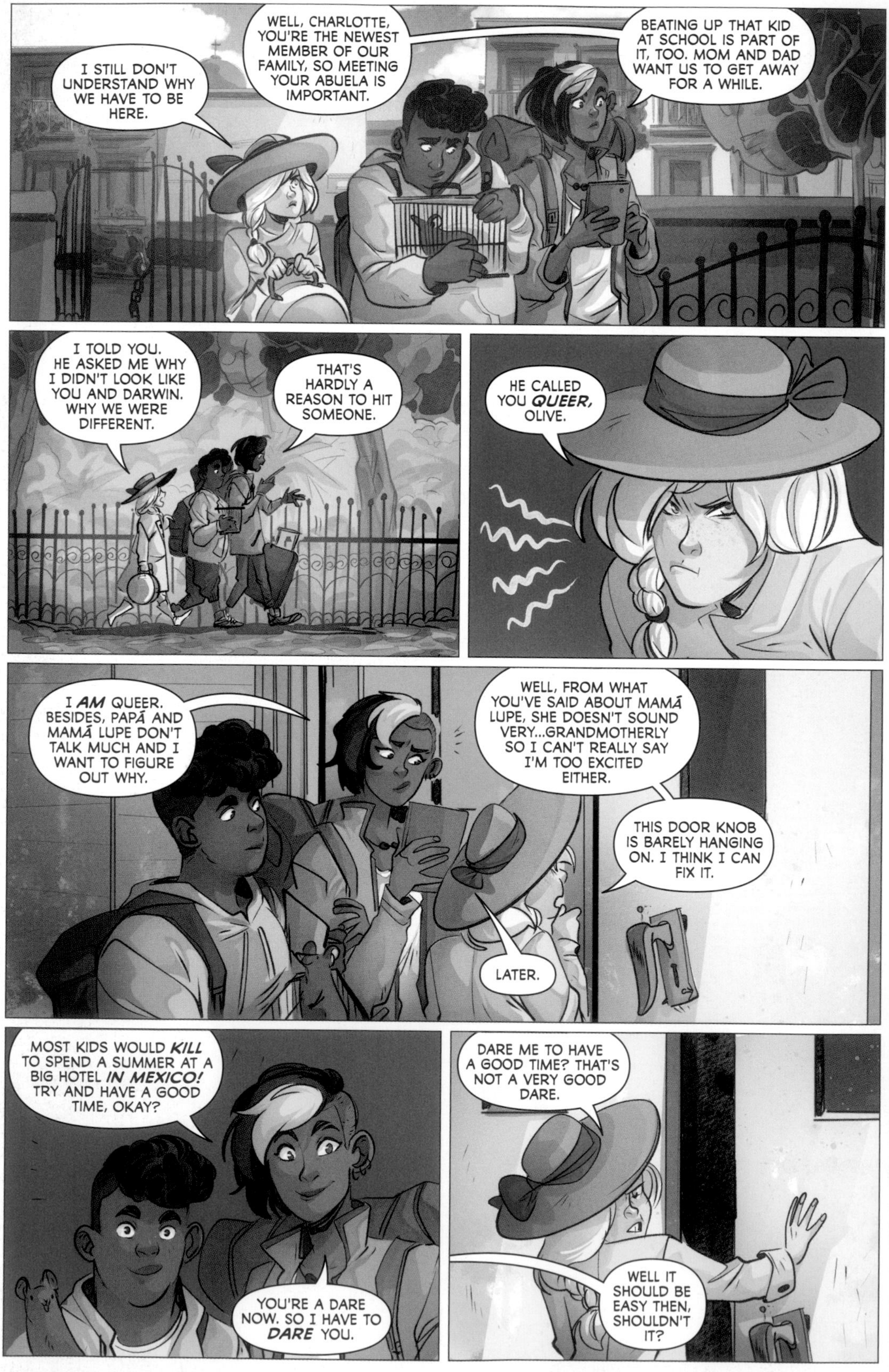
I STILL DON'T UNDERSTAND WHY WE HAVE TO BE HERE.
WELL, CHARLOTTE, YOU'RE THE NEWEST MEMBER OF OUR FAMILY, SO MEETING YOUR ABUELA IS IMPORTANT.
BEATING UP THAT KID AT SCHOOL IS PART OF IT, TOO. MOM AND DAD WANT US TO GET AWAY FOR A WHILE.
I TOLD YOU. HE ASKED ME WHY I DIDN'T LOOK LIKE YOU AND DARWIN. WHY WE WERE DIFFERENT.
THAT'S HARDLY A REASON TO HIT SOMEONE.
HE CALLED YOU *QUEER,* OLIVE.
I **AM** QUEER. BESIDES, PAPÁ AND MAMÁ LUPE DON'T TALK MUCH AND I WANT TO FIGURE OUT WHY.
WELL, FROM WHAT YOU'VE SAID ABOUT MAMÁ LUPE, SHE DOESN'T SOUND VERY...GRANDMOTHERLY SO I CAN'T REALLY SAY I'M TOO EXCITED EITHER.
THIS DOOR KNOB IS BARELY HANGING ON. I THINK I CAN FIX IT.
LATER.
MOST KIDS WOULD ***KILL*** TO SPEND A SUMMER AT A BIG HOTEL ***IN MEXICO!*** TRY AND HAVE A GOOD TIME, OKAY?
YOU'RE A DARE NOW. SO I HAVE TO ***DARE*** YOU.
DARE ME TO HAVE A GOOD TIME? THAT'S NOT A VERY GOOD DARE.
WELL IT SHOULD BE EASY THEN, SHOULDN'T IT?

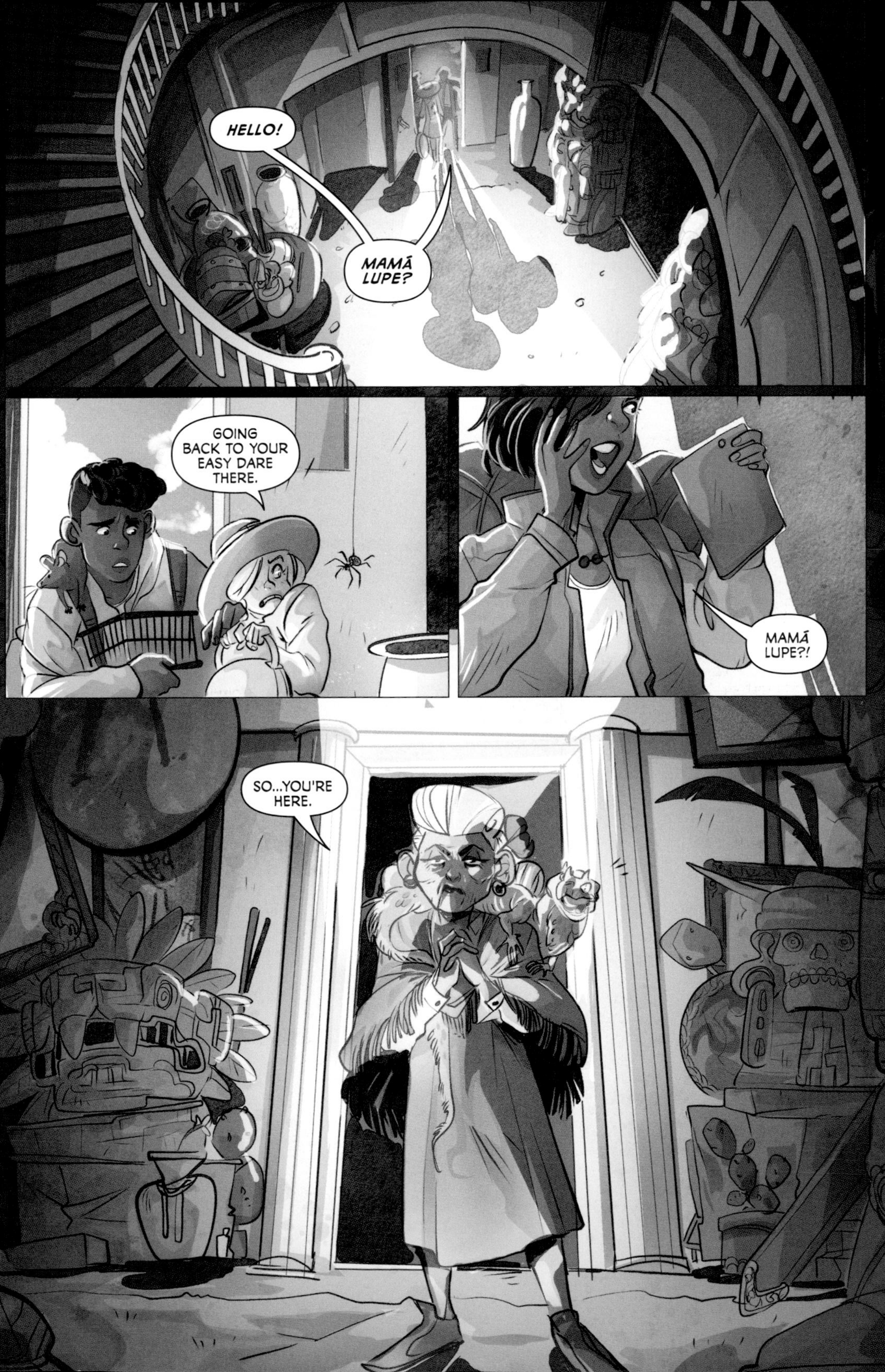
HELLO!
MAMÁ LUPE?
GOING BACK TO YOUR EASY DARE THERE.
MAMÁ LUPE?!
SO...YOU'RE HERE.

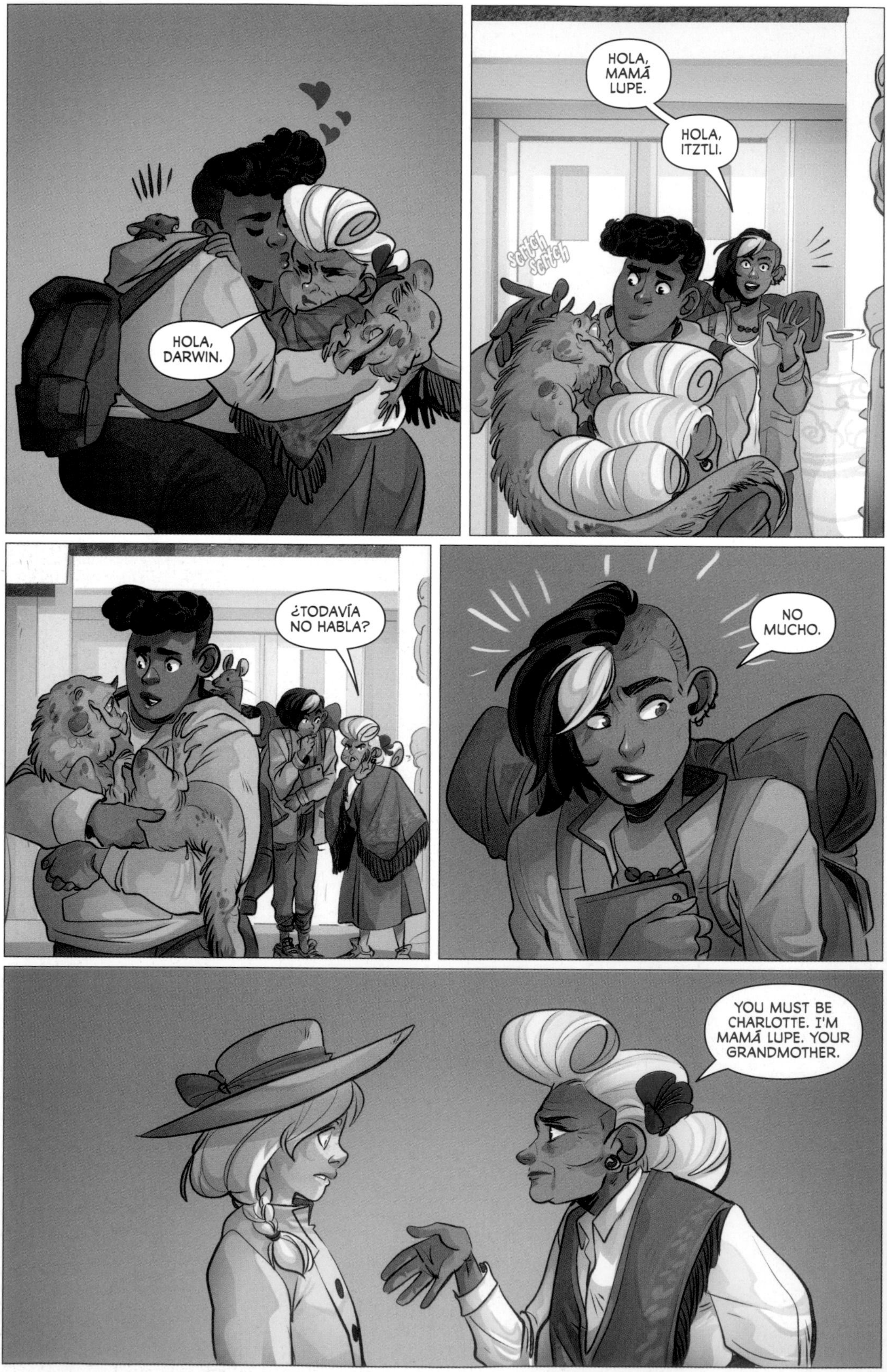
HOLA, DARWIN.
HOLA, MAMÁ LUPE.
HOLA, ITZTLI.
SCRTCH SCRTCH
¿TODAVÍA NO HABLA?
NO MUCHO.
YOU MUST BE CHARLOTTE. I'M MAMÁ LUPE. YOUR GRANDMOTHER.

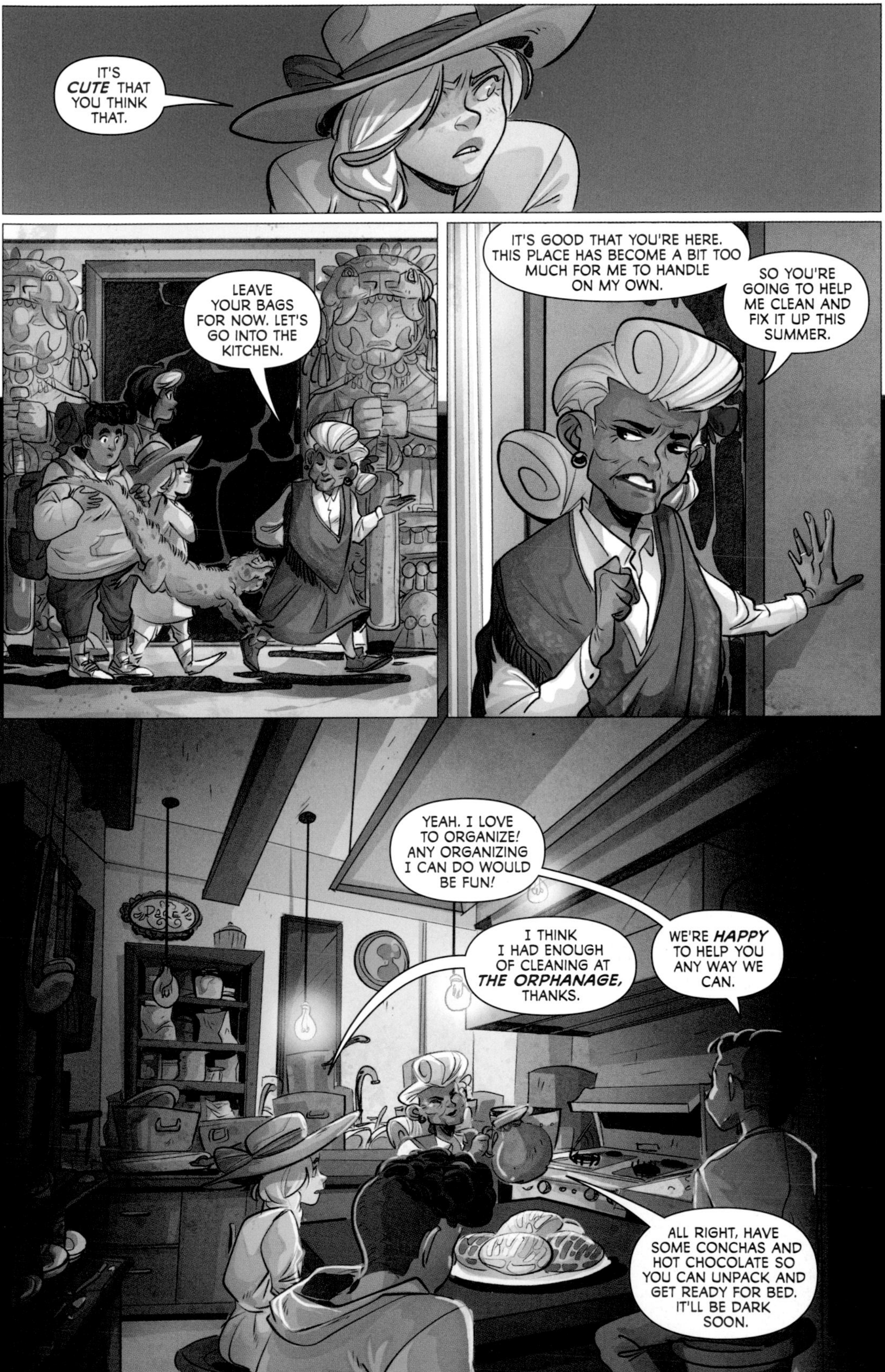
IT'S *CUTE* THAT YOU THINK THAT.
LEAVE YOUR BAGS FOR NOW. LET'S GO INTO THE KITCHEN.
IT'S GOOD THAT YOU'RE HERE. THIS PLACE HAS BECOME A BIT TOO MUCH FOR ME TO HANDLE ON MY OWN.
SO YOU'RE GOING TO HELP ME CLEAN AND FIX IT UP THIS SUMMER.
YEAH. I LOVE TO ORGANIZE! ANY ORGANIZING I CAN DO WOULD BE FUN!
WE'RE *HAPPY* TO HELP YOU ANY WAY WE CAN.
I THINK I HAD ENOUGH OF CLEANING AT *THE ORPHANAGE,* THANKS.
ALL RIGHT, HAVE SOME CONCHAS AND HOT CHOCOLATE SO YOU CAN UNPACK AND GET READY FOR BED. IT'LL BE DARK SOON.

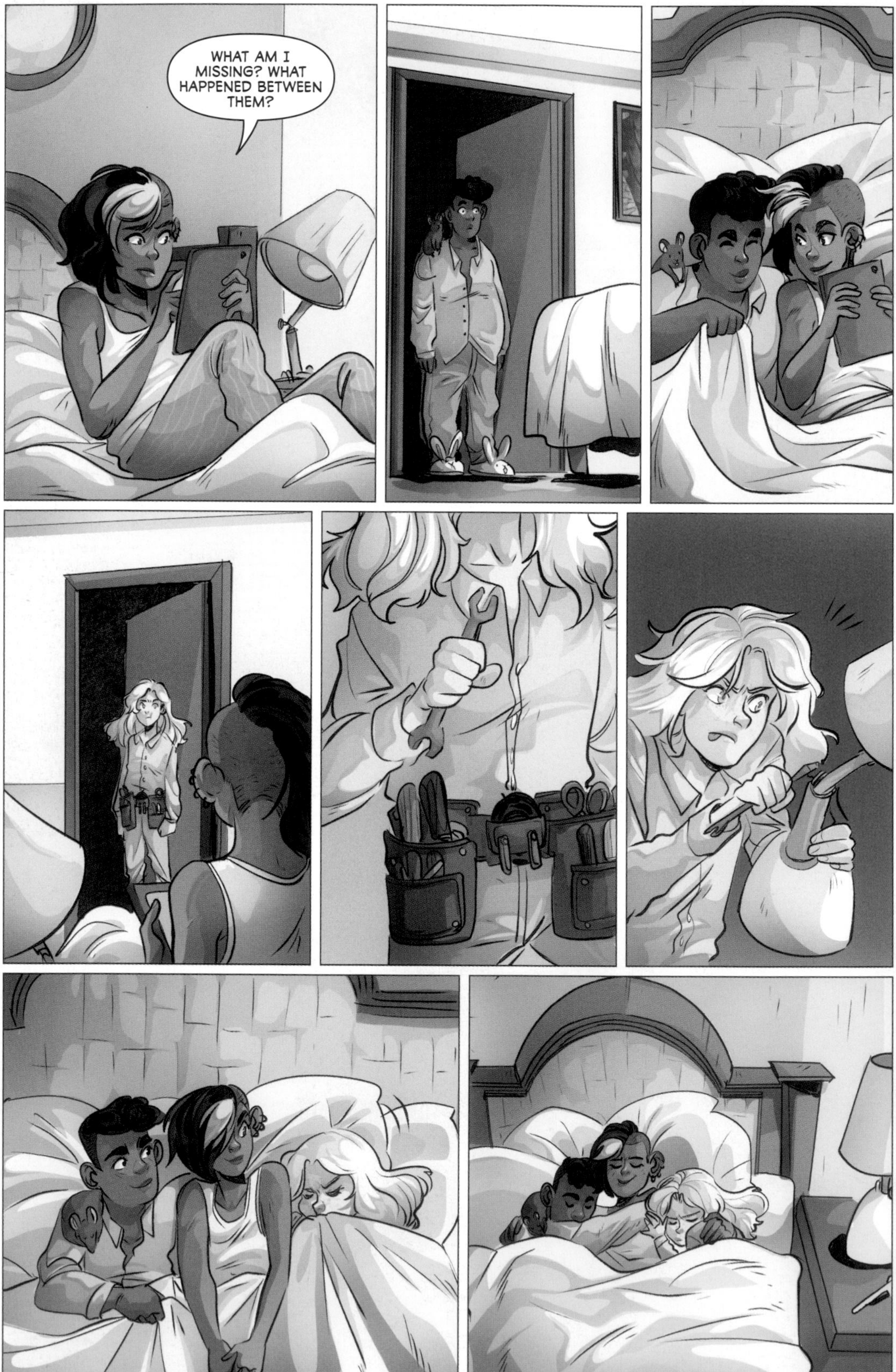
WHAT AM I MISSING? WHAT HAPPENED BETWEEN THEM?

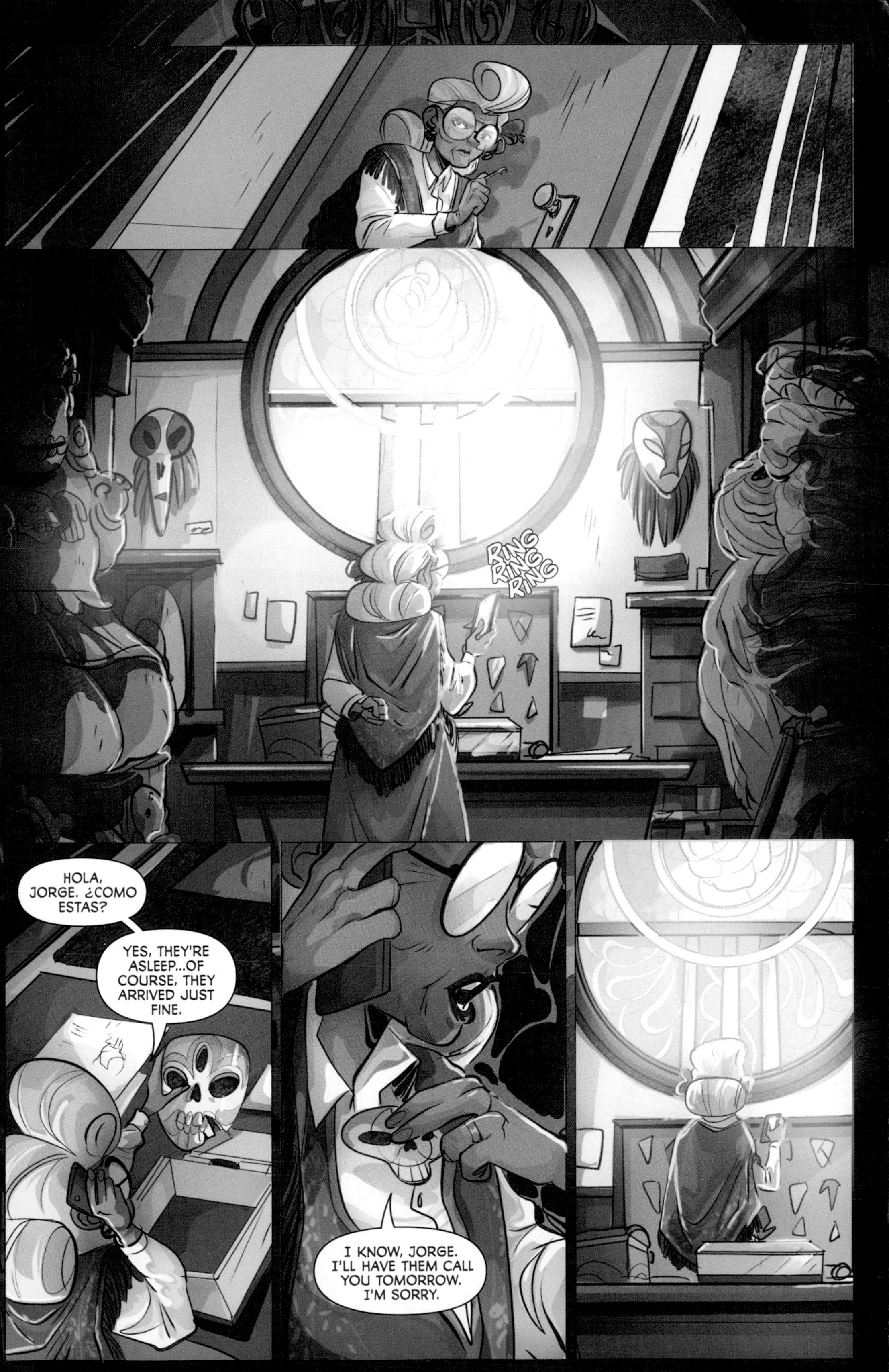
RING RING RING
HOLA, JORGE. ¿COMO ESTAS?
YES, THEY'RE ASLEEP...OF COURSE, THEY ARRIVED JUST FINE.
I KNOW, JORGE. I'LL HAVE THEM CALL YOU TOMORROW. I'M SORRY.

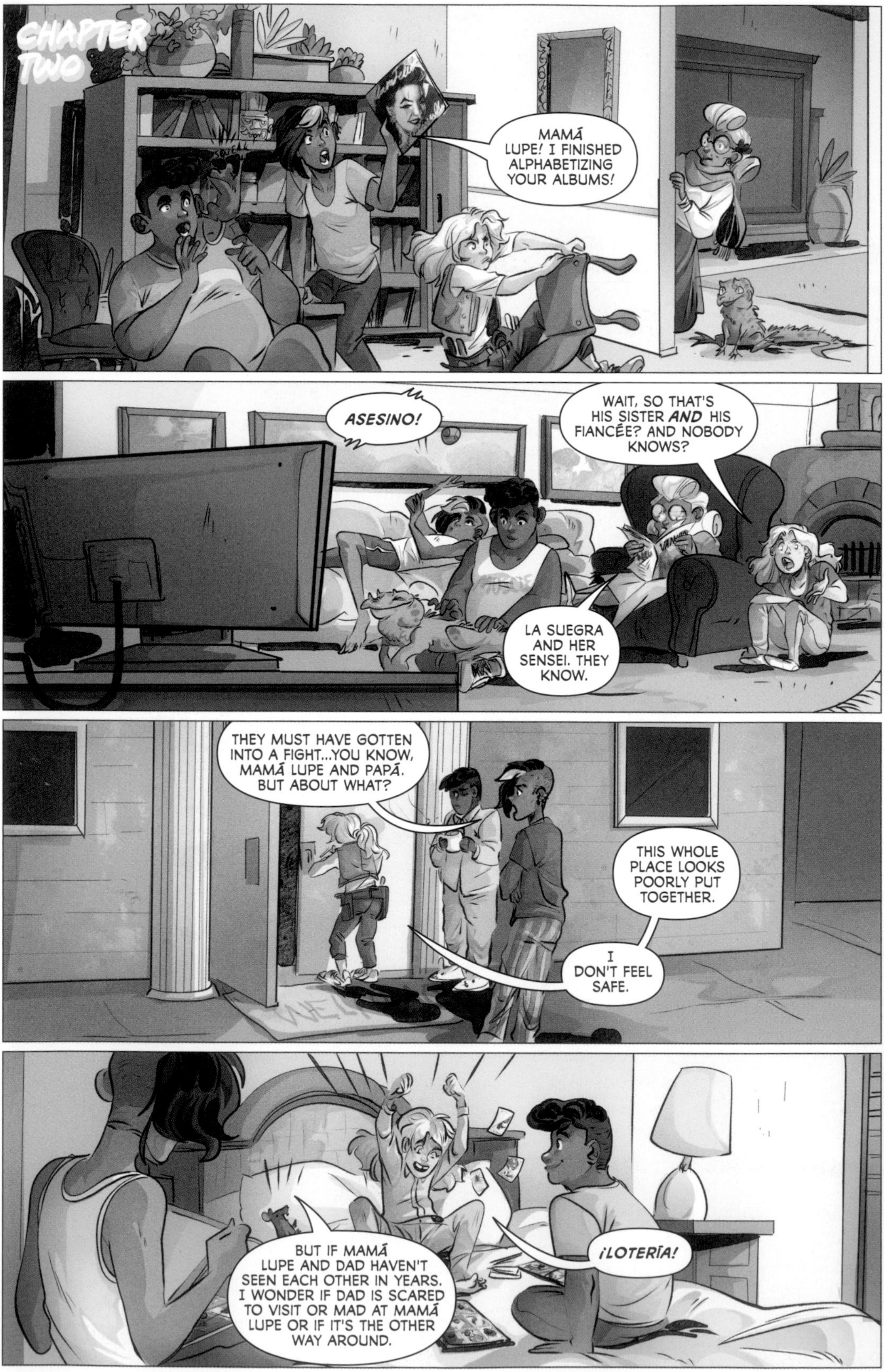
CHAPTER TWO
MAMÁ LUPE! I FINISHED ALPHABETIZING YOUR ALBUMS!
ASESINO!
WAIT, SO THAT'S HIS SISTER AND HIS FIANCÉE? AND NOBODY KNOWS?
LA SUEGRA AND HER SENSEI. THEY KNOW.
THEY MUST HAVE GOTTEN INTO A FIGHT...YOU KNOW, MAMÁ LUPE AND PAPÁ. BUT ABOUT WHAT?
THIS WHOLE PLACE LOOKS POORLY PUT TOGETHER.
I DON'T FEEL SAFE.
BUT IF MAMÁ LUPE AND DAD HAVEN'T SEEN EACH OTHER IN YEARS. I WONDER IF DAD IS SCARED TO VISIT OR MAD AT MAMÁ LUPE OR IF IT'S THE OTHER WAY AROUND.
¡LOTERÍA!

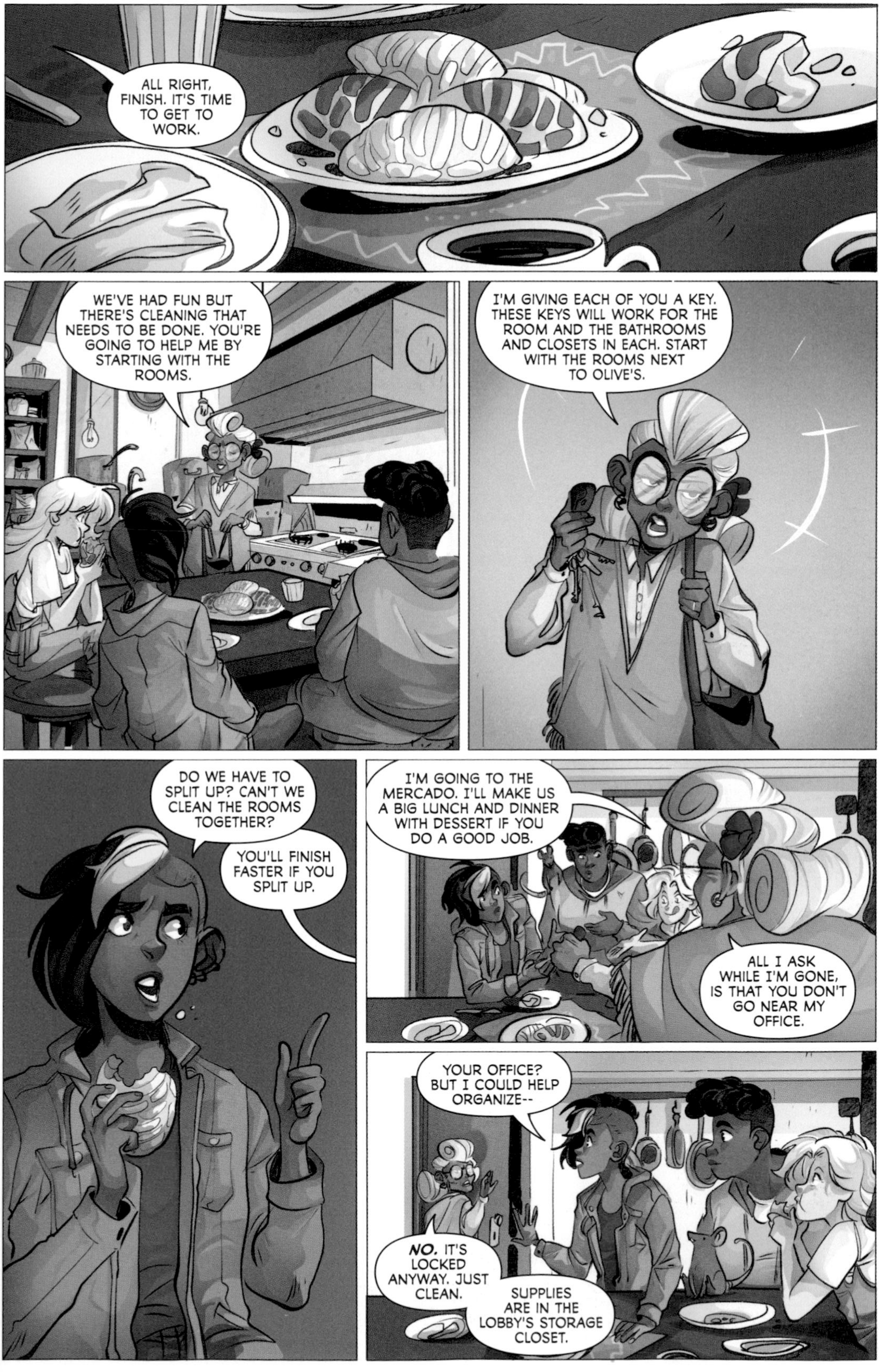
ALL RIGHT, FINISH. IT'S TIME TO GET TO WORK.
WE'VE HAD FUN BUT THERE'S CLEANING THAT NEEDS TO BE DONE. YOU'RE GOING TO HELP ME BY STARTING WITH THE ROOMS.
I'M GIVING EACH OF YOU A KEY. THESE KEYS WILL WORK FOR THE ROOM AND THE BATHROOMS AND CLOSETS IN EACH. START WITH THE ROOMS NEXT TO OLIVE'S.
DO WE HAVE TO SPLIT UP? CAN'T WE CLEAN THE ROOMS TOGETHER?
YOU'LL FINISH FASTER IF YOU SPLIT UP.
I'M GOING TO THE MERCADO. I'LL MAKE US A BIG LUNCH AND DINNER WITH DESSERT IF YOU DO A GOOD JOB.
ALL I ASK WHILE I'M GONE, IS THAT YOU DON'T GO NEAR MY OFFICE.
YOUR OFFICE? BUT I COULD HELP ORGANIZE--
NO. IT'S LOCKED ANYWAY. JUST CLEAN.
SUPPLIES ARE IN THE LOBBY'S STORAGE CLOSET.

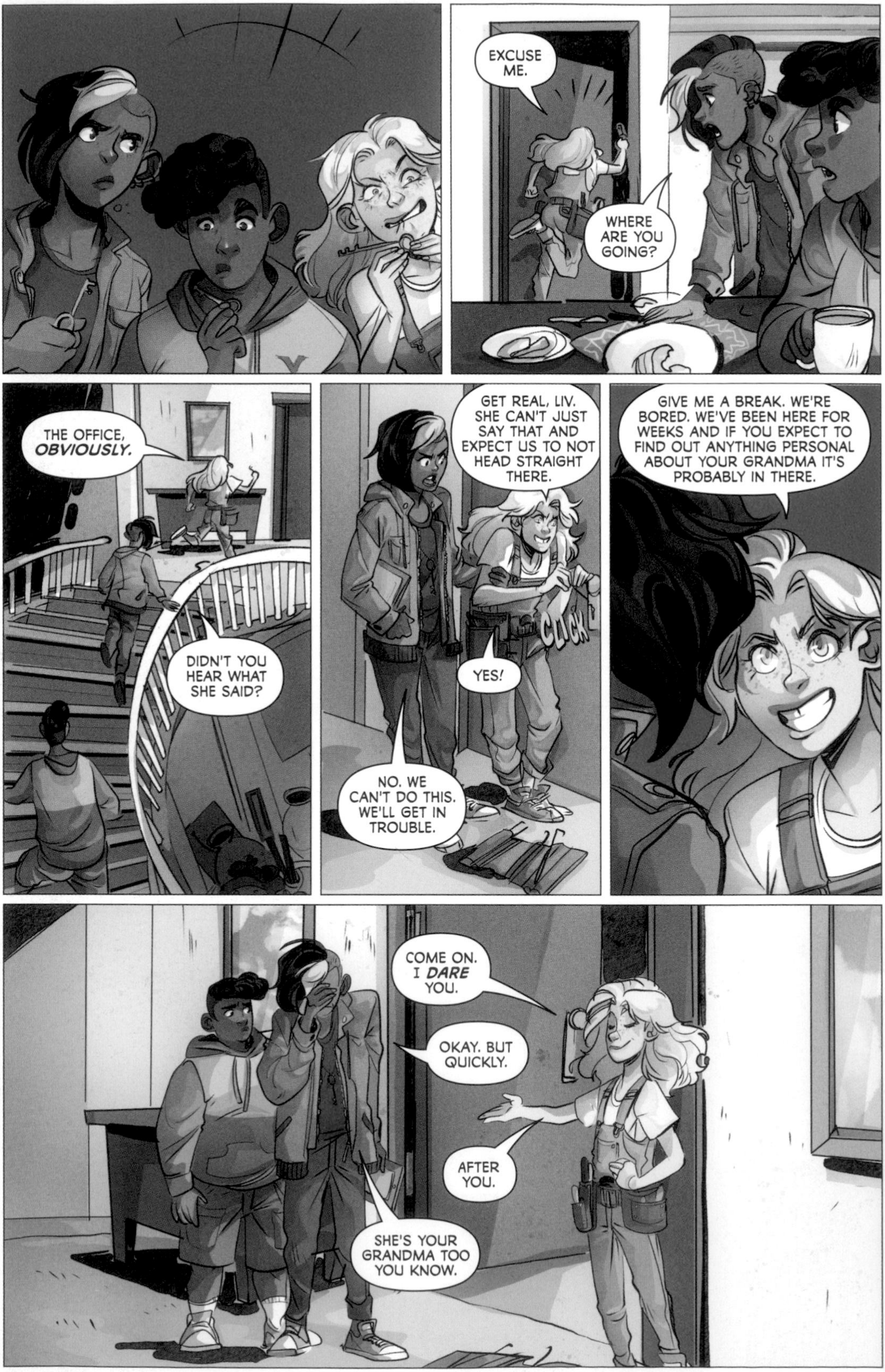
EXCUSE ME.
WHERE ARE YOU GOING?
THE OFFICE, ***OBVIOUSLY.***
DIDN'T YOU HEAR WHAT SHE SAID?
GET REAL, LIV. SHE CAN'T JUST SAY THAT AND EXPECT US TO NOT HEAD STRAIGHT THERE.
CLICK
YES!
NO. WE CAN'T DO THIS. WE'LL GET IN TROUBLE.
GIVE ME A BREAK. WE'RE BORED. WE'VE BEEN HERE FOR WEEKS AND IF YOU EXPECT TO FIND OUT ANYTHING PERSONAL ABOUT YOUR GRANDMA IT'S PROBABLY IN THERE.
COME ON. I ***DARE*** YOU.
OKAY. BUT QUICKLY.
AFTER YOU.
SHE'S YOUR GRANDMA TOO YOU KNOW.

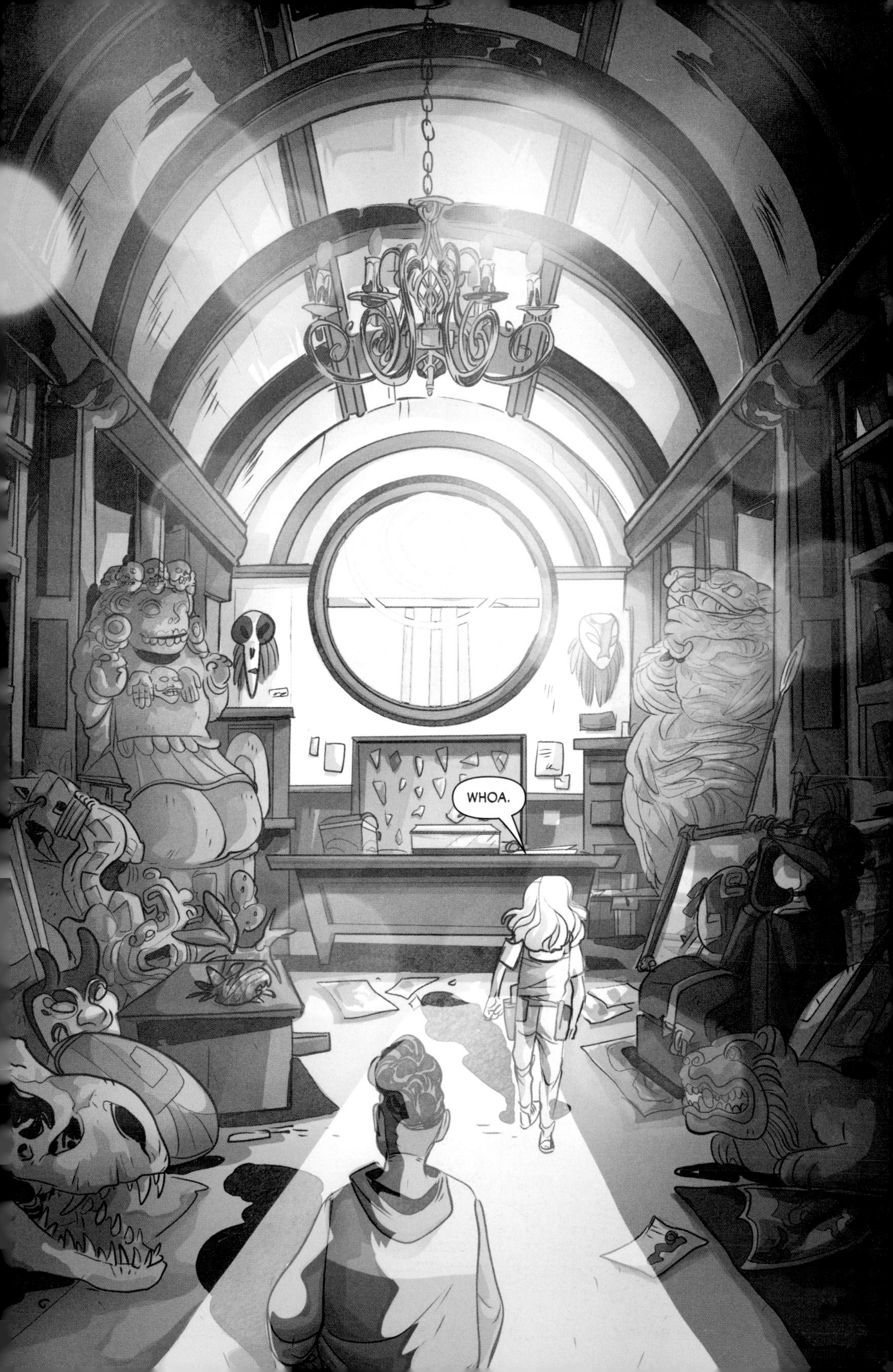
WHOA.

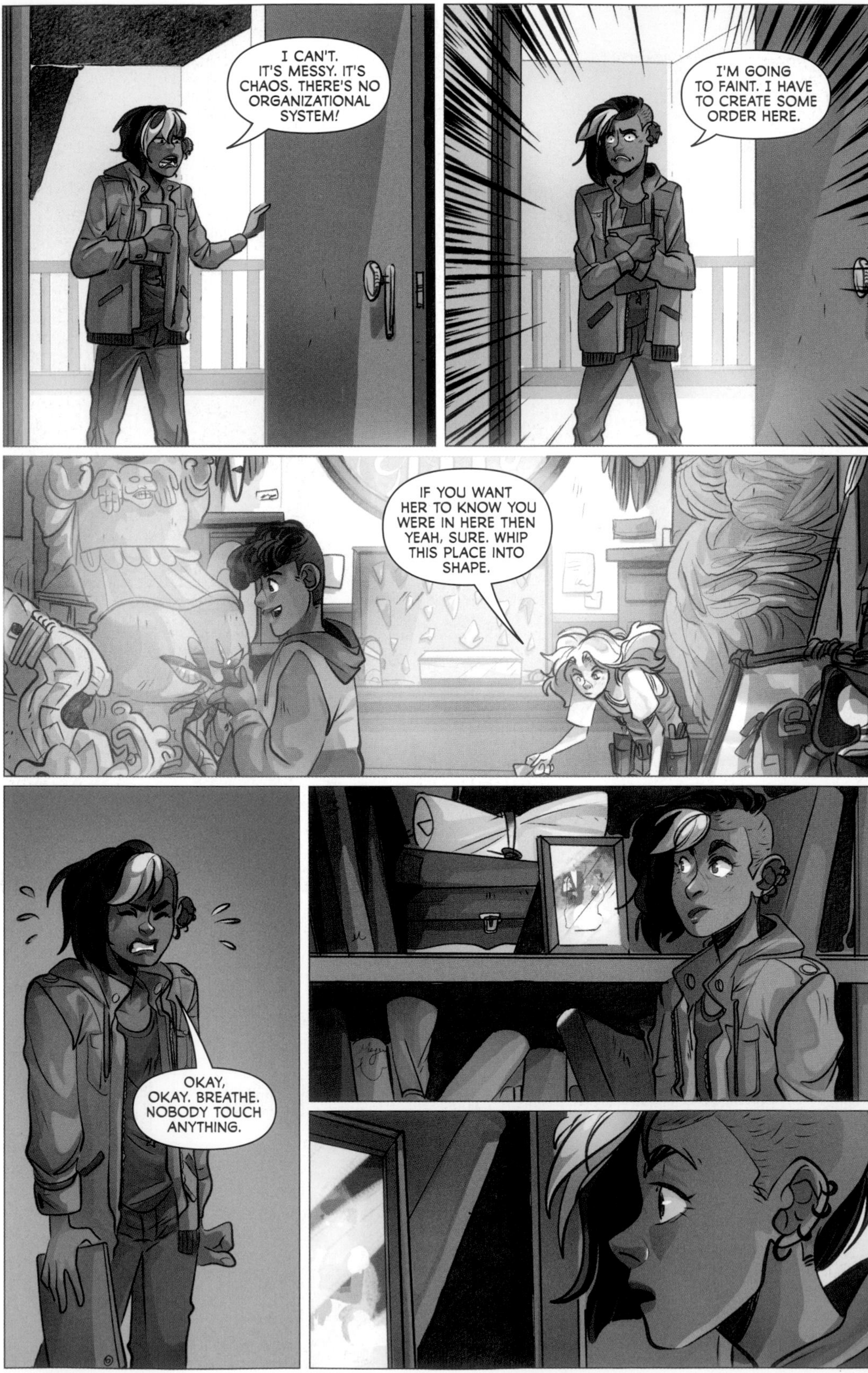
I CAN'T. IT'S MESSY. IT'S CHAOS. THERE'S NO ORGANIZATIONAL SYSTEM!
I'M GOING TO FAINT. I HAVE TO CREATE SOME ORDER HERE.
IF YOU WANT HER TO KNOW YOU WERE IN HERE THEN YEAH, SURE. WHIP THIS PLACE INTO SHAPE.
OKAY, OKAY. BREATHE. NOBODY TOUCH ANYTHING.

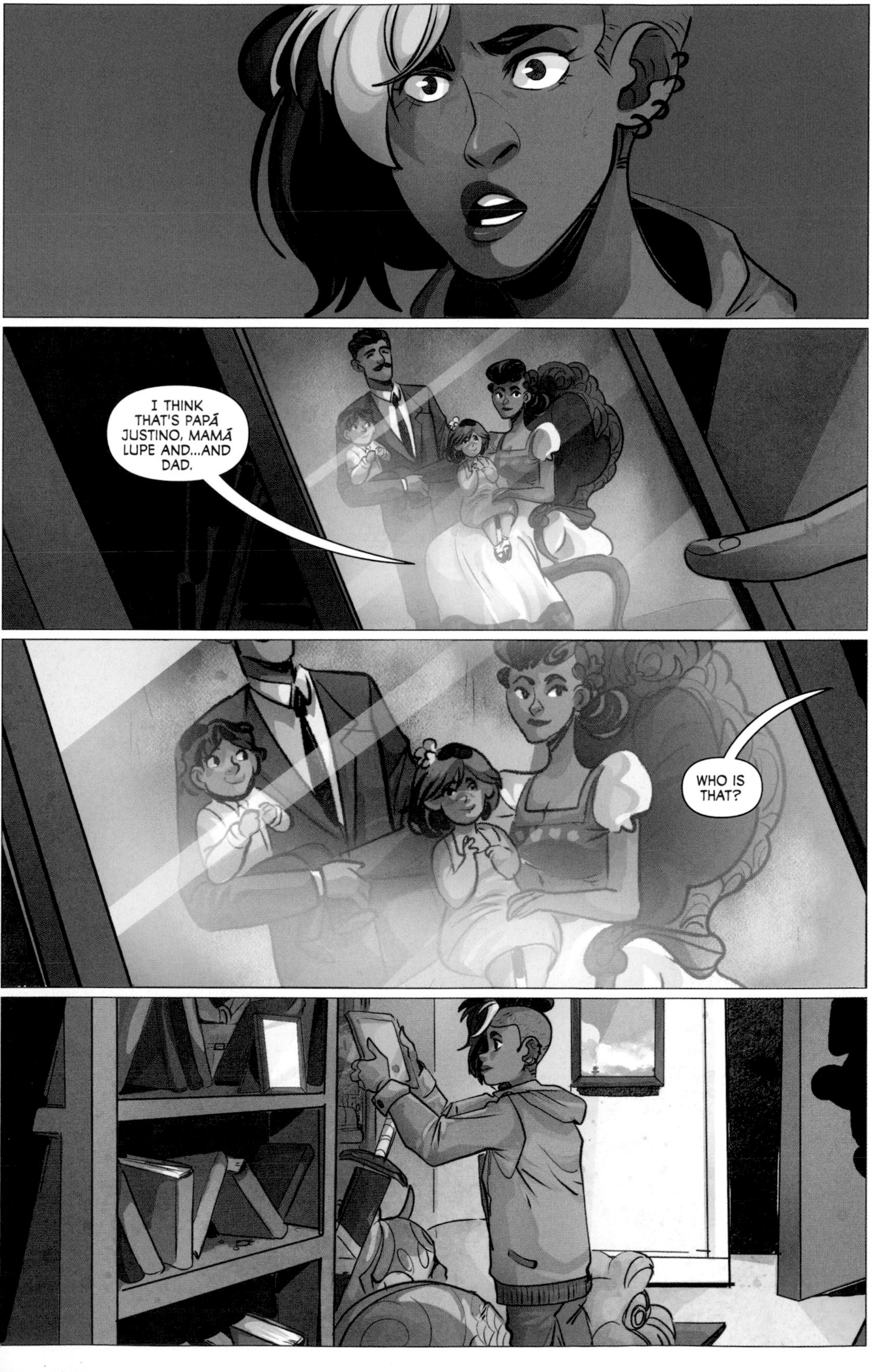
I THINK THAT'S PAPÁ JUSTINO, MAMÁ LUPE AND...AND DAD.
WHO IS THAT?